Murder in Vail

Dean C. Ferraro

Digital Biz Media

Digital Biz Media

MURDER IN VAIL

Published by Digital Biz Media.

www.digitalbizmedia.us

This novel is entirely a work of fiction. The names, characters and incidents portrayed in it are the work of the author's imagination. Any resemblance to actual persons, living or dead, events or localities is entirely coincidental.

Dean C. Ferraro has no responsibility for the persistence or accuracy of URLs for external or third-party Internet Websites referred to in this publication and does not guarantee that any content on such Websites is, or will remain, accurate or appropriate.

Designations used by companies to distinguish their products are often claimed as trademarks. All brand names and product names used in this book and on its cover are trade names, service marks, trademarks and registered trademarks of their respective owners. The publishers and the book are not associated with any product or vendor mentioned in this book. None of the companies referenced within the book have endorsed the book.

First edition, 2022.

www.deancferraro.com

ISBN: 978-1-7378367-3-5 (Paperback)

ISBN: 978-1-7378367-5-9 (Hardcover)

MURDER IN VAIL

ISBN: 978-1-7378367-4-2 (eBook)

Acknowledgments

First, I want to thank all the people that had faith in me and spent some of their valuable time reading my first novel, *Murder in Santa Barbara*. If you're reading this, I guess you liked it. And thank you for your continued support. Also, I'd like to extend a very special thanks to those who provided me with their valuable feedback and positive book reviews. Please, keep 'em coming!

I also want to thank Chaucer's Bookstore in Santa Barbara, CA. And a special shout-out to Scott. The continued sales of *Murder in Santa Barbara* at your bookstore have been truly amazing! I appreciate your support and efforts in getting my book out to so many readers.

Last but certainly not least, thank you to all my readers. *Murder in Santa Barbara* has been a success because of you and has allowed me to continue following my dream as a writer. I think you'll enjoy this second book in the Joshua Rizzetti thriller series as it is filled with more humor, action, and nostalgic 1980s' references to keep you engaged and entertained.

And please remember, the best compliment you can give is to post a positive book review online. So, I kindly invite you to take a couple of minutes and post a review at the source of your purchase. As much as the world continues to change, the power of the written word persists. Thank you again for your continued support.

Chapter One

T HE WOOD CABIN nestled itself into the mountainside, hidden by the hundreds of Colorado Blue Spruce trees towering amidst the twenty-three secluded acres in the awe-inspiring Rocky Mountains. At over nine thousand feet above sea level, the air was thin. In mid-winter, the ground was white. At the outset of a winter storm, the temperature hovered near zero.

Outside, over two feet of snow covered the world-class terrain situated between Vail and Frisco, on the outskirts of Copper Mountain, Colorado. As the sun set behind the majestic Rockies, visibility was limited. The gentle crunch of steps in the fresh snow was inaudible beyond thirty feet. Slow, equally timed strides resembled the makings of human steps. But with the abundance of wildlife searching for winter food, anything was possible.

The old man sat in the dark, save for the natural light glowing from the hearty wood-burning fireplace that warmed the spacious great room of the family-built cabin. It opened into a quaint but functional kitchen. A stainless-steel tea kettle heated up, preparing to scream as the water approached its boiling point. Next to the propane-burning built-in stove that rested atop a massive island, a coffee mug containing a green tea bag waited to be filled. The mug was oversized, disproportionate to the point of being deformed, and multi-colored, evidencing signs it was a gift made from the hands of a child. It was old but well taken care of, just like its owner.

The old man's modest, rustic home was designed by his grandmother and built by his grandfather, long before Vail earned its reputation as a world-class ski resort destination. When they passed, they left their unassuming home and its valuable land to their three grandchildren, who included the old man.

The three siblings had decided that the old man would occupy the residence, as he was the only one who had remained in Colorado after his siblings had moved farther west. As each heir passed, the remaining equitable interest in the property passed to the surviving siblings.

Large cobblestones surrounded the burning logs and narrowed their way up to the tall ceiling, providing a classic log cabin ambiance in the cozy Colorado cabin. The width of the fireplace surround extended ten feet, centered perfectly along the thirty-foot wall perpendicular to the cabin's entryway. On each side of the fireplace, symmetrical built-in bookcases accented the cabin's foremost heat source.

A wide array of literature filled the handmade bookshelves, all well organized by categories. An encyclopedia set, a massive collection of law books, and an Ivy League-worthy collection of reference periodicals consumed every linear inch of the bookcase to the left of the screenless fireplace. To its right, mostly fiction novels adorned the handcrafted bookcase, with titles ranging from *Catcher in the Rye* and *To Kill a Mockingbird*, *The DaVinci Code* and the *Longmire Mystery* series. Keeping them company, a copy of *The Almanac of Famous Quotes* gathered no dust.

Sitting at a forty-five-degree angle facing away from the burning logs that had been ruggedly cut in exchange for the old man's sweat, lay a brown recliner. Its leather was warmed by the fire on its right side, and by the old man's behind on its topside. Reading glasses perched on the tip of his nose hung for dear life as his tipped head faced downward to a torn and tattered notebook. He reviewed his notes for the ten-thousandth time, then jotted down some more.

The crackling fire logs resembled a firework show in the silence of the isolated woods. A mini Fourth of July celebration in mid-winter. Then, abruptly and unexpectedly, the silence ended. A rustling followed by a thump sounded outside, two seconds before the tea kettle sounded its high-pitched whistle.

The old man tossed his notebook and pen on the side table to his left, knocking over a recently received holiday card displayed upright. The envelope in which the card had arrived fell to the floor and under the bottom shelf of the wooden table, with only a corner peeking out underneath.

He hustled to the stove to silence the screaming kettle. For eighty-three, he moved quickly. But still, he was in his ninth decade, so not nearly as fast as he wished. By the time he turned off the stove and removed the kettle from the scorching cast iron top, he heard nothing other than the crackling silence.

Had he heard a noise outside? One could flip a coin. Sometimes, while deeply entrenched in his search for the undiscovered, his imagination got the best of him. Other times, his hearing aid played tricks on him. So, for the old man, if a tree fell in the woods, did he actually hear it? He certainly wouldn't wager on it.

Could it have been an animal desperately searching for winter nourishment? Was it an extreme skier, separated from his buddies, looking for an epic vertical drop? Or was it an intruder looking to rob the old timer of his most valuable asset—the physical manifestation of the product formed between his ears?

Animals scrounging around on his property was common, but this sounded different. Just slightly, but different nonetheless. Extreme skiers passing through was not commonplace, but it wouldn't be the first time. An intruder, looking to snatch valuable physical property, would be gravely disappointed. An intruder, searching for valuable intellectual property, potentially could strike gold.

Ninety seconds later, the front door's vintage wooden doorknob slowly turned, inching clockwise at the speed of a pocket watch's second hand. Each turn was made with precision and total silence, eliminating the odds it was an animal—at least of a four-legged variety. Inside, the fireplace sparkled, now struggling to warm the cozy cabin that cooled slowly as the frozen air seeped into the expanding door opening. After edging to a six-inch crack, the creeping door came to a stop. About shoulder height up the door jamb, a long satin stainless-steel barrel peeked inside the rural home, clearing the path for its holder.

The *Ruger Mark IV's* extended ten-inch barrel emerged like a telescope scanning the room. The long sleek barrel accomplished two things: increasing the bullet's stability and velocity with its prolonged barrel-time; and enhancing its accuracy due to the increased sight radius from the distance of the rear sight to the front sight. Featuring a Computer Numerical Control-machined grip frame, a cold hammer-forged barrel, and a natural pointing checkered synthetic grip angle contoured comfortably to the hand; it was the intruder's weapon of choice.

Prepared to have a shotgun greeting him at the door, the unwelcomed visitor paused. Nothing. His butt cheeks clenched. With his right foot, he gently tapped the door, opening it another few inches. Still nothing. No spring-gun booby trap to blow his head off his shoulders. No "get off my lawn" old man blowing the door from its hinges with a *Remington 870* shotgun. Still proceeding with extreme caution, the trespasser tossed a pinecone into the cabin, expecting a gunshot to follow. He waited. He listened. Nothing.

Led by the long-barreled companion, two black down jacket sleeves crept through the doorway. A hooded head followed. The right shoulder of the insulated, quilted winter attire leaned into the door just enough to open it halfway. The *Ruger* cleared the room, the outdoor air chilled it. Other than the popping of the fire logs, the loudest things in the room were the hideous homemade mug and a brightly colored handcrafted blanket draped over the old man's chair.

Physically fit like a fifty-five-year-old lumberjack, the old man still chopped his wood and fished often, but he no longer drove a car. His diminished eyesight over the years, combined with the dangerous mountain roads—especially during winter—made such a luxury unwise. Rather, a versatile young millennial, who split time as a rideshare driver and other employment, graciously drove the old man to his limited outings.

The great room and kitchen were unoccupied. The cabin's owner appeared nowhere in sight. The dossier on the old man indicated a ninety-eight percent chance he would be home. Other than a twenty-five-minute drive to Frisco once a week for groceries, and every day for a morning coffee rendezvous with his best friend, he was all but certain to be home.

The old man didn't own a vehicle, so the absence of one provided no clue to the intruder. And with the fireplace being the cabin's primary heat source, it would blaze all winter, even while unsupervised. So likewise, that didn't offer a hint as to the presence of anyone.

The hired gun had been tasked with two assignments: secure the old timer's notebook and any other related evidence; and if necessary, expedite the introduction of the Grim Reaper to the seemingly immortal old man.

The burglar cleared the main room and kitchen. No old man in sight. He tiptoed to the lone bedroom. No old man passed out on the bed or dead on the floor. He searched high and low. Still nothing. He simulated his routine in the bathroom. No old man hunched over sitting dead on his throne. He yanked back the shower curtain; no Janet Leigh scream followed. Wherever he was, the old man was not in his cabin.

With no old geezer in sight, the hitman's second assignment was put on hold, perhaps permanently, as it was only required if necessary to accomplish assignment one. Assignment one was the priority; get the notebook.

Returning to the main room, the intruder felt the top of the leather recliner nearest the fireplace. It felt warm. Perhaps recently sat on. Perhaps the effects of its proximity to a blazing fire. The side table next to the recliner was empty. Underneath, a bit of paper peeped out. The intruder squatted, picked it up, glanced at it, and shoved it in his pocket.

Obviously not a Rhodes Scholar, other than clearing the rooms, the hired gun didn't look for other clues to verify if the old man had recently been inside. He didn't see him, so his focus instantly shifted to finding the notebook. If he combed every inch of the property where a notebook could fit, the old man was bound to turn up somewhere.

Primarily tasked with that mission, the search was exhaustive—and destructive.

* * *

THE NEXT MORNING, the old man's flesh had grown cold, and his body had stiffened like a board, lying still as a corpse. The cabin was cold, but its owner colder.

Cold, stiff, and still. Dead? No. But unquestionably lucky to be alive. Cold, because the fire had dwindled, and the front door remained open for hours throughout the biting-cold evening temperature. Stiff and still, because he'd slept the entire night on an old vinyl recliner while confined in a tight five-by-ten-foot dark space—the likes of a nineteenth-century cave.

The hidden area was simple, with nothing other than the chair, a fleece blanket, a flashlight, a no-longer-empty five-gallon bucket covered by a snap-on toilet seat and cover, three-days-worth of nonperishable food supplies, three gallons of water, and a security blanket—a 1961 *Smith & Wesson .22 Center-fire Magnum.*

He looked at his watch. It was 6:35 a.m. His aged eardrums listened intently for twenty minutes, all the while not moving an inch. Not a sound. Not a squeak. Not a creak.

The old man labored to remove himself from the sunken cushion. He groaned as he stood upright. He placed his pen and notebook on his warmed seat, preparing to exit. With the handgun in his right hand, his free hand flipped a latch and then grabbed the handle on the interior wall. Then with a gentle push, the wall crept open slowly as the old man listened closely. Still, not a sound.

In the great room of the cabin, one half of the bookcase to the right of the fireplace opened into the room. From behind it and led by his handgun, the old man ambled out of the hidden safety cove. A true work of ingenuity and craftsmanship, his grandparents' foresight had saved his life, and not for the first time. The old man looked to the ceiling and motioned a sign of the cross. Knowing the afterlife could be on the other end of every breath he took, his relationship with the divine had grown stronger in recent years.

The custom swivel bookcase concealed the private safety space that had been initially designed to keep private and secure the personal belongings of the original owners. Supporting the considerable weight of the books on the shelves, the bookcase sat on four swivel casters that enabled the heavy wood masterpiece to rotate open and shut smoothly on the hardwood floor. The simple, custom trim work was identical to the rest of the bookcase, and symmetrical with the bookcase on the other side of the fireplace, eliminating any suspicion of a hidden room, as well as masking the casters at its base. Finally, the hidden latch that unlocked the secret entryway from the main room was known only to the old man and intended never to be discovered by any other living human. It was simple, yet ingenious.

Randomly aimed into the great room, the old man's security blanket led him into the battle-scarred room. It resembled the aftermath of a warzone! Not a single book remained on the bookshelves. Rather, they lay scattered all around the floor. Most thrown. Many torn. The furniture was flipped. The lamps lay shattered on the floor, with glass from broken bulbs sprinkled everywhere. And in the kitchen, outside its slung-open cupboard doors, pots and pans had been tossed like a mixed salad.

Rarely before had a tornado torn across the high elevation landscape of the Rocky Mountains. The night before, the equivalent of an F5 tornado ravished the quaint, once-charming cabin.

The roaring fire had dwindled to remnants of orangish-colored charred logs and a flickering flame. The old man looked around and took a deep breath. He had his work cut out for him. But first, he needed to increase the room's temperature to something warmer than a meat locker. He moaned paying homage to his stiff back and gingerly grabbed a couple of wood logs from the hearthside log holder. Then, he gently placed them on the fireplace grate, atop the burnt logs, causing more ashes to fall below and a sigh of relief up above.

"Just like how grandpa described how he built this place, one step at a time," the old man said in a feeble attempt to distract himself from the overwhelming task ahead. He picked up a fiction novel, glanced at the spine, and placed it on the shelf. A chuckle followed. Ironically, it was *War and* Peace, as he tried to restore peace to the war-torn room. He grabbed another fiction novel and set it on the shelf. Then another one. Then another. He kept going until the entire right half of the bookcase was filled.

Next, he placed the first volume of a series of Colorado Reports from the 1960s onto the bottom shelf to the left of the fireplace. The retired attorney kept the relic periodicals as a reminder of the effective simplicity of the law, long before the ease and convenience of e-filing and internet-based legal research spoiled a lazier generation. When it came to the old school way of practicing law, the old man was the poster child.

Even with the strength of someone thirty years his junior, the old man struggled to flip up his favorite chair. But strong as an ox on the tail end of its life in the wild, he succeeded.

The sentimental senior rested his left hand on the armrest of his reading chair. The same one that had been tossed on its side. He leaned toward the side table and reached over with his right hand, propping up the holiday card. Pushing himself upright, he glanced under the table, then scanned the floor around it. He didn't see the envelope. Had it fallen to the floor? Was it underneath his chair? Too fatigued from returning to their proper place his mini version of the *Library of Congress*, the old man couldn't muster the energy to drop to the floor and look underneath. That was a chore for another time.

In need of a recharge, the weary man plopped down on his comfy chair, exhaled deeply, and with his brow creasing vowed to himself, "I've come too far. If it's the last thing I do before I die, I am going to solve this mystery."

Chapter Two

COLORADO'S PREDICTABLY UNPRE-DICTABLE weather held true to mid-winter form. Snow flurries, with a high of twenty-two degrees the day before; and when their plane landed at Denver International Airport it was fifty-nine degrees and as sunny as a mid-summer day in Santa Barbara. The two attorneys were back on their feet, unassisted by crutches to which they had become accustomed in the months prior. Having escaped death more than once, Joshua and Kristen were now primed to enjoy their much-needed escape.

The massive airport took up fifty-three square miles, making it the largest airport by total area in the United States. A far cry from the small, roughly one-and-a-half square mile hub from where they had departed seven miles west of downtown Santa Barbara, California, just a few hours earlier. Kristen Laney was an experienced flyer, having gone back and forth from New York to California multiple times to visit her mother while Kristen attended law school at Cornell University in Ithaca, New York.

Joshua Rizzetti, on the other hand, didn't fly much. Unequivocally, he despised it. In the previous year,

Josh had been struck by an SUV while riding his bike and shot only a month after, giving him two brushes with death in as many months. Oddly, those life-threatening events didn't scare him much, if at all. Flying, on the other hand, frightened him to no end. It not only was his biggest fear, but quite possibly, it might've been his only fear.

The long-time best friends, now dating, stood outside the sliding doors closest to the baggage claim area. Kristen had arranged for a ride that would take the couple directly to Vail, with no other stops and no other patrons.

Both travelers wanted to avoid traveling by shuttle, particularly the nuisance of it stopping all over Colorado. Inevitably, it would turn what should be a two-hour drive into a twenty-hour excursion. When Kristen had asked Josh if he wanted to save money by taking an airport shuttle instead of a rideshare, loosening his tight wallet Josh responded, "If we take a shuttle, it'd be faster if we drive from Santa Barbara to Colorado ourselves." So, rideshare it was.

Blending like a *Vitamix*, the popular airline hub crushed out various noises. Cars honked, travelers hollered, jet engines roared, and winds gusted through the covered corridor between the terminal and the covered short-term parking. The sounds of the world on the go stressed Josh a bit, but he endured knowing relaxation was a ski slope away.

Kristen and Josh looked up and down the curbside, having been told their driver would wait in the loading area with a sign that read "Rizzetti."

"Bang!" a booming noise echoed through the covered passageway.

Josh jumped back, mentally taking inventory of his packed boxers. "What the—?" he cried. *Might need a clean pair*, he thought.

"Relax," Kristen said. "It wasn't a gunshot. A car just rear-ended that airport shuttle van over there." She pointed to the lane that veered into the parking garage. The weaving of vehicles in and out of lanes, and their constant acceleration and braking, resembled maneuvers on the bumper cars. Consequently, rear-end collisions should've come as no surprise. But to Josh, thanks to his recent encounters with flying bullets, including one that kissed his gut firsthand, every unexpected loud noise sounded like gunfire—and zeroed in on him.

"I guess we can add loud bangs to flying on the list of things I fear," Josh laughed. "That frightened the crud out of me."

Josh wasn't one to cuss and often wondered what others thought when he opted against using expletives at opportunities not passed up by ninety-nine percent of the population. As he saw it, what was the point of cursing? At best, it was inappropriate around children and served no real purpose other than to make some people uncomfortable. *What the f— is up with that?* he thought to himself while aware of the irony.

"Take a deep breath. We're on vacation." Kristen patted Josh on the shoulder and smiled.

"Oh good, there's our ride," Josh said, pointing to his right toward a Subaru SUV, beside which stood a young lady with a sign that read "Rizzetti and Laney." Fitting the Colorado lifestyle stereotype, a ski rack sat atop the Rocky Mountain region's most popular SUV.

Kristen waved and made eye contact with the driver. The couple grabbed their respective rolling luggage handles and hurried toward their ride, excited to relax and enjoy their two weeks of vacation.

Although both had accumulated several weeks of vacation time from their jobs, they settled on a two-week sabbatical. District Attorney William Tell had insisted that Josh take three weeks, while Kristen's boss, Saladino Perricone, had demanded that she take off a month. Workaholics to the bone, the couple had only requested one week. They compromised on two.

"Hello," greeted the rideshare driver. "You must be Mr. Rizzetti and Ms. Laney. I'm Hannah. Welcome to Colorful Colorado." With the hatchback open, she placed Kristen's luggage in the back as Josh did the same with his. Josh's baggage was twice as heavy as Kristen's. But not by his choice, and not with his stuff. No, Kristen had nearly busted the zipper cramming what Josh referred to as "extra junk into his trunk" with her superfluous accessories.

"Hi, Hannah. Nice to meet you," the newly anointed couple said in unison.

After Hannah's insistence, Kristen sat in the front seat. Josh sat behind Kristen. Other than some melted snow on the floor mats, the vehicle was spotless. The radio played at a low volume, fittingly on Josh's favorite—an eighties' station. Like Depeche Mode, he just couldn't seem to get enough. One-hit wonders were his favorite.

With the precision and confidence of a NASCAR driver, Hannah squeezed between two shuttles and exited the covered corridor toward the ticket toll booth. Abruptly turning to the right, she bolted toward the only empty booth, paid the toll, and exited the airport. After witnessing the fender bender to the Airport Shuttle that nearly soiled Joshua's skivvies, and with a younger and much prettier Richard Petty behind the wheel, the couple had to be feeling vindicated by their pricier choice of transportation.

Interstate 70 flowed smoothly, with only moderate traffic. To Josh's surprise, the road conditions were decent; enough to keep him from needing his third pair of *Hanes* in his first hour in the colorful state. The bright sun had melted any leftover precipitation from the day before, and the sky was clear. It has been years since Josh last visited Colorado, and he had forgotten how beautiful it was. As they passed the Front Range and headed up the Rocky Mountains toward Evergreen, it reminded Josh why so many people were fleeing California for the Centennial State, much to the lament of Coloradoans.

"So, Hannah," Kristen said, "I noticed the ski rack on top. Not to stereotype all Coloradoans, but I take it you're a big-time skier?"

"I am. I dabble as a private ski instructor. Mostly in Vail and Copper Mountain. I do the rideshare gig on my days off during the winter, and most days during the summer."

"That must be fun," Josh said. "Kristen, I think we picked the wrong profession."

"Oh yeah," interjected Hannah. "And what profession is that?"

Kristen responded, "Sadly, we're both attorneys."

"Funny," said Hannah. "My parents wanted me to go to law school. Fortunately, my grandfather talked me out of it."

"Why did he do that?" Josh asked, fully understanding the why.

"Because he was an attorney, I'm sure I'm not telling you two something you don't already know, but most attorneys wish they'd chosen another path. Don't get me wrong, he loved his work. But he dealt with enough miserable attorneys to know that his enjoyment was the exception, not the rule." Hannah's voice faded as if worried her words would fall on offended ears. Hardly. Kristen and Josh smiled and nodded. While they enjoyed their jobs, they certainly understood, Josh more painfully in tune from his days at "The Bakery."

Hannah continued, "He's now retired and subscribes to a local ski magazine. He's too old to ski as much as he used to, but he likes to stay 'hip' as he likes to call it, so he reads up on the local trends."

As they traveled smoothly along the winding interstate that weaved up and down and left and right through the Rocky Mountains, Hannah filled the time with quirky facts about the area. Kirstin focused on the highway, warding off motion sickness.

Josh wasn't as lucky. He tried desperately to focus on a point, but the point kept moving. Left, right, left, right, up, down, up, down, up . . . chuck—likely around the next corner. His face turned pale as he struggled to keep his eyes from bouncing back and forth. His throat thickened. Just as he was about to ask Hannah if they could make a rest stop, if he didn't vomit first, her phone beeped.

Hannah peeked at her smartphone and said, "Looks like there's a major slowdown because of an accident right before the Eisenhower Tunnel. If you're hungry, we can stop in Idaho Springs and grab a bite to eat. There's a great pizza place there, famous for its Colorado-style pizza pies."

The Eisenhower Tunnel was a dual-bore, four-lane tunnel that extended Interstate 70 under the famous Continental Divide of the Rocky Mountains. Idaho Springs was a small, old mining town nestled about five miles from their present location. Kristen was ready to take a restroom break, Josh was ready to puke; so, they both jumped at Hannah's offer.

"Yes, please," the couple blurted in harmony. Josh swallowed quickly, as more than words tried to exit his mouth.

"Sounds like a plan," Hannah said. "It's a charming little historic town. You won't believe it when you see it, but it was a booming town during the gold rush."

The main street that ran through Idaho Springs looked straight out of a storybook. Charming buildings lined Miner Street, housed by cute retail shops with restaurants sprinkled in and surrounded by some of the prettiest mountains in North America. The street was active, with cars parked along the curb and tourists strolling up and down the quaint but lively thoroughfare.

To Hannah's excitement, a truck pulled away from the curb, freeing up a parking spot only one door down from the pizza place. Like pulling in for a pit stop, her vehicle was parked in a flash.

After a fifteen-minute wait, the group of three was seated in the back of the busy restaurant overlooking the outdoor patio area. The crowd included a hodge-podge of young families, older couples, groups on vacation, grungy snowboarders, and local businesspeople enjoying a noontime break that inevitably would lead to an afternoon nap.

Josh eyed a variety of Colorado-style pizza pies scattered on several tables around the room. Each table had the standard supply of grated parmesan cheese, ground chili pepper, napkins, and squeeze bottles of honey. *Honey?* Befuddled for only an instant, Josh's focus returned to the delectable pies loaded with all the toppings. His eyes widened, his face smiled, and his mouth watered.

Kristen was buried in the menu, struggling to make a choice. Everything looked delicious, enhanced by the alluring aroma of fresh-baked dough, garlic, and pizza sauce lingering in the air. Undecided, Josh threw in the towel and deferred to the local.

"Hannah," said Josh, peeking his eyes over the top of his menu. "What do you recommend?"

"You can't go wrong with the traditional pepperoni pie." Hannah smiled and lifted a container of honey from the center of their table. "Unlike any other pizza you've ever had, the best part is the often-neglected afterthought—the crust. Here, it is so fresh. When you get down to the crust, what you do is cover it in honey and then eat it last, like dessert."

"Interesting." Kristen put down her menu "That sounds amazing. Count me in."

"Pepperoni pizza it is," Josh chuckled. "I never met a pepperoni pizza I didn't like. I'm fairly confident, I'm gonna love this one. Judging from the room full of smiles, everyone's either high as a kite, or they're enjoying the pizza."

"Perhaps both," said Hannah, sparking giggles from her guests.

"I've also counted a handful of men with the top button of their pants unbuttoned. That's always a good sign." Josh patted his six-pack abs.

Kristen scoffed. "I'm not going to ask how you noticed that."

Josh was seated facing the windows that overlooked the back dining patio. He glanced at a young boy two tables over, as a long string of cheese stretched from his grinning mouth. With his arm fully extended, the little guy's reach wasn't quite long enough, falling short of snapping the gooey string. His older sister laughed as she flung it with her marinated finger. Her fling cut the cheese but sprayed his face with pizza sauce in the process. The brother retaliated by cutting his own cheese, lifting a cheek, and aiming at his sister.

"Andrew William Schmidt," scolded his mother.

"Aw, come on Drew," his sister cried, plugging her nose. "That's disgusting." Her face cringed as she shook her head at her brother, who seemed aptly named—appearing able to draw fire at will.

Seated to Josh's right, were three men: one mid-life and two seemingly in their late twenties. One of the three had one of those loud voices that carried over other voices, even while attempting to whisper. Booming. Resonating. Echoing. Every time he spoke, his friends shh-shh'd him. Each time they did, it drew greater attention from the curious prosecutor.

Josh, Kristen, and Hannah polished off every last bite of their large pizza. Having first-hand knowledge the Colorado-style pie would make her drowsy, Hannah put away caffeine as if the U.S. Supreme Court was set to rule cola unconstitutional, banning it the following day. She excused herself from her guests and scurried to the ladies' room. Josh's eyes trailed her, expecting a puddle to follow.

A minute later, their waiter stopped by their table. Josh settled their tab; grateful it didn't include tinkle clean-up from their saturated driver.

"So, what did you think?" Kristen asked.

Josh lifted a menu to the right side of his face, and with his left forefinger, placed it against his lips. He shifted his eyes to his right toward the three males seated at the adjacent table. Kristen caught the hint and said nothing further.

Two of the men were Gen Z members, and the third was considerably older—likely the recipient of countless junk mail invitations for AARP membership. One of the young men was topped with curly blonde hair, seemingly permed. A blond version of Greg Brady in the latter episodes of *The Brady Bunch* came to Josh's mind as he tried not to stare. The other youngster was the loud one. Dressed like a hipster, he was cursed with one of those voices that carried no matter how quietly he spoke as if an amplifier had attached to his vocal cords at birth. The early-to-mid fifties man stood out, but not for his age relative to his younger cohorts. Rather, for something more visibly distinguishable.

After two of the men shushed the loud one for the umpteenth time, Kirsten leaned to her left, inching closer to the table that suddenly had Josh's attention. Knowing Josh, Kristen probably figured that her boyfriend overheard the three amigos planning a jewelry heist or were strategizing a bank robbery.

"It's rumored to be worth at least ten million, but nobody really knows" the megaphone mouth loudly whispered, followed by a shush and a slug to his arm from one of his companions. "And we're looking at a twenty percent finder's fee." Two more "shh-shh-es" and a slug to his other arm finally silenced the loud-mouthed zoomer.

Kristen raised her eyebrows. Josh raised his level of attention. But before they could eavesdrop further, Hannah returned. "Ready to hit the road after we pay the bill?"

"I already took care of it," Josh responded. "So, we're good to go."

"Thank you, Josh."

"Thank you for suggesting the local fare." Kristen stood up and rubbed her stomach. "It was both delicious and unique. And I'm a loyal subscriber to *when in Rome.*"

"Yes, thank you," Josh said. "In less than an hour, this Colorado-style pizza made its way from my plate to my stomach to my top five list of favorite pizzas."

Josh peeked over to take a mental picture of the patrons seated to his right as he waited for the two ladies to walk ahead of him. As a seasoned prosecutor, observing the details—especially when his "something-looks-suspicious" radar went off—was engrained in his behavior. If Josh had a dime for every time, after questioning a witness, he had said to himself *If only you had paid more attention to the details, or at least the obvious*, he'd be retired by thirty-five. In this instance, remembering one of the details wouldn't be an issue. One of the men wasn't just memorable, he was unforgettable.

Chapter Three

T HE THREE FORMER colleagues sat in their usual spot outside their favorite coffeehouse on the charming Main Street in Frisco, Colorado. Creatures of habit, even on the coldest winter days, the retired attorneys stuck to their routine. Comparable to the slogan of the United States Postal Service, the seemingly immortal men would meet regularly for their coffee chat through rain, sleet, snow, or blizzard.

The popular gathering spot for locals and visitors alike was inviting, with its welcoming front patio, centered by a custom natural gas firepit. And while it provided some heat and a warm ambiance, it wasn't enough to warm the entire patio area on cold winter days in the Rockies.

Three years prior, the owner of the coffee shop added a portable propane heater to the patio area as a courtesy to the stubborn old men. It was ninety percent out of love and respect for his loyal patrons, and ten percent out of fear that the three old men would freeze to death in the middle of the morning coffee rush. He likely assumed three dead geezers at the doorstep of his coffee shop probably wouldn't be good for business. With such astute business acumen, it was no wonder his coffee shop was the most popular in town.

Frisco was a small town with a population in the ballpark of three thousand people. But for someone living on the secluded outskirts of Copper Mountain, Frisco was like a big city. Paling in comparison, Copper Mountain had a population of fewer than five hundred people.

Frisco's primary street was adorned with several blocks of charming retail shops, a variety of restaurants, a quaint hotel, a local bookstore, a bed and breakfast, and a few motels. One end of the street ran into Lake Dillon, one of the most picturesque lakes in the country, and intersected it near the middle of its nearly twenty-seven miles of shoreline. The other end of Main Street nestled up against a Rocky Mountain backdrop. Decorated to the hilt for every season and holiday and positioned in the middle of several top-notch ski destinations, the town looked straight out of a *Hallmark* movie.

The morning crowd on Main Street was typical for a winter weekday. A few pairs of middle-aged women were speed-walking on the sidewalk, some early-riser tourists enjoyed window shopping and consuming the crisp mountain air, and a fair amount of Gen Z'ers periodically popped in and out of the coffee shop before hitting the slopes in Breckenridge, Keystone, Copper Mountain, and A-Basin.

"Hey, please pick up your dog crap!" George hollered in classic old man, get-off-my-lawn fashion, scaring the human equivalent out of the furry mutt's female owner. With eight decades in his rear-view mirror, the old man saw no harm in speaking his mind with minimal filtration. Statistically speaking, he wouldn't be around long enough to need more friends, so he might as well attempt to improve the world any chance he could get—even if just a bit.

Faking window-shopping, the thirty-something-year-old entitled, female tourist jumped back and scrambled to pull a plastic baggy from her pocket, after pretending not to see her massive, sweater-wearing canine drop a horse-size turd in the middle of the sidewalk. "Yes, sir. I'm sorry," she replied, likely more embarrassed that she was caught playing ignorant more so than being genuinely apologetic.

"Alright, George," said Sam, the medium-rare seasoned of the three old men. "What's eating at you? I've known you for too long not to know when something's up."

Sam stood at a modest five-foot-ten-inches tall, with a thin frame that supported his bald head. The chrome dome sported a bold new look for George's closest friend. Although different, his appearance was much preferred over the laughable comb-over that had been thinning dramatically over the past two years. He was a young seventy-six years old, diligent about taking good care of himself. He walked two miles at least four days a week, including the winter months, and kayaked on Lake Dillon two days a week during the warmer months.

Sam had joined the Summit County District Attorney's Office after ten years of private practice with a large, statewide law firm headquartered in Denver. With offices in Denver, Colorado Springs, Fort

Collins, Castle Rock, and Grand Junction, it was the second largest firm in the state at the time of his departure, just one year after making senior partner.

Unfulfilled, Sam no longer wished to trade his life for money. At that point in his career, he was well-connected, and could pretty much select the job of his choosing. With a strong desire to spend more time enjoying life, his affinity for downhill skiing made snatching the opening at the District Attorney's Office in Breckenridge an easy decision. On day one, Sam was partnered with an eight-year veteran prosecutor to teach him the ropes of criminal prosecution. Almost a half-century later, the two former Deputy D.A.s remained best friends.

George took a sip of his coffee, then curled his fingers around the cup to warm his frozen hands. "I had a visitor last night."

"What do you mean by visitor?" asked Hank, the youngest of the three retired Deputy District Attorneys. "You're too old for booty calls. *Doody* calls, yes. Booty calls, no."

"Hank, don't you mean *duty* calls?" asked George.

"For someone who should be a majority shareholder in adult diapers, I'm pretty sure he means *doody* calls." Sam smiled, chuckling at his own joke.

George raised his coffee cup toward Sam. "People in glass houses, my friend."

"Touché." Sam reciprocated, tipping his cup to his former court partner. "I'm sorry. Go on. So, what do you mean by visitor?"

"An unwanted one." George raised his eyebrows, shifting his sight from one friend to the other.

"*What*?" Hank pulled his head back. "You mean, like an intruder?"

"Yes sir," George said. "And not the random kind. This one came with a purpose."

"You mean—" Sam lowered his cup to the cold frosty table.

"Yep," George responded before Sam could finish his sentence.

"Did he get anything?" Hank leaned toward the firepit but kept eye contact with George, eager for his response.

"Not that I'm aware of. And certainly not what he was after."

"George, my friend," Sam said. "I worry about you out there in your secluded cabin. I'd feel much better if you moved into civilization near me. A condo only two units over from me just went on the market. Like I've said a million times before, it's great being only two blocks from Main Street here in Frisco. We could walk to our daily coffee meetings together."

"I'm too old to uproot myself."

"Uproot!" Sam laughed. "We're talking Frisco, not San Francisco. It's not like you'd be moving across the country. It's less than twenty miles. But a world of difference in terms of convenience and safety. You even can get cell service here."

"Cell service," George said with a smile. "What do I need phone service for?"

"Calling 9-1-1 for starters!" Sam took a sip of coffee, then continued. "And you could keep in touch with your great-nephew."

"I do keep in touch with him," George insisted.

"I wouldn't call sending him a birthday and Christmas cards every year keeping in touch." Hank shook his head. "That's more like just letting him know you're still nine thousand feet above sea level as opposed to six feet underground."

George took a sip of coffee, then nodded his head.

"So, George," Sam continued, "at what point will you decide that this wild goose chase you've been on for years is not worth your life?"

Hank nodded his head. "I concur. I mean—when's the last time you made any new progress anyways?"

"Like I told you guys last week," George said as he stared into the fire, "I think I've had a major breakthrough."

Relative to his friends, Hank Ragsdill was a spring chicken—having just celebrated his sixty-eighth birthday. He stood tall for his generation, peaking at six-foot-two-inches tall on a husky frame. His thick head of hair defied his age, which he further magnified by routinely applying jet black dye to avoid a speckle of gray hair.

Like Sam, Hank joined the District Attorney's Office after leaving private practice. But unlike his friend, Hank came from a small firm, consisting of only him and his business partner. And while the fully retired besties met daily at the local java joint, Hank's busy schedule only permitted him to join George and Sam one or two times a week.

After having taken over the helm of his family's business—Ragsdill Masonry—after the unexpected death of his brother, Hank's retirement from the District Attorney's Office didn't relieve him from working altogether. He didn't seem to mind. Often he mentioned that he enjoyed running the business more than practicing law.

Hank too stayed in top shape for a senior citizen, walking two miles a day, six days a week, and paddle boarding three days a week in the summer. His dark, leathery skin surfaced when he was in high school, working summers for his family's cement contracting business, then darkening in tint and gaining in wrinkles from his paddle boarding ritual on the lake during his senior years. Not letting his late sixties slow him down, the athletic businessman even made use of his Senior's Ski Bum Pass with regular skiing treks down Vail, Copper Mountain, Keystone, and Breckenridge a few times per year.

Sam glared at George and shook his head in frustration. "It took me years to realize it, but lives are worth more than some mythical treasure."

"Gentlemen, at this point in my life, I'm living on stolen time. So, I figure I've got nothing to lose."

"Well, my friend. I do." Sam leaned across the small, round metal table and patted his long-time companion on the shoulder. "I don't want to lose my best friend."

"I hear ya, Sam." George lifted his coffee cup as if to toast their friendship. "But it's no longer about the financial windfall at the end of the hunt. It's about completing what I started. You and I both know how close we were to solving the puzzle when you decided to throw in the towel. And I know I've made some real progress since then. It's so close, I can taste it." George took a swig of coffee.

"That taste, my good man, is your new denture cleaner," joked Hank, clearing his throat. George quickly placed a napkin over his mouth, fending off spraying his friends with Columbian hazelnut showers. Sam's forecast, however, called for a one-hundred-percent chance of scattered showers. He jolted his head to the side to avoid misting his friends, instead spitting a vanilla nut blend into the fire pit.

"Well played, Hank. Okay, how about this?" George rubbed his thumb, pointer, and middle fingers together. "I'm so close, I can feel it." He followed with a deep inhale. "I can smell it."

"That smell, my friend, is your adult diaper ready to be changed," jabbed Sam, smiling as he gave a nod to Hank. The two chuckled.

"Oscar Wilde was spot on—*true friends stab you in the front*." George picked up a plastic knife from the table, pretended to pull it out from his chest, and extended it to his friend. "Sam, I believe this is yours."

The three sounded out with their synchronized, old man laugh-cough combination.

George raised his cup and toasted his friends. "To true friends." He paused., then smirked. "And to you guys as well."

The three long-time co-working crimefighters of the Summit County District Attorney's Office tapped their coffee cups together. Sam and Hank repeated, "To true friends."

Chapter Four

HIS FACE WAS creepy, yet almost artistic. Straight out of a low-budget horror film. Almost the entire left side of his prematurely wrinkled face had been burned, with raised skin scarred to a reddish-purple hue. It was charred to the point of being numb to the light touch. The artistic element, however, was not in the scar itself. It was in the unscarred portion of his branded cheek, perfectly shaped like a snowflake. The precision of its shape resembled the masterpiece of a talented tattoo artist.

The boss answered his burner phone, "So? Don't keep me waiting."

"We got nothin'," responded Scarface. "It wasn't there. Neither was the old man."

"What do you mean?" the boss snarled. "It has to be there. Where else could it be? The old man is a hermit."

"Nate turned the cabin upside down. Nothing but the bare essentials and a bunch of boring books."

"Could it have been hidden in the books?"

"Not a chance. He said he tore through every one of them. Nothing."

"Well, it's got to be in there somewhere," argued the head honcho, raising his volume. "How do we know he didn't find it and keep it for himself?"

"Not a chance," Scarface challenged with conviction. "First of all, he isn't smart enough for the notebook to do him any good. And second, his loyalty to me is second to none."

"Well, he's new to our crew. So, his allegiance to you doesn't necessarily mean unwavering loyalty to me. Does it?"

"You can trust him," Scarface assured. "Trust me."

"I trust no one. Speaking of, where are we with our other problem?"

"Our inside source told me the guy's thinking about cutting a deal."

Slamming his fist down loud enough for Scarface to pull his phone away from his ear, the alpha male scowled, "Which would be a breach of his deal with me!"

"Yes, sir. It would."

"Now, we can't have that. Can we?"

"I suppose not," replied Scarface. "Would you like to do something about it?"

"Let me think about it," huffed the leader, abruptly followed by a beep, ending his call.

Scarface pulled away the phone that was pressed against his scarred cheek and glared at the screen. Did he get disconnected or was it a hang-up Two seconds later, his phone rang. He answered, "Yes, sir. What—"

Before the highest-ranking minion could finish, an authoritative tone interrupted, "I thought about it.

Take care of it!" he commanded, then hung on a three-second pause. "Permanently!"

A beep sounded. "Call Ended" flashed on the recipient's phone. Message received.

Chapter Five

JOSH AND KRISTEN sat in comfort by the fireplace in their one bedroom, one bathroom condo. It lay perched on the third floor of a classically Bavarian-designed building in the Lionshead Village of Vail, an area oozing with European charm.

The public, touristy section of Vail was separated into two main retail areas: Vail Village and Lionshead Village. Josh chose a condo in Lionshead Village because of its convenient location above a coffee shop, pizza restaurant, and the local outdoor ice-skating rink. To boot, it was just a stone's throw away from one of the thirty-three ski lifts at the world-renown resort.

Location was a priority for Josh, and not just while on vacation. His quaint bungalow home in Santa Barbara was conveniently located within walking distance to his work at the District Attorney's Office, the restaurants and retail shopping on the famed State Street, and the sandy shores of Cabrillo Beach along the Pacific Ocean. While on vacation, a prime location was equally important for the fit thirty-something-year-old. He loved to wake up early in the morning, walk to grab a coffee, and take in the local surroundings.

Josh scored an ideal spot for part one of their vacation with the ideally situated cozy condo in Vail. They had reserved four days of lodging in Vail, with plans to ski one day and ice skate another day. The rest, they'd play by ear. Despite the massive expanse of Vail's ski terrain, by far the largest in Colorado and covering over five thousand skiable acres, its two retail villages were relatively small and did not offer a lot to do for more than a few days. Unless one was adamant about skiing 24/7 or blowing thousands of dollars on overpriced retail items, Vail could be experienced in a day or two.

For the remaining ten days of their escape, they appropriated accommodations in neighboring Summit County. Part two of their vacation awaited them on the *Main Street to the Rockies*. They had booked a prime location at the Lake Dillon Bed and Breakfast, roughly twenty-five miles east of Vail and nestled in the heart of the delightful retail district of Main Street in Frisco.

The temperature outside was a snugly twenty-nine degrees. A sporadic assortment of small snowflakes trickled down as the two over-worked attorneys sipped hot chocolate and cozied up to the gas fireplace. The cobblestone surround of the fireplace created a warm ambiance while the gas logs supplied toasty air. A faux wood, rustic mantle above the opening completed the cozy atmosphere. The flame blazed exceptionally strong for an indoor gas fireplace, requiring Josh to crack a window to prevent the five-hundred-seventy square foot condo from turning into a sauna.

Kristen's eyes fixated on the page that she reread three times, entrenched in the spicy scene in her latest book. She fancied a variety of fiction, but romance seduced her weak spot. She found two lovers engaged in a grind a proven source of relief from her day-to-day grind as a business attorney.

Josh, on the other hand, preferred non-fiction while on vacation. Most notably, he loved to read the local newspaper while visiting personally unchartered destinations. He found getting a glimpse of the local events to be a sure-fire way to get the most out of his vacation. What better way to enjoy a place than to mix it up with the locals in their native activities? Not to mention the humor he often found reading the newsworthy happenings of an unfamiliar town.

Josh flipped the next page of the Eagle County Daily Tribune to page five and busted out in laughter after reading the headline: "Open-bed condom truck dumps entire load after rear-ending someone on I-70."

"I'm guessing the paper's weather forecast called for chocolate showers," snarked Kristen as she watched Josh spray cocoa mist into the sizzling fire.

Still in hysterics, Josh couldn't muster more than three words amidst his laughter. "Check this out." He showed the article headline to Kristen, on the verge of peeing his pants. She read it, then did a double-take as if questioning what she had seen. She read it again.

"Okay, that's beyond hilarious. Definitely spit-worthy," she chuckled. "And I thought what I'm reading is hot and heavy." She marked her page and set her book on her lap. "So, what else did you find?"

"There's an opening for a Deputy District Attorney in Breckenridge, Colorado."

"Really?" Kristen said, disenchanted by her partner. Her stare burned into her mate hotter than the gas-infused flames. "We're on vacation and you're job hunting. Come on now."

"In the words of Frankie, 'Relax.' I'm just noting an observation. Although, it would be pretty cool to live out here. Figuratively and literally." The eighties' music-obsessed prosecutor envisioned life as a Deputy District Attorney in the Rocky Mountains—taking in a few black diamond runs during a lunch break. He undoubtedly could think of worse places to fight the good fight.

"Okay, enough daydreaming about trading in your surfboard for a snowboard," Kristen said, shivering from the freezing air sifting through the edged-open window. "In the lyrics of The Go-Go's, 'vacation's all I ever wanted.' So, did you find any must-attend local events for us while we're here?"

"Well, since you appear to be frozen, in the words of Anna, 'Do You Want to Build a Snowman?' Or, in the words of Duran Duran, are you 'Hungry Like the Wolf?'"

"Huh?"

"Do you want to build a snowman or go for a hunt?"

"Those are my two choices?"

"Well, there's a couples' snowman building contest scheduled for tomorrow. There's also the annual Vail Village Scavenger Hunt in two days."

"A scavenger hunt," Kristen said, raising her eyebrows. "That sounds unique! And fun!"

"Yeh, it's definitely unique. They've been doing that event here for years. It started as a real-life treasure hunt, riddled with cryptic clues, all in search of the hidden golden treasure of Vail Valley."

"The newspaper mentions all that?" Kristen asked.

"No. Not exactly," responded Josh. "I started hearing the story of the hidden treasure from when I was as young as I can remember." Gazing at the fire, Josh's mind wandered. "You know how I told you about my quirky great-uncle who lives in Colorado?"

"Yes," Kristen said, then paused. She grabbed her book from her lap, placed it on the end table next to her chair, and rubbed her hands close to the fireplace. "Don't tell me your uncle is a treasure hunter?"

"Well—"

"Are you serious?" Kristen interrupted.

"Well, not exactly."

"Then *what*, exactly?" Kristen shifted to cross-examination mode.

"Easy, shark!" Josh stammered. "I thought I was the litigation attorney, and you were the paper-pushing lawyer."

"I'm still waiting for your response," Kristen said, then cleared her throat. "Mr. Rizzetti." She looked to her left to a space occupied by an imaginary judge. "Your Honor, please instruct the witness to answer the question."

"Objection, Your Honor. She's badgering the witness."

"Oh, Mr. Rizzetti. Poor fragile Mr. Rizzetti. This isn't badgering. Trust me, when I badger you, you'll know it." Kristen snickered. Impersonating a judge, she hammered her fist on her lap. "Objection over-ruled. The witness shall answer the question."

"Okay, okay. I guess you could call him a treasure hunter," Josh muttered defensively. "But it's not how it sounds."

"You mean *crazy?*"

"Like I said," Josh jumped in quickly, "it's not how it sounds. He's an extremely intelligent, well-educated man. Brilliant, actually. He finished second in his law school class at the University of Colorado and was a prosecutor for the Summit County District Attorney's Office for decades."

"So, is that the surprise you were telling me about on the plane?" asked Kristen.

"Sort of," Josh replied. He now regretted not filling in Kristen when they had scheduled their trip. "He lives nearby. And I would love to visit him, and for you to meet him. He's gotta be close to ninety years old, so this might be the last chance I get to see him."

Kristen dropped her head, shaking it side to side.

"I'm sorry," Josh whispered. "I know I should have said something to you months ago. I totally get it. This is our vacation, not a family reunion."

"Rizzetti, Rizzetti, Rizzetti. What are we going to do with you?" Kristen looked up, glared at Josh, then smiled. "You know me better than that. Of course, we can visit your great uncle. After all, he's family! Truth be told, that's a nice surprise. I remember you talking about him, but I don't think you ever mentioned ex-actly where he lived. But that makes sense. You told me your grandparents were from Colorado."

"Thank you." Josh leaned over and kissed Kristen on the top of her head.

"Now I'm super intrigued by this scavenger hunt. We gotta partake in that event. Most definitely. That sounds like a lot more fun than building Frosty."

"Sounds like a plan." Josh flipped the page of the local newspaper. He pulled his head back and grumbled something incoherent. The headline on page six caught the trial attorney's attention. He read aloud to himself, "The Midnight Vandal is trying his luck with a jury." He read on, then mumbled, "Hmm. No way!"

Kristen swallowed a sip of hot chocolate. "What is it?" She scooted closer to the fire. The chill from the cracked opening of the window now surpassed the heat from the fireplace.

Josh hopped up and closed the window, then pointed to Kristen's mug, as if to ask "Refill?" She held up her left hand and shook her head. "Remember a few years back when I attended that week-long training course at Northwestern University organized by the National District Attorney's Conference?"

"Yeah. Why?" Kristen set her mug on the flagstone hearth and rubbed her hands together near the fire.

"The Deputy District Attorney I hung out with that week was from Colorado. At that time, he worked for the District Attorney in Denver. He must have relocated. It says here he's the one prosecuting this *Midnight Vandal* character in Summit County. The case is set for trial next week. When we hang out in Breckenridge, I'd love to surprise him and stop by to say hello."

"Sure," she responded in a flash, eager to agree.

Kristen was the social butterfly of the newly formed couple, frequently coaxing Josh to step outside of his comfort zone, at times dragging him kicking and screaming. Oddly, for a man who made a living persuading twelve strangers to determine someone's fate, Josh preferred solitude over social. That was his comfort zone. And he liked it. After all, it was, well—comfortable.

Other than their happy hour group of friends back in Santa Barbara, Josh mingled very little. The polar opposite in that regard, Kristen embraced meeting new people. Her philosophy—*You can't have too many friends.* Josh's motto—*I've got enough friends.*

Chapter Six

OBSESSED WITH STAYING in shape, Josh spent only a small fraction of his workout time strengthening his legs. Regardless, snow skiing worked leg muscles he forgot he had. And after a full day of skiing down the seemingly countless acreage of Vail, followed by an hour of ice skating later that evening, his legs were aching.

But the pain didn't sideline the adventurous couple. Realizing they would struggle simply to walk the day after their first day of skiing, the ambitious pair had opted to go ice-skating a couple of hours after finishing up on the slopes, preempting the real pain that would intensify the next day.

Their strategy worked, even though it would produce even greater pain later. With their adrenaline flowing and the onset of muscle soreness caused by the microscopic muscle damage from skiing still delayed, the couple mustered enough energy to enjoy some leisurely ice skating under the moonlight. The crowd at the open-air rink was light, lessening Josh's embarrassment as he struggled to keep pace with his polished partner. While attending law school in New

York, Kristen became obsessed with ice skating and developed quite a knack for it.

Now, the day after, Josh paid the price for having let his pride overpower his common sense. And despite his burning thighs triggering vivid flashbacks of the painful feeling of waking up the morning after a hard-fought football game back in his younger days, Josh ignored his screaming leg muscles and stuck with his routine, enduring the pain through his morning coffee walk.

Ignoring his body's plea for him to sleep in that morning, he remained consistent with his vacation morning ritual, waking up at the crack of dawn and dragging his heavy legs on a stroll for his daily cup of joe. Slogging in agony, he headed to the nearby coffee shop in the village.

With most vacationers having more sense than Josh, and wisely choosing to sleep in, he was the first customer of the morning.

Kristen, clearly the brighter of the two, was out like a rock when Josh slipped away. And although she too enjoyed an early morning coffee walk and had expressed her desire to join him, Josh thought it wise to let her sleep.

The evening before, Kristen had asked that he awaken her when he woke. Astutely, Josh ignored her words and listened to her actions. The predominant signs indicated that he'd be wise to disregard her request. Before they'd crashed only seconds after their heads hit the pillows, she was experiencing "miserable pain," as she phrased it. And before that, she was moaning all night long. And not the good kind. Given all that,

Josh felt confident Kristen wouldn't be heartbroken if he gave her the extended slumber time. Truth be told, she'd be grateful.

It was a short amble from the front door of their condo building to the morning scent of Black Diamond Roasters; just a hop, skip, and a jump past the promenade's ice-skating rink.

Josh's legs were burning, but nothing compared to the heat that scorned him as he opened the door to the village café. A rush of well-heated, vanilla-nut-coffee-roasted air blew past him. Too hot, in fact. Never thinking of it before, now he knew what it felt like to be in the mouth of a hot air balloon as the propane-fueled burners torched air into the giant balloon.

Psychologically speaking, the heated breeze fueled his mind causing Josh to ponder one of life's peculiar mysteries. *Why do businesses in cold climates feel the need to overheat their establishments?* After all, their patrons assuredly will be bundled up in warm clothing to endure the harsh outdoor elements. So, comfortably warm room temperature would suit people just fine, eliminating the need to go from layered to unlayered, then layered again. *Customers are humans, not chocolate cakes.* And rivaling the temperatures in Death Valley in mid-July was not only unnecessary but wasteful.

Tempted to strip naked, the law-enforcing attorney thought twice, then refrained. But not for his own sake. Kristen would be inflamed if she had to bail him out of jail for indecent exposure during her vacation. Carefully, he weighed his options. The coffee shop may have been hot as hell, but Josh thought *Hell hath no fury like a woman scorned*, so he opted to endure the heat less likely to chap his backside.

Normally a coffee-with-cream-and-sugar man, Josh ordered a hot mocha with whipped cream, enjoying some variety while on vacation. Standing below the "order pick-up" sign, Josh overheard the young male cashier talking to the barista who was topping his mocha with whipped cream. It grabbed his attention when heard the barista say the words *law school*.

The cashier replied to his co-worker, "I took this year off to save money for law school in the fall. I'll be receiving student loans, but I'm resolved to mitigate my debt as much as possible."

Josh smiled with empathy, while simultaneously appreciating the phraseology of the youngster. *Already speaking like an attorney*, Josh thought. Reminded of the struggles of his past, and the financial burden of law school, the fiscally wise attorney pulled a ten-dollar bill from his wallet, folded it in half, and placed it in the tip jar. The cashier made eye contact with Josh.

"Good luck in law school," Josh said, giving a nod and a grin. *Don't do it! Change your path before you become a slave to billable hours*, he couldn't help but think. But for the grace of God and the job offer from the District Attorney, Josh narrowly escaped the misery of having to track and bill every move he made—from legal research, to document drafting, to wiping his nose as well as other body parts not openly discussed at parties.

With a smile and a thumbs up, the proud young man responded, "Thank you, sir."

The barista placed a large cup on the counter. "Here's your mocha, sir."

"Thank you," Josh replied, wondering at what point he had aged from a young man to a sir. Then he grunted like an old man as he plopped down in a comfy chair closest to the indoor fireplace of the delightful coffee shop. His newly developed groan answered his question.

Josh sipped his mocha and reminisced back to his early twenties. He too, took a year off between college and law school to save money for the second poverty phase of his young life. He had worked two jobs during his year off, painting houses and canvassing for a political campaign. An odd combination, but they both paid more than minimum wage. So, for that, they served their purpose.

From birth through high school, Josh had experienced little change. He grew up in a middle-class family, in a middle-class neighborhood, in a middle-class town. To his knowledge, they never lacked anything. At the same time, they didn't live at the top of the hill. And as much as his parents would have loved to pay for his college education, it wasn't in the budget. So, the day Josh left for college, he'd gone from lacking for nothing to lacking for everything. How's that for change?

Like many other students at Cal Poly Pomona, Josh had paid his way through college. Fortunately, back in Josh's college days, that was feasible. Extremely difficult, but feasible. From the age of eighteen, Josh worked hard for everything he had, as little as it may have been. College classes all day, working all night, leaving him no time to pursue his true passion—base-ball. And sadly, while having to sacrifice his dream of one day playing in the Bigs in exchange for sheer survival, Josh lived in utter poverty.

Even the mundane task of grocery shopping wasn't free from hurdles. The days of adding up items Josh placed in his grocery cart to avoid the embarrassment of asking the cashier to set aside food at check-out remained forever embedded in his head. That look of pity from a total stranger—who knew Josh's eating habits better than his mother— after the starving student was forced to set aside the three-for-a-dollar frozen burritos from his cart because the change in his pocket wasn't enough to supplement his paper bills, was bearable only once, perhaps twice.

And that was just college. Law school was much worse, spanning three years when Josh needed a telescope to look up to catch a glimpse of the poverty line. In retrospect, his lavish college life mirrored an episode of *Dynasty* compared to his three years of law school, when low-budgeted *Top Ramen* replaced the extravagant frozen burritos. If law school taught him nothing else, the starving student learned to appreciate the delectable taste of a good bean over a bland slimy noodle. *Oh, the finer things in life*, he recalled.

As days of yesteryear raced through Josh's mind, he felt honorable leaving the generous tip. Seconds later, remembering more specifics about his higher education monetary scarcity, he wished he had left a twenty, or better yet, a C-note.

Josh relaxed next to the warmth of the fireplace to his right. Facing the front of the coffee shop, he watched as more early risers popped in for their morning caffeine fix. He couldn't help but laugh at the coffee vernacular that had evolved over the years. When had the world gone from "I'll have a black coffee" to "give me a Grande iced skinny hazelnut macchiato, sugar-free syrup, triple shot, heavy whip with mocha sprinkles?" And what about that order says skinny or sugar-free? Shouldn't it be more like "I'll have a large cup of instant diabetes with room for ten pounds around my butt . . . to go please?"

And of course, the response from the cashier, "That'll be sixty-three dollars and forty-four cents. Oh, wait. I'm sorry. You said Grande, didn't you? Forgive me. That'll be seventy-two dollars and three cents."

He stared into the fire and took a deep breath. Setting aside his distracting thoughts, he enjoyed the moment. Near brushes with death could do that to a man. Perhaps a blessing in disguise, reminding him to stop and smell the roses. Or in this case, the roasted coffee beans. After all, he was on vacation in the majestic Rocky Mountains with the love of his life. Suddenly, his legs didn't ache as much. *The mocha tastes chocolatier*, he thought. *Is that a word? It is while I'm on vacation*, he responded in his head. Josh smiled after another sip and a giant exhale. He couldn't remember the last time he felt so relaxed.

Josh glanced over to the unfinished pine coffee table two feet in front of him. A stack of several clusters of the local newspaper was spread out in an accordion-like fashion across the top. He set his cup down and grabbed the daily paper, thirsting for a taste of the local scoop. A short article on the bottom of the front page jumped out at him, "Snow Flurries Possible for the Annual Scavenger Hunt."

As Josh read the details of the upcoming event in which he and Kristen intended on participating, a handful of worm-catching patrons entered the coffee shop. Entrenched in the paper, Josh fell into the depths of a captivating story. The scattered chatter, machine-generated grinding noises, and background music escaped his attention as he continued to read undistracted until he heard a familiar voice. It wasn't unique, but it was distinctive enough to draw his attention and pique his curiosity. With his head still buried in the paper, he couldn't pinpoint how, from where, or why it sounded familiar. But he had heard it somewhere.

Thirty seconds later, Josh finished the article and looked toward the counter from where the voice had boomed. As customers waited at the drink counter, he recognized the patrons thanks in large part to the man with the burned face. Two of the *Three Stooges* he had noticed at the pizza place in Idaho Springs were now patrons in the same coffee shop sixty-five miles away. Showing no signs of recognizing Josh, they grabbed their drinks and sat at a table, once again about ten feet away from the attentive attorney.

It was Scarface and the mega-mouth hipster. Curly wasn't with them. *Small world*, thought Josh but didn't think much more of it until his caffeinated ears alertly overheard their conversation shift to a familiar topic. With his mind on the scavenger hunt, Josh couldn't help but hear Scarface when he referenced their intention of partaking in the local annual event that evening. *An even smaller world*, Josh thought.

The Annual Vail Scavenger Hunt derived itself from the infamous prosecution of a local white-collar criminal who, along with his business partner, victimized hundreds of wealthy Colorado residents, and thousands of people worldwide, about two decades prior. At the time, the news was the biggest story in the Rocky Mountain region. Two "gentlemen" from Summit County, Colorado scammed thousands on their way to making millions.

For three years, Opulent Ores Inc. had run a website that claimed to provide a simple way for customers to invest in precious metals. To build their clientele, they created a facade of exclusivity, with marketing that claimed the membership was limited to select applicants only. In truth, anyone with a credit card and a pulse was accepted. Users could buy, hold, and transfer gold and silver on the company's online platform, e-Fortune.com, and convert their investments to cash at ATMs worldwide. With the value of the gold market progressively increasing, the business model enticed ambitious investors with a rewarding return on investment.

For a while, the business flourished and generated massive amounts of revenue. But like most scams, it couldn't stay off the radar forever.

Following the emergence of a few red flags, the gig was up. After an investigation, it became evident that the company was engaged in more than just trading in precious metals. Operating without a license, Opulent Ores was working almost solely as a money-transmitter, earning the owners millions from user transaction fees alone.

The e-Fortune website hyped no fees for creating or funding an account. That much was true. However, there was a cost to switching virtual holdings back into real money. Federal and state investigators determined that at the company's pinnacle about $12 million per month was funneled through Opulent Ores and its e-Fortune website, and practically none of it had come from buying and selling precious metals.

Shortly before the hammer fell, the owners suspected the FBI was closing in on their scam. Seemingly overnight, a leak surfaced, indicating that one of the owners was requesting to testify in exchange for a sweet plea deal. The following day, the rumored turncoat disappeared. Two weeks later, with enough evidence to prosecute, the feds arrested one of the suspected scammers on a multitude of felony charges. Immediately upon his arrest, all his personal and business assets were frozen. The next day the newspaper headline read: "Feds Strike Gold, Arresting Mastermind Behind Multi-Million-Dollar Scam."

Fortunate for the captured outlaw, the opulent ore oasis was more than a precious metal mirage. At least for him. Hit with a rare dose of reality at the outset of their scam, that particular owner had planned for the worst contingency. In part, they had been purchasing gold throughout their con game to hedge their bet. In the event of getting caught and having their ill-gotten gains returned to their victims in the form of restitution, the fall guy had stashed the gold for future financial security in the off chance he didn't die in prison. The how and where was a mystery, and allegedly only known to him.

The conversation between the two men clutched Josh's attention. He pretended to read the paper while he listened to the high-volume hipster ask questions of the scar-cheeked skipper.

"So, what's the real story behind this scavenger hunt?" the youngster asked.

"Twenty-something years ago, a couple of white-collar criminals scammed investors out of millions of dollars." Scarface scanned the room, then leaned in. "Right before they were to be arrested, rumor has it that one of them was going to snitch in exchange for a plea deal."

"Some partner," snickered the hipster.

Scarface continued. "But before he could, he disappeared. Ultimately, only one guy was arrested and convicted of a boat load of felonies. Legend has it that he had hidden millions of dollars worth of gold during their scam and possibly murdered his partner trying to save his own ass. That, or the partner fled to parts unknown never to be seen or heard from again."

The youngster crinkled his eyebrows. "So, what does this have to do with the scavenger hunt?"

"Well, the scam artist was convicted on several federal charges. But the state was convinced he had killed his partner as well. So, the District Attorney's Office was determined to prosecute him for first-degree murder."

"What made them think that? Did they have any proof?"

"Apparently not enough to prosecute him," replied Scarface. "But not long after he was imprisoned, he started releasing clues to the press. Almost like short riddles. Hinting at the location of something. Some believed the clues would lead to the gold. Some believed it would lead to the dead body of the missing partner. Others believed he did it for kicks, just for a good laugh as he rotted away in prison."

"And the scavenger hunt?"

"Some local publicist came up with the idea several years ago. She thought it would be a good fundraiser to help pay back some more money to the local victims of the scammers. Obviously, the restitution paid by the convict didn't come close to covering what the victims lost. Not surprisingly, the cons probably lived a luxurious lifestyle during their scam and blew almost all the cash. At least from what could be recovered. That, or they managed to stash a chunk for a rainy day."

"Is there a Joshua Rizzetti here?" hollered the cashier. Shocked, Josh peeked over the top of the newspaper. The cashier looked around, finally making eye contact with the fake-newspaper-reading patron. Josh tossed the paper on the table and walked toward the employee. Scarface and the loud hipster stopped talking and both stared as Josh drifted toward the counter.

Assuming the approaching customer was the beckoned one, the cashier spoke. "Joshua?" he asked.

Josh nodded.

"A sweet lady named Kristen called." The future law student's voice faded, gradually lacking in confidence.

"She ordered a large chai tea latte and said you would pick it up and pay for it on your way out. Does that sound right?"

"Huh, how nice of her," Josh chuckled. "Yes, that sounds right."

"Okay," sighed the relieved cashier. "Just let us know when you're ready for that."

"Sure thing." Joshua dropped another ten-spot in the tip jar. "In about fifteen minutes should be good. Thank you." *I'm gonna be broke before I get out of this coffee shop,* he thought. His face smiled; his wallet cried.

"Yes sir."

There it was again. That dreaded "s" word—sir. *How dare that youngster to use such foul language*, thought Josh.

Now feeling increasingly self-conscious about his age, as much as a thirty-three-year-old fit male could, he seemed to be walking slower as he plodded back to his fireside seat.

Josh drifted back toward the fireplace. As he passed the two suspicious characters, about five feet to his left, they appeared preoccupied. Hipster took a sip of his drink and looked away. Scarface pretended to drop a napkin to the floor, tilting away from Josh, and reached to the floor.

The observant prosecutor recognized the window of opportunity and glanced toward the wannabe B-rated daytime television actors. Scarface's jacket crept slightly above his right hip, revealing a handgun tucked in his pants. Josh scampered back to his seat, grabbing the paper and seating himself in one quick swoop.

He exhaled a painful sigh as he sat down. There it was again, the old man's noise. To put his mind at ease he quickly brushed it off, convincing himself it strictly was a case of day-after-skiing pain. He avoided the temptation of eavesdropping and returned to reading the local paper.

Josh flipped to page eight and read the title of the top-page article: "New Marijuana Law Quickly Passed Through Joint Committee." Josh chuckled loudly, then quickly muted himself. He moved down to the next article, written by the same columnist. The title read: "Local Tremble Pleasures Five Women for an Entire Day." Josh busted out in laughter, then read on.

> One of five lucky ladies summed up their elation in a few sentences, saying "The minister surprised all five of us at the same time with his big gift, making all of us scream with excitement. It was a day of sheer enjoyment. We all were exhausted, but extremely satisfied." Local Minister Mack U. Tremble, in his annual spirit of giving, delivered an unexpected thrill to the five grateful female recipients. "I find great joy in giving pleasure to others," Minister Tremble professed. For the third year in a row, the generous clergyman gave five women a glimpse of Heaven, providing a generous holiday shopping spree to the matriarchs of five needed families. Having grown up in poverty, he

experienced firsthand what it was like to
be without after the holiday season . . . .

You can't make this stuff up, thought Josh. Somebody
at the local newspaper had missed his calling. *Forget
being a writer. This guy's a comedian.* Seventy-five seconds later, Josh wiped the tears from his eyes and
finally stopped laughing. He doubled back to read
the name of the writer. Every hysterical headline and
article were by the same columnist, "Hugh Morris."
Hugh Morris, Josh recited in his head. *Hugh Morris*, he
repeated speedily. *Humorous. This guy is a comedian.*
Josh's laughter returned in full force.

He bounced to the next article, and one more serious in nature. Quickly, he regained his focus. Engrossed in an article expressing the struggle of mountain towns being able to provide affordable housing
for local workers, Josh didn't notice it when a pretty
young lady sat in the chair beside him.

"Is this seat taken?" the lady asked.

Josh didn't blink, let alone hear her. If he did, he
didn't think she was talking to him. Immersed in the
editorial piece, he didn't even flinch. When focused,
Josh had tunnel vision. Pathetically, to such an extent
as to miss a hot female flirting with him.

"Want to come back to my place?" the female
propositioned. "My boyfriend isn't there."

Snapping from his reading trance, Josh looked up.
The woman of his dreams smiled at him. Josh made
eye contact with the cashier, mimed a drinking motion with his hand, then pointed to the young lady.

"Let me get you a drink, pretty lady," offered Josh. "Let me guess, a large chai tea latte."

"Is that how you woo all of the ladies?"

"If only," Josh joked. "Unfortunately, I'm not rich enough to buy just anybody a seventy-two-dollar chai tea latte."

"You really know how to make a woman feel special." She smirked and tossed him a wink.

"From the classic eighties' lyrics of The Outfield, 'I just wanna use your love tonight.'"

"Wow, aren't you a bold one?" She shook her head. "Young man, you're 'Livin' on a Prayer.'"

"Please," Josh begged, "if 'You Wanna Be Startin' Somethin' you need to 'Take Me Home Tonight.'"

"In your dreams," she said. "Even though 'Girls Just Want to Have Fun,' don't 'Push It.'"

"Instead of shaking a little Salt-N-Pepa on me," Josh remarked, "why don't you 'Pour Some Sugar on Me?'"

"Michael Jackson said it best. 'Beat it.'"

"Ouch, my lovely queen," said Josh. "I guess 'Another One Bites the Dust.'"

The pretty lady tilted her head to the side in a sympathetic fashion. "Hey, 'Don't Stop Believin'.' You're young and not so hard on the eyes."

The quirky couple laughed at their spontaneous improvisation. "Kristen, I'm impressed with your eighties' music references. I'm rubbing off on you."

"God help me." She giggled. "Just kidding. From the lips of The Romantics, that's 'What I Like About You.'"

"I knew it," Josh snarled. "You're using me for my eighties' trivia expertise."

Kristen grinned, leaned toward Josh, and patted him on the shoulder. "What can I say? Oddly enough, it's your most endearing quality. Useless, but endearing nonetheless."

"Don't forget how useful it can be. Not too long ago, it was life-saving."

"True. But how often does that happen? Once in a hundred lifetimes. A thousand, maybe?"

"Mr. Rizzetti," hollered the barista. "Your chai tea latte is ready."

Josh stood up. Kristen eyed him as he strolled to the counter. Halfway through, her eyes were diverted. The man with the branded face was hard to miss, marked like cattle at the hands of his rancher. She briefly stared, almost uncontrollably. Then, catching herself, her head turned to Josh, but still peeking at Scarface out the corner of her eyes.

Josh returned in Kristen's direction, holding up her drink. She smiled. From his periphery, his vigilance spotted the two strangers watching him. He handed Kristen her cup and fell to his chair.

"Nice grunt, old man."

"It's from the skiing."

"You go ahead and tell yourself that." Kristen winked as she leaned toward Josh and patted him on the knee.

Josh slowly glanced at the men. Whipping their heads back, the men swiftly looked away.

To Josh, their behavior appeared a bit odd. But, being on vacation, he convinced himself it was nothing. He hadn't fully shifted his mindset from prosecutor to vacationer. The peculiar duo's seemingly nosey behavior was in his head. They probably were checking out his beautiful girlfriend. Who wouldn't?

"So, treasure hunter," declared Kristen, "are you excited about the scavenger hunt tonight?"

The curious duo, in the middle of a conversation, stopped. They glanced toward Kristen. Josh sensed it and whipped his head to face the odd pair. In a flash, they refocused on each other.

Josh gazed into Kristen's eyes and whispered, "I can't wait 'Til Tuesday," throwing up air quotes for his last two words.

Kristen's scrunched her brow. "Tuesday?" she replied. What Josh said made no sense to her. She glared at him with uncertainty. "What's Tuesday?"

Confusion was written all over her face. Until it wasn't. Suddenly, it made some sense. Kristen looked to the fire as if searching for the meaning of the code. There was a ninety-nine percent chance the answer was buried in the archives of eighties' music. Inevitably, when Josh spoke gibberish or nonsense, the answer usually could be found in something eighties. Getting used to it was an acquired taste for Kristen, so she took it in stride, *One Day at a Time*. Stumped, she shook her head ever so subtly.

Josh murmured, "Hush, hush—"

Suddenly, it clicked. Kristen nodded at Josh. He was telling her that "Voices Carry," based on the mid-1980s' hit song that won a video music award for Best New Artist. Lucky for Josh, Kristen was a quick study, in large part due to her extraordinary memory. What was learned by him from a lifelong obsession with 80s' music, was retained by her from Josh merely citing a song and its artist—once. The presumably worthless 80s' knowledge proved more than useful when it served as the tipping point to solving a murder in Santa Barbara just a few months earlier.

Giving deference to Josh's judgment, Kristen engaged in small talk, sipping her scorching-hot latte in between sentences. If the blisters forming on Kristen's lips were any indication, the coffee shop never got word of the hot coffee lawsuit against the famous food chain that garnered global news when an elderly woman suffered third-degree burns after spilling a cup of liquid lava on her lap. While the final monetary hit suffered by the restaurant was undisclosed through a subsequent settlement, the jury had imposed a steamy three-million-dollar punitive damage judgment at trial.

Kristen weathered Josh's strange behavior, figuring he was hot onto something—other than coffee.

Chapter Seven

THE ONCE GLOOMY cold cinderblock walls that epitomized depression in every sense of the word, were now just walls. What he once believed intolerable, was now livable. What he once thought unprecedented, was now commonplace. The inhumane, now palatable. The outlandish, now mundane. With enough repetition, man could get used to anything. Somber is the soul that surrenders to savagery.

The light blueish-green, teal-painted walls worked their magic, evoking tranquility and trustworthiness. The prisoner lay on his hard bed, calm as the sunset, which he hadn't seen in years. If ritual had taught him anything, it was invariability.

Daily, he woke up behind bars. Nightly, he fell asleep behind bars. Unfailingly, he spent the hours in between confined in the seven-by-ten-foot cell. Forty-three going on eighty, the broken prisoner stared at the metal cage, now trusting he would die with the same view. Albeit hardened, he just laid there in his tranquil and trusting state of mind . . . waiting to die. Callous is the spirit that capitulates to cruelty.

What day it was, he had no idea. And really, what did it matter? The once optimistic attitude that he would eventually see the light of day had now dissipated with his diagnosis—cancer. A fitting end for a man who was a cancer on society; victimizing thousands of innocent, trusting, hard-working people who fell prey to his scam. According to the newspapers, at least three had committed suicide after suffering financial ruin. But with a projection of fewer than six months to live, life's karma finally had caught up with him; a female canine in all her glory.

After the investigation had been completed, and with the fall guy facing enough federal charges to lock him up for a few decades, it was alleged that two men were behind the scam. One was in custody, awaiting trial. The other, missing, along with a substantial though undetermined amount of gold and cash. At the time of the trial, the value of the missing gold was believed to be considerable. Now, more than two decades later, its value had increased by more than six-hundred fifty percent. In real dollars, the price of gold had escalated exponentially, from roughly two-hundred-seventy-two dollars per ounce to more than one-thousand-eight-hundred dollars per ounce. Its ROI, borderline criminal.

Two theories surfaced as to the whereabouts of the missing scam artist. The most prominent one—he fled the country, likely to a non-extradition sovereignty, with access to millions tucked away in a private Cayman Island bank account. Sipping fruity umbrella-capped drinks while admiring clear blue waters, leaving a dark cloudy wake in his past. The other—he was dead. Killed by his partner and never to be discovered.

"William!" shouted the guard. The prisoner did not respond. "Bill!" Still, no response. The prisoner's eyes were open but fixated above as if staring through the ceiling and into the foreign sky.

"Hey, Clybourne!" The guard rattled the bars. Liberated from his trance, the prisoner popped up.

"Yes. What's up?"

"You have a visitor."

"I'm sorry," the prisoner reacted. "With so little human contact, I think my hearing has gone bad. It sounded like you said I have a visitor."

"I did."

"Cody, knowing I'm on my last leg," the prisoner confided, "I appreciate your effort to take my mind off it. But I haven't had a visitor in over twenty years. So, good try, but I'm not in the mood. Today, I just want to feel sorry for myself."

"Roger that, William."

"Thank you," the prisoner replied. "As much as I could use a good laugh, I'm just not feeling it today."

"All kidding aside," said the guard, "really, you do have a visitor. Seriously."

William Clybourne examined the face of the guard. It was a face who knew him very well. It was one of the few faces he had laid eyes on in years. A familiar face. Not so much a friend, but a relationship as much akin to a friendship as could exist between a guard and his prisoner. Stone-faced, William just stared at the guard for thirty seconds as if not knowing what to do next, confronted with a concept foreign to the isolated caged mouse. The guard countered with a stoic gaze.

"Oh my God," whooped the prisoner. "You are serious." He paused. "Who is it?"

"It's a young man."

"Can you be more specific?" William asked, elevating his body along with his curiosity. "Did he give a name?"

"Geoffrey with a 'G.'"

"I don't know a Geoffrey." William scooted to the side of his bed and leaned forward to stand.

"Perhaps you should. He says he's your son."

The prisoner dropped to the ground as if shot by a firing squad.

Prison visits were scheduled in advance. Names not on an inmate's approved visiting list could be authorized by the Administrative Head or Executive Director of the prison. William's list had one name on it—his attorney. A man he hadn't seen since his last appeal over a decade earlier. He had no friends, and his only family—if any— was one person, and one whom he had never met.

Eight months before he went to prison, William's girlfriend had dropped the bomb on him—she was pregnant.

Having swindled enough wealth to last many lifetimes over, and without her knowing his business was a scam, the life-changing news exhorted change in the con man. He was ready to get out. He needed to get out. But, unbeknownst to him at the time the feds were closing in, it was too late.

It all came crashing down on William Clybourne before his soulmate gave birth. And with the cat out of the bag for the world to see, the devastated and naïve prospective mother cut off all contact with the soon-to-be convicted felon and vanished. Faster than the dark-shaded feds rushing Clybourne's office, his pregnant companion was off the grid.

Whether a healthy child was born, he didn't know. Was it a boy or a girl? He could only speculate. A boy? Maybe. But other than a prison guard rumor that had floated around about six months after William's ex was due to give birth, he couldn't be certain. The child's name—a mystery. Did she put the child up for adoption? He had no idea. Where did the child live? Anybody's guess.

Haunted by secrecy prescribed by his lost love, the inmate choked on his own medicine.

Upon his incarceration, William's life took a dramatic turn one would expect when losing one's freedom. His home state, on the other hand, remained the same even after his conviction. But unlike the surroundings of the majestic world-class ski resorts of Summit County, his new home resided at the Federal Correctional Institution in Florence, Colorado, about forty-two miles southwest of Colorado Springs. A medium security facility, William was placed there due to his risk of escape. With allegedly millions in assets—gold, money, or both—the scheming trickster had over a million reasons to attempt a prison break.

The visitation policy for federal inmates automatically approved visitation from immediate family members. However, the determination of "immediate family" members was contingent on who prison officials included in the prisoner's Pre-Sentence Investigation Report, a.k.a. his PSR. Not knowing if he had a child when he was convicted, William's PSR included zero immediate family members.

Special visits by non-immediate family members could be granted for certain reasons but required the approval of prison officials. With less than six months to live, and the visitor showing proof of his relation to the inmate, his visitation of Geoffrey was permitted. Perhaps it was hoped that the prisoner would come clean, and disclose the answers to the decades-long mysteries: What happened to his partner; and where were the gold and unfound money?

Three rows of five tables each occupied the visitor's room. Symmetrically aligned in perfect fashion, the all-in-one, four-seat-one-table white metal furniture pieces were clearly the result of an obsessive-compulsive designer. The walls looked cold. The pumped-in air was overly warm, producing a borderline sleep-inducing effect. Intentional? Likely. Sleepiness equaled calmness. And in prison, calmness was more valuable than the Federal Reserve Building's three-story gold vault nested eighty feet below street level in Manhattan.

At first glance, when the guard escorted William into the visitor's room, it looked empty. With his prisoner to his front, the guard closed the door behind him. He uncuffed the bewildered inmate. William's eyes stared at his feet, seemingly stuck in the downward position one might expect from a dejected captive human. When his hands were freed, at the far end of the room the frame of a man stood up from the corner table and gazed forward.

William raised his heavy eyes. Standing in place, he looked frozen. He stared back. The room was silent. For thirty-three seconds, the two familial strangers locked eyes. No words. No movement. Just staring. Like two boxers before a championship bout.

Finally, William slowly shuffled forward, as if thawed from his frozen state by the heated room. Triggered in part by the guard's nudge from behind.

"Go ahead," Cody instructed, followed by a second prod. "What've you got to lose?"

William reached the family table. A Thanksgiving family dinner, this was not. The inmate and his off-spring just stood there, staring. William didn't know what to say, so he said nothing. The young visitor sat down. William followed his lead, sitting opposite the table.

For three minutes, the two simply stared at one another. Finally, the son spoke. "So, you're my father?"

"You have my eyes and your mother's nose." William paused, then continued. "Even though I didn't know if you were a boy or a girl, I've thought about you every day—"

"Don't!" scowled the young man.

"May I ask you your name?"

"Geoffrey, with a 'G.' I go by Geoff. Geoff Summons."

"It's nice to meet you, Geoff," he said. William beamed. "With a 'G.'" He optimistically extended out his right hand. Geoff gazed at the prisoner's hand, and just staring at the number "3" tattooed on the back of it, he left his father hanging.

The two sat in awkward silence for the next two minutes. From the look on his face, like a shadow covering it, William must have been contemplating telling his son that he was terminally ill. If the young man had any intention of ever visiting again, fate might not be willing to accommodate such a wish.

"So," Geoff said, breaking the tension, "they tell me you're dying."

"That's what the doctor tells me."

"I'm sorry to hear that."

William's head drew back, visibly surprised. "Thank you for saying that."

After the brief exchange, quadruple the silence followed. Either both didn't know what to say, both were afraid to say what he was thinking, or one of each. William looked over his left shoulder as if looking for Cody to rescue him. He saw Cody's back, as he opened the door for a replacement guard to take over, while the former stepped out for his scheduled break.

Typically, Cody was the guard assigned to deal with William. Relative to the other prison guards, Cody was small in stature. While most wore XXL snugly, a medium shirt left room to spare for the narrow-shouldered, five-foot-eight guard. But unlike most inmates, a massive physical presence wasn't necessary to keep the cerebral prisoner in line. William, a non-violent, mostly isolated prisoner posed no threat to instigate an insurrection, not even to a guard the size of a teenage girl.

The new guard simply folded his arms, and with a stoic face and statuesque posture, stiffened. Towering at six-five, this guy fit the mold. An intimidating physical presence. With a muscular build, carrying two-hundred-fifty-nine pounds, he could've moonlighted as an NFL tight end. But with only two months under his belt in the prison system, the administration eased the giant into the life of a prison guard. When it came to institutionalized felons, size didn't matter. Nor did the skull and crossbones tattoo on his neck.

If he said the wrong thing, the imprisoned absentee father would crush his son more than he already had—assuming such a feat was possible. An awkward silence ensued. A courtyard shiv in the chest was looking pretty good right now for the floundering felon.

William rolled the dice and spoke again. "So, how is your mother?"

"She died."

Immediately, the prisoner fell silent, struggling to remove his foot from his mouth.

The pain of a well-placed shiv would have been less painful, while simultaneously putting William out of his misery. Of all the things he could've said, he picked the one thing that dumped a fifty-five-gallon drum of salt on his already-wounded son. What to say next? At this point, it couldn't get worse. William's instincts took over, and rather than force it any longer, he simply spoke unbridled.

"I'm so sorry." He lowered his head. "Jessica was an amazing woman. Better than I ever deserved."

"That goes without saying."

"Fair enough. I deserve that," uttered William. "When? How?"

"Six months ago. Car accident."

"That's terrible. Do you know if she suffered?"

"Other than the past twenty-plus years?"

"I deserved that as well." William hesitated. Delicately, he continued. "From the accident?"

"She was rushed to the hospital. She lost a ton of blood before she got there." The heartbroken young man's voice cracked. "I arrived about twenty minutes before she—" He wiped a tear from his right cheek.

William's eyes watered. His mouth opened, but no words escaped.

"Oddly by chance, she told me about you a few weeks before the accident. And then a little more, minutes before she died. I'm thankful she did, but I hate that you were the last thing on her mind."

"I understand why you feel that way," agreed William. "But I knew your mother as well as anyone. And believe me, you were the last thing on her mind. I'm certain of that."

"Mom told me your name, how you two met, that you were in prison, and some other rather random things. Enough info to look you up. Needless to say, when I searched your name, no shortage of articles came up. It took me six months to drag myself here. Countless times I scheduled a visit, then talked myself out of it. Two weeks ago, one of the prison administrators contacted me and told me you were dying. He figured I should know in case I wanted to see you before you die."

"So, apparently you did."

"Actually, no," replied Geoff. Confusion spread across William's face like chickenpox. "But I happened to be reading a book at the time. And a quote in the book spoke to me. It read: 'At the end of your life, you'll regret more the things you didn't do, than the things you did.' So here I am. Hopefully with no regrets."

"I'm so glad you did. I can see that your mother did a wonderful job raising you. You were probably better off without me."

"Judging by your career choice and your housing accommodations, probably so," Geoff said looking around the room, then gave a nod. "But rarely is a child better off without a father."

"Touché."

Geoff shook his head as if waiting to hear something that hadn't been said. With ample time to say something more, prophetic or otherwise, the terminally ill prisoner turned terminally mute.

"Do you have anything else you want to say to me?" Geoff asked. The painful look in his eyes spoke volumes as they glared into the clueless convict across the table. Sadly, for the expectant young man, they fell on deaf ears. In less than fifteen minutes, he discovered that his father was deaf, dumb, and mute. Obviously, he didn't win the genetic lottery from his father's side.

Thwarted, the disheartened visitor slapped both hands on the table, stood, and marched toward the exit. The jailer standing guard reached to open the door.

"Wait, son. Please!" yelled William. Without flinching, his son stormed toward the exit. "Come back next week and I'll tell you everything."

Geoff stopped in his tracks and sighed, now standing beside the guard who leaned against the open door. The wounded visitor turned around, then held a glower at his father, a glutton for another bucket of salt.

"I mean it," hollered William. He stood and took two steps toward his son. Sharply, he stopped moving and started talking again. "I'll tell you everything. What happened? Where the gold is. And more. I promise. Everything! You deserve it!"

Geoff shook his head with disappointment. "So sad. That's not what I need to hear from you." He spun and stomped out the door. The mountainous guard didn't balk, standing rigid with his ears peeled.

Then, as if a power outage was restored, the light bulb turned on for the relationship-deprived father. William yelled, "I'm sorry son!" In a flash, he broke into tears, and with his voice weakening by the word, he cried, "I'm so sorry son."

Chapter Eight

THE NEXT MORNING, the giant prison guard tapped on the prisoner's cell bars. William laid motionless on his bed, counting cracks in the ceiling. His circumstances had changed dramatically in the past couple of hours. Still imprisoned, yes. Still dying, yes. But the dream of one day reuniting with the love of his life was shattered. And the question of what happened to his child was now answered.

With his soulmate dead, the decisive factor that kept him in check was gone. The canary was free to sing. Now, if only his son would come back. He could tell him everything. The human vault was ready to crack, dying to reveal his secret—literally. His reason to remain under lock and key concerning the mystery that hovered over Summit County, Colorado for two decades had gasped her last breath.

Taps turned to bangs, as the impatient guard knocked his nightstick along the bars like a xylophone. "Hey, William. Get your ass up! You've got a phone call."

Clybourne jumped up with unusual excitement. He must've thought his son was calling to tell him he'd schedule a follow-up visit. That he forgave his father.

That he wished he had a chance to get to know him. Visibly anxious to find out if his dying wish had been granted, he stood at attention as the mountainous guard opened his cell.

The hallway was empty and eerily quiet. A second guard stood with the phone receiver in hand, holding it out to the approaching prisoner. With a clean-shaven head and twenty-inch neck that seemingly merged with his muscular shoulders, this guard could've eaten William as an appetizer.

"Thank you," William said, grabbing the phone with trepidation.

The two brutes stood ten feet from the inmate, facing the other way. They looked like professional bodyguards, scanning the crowd for psycho fans ready to rush the iconic lead singer of a famous rock band.

"Hello."

"Hello, William. It's been a while," sounded a voice from his past.

Shock fell upon the prisoner's face. "It has been a while," William said. "Why are you calling me?"

"It seems we have a change in circumstances."

"What do you mean?" the puzzled prisoner responded. "I've kept my end of the bargain for twenty years. Or however long it's been."

"A little birdie told me that you recently learned that your incentive to keep quiet met her maker a little earlier than expected."

"Yeah, but I literally just found out. I haven't said a word."

"You need to keep it that way."

"Do I? Let's recap. I agreed to keep my mouth shut—not tell anyone what I know—in exchange for Jessica's safety. Our deal included you not laying a finger on Jessica, and in return, I'd give you half the proceeds when I got out." William held a dramatic pause, his nerve sprouting. "Well, she's dead and I'll be dead long before getting out of this hell hole. So, if I want to sing like a canary, I'll sing louder than an eighties' hair band. Heck, when I'm done, when people hear Sing Sing, they'll be thinking of this prison, not the one in New York."

"Oh really?" responded the undaunted voice.

"Really!"

"Has your son heard you sing?"

William drew silent, shifting from insolent to speechless. Though he'd just met his son, the fact remained—Geoffrey Summons was *his* son—a fact previously privy to only Jessica Summons.

"What's the matter canary? Cat got your tongue?"

* * *

TWO HOURS LATER, Geoffrey with a "G" called the prison administration and requested a follow-up visit with his father. The Administrative Head approved it and scheduled the visit for the following week.

Chapter Nine

BY ROCKY MOUNTAIN winter standards, the weather was ideal for a touristy outdoor activity. The bright sun had settled beyond the western horizon of the Continental Divide, dropping the temperature slightly below freezing. And in classic Colorado weather fashion, the climate dramatically changed in the blink of an eye. Clouds moved in, pushed along by a gentle breeze. The temperature cooled to a comfortably numb twenty-seven degrees. Snowflakes the size of golf balls lightly floated to the ground, adding to the ninety-four-inch base of white powder that canvassed the pristine mountain.

A day earlier, Josh had overheard a local summarize Colorado weather by vocalizing, "if you don't like the weather, wait ten minutes." What made no sense to him then, made perfectly good sense now.

Blue Bison Pizza Company, the primary sponsor of the annual event, hosted the scavenger hunt kick-off presentation at their Vail location, ideally situated in Lionshead Village. Their sizable outdoor patio was large enough to accommodate the participating teams, and their outdoor propane heaters and massive firepit provided a taste of warm comfort, sprinkled with just enough touch of cold to acclimate the competitors to the impending outdoor conditions of the hunt.

Josh and Kristen were the first ones to arrive. And rather than eat somewhere else and inevitably feel rushed, they opted to grab a pizza at the reputable pizza place. While on the slopes, they had heard no less than ten people rant and rave about the Blue Bison Pizza Company. And after relishing their lunch detour in Idaho Springs that spoke so highly of Colorado's pizza pies, why limit themselves? That first meal after their arrival in the Centennial State proved more than enough to convince the pizza-loving couple that it was a must-have meal for the Vail visitors.

The food did not disappoint. True to form, Josh ignored Kristen's advice and ate too much, prompting him to undo the top button of his pants. Kristen had warned him not to overeat, saying, "We don't want your bloated belly and overstuffed butt dragging around the village, or we'll never win the scavenger hunt."

Falling on sausage-stuffed ears, Kristen's prudent warning fell mute to Josh's ravenous appetite. The Wallowing Pig pizza pie, loaded with Canadian bacon, Italian sausage, salami, prosciutto, maple-glazed bacon, tomatoes, and mozzarella penetrated Josh's gut before Kristen's words could do likewise to his thick skull.

While the two were in it for the fun, their competitive nature was not to be contained. Make no mistake about it, they were in it to win it. And if Kristen could scrounge up a wheelchair to transport Porky around quicker, the scavenger hunt would be theirs for the taking.

By the time Josh paid their bill, six other pairs of contestants had gathered around the temporary podium positioned a few feet in front of the firepit, facing the zealous entrants. The host speaker approached the podium, then glanced at her watch. The 6 pm official start time was a few minutes away.

The host looked around at the seating set aside for their event. Only two empty seats remained. She stared at her watch, patiently waiting for the last minute. At 5:59 pm, two men hustled into the vacant chairs. A small world turned itty-bitty, as Hipster and Scarface from the coffee shop plopped down, panting from exhaustion.

The rules were simple: follow the first clue to the next clue, and so on, until your team found the final treasure. The first team to reach the final treasure would be the winner. And, to prevent one team from riding the coattails of another team, not all clues were the same, and those that were the same were arranged in random order. Simply put, each team was to follow its own clues. And although each team's journey would be unique, they all led to the same destination.

Each participant was given a custom sweatshirt. On the front side left chest of the sweatshirt was the Blue Bison Pizza Company's logo, surrounded by the self-promotion phrase "17th Annual Vail Scavenger Hunt" imprinted circularly. Scattered randomly throughout the back of the sweatshirt were logos of other participating local businesses co-sponsoring the event, all of which donated graciously to the event's worthy cause.

"Hello scavengers," greeted the middle-aged lady who looked as if she and her plastic surgeon spent quite a bit of time together. "Welcome to the Seventeenth Annual Vail Scavenger Hunt. I know you're all eager to get started, so I'll be brief. You all received a copy of the brochure that articulated the origin of our event as well as our cause and explained the rules for the participants. So, I won't repeat that, unless anyone has any questions." She paused and scanned the crowd, allowing for any questions.

"I have a question," Scarface broke in. "I heard that this year at least one of the clues will be an original clue from the tragic event that prompted this scavenger hunt fundraiser. Is that true?"

"Good question," the Botox-infused plastic lady responded. "My response is, sort of, but not exactly. While we did not copy any original clues, each team has one clue that closely imitates an original clue. For instance, if an original clue came from a Dr. Seuss rhyme, then we may have used a different Dr. Seuss rhyme. Does that make sense?"

"So, no original clues?" Scarface asked in a disappointed tone.

"Yes and no," answered the host. Scarface looked like he wanted to put a bullet through the lady's head. "If and when a team reaches the final destination, included with the prize is an original clue or message, as written by the *Gold Scammer*. One that may or may not have been released to the general public."

Josh stared at Scarface, observing his response. Seemingly spirited, Scarface nodded his head, leaned toward his partner, and whispered something in his ear. Hipster shrugged his shoulders. Scarface glanced around, scanning the group of competitors. He turned back to Hipster, then gave him a nod.

"Remember," recycled face continued, "our goal here is to provide you with a safe, fun activity, and help raise money for the victims of the *Gold Scammer*.

An hour earlier, as Josh and Kristen waited for their mouth-watering pizza, the well-informed lawyer detailed to Kristen what he had learned about the history of the event. Fueled by the heavenly smell of roasted garlic, Josh fed a flavorful rendition of the fundraiser's past.

At the scavenger hunt a year earlier, all teams were given the same clues in the same order. As should've been expected, that led to a bottleneck effect. To make matters worse, each clue led to the next "made-up" clue, plus an original clue from the *Gold Scammer*, referred to by some locals as the *Golden Riddler*. Poor planning led to pandemonium. Each subsequent destination had the exact number of subsequent clues as there were teams participating. That allowed each team to move on to the next clue whether they were the first to arrive or the last.

Due to the scavenger hunt creator's lack of foresight, mayhem followed. The problem—each location had only *one* copy of the original clues from the imprisoned scam artist. That meant the first team to arrive at a clue would be the only team to get a copy of that original clue, the collection of which could lead them one step closer to the real multi-million-dollar treasure.

Not surprisingly, when three teams had arrived at the second clue at effectively the same time, a brawl ensued. Three participants were hospitalized, one being an elderly lady who suffered a concussion. Funny thing was, she wasn't the participant who sustained the worst injury. A thirty-something-year-old fitness trainer suffered a broken nose when the feisty old lady popped him between the eyes. Giving proper credit to her Smokin' Joe Frazier-like heavy left hook, blood streamed along the young man's lips faster than cool water down the Colorado River.

Josh soaked in the setting. Aptly creating a shadowy ambiance, mystery music played in the background, courtesy of the host's music app. Taking it a step further, each team was handed a red-colored sealed envelope. While a little cliché, the red hue added to the mystique, and the music set the mood.

A mystery envelope in hand—the inaugural piece of the puzzle—paved the competitors' path to the treasure, or in this case, a handful of gift cards to a few local eateries. Of course, considering the exorbitant restaurant prices in Vail, those could be worth millions—the equivalent of the average cost of a nice meal for two at the upscale resort.

The host pulled a gun from her side, startling a few of the participants. Kristen smiled, visibly appreciating the effort the sponsors put into the event. Josh, a little spooked, snapped back. After his shock settled, he chuckled. Mostly sniggering at himself. Next, the host fired the blanks-loaded gun in the air. Three seconds later, a bird plummeted to the ground, two feet from the fire pit.

"What the—" shrieked a collection of the competitors. The group looked up. Leaning against the second-floor balcony railing directly above the restaurant patio, a young man hung over the edge, almost crying in laughter. "Gotcha!" he bellowed, then waved to the stunned scavengers.

The host stepped toward the fake fallen fowl, squatted down, picked it up, and raised it above her like a trophy. The crowd laughed.

Josh leaned into Kristen and giggled, "I love it. These are my kind of people."

"You mean corny? You got that right."

"Alright folks," the host said. "We're here to have fun. Nothing else but have fun. It's not life or death. Other than the fake featured fowl here, there's only one other thing I want to see killed during this scavenger hunt." She hung on a dramatic pause. The participants appeared shocked again, then exhaled a collective sigh upon her closing remark. "Kill some time having a safe, challenging, and enjoyable scavenger hunt. Scavengers . . . let the hunting begin!"

The brochure indicated that the clues would be progressively more challenging. Josh and Kristen sure hoped so, because the first challenge took the two geniuses less than a minute to figure out. Their first clue read as follows:

Whether you wear your hair in a bob, or peg your opponents with quick witt,

You will feel at home here, while spectators watch and sit.

If you play here long enough, you'll ache with sore feet,

Then go sit and relax, behind the source of outdoor heat.

"Wow," Josh said. "That took me all of five seconds to figure out. But I won't spoil the fun. Did you figure it out?"

"I'm pretty sure," Kristen responded with confidence. "Well, when I hear 'hair in a bob,' I think of the most famous hair-bob wearer of all time—Dorothy Hamill. And of course, 'spectators watch' and 'sore feet.' It's got to be the ice-skating rink. And my favorite part of the rink here is that it has a fireplace at the far end. Ergo—the 'source of outdoor heat.' So, the next clue should be behind that fireplace." She pointed to the ice-skating rink no more than thirty yards from Blue Bison Pizza.

"For someone who's indifferent about the Olympics," Josh remarked, "I'm impressed. A little more subtle were the words 'peg,' as in Peggy Fleming, and 'witt' with two Ts, as in Katarina Witt. Two of the most famous figure skaters of all time."

"I guess before we get too cocky, we should go confirm our genius and grab the next clue."

"Good point." Josh puffed-up. "But we're confident, not cocky. Confident means we can back it up. Cocky means we can't."

"Until we verify our conclusion, your comment alone states cockiness."

"Fair point," replied Josh. "Let's go turn arrogance into assurance."

Relative to Josh's cannon for an arm, the ice-skating rink was only a stone's throw away from their starting point. As the dynamic duo raced to grab their next clue, the other contestants scattered in all directions.

The hunt was on. And for the vacationing couple, they were spot on in solving their first clue. Kristen opened the next envelope that was taped to the back of the stone fireplace that topped the outdoor rink.

"I must say. This is awesome," she said. "Okay. Here we go. Our next clue reads:

1. *What is the name of the Indian tribe that once occupied the Vail Valley prior to the gold rush? Say it out loud.*

2. *Hearing the pronunciation, answer this: "What movie contained the famous scene in which the main character pronounced that word using his local vernacular, rather than the intended word's proper pronunciation?*

3. *With that in mind, go to where the flower is plentiful. However, don't think of this as a garden variety clue. And if you knead to use your smartphone, feel free. After all, it's the greatest thing to happen since sliced bread!*

"This clue sounds like it's calling upon each of our strong points," said Josh. "The first part is history related. That's all you. The second part is useless movie trivia—definitely up my alley."

"Well, I'm not certain about the Vail Valley area, but I know the Utes settled in parts of Colorado and Utah. But, let me check to be certain." Kristen had begun searching her smartphone mid-statement. Quickly, she blurted, "Bingo—the Utes."

"Did you say Utes?" Josh replied immediately. "You mean yoothz,"

"Huh? No, I said Utes."

Josh tilted his head and raised his eyebrows, looking at Kristen with a *Come on!* look. "Really? Our little word exchange doesn't ring a bell? Especially as an attorney, hint hint."

"You're the movie watcher. Remember? I'm the book reader."

"The clue is referring to *My Cousin Vinny*," Josh chuckled. "Remember, the famous exchange between Joe Pesci and Fred Gwynne. You know, Vinny and the judge. 'Did you say yutes? . . . What is a yute? Oh, excuse me Your Honor. Two yoothz,' Ring a bell?"

Kristen laughed with a subtle nod. Then in her best Marisa Tomei/Mona Lisa Vito accent, while mimicking another scene, berated, "'He has to! By law you're entitled. It's called disclosure you dickhead.'"

Josh busted out in laughter. "I love it! That's classic! So, you did see it?"

"My Evidence professor at Cornell made us watch it. Best homework assignment ever. My study group made a drinking game of it. I had to drink every time Mona Lisa Vito gibed a snide remark. Given that, it's a miracle I remember any of it." Kristen refocused. "Okay *Siskel and Ebert*, let's get back to our scavenger hunt. Let's see. Clue number three."

Josh responded with two thumbs up. Kristen replied with a smile and laughed, "I should've seen that coming."

"Okay," Josh thought out loud, "it says to go to where the flower is plentiful, then spells knead with a 'k' instead of using the correct *need* with an 'n.' So, maybe the flower is really *flour*, like the all-purpose bread kind. Not the garden kind."

Kristen nodded. "Yep. I agree. That's also consistent with the reference to *sliced bread*."

Their heads whipped up. Their eyeballs popped out, nearly bumping corneas. "A bakery!" they whooped in unison.

"Do you have your village map?" asked Josh.

From her right coat pocket, Kristen pulled out a brochure and unfolded it. "Got it." She pointed to a spot on the map. "There it is. *Vinny's Pastry Shop*."

Josh rushed three steps in the direction of the bakery. Suddenly, he stopped on a dime and twisted his hips to face Kristen. And as if waving her to round third and head for home, he swung his left arm in a full circular motion and with machine-gun-paced repetition wailed, "Let's go, let's go, let go!"

They hoofed it to the far end of the village. The depleted oxygen level of the high elevation took its toll, forcing them to stop for a breather more than once. On the way, they witnessed one team storming in the opposite direction, while a middle-aged married couple stood in front of a clothing shop looking confused and arguing over what their clue meant. *What if that's me and Kristen in ten years?* Josh thought.

Cursed with nothing but bad relationships in his past, Josh worried about that often—certainly more frequently than circumstances warranted.

The two amateur sleuths once again were on target with their clue-solving ability. Two-for-two so far.

The pastry shop was closed. Outside its bay window, in which were displayed a variety of enticing treats, a dozen cramped patio chairs equally spaced sur-rounded four modest tables. Underneath the closed sign that hung on the interior of the glass door was a taped sheet of paper that read: "Ride the horse in the direction that it's going. – Werner Erhard."

To the right of the entry glass door, about six feet up a transom window, was a Denver Broncos poster, logo and all. The bronco stood on its hind legs, with its front legs pointing up and directly toward an outdoor porch light that illuminated the bakery's entrance and part of its patio. Taped to its base was a letter-size brown envelope. Josh reached up and yanked it down.

To Kristen's surprise, he didn't tear it open right away. Rather, he simply smiled and inhaled deeply. An aroma of fresh baked goods hovered around the pastry shop, seemingly pulling passersby into the grasp of the sweetly scented bakery. Josh glanced at a patio chair, then at the bay window, as if tempted to throw a piece of outdoor furniture threw the window clearing a path to pastry nirvana.

"What are you doing?" asked Kristen, throwing her hands up.

"Sometimes, you have to stop and smell the pas-tries."

"Easy, *Famous Amos*," Kristen prattled, taking a quick whiff. "You look like you're about to do more than just smell. And after that pizza, you're looking more like a stuffed éclair. Now, stay focused." She snatched the envelope from her sniffing sidekick.

Sure enough, inside the envelope was their next clue.

"I gotta say," Kristen said, pointing to the eclairs in the display window "we make a great *cream*."

"Ha-ha, very punny!" Josh said as Kristen unfolded the paper inside the envelope. "It's like we're a *batch* made in heaven." He pointed at the envelope. "All kidding aside, I think we're pretty good at this."

"As a *batter* of fact, I agree. If we're wrong, we can *bake* it 'til we make it."

"This conversation reminds me of my punny departure when I resigned from my first law firm job at *Marble, Wheatly and Rhye*." Josh leaned against Kristen's shoulder to shoulder and raised her hand to hold the clue up.

"Oh, yes. The law firm also known as 'The Bakery.' Leave it to three men with those last names to form a law firm. If they were three women, they would've had the sense to open a confectionery."

"Baked goods or not, I gained twenty pounds working there just listening to our receptionist answer the phone, 'Marble, Wheatley and Rhye. How may I help you?'" Josh rubbed his belly. "I'll tell you how you can help me. I snacked on three loaves of bread and a glazed donut every time the phone rang. I learned the hard way . . . sometimes you can't help but cave into your cravings."

"Okay *Pillsbury* Doughboy," Kristen said, poking her index finger in Josh's gut. "Sometimes, you're like an eight-year-old boy. Focus. Please, focus."

The potent legal minds glided through their next two clues. With each passing of their competitors, their nimble legal brains grew with confidence. Other pairs looked confused, argued some, or split in different directions. "Let's just throw in the towel before we get a divorce," Josh overheard one couple say as they headed back to the scavenger hunt home base at the pizza place patio.

Thank God that's not us, Josh thought. *At least not yet.*

Josh shook his only insecurity from his brain. *Be present*, commanded his inner voice. After all, Josh had been laughing incessantly since the hunt had begun, and a smile was glued to Kristen's pretty face from the word go. The couple was having an absolute blast. The time had flown by—faster than a runaway semi torpedoing brakeless down a steep decline west of the Continental Divide.

Now, seemingly having deciphered their final clue, the couple hustled toward their final destination. A couple clues ahead of their closest competitors, nothing stood between the cruising couple and their victory in the Seventeenth Annual Vail Scavenger Hunt, until . . .

Chapter Ten

KRISTEN WAS EAGER to see more of Colorado. Prepping for their final full day in Vail, she had packed up everything, save for the clothes they would wear the next day. She figured they could wake up, shower, and catch a ride to their next short-term home, the bed and breakfast in Frisco. Her preparation proved prophetic, but not for the reasons she'd expected.

After participating in the scavenger hunt on their last night in Vail, the couple knew they would be exhausted. With that in mind, Kristen planned accordingly. Similarly, Josh had planned their trip transportation arrangements down to the day.

Knowing how unpredictable and dangerous the winter roads in the Rockies could be, Josh had strategically planned their local post-arrival travel arrangements long before they landed in Denver. His plan included rideshare from the airport to Vail; rideshare from Vail to Frisco; then reserve a rental car locally in Silverthorne for convenience to get to the nearby attractions and ski resorts in Summit County; and finally, rideshare back to the airport.

What they didn't anticipate for their last night in Vail was a late-night interview with the local police detailing their startling scavenger hunt find—the dead body.

The scavenger hunt host had specifically prohibited killing anything other than time having fun. And whether a participant or not, somebody had disobeyed both the event's rules and the parameters of human decency. And like murder magnets, the power couple was the one that unwittingly attracted the surprise corpse, and of the murdered variety.

The following morning came sooner than expected. Within seconds of waiting curbside, the Frisco-bound visitors' lift arrived. And with their small world shrinking by the day, the driver popped open the hatchback of her *Subaru*. Jumping out to help the customers, the motorist peeked from around the rear of her vehicle to greet her customers. Taken by surprise, Hannah smiled and laughed.

"Well, if it isn't my favorite California couple," the spunky ski instructor/rideshare driver shouted.

"Hey Hannah," Kristen said. "I feel like we're a trendy celebrity couple with our own private chauffeur."

Hannah shuffled up the curb to help load their luggage. Josh handed their baggage to Hannah, which she tossed one by one inside the hatchback.

Josh flashed a forced grin, giving Hannah a friendly nod. His expression appeared lost. His mind, clearly wandering. Gazed into the distance, he wasn't in a chatty mood.

"How's your trip so far?"

"That's like asking—other than your husband getting killed, how was the play, Mrs. Lincoln?"

Confusion draped over Hannah's face. "Sorry, cryptic messages go right over my head."

"No, I'm sorry," Josh said. "That was a little snarky of me. My mind's a little preoccupied right now."

"I don't get it."

Kristen opened the front passenger door before Josh dug any deeper. "Did you hear about the dead body found during last night's scavenger hunt?"

"I heard something about it when I was waiting in line for coffee first thing this morning." Hannah pressed a button on her key fob, triggering her hatchback to close.

"Well," Josh chimed in, "you're looking at a couple of murder magnets."

"No way! I heard a couple of tourists found the body," Hannah wiggled her right pointer finger back and forth from Josh to Kristen to Josh. "It was you two?"

"Yep, it was us," Josh replied, having become too familiar with murdered bodies. "We participated in the scavenger hunt last night. And, well—let's just say we found more than we bargained for."

Hannah shook her head in disbelief. "I've heard some crazy things chauffeuring tourists around. They've found everything from diamond jewelry to Hollywood screenplays. But this easily tops the list. No question about it."

The three loaded into the Subaru and Hannah piloted them twenty-six miles east on I-70 to their next destination—Frisco, Colorado. The entire ride,

Hannah fired questions faster than reporters at a post-presidential-scandal press conference. Kristen responded while Josh's mind ventured in all directions. *How? Why? And why is it that murder keeps crossing my path—outside of the courtroom?*

* * *

THE TOP FLOOR suite at the Lake Dillon Bed and Breakfast, vacant the day before, was available for an early check-in for the attorney duo. Hannah dropped them off in front and rushed off, stating that she had a weekly appointment that was awaiting her arrival.

As Josh opened the front door to their new home away from home, he told Kristen, "A new location, so we'll call this a new vacation. Murder. What murder?"

The gracious manager radiated with early-bird zeal and greeted her cold guests with a warm reception, "Welcome to Beautiful Frisco, Colorado, the Main Street to the Rockies." Her blueish-white hair styled in a pixie cut accentuated her hazel-green eyes and gave extra volume to her thinning coat. A pair of thick-rimmed eyeglasses donned a vintage look while underlining her sparkling eyes. And with a giant twinkle blanketed over her face, Josh was certain she was born with a grin that saw more daylight than summer solstice in Alaska. Josh envied that. Who wouldn't?

Although still visibly shaken from the recent discovery of a murdered body, Josh and Kristen couldn't help but smile at the chipper inn keeper's kind-hearted greeting, casting a beam that could brighten the darkest depths of the Pacific Ocean's Mariana Trench.

For the cerebral prosecutor, sporting a constant smile was something to which he could only aspire; realistic that such a state of serenity was unattainable. For Josh, it was different. His mind worked at warp speed, never coming to rest. All day, every day. Born old, with the burdens of the world weighing heavily on his altruistic conscience and broad shoulders. Born to right the world's wrongs, with injustices ostensibly increasing exponentially. Holding that onus, smiling required a conscious, focused effort. *Ignorance is bliss,* Josh thought. *Oh, what a slice of Heaven to be ignorant for just a day.*

The blazing fire in the lobby toasted the rustic, log-cabin-style common area. A brown leather sofa faced the fireplace and was flanked on each side by tan microsuede recliners. Centered in the seating area laid a weathered wood coffee table, held up by four massive timbered legs, reminiscent of railroad ties. The décor, while minimal in quantity, was authentic in quality.

A pair of archaic skis, made from laminated timber beams and centered with the old, classic leather straps for bindings, hung from the wall at a forty-five-degree angle to the upper left of the cobblestone fireplace chimney. To its right, two framed, animated-art ski posters, with colorful captions, added personality to the cozy space. One poster portrayed a young female skier, with her scarf flowing mid-air behind her, with the saying: *Ski Like a Girl! You won't get lost and you'll get there faster!* The other showed a red-headed female skier, mid-jump, with the caption: *I Know I Ski Like a Girl. Good Luck Keepin' Up!*

Their suite was located on the top floor of the three-story structure, and complete with its personal balcony overlooking Main Street. The organized couple didn't piddle around one bit before settling into their new accommodations. Josh unpacked their suitcases and methodically folded them into a pinewood dresser. Kristen organized their toiletries in the restroom, then drew open the curtain to the sliding glass door, exposing the sunlight peering over their quaint balcony.

The B&B suite resembled a condo-hotel room hybrid. Other than the bathroom, it contained only one room. However, the space was large enough to house a king-size bed, flanked by a kitchenette on one end of the room, and the other side sporting two, plaid upholstered armchairs positioned side by side and angled toward a gas fireplace. On the far wall immediately adjacent to the bed, neighboring to the right of the sliding door, was the pinewood dresser topped with a stained-glass lamp and five books sandwiched by wood-carved black bear book ends. And above the fireplace mantel hung a wall-mounted fifty-inch HD television.

The kitchenette was equipped with a faucet and sink, a small refrigerator, microwave, one electric stovetop eye, a coffee maker, and a blender. The cupboards above the appliances kept the bare essential cooking supplies to make one feel at home, at least temporarily. With morning coffee and evening margaritas five steps from their bed, the young attorneys had all they needed. Each of them having survived three years of law school proved that one could live temporarily on morning liquid caffeine and evening alcoholic libations. And blessed with the convenience of accessing both within stumbling distance of a medium-soft hybrid mattress couldn't have been more strategically engineered.

"Shall we take a walk on Main Street and grab some coffee?" Kristen asked.

"My brilliant lady," Josh responded, grabbing their jackets, "you read my mind."

Kristen smiled, feeling refreshed in their new surroundings, "Great minds, young man. Great minds . . ."

The hospitable manager of the bed and breakfast directed her new guests to the nearest coffee shop as she filled the brochure rack with the staple attractions. She handed Kristen brochures for the host's two favorite activities she recommended to out-of-state visitors: Frisco Adventure Park, famed for its epic snow tubing; and Frisco Historic Park and Museum, notable for its collection of original historic buildings and exhibits, and conveniently located on Main Street and only a couple blocks from the doorstep of the B&B.

Josh, true to form for a cash-conscious government employee, grabbed a brochure on which its front fold read "LOCAL COUPONS" in big block letters. Was that necessary for him? Probably not. But Josh was old school and programmed to save a buck anytime he could. Was that necessary for Kristen? Most definitely not. Although she grew up with modest means, she had recently become a multi-millionaire thanks to the most recent wealthy new client she had acquired for her firm.

But despite his partner's newfound wealth, the traditional young man insisted on paying for most of the couple's outings. Kristen found it romantic. And Josh, hardly known for romance, eagerly took the points when he could get them. With that, he folded the brochure and shoved it in the right rear pocket of his jeans.

The temperature outside was in the high twenties. With the sun out in full force, surrounded by blue skies, it felt much warmer at altitude. While many outsiders thought it a myth, living at a high elevation several thousand feet closer to the sun made a significant difference. For locals, sunny days felt hot if the temperature was north of twenty-five degrees; the sun's canopy demonstrated its powerful heat.

Josh, prone to overheating, removed his jacket the second the sun hit his face. He tied the arms of his jacket around his waist and embraced the cool relief of the crisp mountain air. His long-sleeved Ole Miss Law sweatshirt was more than enough to keep him warm, especially while walking at his usual vigorous pace. Kristen, on the other hand, was bundled up like an Eskimo.

Given the early morning hour, Main Street was quiet, with most of the retail shops and restaurants not open at such an early hour. But that didn't stop Kristen from browsing. She peeked through the window of five shops in the short block and a half stroll from the bed and breakfast to the coffee shop. The window-shopping fascination dumbfounded Josh. He didn't understand it. But then again, what man did?

The exterior of the local coffee shop was inviting. The outdoor façade exemplified classic log cabin construction. The exterior front presented with thick panel siding that mimicked the look of old-world log cabin cladding. Installed with shiplap construction, the smooth round machine-profile cut left a rustic, irregular appearance that closely replicated historical log cabin homes.

To the left of the glass door entrance to Mocha, Mountain Java was a fifteen-by-fifteen-foot slab patio, centered with a blazing firepit ringed by five wrought iron tables accompanied with four chairs each. Two of the five tables were occupied with early-rising regulars.

Josh's attention was split as he and his best friend-turned-girlfriend approached the popular local café. His eyes shifted from the coupon brochure he'd removed from his pocket to the general direction of his travel. Were it not for a chivalrous customer exiting the coffee shop, who kindly held the door for the attractive female lawyer, Josh would have faceplanted smack dab into the recently-Windexed entry door.

A lightly caramelized, almost nutty aroma filled the air throughout the entrance and foyer of the charming establishment. Not surprising, as the popular local café hardly lacked options. The selection of coffee was like a UN Convention on coffee beans. Kenya, Brazil, Costa Rica, Tanzania, Guatemala, Colombian, Hawaiian Kona, and more. The vast selection of java overwhelmed the indiscriminate tourists while the aroma exhausted their olfactory senses.

"Good morning," greeted the spunky cashier. "Welcome to Mocha Mountain Java. How may I help you?"

Recognizing the paralyzing look of her unfamiliar customers, the adorably generic, makeup-less employee proposed a local fancy coffee drink called *Mountain Mogul Mocha Madness*. Kristen, craving something chocolaty, indulged. Josh, captivated by the indigenous alliteration and snowed by the radiant recommendation, caved into the mountain mocha malarky and ordered the same. Lumbering ever the voracious appetite, he added a breakfast burrito to fuel his morning.

"Shall we enjoy our morning boost outside by the fire pit?" Kristen asked Josh as Plain Jane placed their order on the counter while tossing the patrons an affirmative smile and a nod.

"Great minds . . ." Josh said, grabbing his drink and burrito after handing Kristen her liquid chocolate delight. Excited by the hype, she snuck a quick sip before Josh's hand relinquished its hold.

Josh and Kristen sat down at one of the vacant tables surrounding the outdoor firepit. Josh faced the coffee shop entrance, with the firepit to his left, and an occupied table to his rear. Kristen quickly sat closest to the firepit before Josh had a chance to pull her chair. Josh set his food and drink on the table and pulled his chair out to sit. But, before his rear hit the seat, he heard one of the men at the table behind him speak. It wasn't loud, but it seized Josh's attention. He popped upright and turned a one-eighty.

The voice Josh heard was facing away from him, so visual confirmation was not immediate. But facial recognition wasn't necessary. It was a voice Josh knew well but hadn't laid ears on in quite some time.

"Uncle George!" Josh shouted.

Startled, the old man whipped his head and body around at the speed of an old carousel. He made eye contact with the familial set popping out at him prompting a cheerful grin to drown the old man's face. "As I live and struggle to breathe," he said, "Joshua George Rizzetti!"

"Uncle George Dellucci."

"What is this, a mafia reunion," snarked one of the old man's companions, "or another sequel to the *Godfather*?"

The old man struggled to scoot his chair out, eager to stand for a proper greeting with the young man who was the closest person to a son he'd ever known. Josh rushed to his aid and helped the old man to his feet. The two embraced tighter than a vice grip, neither wanting to let go. Kristen stared with jubilation, wiping the frozen tears freely flowing down her cheeks. Seconds before the family reunion participants' hug would've frozen them into a human ice sculpture, the embrace disengaged. Even so, Kristen's tears still poured heavier than a Colorado hailstorm.

"Please, Uncle George, sit."

"What in the world is my favorite relative doing in Colorado?" the energized old man asked. "And more importantly, what is he doing in the company of such a lovely young lady?"

"I'm sorry," Josh said, finding his manners. "Uncle George, this is my girlfriend, Kristen Laney. Kristen, this is the infamous Uncle George."

Kristen stood and walked around the table as George gestured to shake her hand. Kristen insisted on a hug. He happily obliged. "It's a pleasure to meet you, sir."

"The pleasure is all mine," George said, sharing a smile and a wink. "And please, call me George. I'm much too young to be called the s-word."

"Certainly . . . George," Kristen chuckled. "I see where Joshua gets his charm."

"Kristen, Joshua," George said, pointing to his cronies, "these are my friends, Sam and Hank. Sam, Hank, this is my great-nephew, Joshua, and undoubtedly his better half, Kristen."

An exchange of greetings warmed the frigid air. They all sat, leaning toward the fire and engaging in small chit-chat. In the presence of five attorneys, not even the frozen temperature could chill the conversation. Getting in a word required strategic timing, but even that didn't guarantee one's success.

Josh explained to his uncle how they planned on surprising him with a visit later that day after they settled into their newest vacation spot in Frisco.

"You're just saying that because you accidentally ran into me. You wouldn't want to waste any of your vacation time dusting off this ancient artifact." George snuck a flirtatious smile in Kristen's direction. "Especially with such exquisite company."

"You got me, Uncle George." Josh giggled. "When I saw you, I whispered to Kristen as we were exiting the coffee shop, 'There's my uncle. Cover me so he doesn't see me.'"

"So, how long are you two visiting the Centennial State?" asked Hank.

Kristen responded, "We're here for nine more days. We spent some time in Vail. Went skiing and ice skating. Did some touristy stuff. And just got into Frisco this morning. Now we're going to hit a few of the local slopes in Summit County. At the very least, Keystone and Breck."

"Listen to her," said Sam, smiling and pointing to the refreshing young female face. "Breck. You fit right in. You sound just like a local."

Abruptly, giggles turned to gasps. A car screeching to a sharp stop had the same effect on their conversation, slamming the brakes on the welcoming coffee shop banter. Fortunate for the distracted driver, Main Street had recently been plowed. Heads turned quicker than Sam Duggan's phony-whiplashed melon reacting to the Mr. Brady-tossed briefcase slamming to the courtroom floor in "The Fender Benders" episode of *The Brady Bunch*.

The dog-walking lady crossing the street unexpectedly needed two plastic bags, one for her cocker spaniel and one for her. The distracted driver dropped his phone mid-text and squirmed an apologetic wave to his near victims. Rover just froze, too frightened to poop. Scared shitless—literally. His owner was not as lucky. She grabbed her dog and rushed to the curb. Plastic bag aside, an adult diaper would've served her better.

A small, shack-size building occupied the corner retail space closest to the near-accident. A park bench sat beneath its front bay window. "Are you okay, ma'am?" asked the salt-and-pepper-haired man warming the bench, setting aside a pair of binoculars. Raccoon's eye-like impressions encircled his eyes. She nodded; Rover barked.

Josh watched the exchange from across the street, having noticed the peeping-tom-like perv scoping Main Street with his high-end binoculars. His eyes shifted up and down the street, waiting for a patrol car to pull up on the deviant spectator.

"What's with the park bench peeper over there?" asked Josh.

Sam responded, "That's Tom Robard. He's a friend of mine."

"Seriously?" Josh teased. "The peeping tom's name is Tom?"

Sam defensively shook his head. "He just took up bird watching. He recently retired from forty years in construction. After four decades of physical labor, sitting is his new favorite hobby. And he told me *that bench* is a gold mine when it comes to spotting several types of birds."

Hank, ever the wise guy, jumped in. "Bird watcher, voyeur. Toe-may-toe, toe-mah-toe."

"He certainly looks the part," remarked Kristen. All the men whipped their heads toward her in shock. She shrugged, "Sorry, but he kinda does," she added, drawing chuckles from her all-male audience.

"I like this girl," declared George. "Josh, you out-kicked your coverage." Like great-uncle, like great-nephew; George was an avid football fan and a Denver Broncos enthusiast since their inception. Having predated even the notion of a pro football team in Colorado, he facetiously claimed that he coined the phrase, *Broncos Country*.

"Shh," Josh muttered to his great-uncle. "She hasn't figured that out yet."

George swiftly changed the subject. "So, Vail, huh?" said the spry old man. "We were just talking about the dead body they found near the slopes last night during the annual scavenger hunt. Did you kids hear about that?"

"Hear about it?" replied Josh. "We saw it!"

"What do you mean, you saw it?" asked Hank.

"We're the couple who found the body," the synchronized couple confessed.

"Do you know who the victim was?" Sam said while giving a friendly wave to his peeping friend across the street. "They didn't identify the victim in the newspaper. I'm assuming they want to notify next of kin first."

"No, the police didn't give us any information about the victim," responded Kristen, still visibly shaken from their discovery. "Although, I did overhear a couple of cops talking at the scene. It sounded like they knew who he was. So, I'm assuming he's a local."

"Wow," declared Sam, turning to George. "What are the chances? The phony scavenger hunt leads to your great-nephew finding a dead body. And the original scavenger hunt almost led to us finding your dead body."

"You simply can refer to Joshua as my nephew. *Great* makes me sound too old. Plus, he's more like a son to me."

"Uh, hello! My *label* is what you took as the focal point of Sam's comment?" Josh stared at his oldest living relative, numbed with shock. "What the heck is he talking about? *Your dead body!* Uncle George, is that wild goose chase now putting your life at risk?"

Chapter Eleven

"IT'S JUST AS I remember it," Josh said, glowing as he entered the rustic handiwork of his great-great-grandfather. It was rather remarkable. And for its time, awe-inspiring.

"Wow," admired Kristen, scanning the room with the detailed precision of a contract-review attorney. "If walls could talk."

"My apologies," uttered George. "You could hang meat in here right now."

"Speaking of meat," said Josh. "Why don't you two get the fire going and I'll bring in the groceries."

After morning coffee, George was set to restock his food supply with his weekly trip to the grocery store. The weekly ritual consisted of his rideshare driver picking him up at sunrise and taking him to the coffee shop. There, he would chit-chat with his buddies for a couple of hours, after which his ride would assist him at the grocery store, then haul the old man and his edibles back to his cabin. In light of his unexpected but highly welcomed visitors, phoneless George had Sam cancel his ride to the store and return home.

Within minutes, with the fire burning at full tilt, George and Kristen perched beside it while Josh put the groceries away. Josh insisted, although unnecessarily. The other two didn't put up much of a fight, eager to chat like a couple of schoolgirls. The old man laid down the Spanish Inquisition, determined to learn more about his great-nephew's better half.

George couldn't get enough of the charming young lady. For a man who was always the smartest one in the room, he was engrossed in conversation with someone of equal intellect. She was pretty to boot. What more could a man of his age and social seclusion ask for?

In return, Kristen learned more from George about Josh's maternal ancestry in thirty minutes than she had from Josh in several years. Enlightening—a gross understatement. George was the uncle of Josh's mother and the younger brother of Josh's maternal grandfather. Josh's mother's maiden name, Dellucci, was George's last name. Joshua's middle name, George, was in tribute to his great-uncle.

Once tighter than a ski racer's bindings, a falling out between George and Josh's mother several years earlier left Josh as the only relative who regularly kept in touch with the old man. Josh never knew the full story as to what caused the riff, nor did he care. Or so he said. A special bond existed between the former and current Deputy District Attorneys, formed when Josh was eight during his first visit with his great-uncle in the Rocky Mountains. Fishing, hiking, and starting a campfire from scratch; Josh learned it all and more from his Uncle George.

Josh's second visit to his uncle's cabin had come when the youngster was twelve. After much begging,

Josh's parents reluctantly allowed their son to spend three weeks of his summer vacation with George. That trip changed the impressionable boy's path forever. He had arrived in Colorado as a boy, on the verge of becoming a young man. He left the Centennial State not only a wiser young man but also inspired as to the direction of his life.

At the time, George was a couple of years from retirement. The career prosecutor had scheduled vacation time for the majority of Josh's stay with him. However, at the request of his curious young great-nephew, he had scheduled a jury trial to take place during Josh's stay. He anticipated the trial would take two to three days. George forewarned Josh that boredom was a likely possibility, knowing the boy would get restless numbing his butt while listening to adults bore him to death.

As it turned out, the young Josh wasn't bored. And if his butt had grown numb, he hadn't felt it. Contrary to being bored stiff, the inquisitive, impressionable straight "A" student was mesmerized by the process.

Even more appealing to Josh was the Summit County Deputy D.A.'s artistry of words, captivating presence, and incomparable ability to sway the opinions of twelve strangers to not only accept his viewpoint but to embrace it. Josh had seen it in their faces, confirmed by their posture and mannerisms. Those who initially appeared standoffish to the prosecution, looked as if they wanted to give George a standing ovation as he wrapped up his closing argument.

Atticus Finch eat your heart out, thought Josh. *Step aside, Perry Mason. Hang it up, Ben Matlock.*

Joshua made some sandwiches. Kristen made conversation. And George made the most of his delightful guests. Promising George they'd have more visitation time during their vacation, the couple chatted with him over lunch, then planned to hop back into their rental car and head to Breckenridge.

Chapter Twelve

COLORADO'S FIFTH JUDICIAL District stood tall in a skier's paradise. Consisting of four counties, it included Clear Creek, Eagle, Lake, and Summit Counties. For snow junkies, the choices for world-class skiing seemed never-ending. Loveland, Arapahoe Basin, Vail, Beaver Creek, Copper Mountain, Aspen, Keystone, and Breckenridge. A buffet of ski lovers' delight.

In addition to being the home to one of the most visited ski resorts in the western hemisphere, Breckenridge was home to the Summit County District Attorney's Office. And for nearly forty years, George Dellucci spent most of his waking hours prosecuting crimes out of that office. Assaults, thefts, and robberies comprised most crimes prosecuted by the newly retired attorney, but his experience covered the entire felony spectrum, including murder.

Twice during George's legal career, the outgoing District Attorneys had urged George to run for office and take over the reins, but George was a blue-collar prosecutor through and through. His place was in the trenches. "I'm an ass-kicker, not an ass-kisser," was his repeated response to the flattering proposal.

"Leave the politics to someone else, like Sam," George had responded more than once, recommending his partner for the top position on several occasions. But Sam, like George, preferred the daily action of criminal prosecution. They loved the adrenaline of a jury trial. They thrived on the challenge of verbal persuasion. Simply put, they preferred litigation over administration.

Hank, on the other hand, routinely expressed his interest in one day holding the highest prosecutorial position in the county, but ultimately never did. The endorsement of the exiting District Attorney was vital to get elected, but always playing second fiddle to George and then Sam during his prosecutorial tenure, Hank's timing was ill-placed.

Despite never pursuing the top spot with the Summit County District Attorney's Office, George more than left his mark. After his retirement, when the county sprung for an updated building, they named its law library after him, even gracing it with a bronze plaque to the right of the door's entrance to celebrate the local legal legend. In a manner of speaking, it was musical buildings. The Summit County Family and Intercultural Resource Center re-purposed the former D.A.'s headquarters into its new Breckenridge Office, and the prosecutors moved into the former location of one of the local library branch buildings, honoring George in the process.

After lunch, George had insisted that Josh and Kristen journey over to the District Attorney's Office so Josh could catch up with his friend.

"We can have dinner together later this week," he said. George recognized the importance of the youngsters doing their thing. "Go, see your friend, and have a young folks' night out. I'm not going anywhere."

With their elder's blessing, they left his cabin in Copper Mountain and arrived at Breckenridge less than an hour later. Josh held open the front door for Kristen with his right hand, looking at his watch on his left. His chrome *Fossil* piece showed 2:45 p.m. Risking that his friend may be in court, Josh decided to give the surprise visit a chance. He didn't call ahead, hoping to get the opportunity to shock his fellow prosecutor.

Kristen unzipped her coat. Josh stripped his off. Like most government buildings, the heat was cranked far too high for Josh's comfort. The sweaty prosecutor wondered what the deal was with that. Was it intentional, to make sure they spent all their allocated funds to avoid cuts in next year's budget? *How ironic—if their security blanket to shield their finances was an exaggerated heating bill*, he thought.

"Good afternoon. How may I help you?"

Kristen smiled at the receptionist. Josh responded, "Good afternoon. Is Austin Willis in?"

"May I ask who's inquiring?"

"My name is Joshua Rizzetti. I'm an old friend of Austin. He doesn't know I'm here. But, if you don't mind, I'd rather you not give him my name. I'd like to surprise him."

The receptionist looked at Josh with skepticism. She'd been with the D.A.'s office for six years. She knew better than to let a stranger with a good story and a handsome smile charm his way past the front line of defense. With a chocolate bar in front of her keyboard and a can of soda to its right, she didn't need his sweet talk.

Josh pulled out his Deputy District Attorney badge, sandwiched in a leather wallet-like case. He flipped it open and set it on the countertop that edged over the receptionist's computer screen. The badge was on one side, his government I.D. on the other. As the thorough receptionist inspected it, Josh gave more detail.

"I'm a Deputy District Attorney in Santa Barbara County, California. I met Austin at the National District Attorneys Association Conference at Northwestern a handful of years ago." He opened his right palm toward his companion, "And this is my girlfriend, Kristen Laney. She's also an attorney. The rich kind. Not the government kind."

Looking partially satisfied, but erring on the side of caution, she searched the Santa Barbara D.A.'s website. She glanced up from her computer screen, then stared at Joshua Rizzetti, seemingly painting suspicion of him smuggling a bomb onto a plane. Lips pressed together, her face a cold blanket; she perfected the expression of all-in at the poker table. Then, her eyes drew down to the screen again, then up to Josh. With her final glance, he reckoned he was out of luck. The longer he stood there, the more he was certain she'd have to let the cat out of the bag and get verification before she would let this strange out-of-towner beyond the locked door.

Without warning, she smiled. "Okay, you're good," she confirmed, sprinkled with a giggle. "I'll tell you what," she continued with a sneaky look on her face, "I can take you two to our small conference room. You can sit with your back to the door. I'll tell him that a victim from one of his cases is here to talk to him and send him to the conference room."

"Perfect. I love it. Thank you," Josh said, dipping a nod. "If you ever move to Santa Barbara and need a job, I'll be sure to put in a good word for you at our office."

The impromptu visitors sat quietly in the small conference room of the D.A.'s office. The room was simple, with nothing but an oval mahogany conference table eight feet in length surrounded by six evenly spaced office chairs. To Josh, the room was not much different than one of the conference rooms at his workplace. Compared to Kristen's firm, it was a supply room cabinet. They had storage closets bigger and dressed in more pricey furniture. The two visitors sat with their backs to the all-glass wall that separated the meeting room from the main hallway.

Austin reacted with surprise when he received the call from the receptionist. He checked his calendar; his afternoon was blank. Before marching to the meeting room, he second-guessed himself and buzzed his Victim Witness Coordinator. Perhaps he neglected to mark it on his calendar. Turned out, he didn't. Visibly perplexed by the unexpected pop-in, the Deputy District Attorney traipsed down the hallway and entered the modest conference room.

The Rocky Mountain prosecutor stood at six-feet tall, sporting a slender build and short blond hair. Although only slightly shorter than his California Coast counterpart, he was much thinner. In large part due to his weightlifting regimen, Josh modeled the look of a middle linebacker, while Austin carried the physique of a skinny receiver. Evidently, while Josh was pumping iron, Austin was shredding packed powder.

Directed to the back of two heads, Austin said, "Good afternoon, how may I help you?" He drifted to the opposite end of the table, looking down as he pulled out a chair.

Josh stood up and smiled, not saying a word.

Austin raised his head, running a gaze up and down Josh. He adjusted his tie. His facial expression remained unchanged. It had been a while. And only spending a week together, mostly in seminar classes. it's not like they'd grown up as next-door neighbors. Austin peeked at the seated woman.

"Ma'am," greeted Austin with a nod of his head. Turning back to the man, he glued in on the visitor's eyes. His mouth shifted ever so slightly but didn't breach a smirk. Holding a full house in his hand, he maintained a world-class poker face. "Hello sir, my name is Austin. How may I help you two?"

A dash of surprise dripped from Josh's face. "You don't remember me?" he asked, feeling a tablespoon of disappointment.

After a long pause, while shaking his head, Austin responded. "I'm sorry. Should I?" Again, a dramatic pause followed.

Josh's mouth opened wide. But before flies could enter or words could exit, his fellow prosecutor interrupted the visitor's response with unbridled laughter. "Joshua Rizzetti!" he blurted. "My good buddy! What in the *world* are you doing here?"

Josh busted out in laughter. "Ha-ha! Very well played my friend. I thought I'd spoil our vacation by paying you a visit. How the heck are you?" His pointer circled his eyes. "Judging from the raccoon eyes, I can see that the slopes are treating you well."

Austin hustled around the table. Josh met him halfway. Like two brothers hugging after one returned from combat, they firmly embraced. Kristen observed intently, impressed with the connection. And more than a bit surprised given that Josh wasn't much of a social butterfly. Heck, he wasn't even a semi-social moth. And here he was, a transformed caterpillar leaving the protective shell of its chrysalis, flying free with another butterfly.

Kristen beamed, admiring the colorful wings of her surprising boyfriend. And making it more impressive, it was a friend he had made without her assistance.

"My girlfriend and I are here on vacation," Josh said. Releasing his bear hug, Josh extended his arm toward Kristen. "Kristen Laney this is Austin Willis. Austin, this is Kristen."

Greetings exchanged. They chatted around the table like girl scouts around a campfire. Even absent the smores, the conversation was rich. Josh spouted off Kristen's resume, clearly proud of her accomplishments. Kristen modestly sat with a shroud of embarrassment over her face.

"Ivy League, huh?" Austin complimented. "So, you're smart, beautiful, and delightful. Seems like your only flaw is your poor judgment—dating this schlepp."

"How about you?" Josh asked. "If memory serves me, you were on the verge of starting a serious relationship last time we caught up. Madison was her name. But that was a couple of years ago. I'm sure she came to her senses and dumped your sorry butt by now. Am I right?"

Kristen just shook her head, undoubtedly pondering the paradox that's baffled women's minds for centuries—the reason why the more grown men like one another, the more they insult each other.

Austin lifted his left hand facing up, pressing his thumb on a wedding band. "We tied the know about six months ago. And I must say, for a guy who couldn't remember his hotel room number, I'm impressed you remembered her name."

"Hey, in my defense, it wasn't me who forgot my room number. The two pitchers of margaritas were responsible for that."

"Congratulations!" Kristen said.

"That's awesome. Congrats!" Josh said. "The capital couple."

"The capital couple?" Austin said with confusion.

"Yeah," said Josh. "You both have the name of a state capital."

"That's kind of cute," Kristen remarked. "Sounds like fate."

"You can name your kids Cheyenne and Jackson," Josh snickered.

"I know my wife would love to meet you both," Austin said. "Hey, if you're free, why don't you let us take you to dinner tonight?"

Kristen and Josh made eye contact. Josh waited for a signal. He was sure Kristen would be game. But just when it seemed that he thought he had her pegged, he'd be dead wrong. So, Josh kept his mouth shut, certain that if he opened it his foot would fly into it. And being a man with a voracious appetite, he didn't want to spoil it before dinner—preferring bruschetta over boots.

Kristen turned to Austin. "We'd love to. But it's our treat. We insist."

"Great. Let me call my wife and let her know. I was thinking pizza or burgers, but since you insist on buying, steak and lobster it is." Austin laughed. "I have a few things to wrap up here. Then I can go pick her up and we can meet you. Where are you staying?"

"We're over at the Lake Dillon B&B in Frisco. Do you know it?"

"Yes."

"Of course you do. Nobody knows a county better than a first responder or a prosecutor."

"Don't we know it?" Austin said. He looked at his watch. "You know, there's a wonderful restaurant one block from the B&B. Charming ambiance, great food. Why don't Madison and I meet you in your lobby at 6 pm and we can't walk over from there? Or since the temperature is below eighty, do we need to drop off you heat-dependent Californians two inches from the front door?"

"Are you kidding? Josh loves the cold," Kristen said. "And truth be told, I'm getting used to it. Plus, the weather is supposed to be relatively moderate tonight and I love the walkability of Frisco's Main Street."

"Perfect," said Austin. "It's a date. Or should I say, double date?"

"We look forward to it." Kristen smiled. "I can't wait to meet your wife."

"Hey, it just occurred to me," Austin said, crinkling his eyebrows. "Last time we spoke, I was still with the D.A.'s office in Denver. How did you know I was here?"

"The *Midnight Vandal*," responded Josh.

Austin looked befuddled. "The *Midnight Vandal*? How is that possible?"

"I read in the paper that the trial of the *Midnight Vandal* is coming up, and it mentioned your name as the prosecutor. We'll still be in town. I'd love to watch you in action."

"Yeah, me too," Austin said in a disappointed tone.

"What do you mean?" Kristen asked.

"There's not going to be a trial," responded Austin.

"Oh. He pled out?" Josh said. "How much time is he getting?"

"Life," Austin said. Then, after a long pause, he continued. "Without the possibility of parole."

"Wow!" exclaimed Josh. "I knew California was lenient on crime relative to the rest of the country. But man, life without parole on vandalism. I thought we were in Colorado, not North Korea. How is that even a potential sentence for vandalism?" His tilted head and squinted eyes exposed his confusion. "Surely it's not."

"You're correct. It's not."

"Huh?" Kristen said. "Then how in the world—"

"He was murdered yesterday."

"Murdered!?" Josh and Kristen blurted in harmony.

Chapter Thirteen

"CRASH!" THE SOUND of glass shattering seemed amplified in the quiet restaurant. Smooth jazz provided the background ambiance but was in between songs when the startling noise breached the dead air. The abrupt swing from Miles Davis to *Crash* Davis was as peaceful as a Louisville Slugger-toting Durham Bull in a China shop. The guests, occupying one-third of the restaurant's capacity, almost fell back in their chairs. One actually did.

For Kristen, the timing couldn't have been more inconvenient. After completing her last swirl like a seasoned sommelier, she began sipping her glass of red wine. The second the easy-drinking red hit her lips, the swinging kitchen door had launched four water glasses from the serving tray of a distraught waitress.

Naturally, the delightful Malbec, a tangy and fruity red vino, stained as well as it tasted. Along with her glass, Kristen's head dropped to her shirt, peering at the blood bath gushing over her midsection. Near tears, she glared through Josh. Distressed—a colossal understatement. She was keen on making a good first impression with everyone she met and doing so in an alcohol-soaked blouse lessened the odds.

Like the floor's impact on the glasses, tears broke the surface. "Thanks, Joshua Rizzetti."

Kristen said his full name. He didn't know why, but he knew it was bad. Somehow, with one foot already in the doghouse, Josh squirmed in his chair. After a great pause, he dared to open his mouth and said, "What did I do?"

"I asked you what I should wear. And you picked the white blouse over the burgundy dress."

"Of course I did," Josh agreed. "It's freezing outside. Literally. But you're right. Sorry. My bad."

Josh paused. Should he dare attempt to lighten the mood with one of his witty comments? In a heartbeat, he took a swing. If he was wrong, he'd be nibbling on *Purina Dog Chow* rather than feasting on Fettuccine Alfredo. "Knowing what a drinking problem you have; I should've known better. The problem . . . getting the wine from your glass to your mouth."

An awkward silence ensued, and heads shifted around the table. Kristen glared at the amateur co-median. She tried to fight it, but her frown began to flip. Then, all at once, the two couples burst out in laughter. Almost certain his joke would strike out, Josh's sarcastic snipe hit it out of the park. *Bring on the Fettucine Alfredo. And throw in some garlic bread.*

Two prosecutors, a business attorney, and a com-mercial real estate broker were having dinner in an Italian restaurant . . . rang like the beginning of a joke. Unfortunately, along with a full glass of red wine, the joke was on Kristen. But true to her nature, and her middle name, she took it with grace and shook it off with levity.

"Do you want me to run to the B&B and grab you a clean shirt from our room?"

Kristen hesitated, seemingly a little out of sorts. She glanced at her blouse, then responded, "Umm, no thank you. I'm fine."

Madison looked at Kristen with empathy. Every woman had been there at one time or another. And although they'd known each other for all of twenty minutes, they clicked instantly. The extent of that bond only could be characterized by what transpired next.

She too favored red wine with Italian food, so Madison grabbed her dinner spoon, scooped her Cabernet-Merlot blend from her long stem wine goblet wine, and tipped a tablespoon of the Napa Valley red blend over the front of her light gray sweater. For good measure, she repeated her lunacy. Not quite to the extent of Kristen's blouse— which looked as if she'd been on the losing end of a mob hit— the stain stood out like a sore thumb. A big, swollen, bloody thumb.

"Oh my—" Kristen gasped. Heavily shocked, but even more touched.

"What the—" Josh and Austin cried together, sharing in astonishment.

Speechless, Kristen locked eyes with Madison, puppy-dog expression and all. A tear drizzled down her flustered cheek. Without a sound, she mouthed to Madison "Thank you," followed by a smile more genuine than a peach cobbler out of Georgia.

Josh reached to his right, placing his hand on Austin's shoulder. "In the famous words of Oscar Wilde, 'Women are made to be loved, not understood.'"

Kristen shook her head. Madison requited, "Sisters are like fat thighs . . . they stick together."

Emotionally floored, Kristen beamed brighter than the Colorado Sun. Josh smiled, grateful that the two ladies hit it off at jump street. He knew it was a long shot, two female strangers genuinely enjoying each other's company. History, observation, and a pulse taught him that. So, he was even more appreciative. Stunned, really. But still thankful.

Whether they'd admit it or not, Josh's experience taught him that when it came to friendships, women were fickle. For guys, one simple common interest could lead to a lifelong friendship, ball games, poker nights, and bar hopping. For gals, they could have ninety-five percent in common, but with the slightest display of a tiny quirk or a misplaced comment, they'd never talk again. Kristen once told him, "Men can enjoy all day on a golf course with a caddy, while women can't enjoy all day drinking wine without being catty."

In the moment of the brief exchange of mental and emotional solidarity between Kristen and Madison, Josh imagined what life in the Rocky Mountains would be like for him. Not that he wasn't happy. Without regret, he loved his life and friends in Santa Barbara. His tight-knit group of five, self-named the *Happy Hour Gang*, was inseparable. But admittedly, after he and one of the formidable five—namely Kristen—had started dating, it felt different. Not bad different, just different. Now that the two of them were a couple, hanging out with three single people made them feel less like one of the gang and more like a fifth wheel.

But it wasn't so much the absence of another couple for the new lovebirds to hang out with that created the void in Josh. It was more like a seven-year itch. And like clockwork, after seven years in Santa Barbara Josh had caught a bad case of *Toxicodendron diversilobum*—Pacific poison oak.

Until recently Josh had never thought of it. But suddenly, he realized that since becoming an adult, he had never been in one place for too long. After four years of college, followed by a year of saving money, he moved from California to Mississippi to attend law school. Next, after three years of law school, he moved from Oxford, Mississippi to Santa Barbara, California.

Now almost seven years later, he was well-settled in Santa Barbara. But the onset of a minor itch had surfaced. And like a mosquito bite, he'd given it a gentle rub, only to find that it escalated the itch—profusely!

In a flash, it dawned on him. Perhaps he should discuss this with Kristen. *Perhaps?* Of course, he should. *Should?* he thought. *Need to!* A true foreigner to long-term relationships, Josh struggled with his *learn-as-I-go* strategy. Ignorance is bliss—hardly! For the rookie romantic, ignorance created angst.

Wine. Spilling. Appetizers. Dinner. Death by chocolate for dessert. More wine. Even more conversation.

Madison vented to Kristen recapping her day; shaken from a heated confrontation she'd had with a disgruntled investor earlier in the day. The commercial broker almost broke down in tears. Kristen listened intently, with the occasional tilt of the head or nod.

Josh filled in Austin on the details of his recent misdemeanor prosecution that nearly got Kristen and him killed—twice. Austin detailed some quirky specifics of past local events that had transpired, all in relation to the decades-old search for the golden treasure. And steadily accompanying their dialogue, more wine.

With a newly formed couple kinship, the foursome jawed and laughed until the manager kindly pushed them out the door. Austin, not wanting to end his career, or later be forced to prosecute his wife for a DUI, summonsed a ride from a phone app. Madison suggested he get one for their tipsy friends, "I'm not sure they can walk a block without getting hurt."

"We'll be fine," Kristen said, throwing her arms up to maintain her balance.

The foursome huddled outside the restaurant, awaiting the local couple's rideshare. A small SUV slowed as it passed them on the opposite side of Main Street. Creeping down, the driver-side window revealed the top half of a face, its eyes staring at the two couples.

While the three others laughed and chatted, Austin appeared to be the only one keeping an eye out for their rideshare. He spotted the *Subaru Outback* slowing to a crawl. "I think that might be our ride," he said.

The SUV rolled past, traveling another fifty feet or so, then whipped a U-turn in the middle of the block. "Yep," said Austin. "It looks like it's coming for us."

Madison and Kristen reached into their respective purses, intending to exchange business cards. Having drunk more than the night of her *My Cousin Vinny* homework assignment in her days at Cornell, Kristen fumbled, then dropped her purse. Instinctively, Josh, Kristen, and Madison all leaned forward and reached down for the purse as Austin waved down the vehicle. As if choreographed by *The Three Stooges*, the three inebriated heads knocked with considerable force, allowing gravity to do her thing.

Simultaneous with the cranial conking, the SUV edged closer to the couples' curbside location. With Austin pressing something on his phone app, the *Outback's* passenger window rolled down.

"Bang! Bang!" Two bullets ripped through the open car window.

Pedal to the metal, the SUV bolted up Main Street, straight toward Lake Dillon with enough speed it could've skimmed across the massive reservoir without taking on a drop of water.

Austin launched himself toward his charming new wife. Fresh off her head-butting with Curly and Moe, Madison was halfway to the ground when her husband finished the tackle. Austin's adrenaline-induced sack of his wife propelled the two of them on top of Josh and Kristen with enough force to crack several wine-saturated ribs. At that moment it became evident that the Denver Broncos had overlooked their next legendary sack master in the latest NFL draft, a prospect cleverly disguised as a slim Deputy D.A. from Summit County.

"Oh my God!" Austin and Josh both shrieked, looking at their significant others who lay motionless, flat on their backs, with red stains covering their midriff. If they were lucky, only broken ribs were on their after-dinner menu. If not, they'd passed up a second serving of death by chocolate for death by gunfire.

Chapter Fourteen

T HE VACATIONERS' ITINERARY tentatively had penciled in snow skiing for the day. Two bullets fired the night before poked a hole or two in those plans. Statistically, most law-abiding citizens don't get shot at once in a lifetime. For Josh and Kristen, this made twice in less than twelve months.

Subconsciously, Josh feared that their relationship would end in a similar fashion to all his past relationships, with him getting dumped. If recent events were any indication, they'd be lucky if that's how it ended. More likely, it would terminate in *death do us part* well before they could exchange *I dos.*

Fortuitously, the drunken brain bashing of *The Three Stooges* likely saved their lives. After securing the crime scene, the CSI unit found two bullets impaled in the wall to the left of the restaurant's entrance. More notably, they were lodged roughly four feet up, and directly in line with the path coming from the location of the vehicle's passenger-side window at the time of the shooting and toward the concussed winos.

Dodging the alternative, Kristen and Madison cried with relief knowing their tops were stained only with red wine. Not surprising. What woman wouldn't prefer a Bordeaux blend over a blood bath? Their clothes were replaceable, they were not.

The morning after the shooting, Kristen's state of being could accurately be described as rattled, but not terrified. Sadly, this wasn't her first rodeo. Nonetheless, she certainly wasn't up for skiing. More important to her, she insisted on comforting her new friend, who understandably wasn't coping as well.

For Madison, frantic-borderline-hysterical more accurately depicted her demeanor. Not unlike most professional women in their thirties, she had never been the target of a shooting. So, for her, brushing it off like it was a split end didn't come as easily as it did for her new friend.

Outside the Willis couple's home, a man circled the perimeter. Gun holstered and ready to fire, he peeked in on the commiserating women who sat huddled on a sofa sipping tea.

The question remained—*who* was the target? It could've been any of them. Madison had been on the receiving end of a heated argument with an ill-tempered investor less than ten hours prior to the shooting. Austin was the prosecuting attorney of a defendant who just had been murdered, only a week before his scheduled trial. And Josh and Kristen found more than they had bargained for while competing in the scavenger hunt—stumbling upon a dead body. And worse, the body wasn't simply dead—he had been murdered.

Madison saw the shadow cut across her living room window out the corner of her eye. She jerked back in fear.

"It's okay," comforted Kristen, grabbing Madison's tea for a refill. "It's just a uniformed officer doing his job."

"I think the most unsettling thing about last night," Madison said as her trembling hands took her cup from Kristen, "is that we don't know who the target was. Or should I say, who the target *is*?"

"You're right. Until then, we all need to have our heads on a swivel." Kristen placed her left hand on Madison's right knee. "But you know what, Josh and Austin will figure this out."

* * *

THE SUMMIT COUNTY District Attorney had insisted that Austin stay home with his wife. However, knowing she was in great hands with her new friend, Austin had other plans in mind. Who was the shooter? Who was his target? And why? They had to figure it out before one of them ended up dead.

And while Austin convinced his boss to let him come into the office, the District Attorney urged his deputy to let one of his colleagues handle his caseload for the day. No coaxing needed, the *Midnight Vandal* prosecutor and his fellow Deputy D.A. from the left coast buckled down in the library of the District Attorney's office, resolved to make some headway as to the motive and target of the *Frisco Firing*, as it had been coined in the local newspaper's daily edition.

"Okay, Counselor," Josh said. "We're on your turf. So, where should we start?"

"Since it appears that any one of us could have been the target, we could flip a coin."

"True," replied Josh. "So, let's try to eliminate the least likely target and go in reverse. That might be more efficient so that we don't go down a rabbit hole unnecessarily."

"Good idea," Austin agreed. "Well, my heart might be speaking instead of my head, but it's got to be Madison. She's least likely to be the target, right?"

"That'd be my guess too," Josh said. "But you'd know better than I. From what little I know, she's a sweetheart, compassionate, likable, and professional. Absent her having dealt with a total psychopath yesterday, I can't see anyone targeting her."

"Yeah, I can't see it either. While she does deal in a lot of stressful, high-end commercial transactions, she is very thorough with her clients. Most are well-educated, and of course, wealthy. They know the risks. Even so, her due diligence is off the charts." Austin exhaled deeply. "So, all that being said, my head agrees with my heart. I didn't think her run-in yesterday with a pissed-off client would've warranted a drive-by shooting."

Josh was seated on the long side of the large, rectangular conference table. With pen in hand and canary legal pad plopped on the table, he crossed off one of the four names he had written down. The savvy crime fighters agreed, someone marking Madison for murder was improbable, nigh inconceivable.

Austin sat opposite the table from Josh. His laptop open, with his fingers on the keys, he appeared eager to research. What? They didn't know yet. But if they brainstormed long enough, then surely the two adept attorneys could unveil something conceivable. And if lucky, something promising.

It had come as no surprise to Josh that he and Austin hit it off when they had first met several years earlier at a conference attended entirely by total strangers; strictly new prosecutors throughout the United States. In terms of age, Josh had inhaled his first breath one year earlier than Austin. Socioeconomically, they both grew up middle class. Educationally, both graduated from public universities as undergrads and again as law school grads. Likewise, both paid their own way while earning their degrees, working part-time, carrying a full-time load, and living in poverty the entire time.

The most noticeable difference between the two rested in their geographic mobility. Austin was a Colorado boy, through and through. Born in Denver, and raised in Colorado Springs, bachelor's degree from Colorado State University in Fort Collins, and his J.D. from the University of Colorado in Boulder.

Josh possessed a bit of a nomad quality. Being born, raised, and having attended school in his home state of California, Josh graduated college from Cal Poly Pomona, However, with a strong desire to explore the country, he only applied to out-of-state law schools to pursue his juris doctorate. With acceptances from several law schools scattered across the U.S., he made his decision immediately after a visit to the Law Center on the beautiful campus of the University of Mississippi.

*　*　*

WARM SPRINGTIME AIR laid thick over the beautiful college town of Oxford, Mississippi. The twenty-two-year-old college graduate had chosen the fourth oldest state-supported law school in the United States for his first visit. A university that could tell more stories than a children's librarian. Home of The Grove, the most iconic tailgating venue in all of college football. Home of more former Miss Americas than any other university. Home of the Ole Miss Rebels.

A university filled with history, both good and bad. Proudly, claiming home to Rowan Oak, the former home of Nobel-Prize-winning writer William Faulkner. Infamously home to the death and bloodshed during the integration and entrance of James Meredith—the university's first African American student—onto the campus of the deeply rooted southern college. The bullet-marred columns of the historic Lyceum, the university's administration building, perpetually exhibiting a reminder of its tumultuous past.

Joshua had never been to the Ole Miss campus before his visit to its law school. He'd never been in Mississippi. In fact, he had never traveled east of Arizona. He knew exactly zero people within a thousand miles. After arriving by plane in Memphis, Tennessee, he hopped on a shuttle that dropped him off eighty-five miles south in front of his motel in Oxford. From there, all his travels would be by foot. No rental car. No buses. No taxis. Unquestionably, no rideshare apps. Just his two legs and a decent pair of cross-trainers.

His first full day in town, he spent touring the campus. On his walk from the motel to campus, Josh nearly got whiplash, swiftly turning his head side-to-side as gorgeous co-eds floated by him, speed-walking to squeeze in their morning exercise before finals. The beautiful young ladies stared back at the strongly-jibbed Californian; but likely for his wide-open jaw—not for its shape—as he drooled his way to campus.

First, a visit to the law school, where a gracious staff gave him the grand tour of the law school building, even offering him a drive back to his motel afterward. But with his motel just a mile off campus, Josh politely declined the ride, with the intention of roaming around the immaculate university grounds to immerse himself in the Ole Miss atmosphere.

Next stop, the Lyceum. The university's administration building was the template for its prominent logo and the symbol of its history. Sitting at the top of the loop of The Circle, the stunning Greek Revival-style building, with its majestic white columns, stood as the pillar of the campus. Joshua exited the building, ran his hands down one of the storied columns, then strolled across The Circle and stopped to admire the adjacent park-like setting of The Grove.

Turning back, Josh looked around, admiring the beauty, smelling the freshly cut green grass, and soaking in its history. Evidently looking like a lost tourist—partly because he was—a young pretty student approached him and asked, "Are you lost? You *look* lost."

"No, I'm just—," he stuttered. "Well, kind of. I'm just visiting and I, uh—" The future courtroom orator was off to a stellar start. A simple conversation with a sweet-accented hotty and Joshua's mouth was gelatin. Finally, his pulse started to decline, as did his incoherent babble. He introduced himself and explained the purpose of his presence and the plans for the remainder of his trip—namely, winging it.

"Well, my friends and I are fixin' to go out tonight to one of the bars off the Square. Would you like to join us? We can have some drinks, dance on the tables, and show you a typical college night in Oxford."

Joshua had heard a tad or two about southern hospitality. Now it was time to experience it firsthand. He fervently accepted and . . . a few months later, moved to Oxford, some eighteen-hundred-fifty miles away from his hometown, and went on to earn his law degree from the University of Mississippi. From that point forward, Hotty Toddy meant more to Josh than most.

*　*　*

Now, with an itch to wander once again, privately Josh was contemplating trading in his surfboard for a snowboard. Problem was, he hadn't shared his thoughts with Kristen. Justifying his secrecy, he couldn't pinpoint whether what he was feeling was just a slight tickle or a full-blown poison oak rash.

"So, Austin," said Josh, "what's your take on the murder of the *Midnight Vandal*? Do you think his death was related to your criminal case against him?"

"Well, why don't I get your take on it?" Austin responded. "His case was set for trial next week. I'm sure you read in the paper that he was the only one caught and charged. But I think he must've had an accomplice who disappeared when the cops arrived. After all, it seems odd for somebody to take a jackhammer to a commercial property, on Main Street, and expect to get away with it. Not without a lookout."

"I totally agree," Josh said, scratching the stubble on his chin, taking a vacation from shaving while on break. "Now, do you know if this was just some random act of vandalism? Or was it some vendetta against the property owner?" He paused. "Was he digging for something?"

"All excellent questions, my friend," replied Austin. "Random? Not likely. Vendetta? It was city property. Under and around the town clock on the corner of Third and Main, to be specific. So probably not." He hesitated and nodded his head. "Digging for something? Certainly feasible. Presumably gold. With those things in mind, I offered him a sweet deal with no jail time if he gave up his cohorts or any other valuable information. But, from the word go, he was adamant about going to trial. I'm guessing he was motivated to keep his mouth shut."

"Hmm. Interesting. So, it's possible that he was protecting his co-conspirators, or keeping his trap shut for some other reason. Perhaps, he was offered some incentive. You know, to keep silent and do his time, in exchange for a nice payday for his silence."

Austin tightened his lips and nodded his head. "Josh, with a mind like yours, we need you to come work for us," he said, tapping his pointer at his companion. "I think you are spot on. Just a few days ago, the defendant's attorney contacted me, indicating his client was considering cutting a good deal in exchange for him providing significant information. Groundbreaking, he said—no pun intended. Next thing you know, he's found murdered the night before we were scheduled to meet."

"Whoa!" uttered Josh. "Murdered to guarantee his silence. The number one deterrent to keep a man from squealing." Josh placed a comforting right hand on Austin's left shoulder as if to soften the blow of what came next. "I hate to say it, my friend. But speaking from experience, prosecuting a criminal case wherein an essential person to the case is murdered means one thing for sure—*you* were the target of the shooting last night."

"Possibly. And ordinarily, I'd agree with you one hundred percent," Austin said, parroting the action of his friend, putting his right hand on Josh's opposite shoulder. "But it's just as likely that you and Kristen were the targets."

A look of confusion swathed Josh's face. His head pulled back, and his eyebrows crinkled as he lowered his right arm. Almost uncontrollably he blurted, "Whatcha talkin' bout Willis?" instinctively demonstrating his best rendition of Arnold from the 80s' comedy *Different Strokes*. "How do you figure?"

"True, I was prosecuting the *Midnight Vandal*. And given there appears more to his case than property defacement, I'm entangled in the crosshairs. But I'm not the one—or should I say two— who found *his* dead body."

"You mean— "

"Yep., The body you two found during the scavenger hunt was the *Midnight Vandal*," Austin said with an emphatic nod. "So, I'm thinking— "

Josh interrupted, "That we might've seen something we weren't supposed to see."

"Exactly! Or *heard* something."

Josh paused and scratched his stubble. "Now that you mention it, I have an idea of what that might be," Josh said, recalling their deadly discovery. He continued, spilling to Austin the details of their adventure.

When Josh and Kristen had discovered the body, it had been covered in a pile of snow. Likely, it was the intention of the killer to delay its discovery or perhaps heaped in a panic to avoid being seen by an approaching witness after the killing. Whatever the reason, Josh didn't know. What he did know, was that he'd tripped over something, kicking aside snow in the process. And when he had turned back, the eyes of a blood-drenched face stared blankly into the night.

Eager to win the event, Kristen already had hustled ahead of Josh and pushed eight paces ahead of him when he tripped. Once he had discovered the dead body, Josh hollered for Kristen to stay clear and call 9-1-1. As Kristen made the call, he leaned in to check for a pulse. As Josh's two fingers neared the victim's neck, the eyes blinked twice and the mouth moaned something incoherent, then all signs of life vanished. Josh confirmed. No pulse.

Knowing it'd be several minutes before first responders arrived, Josh and Kristen waited anxiously, as their scavenger hunt prizes slipped away from their riddle-solving grasp. Shockingly and quicker than expected a police unit arrived, shortly followed by the paramedics.

Kristen had given her statement first, with little to say other than she had called 9-1-1 when Josh told her to, and she simply repeated to the operator what he was saying. Competitive to a fault, Josh then insisted that she finish the hunt while he stayed back to give his statement. So, after receiving clearance from one of the investigating officers, Kristen edged out another couple to the final clue, securing victory for the touristy, scavenger-hunting, dead-body-finding couple.

Meanwhile, after Josh had completed giving his statement, he caught a glimpse of the entire body before it was zipped up in a body bag. The bloodied face, he could not decipher. But a quick scan by the observant prosecutor highlighted one thing of note, a distinctive mark on the back of the victim's right hand after the medical examiner had unraveled a gauze wrap that was covering it.

"I kept telling myself that the unique scar I had seen was just a figment of my imagination. That it was probably a random burn, embellished by some shadow or poor lighting. But now that you tell me he was the *Midnight Vandal*, likely with ties to others determined to find the gold treasure, I can see how our discovery of his body would put us at risk." Josh sighed. "Whoever's behind his murder doesn't know if he was able to start singing before he gasped his last breath. So, to hedge their bet they figured they'd silence every potential witness."

* * *

FEELING LIKE THEY had made some progress, in need of refueling, and concerned with the welfare of their fairer-sex partners, the collaborative counselors turned into caring companions. On the way to Austin's home, to surprise the young ladies with lunch and distract them from fear of early mortality, the young men picked up lunch from Madison's favorite eatery, Sushi at the Summit.

Starving and surprised, the ladies screamed with joy, beholden to the gesture and ecstatic with the choice of cuisine. Madison's favorite restaurant, Kristen's favorite food. Gleaming with pride, the two waiters patted the shoulders of the other.

The break served them well. Kristen and Madison enjoyed the needed relief from reality; Josh and Austin felt re-energized. The latter's plan was to return to the office with a goal to make more headway, followed by a scheduled break on Austin's calendar, then back to racking their brains. The scheduled break was a mandatory in-office seminar.

Once a year, an attorney conducted a continuing legal education workshop at the Summit County D.A.'s Office. While the topic changed annually, the focus never strayed from the practice of criminal law.

Mandatory Continuing Legal Education, MCLE for short, was a required form of career development for attorneys via professional education, intended to maintain and increase the professional competency of active attorneys. In Colorado, attorneys were required to complete forty-five MCLE hours every three years. California required twenty-five hours, also covering a three-year period. Lucky for Josh, most accredited courses in Colorado qualified for the credit in California as well—as did this one. And since Austin had to attend to receive one-point-five credits of MCLE, Josh decided he'd do the same.

The one-and-one-half-hour seminar was scheduled to begin at 2:30 in the afternoon. The topic, *The Hurdles When Prosecuting the Perfect Murder*.

Chapter Fifteen

T YPICALLY, THE ANNUAL seminar was strictly for the Summit County Deputy District Attorneys and their boss. But getting pre-approval from the D.A. and the MCLE instructor, two young local criminal defense attorneys also patiently sat in attendance.

Still wet behind the ears, the two newly admitted lawyers were keen on soaking in experience through education whenever possible. And with a reputation that proceeded him, they couldn't miss listening to this particular speaker, a lawyer praised as one of the best. That, and quite possibly the computer-dependent Generation Y attorneys sought to be amused by an attorney who pre-dated the written word, citing legal precedent carved in the side of cave walls.

Every chair in the large conference room was filled, save for the head of the table. Behind the head chair stood a four-by-six-foot whiteboard. No PowerPoint or fancy software projecting to a large HD screen for this instructor. This guy was the founder of the old-school method. If they had provided him with a chalkboard, he would've felt more comfortable. Stone tablet and a chisel, even better. As it were, the whiteboard would suffice.

Excited about the topic, the attorneys ceased their chatter as the D.A. stood to introduce their guest speaker. MCLE topics varied dramatically, from Alternative Dispute Resolution to Water Law, and everything in between. To participate in courses related to one's area of law was preferred, but not always possible. Some areas of law had a countless variety of options, while others were limited. The practicality of Estate Planning Basics for the Wills and Trusts Attorney, this was not. The snooze-fest of Document Management and Retention, hardly.

Mimicking Jack Nicholson's voice, the D.A. bellowed, "Ladies and gentlemen, our much-anticipated annual speaker needs no introduction. So, without further ado, let's welcome a retired legend." Applause followed.

The closed door to the front of the conference room opened. The MCLE speaker entered. The applause faded to a halt. Not a second of silence ensued when Josh stood up.

"Uncle George!"

Josh whipped his head toward Austin, practically spraining his neck. Visibly stunned, Austin babbled, "Say what?"

"That's my great-uncle!"

Less stunned than his favorite relative, the composed lecturer simply said, "Oh, what a nice surprise. Everyone, this is my great-nephew, Joshua Rizzetti. He's a Deputy D.A. visiting from California."

Mumbling and smiles littered the room, then ceased immediately when the elder attorney spoke again. "Son, please take a seat, and let's get started."

Silence fell on the room. Josh's sense of shock settled in his throbbing head, along with his butt in the soft leather chair. He shifted his cheeks a smidge, producing an awkward faux-flatulence sound, too loud to go unnoticed. Curious heads turned, save for his hearing-impaired great-uncle. With the slight tilt of Josh's smirking face directed in sync with his pointing thumb, he accused an unwitting Austin in jest.

Reading glasses dangled from the wrinkled neck of the guest speaker. To both save time and assist the elder MCLE instructor, George had mailed in his outline to the D.A.'s office a week prior, requesting the D.A. to have an employee prepare the whiteboard in advance.

Trusting his work was in place, George flipped the two-sided portable magnetic whiteboard, revealing his outline, including the sub-headed first topic "Prosecuting Murder without a Body." A female Deputy D.A., seated closest to the dry erase board rolled her chair two feet to her left, reached toward the board, and secured a double-pin lock into the side of the frame, holding the display in place.

"Thank you, my dear." The old man flashed her a wink and a smile, then fidgeted with his glasses before continuing.

"The Hurdles When Prosecuting the Perfect Murder," George announced, circling the title with a black dry erase marker grabbed from the tray framing the bottom of the board. "Now, we all know there is no such thing as perfect. But, when all it takes for a jury to acquit is for them to find reasonable doubt, *near perfection* will send a guilty defendant walking free every time. So, for purposes of today's presentation, we'll call near perfect, perfect. Because either way, it's perfectly certain a *not guilty* verdict will follow."

George took a sip of water from the glass in front of him, then continued. "The first type of 'perfect' murder is when there is no dead body. Although it's statistically unlikely that you'll ever be faced with such a sui generis court case in your career, if you have the opportunity to try this one-of-a-kind case, it's stuffed to the gills with challenges. And to hook the fish, you must first overcome the most difficult of obstacles. Can anyone tell me, what is the most onerous hurdle to leap over in this type of case?"

Dead air filled the room, seemingly impossible for a room full of lawyers—let alone litigation attorneys. Did the retired prosecutor stump the entire room with his first question? How else could one silence a room full of attorneys? Or was it reticence, doubt, hesitation? Was it that no one wanted to be the arrogant individual so bold as to blurt out in confidence, only to be proven wrong, then shrivel in his place with self-inflicted shame?

Never lacking in *Pelotas*, Josh raised his hand. George took a deep breath as if waiting for someone else to give it a shot. No nepotism here. He gazed around the room. Apparently, Josh was the only one who remembered deodorant, for no other armpits peaked from the suffocation of the clenching arms.

Rescuing the extended-arm participant from embarrassment, assuming Josh too had forgotten his *Speed Stick*, George limited the prolonged exposure of his young protégé's armpit. "Yes, Mr. Rizzetti,"

"Jury trust?" Josh responded in a confident tone, curiously tainting it with a question mark.

George didn't reply, but rather scanned the room as if looking for the correct answer, leaving his great-nephew to float on a cloud of uncertainty.

Josh's body sank in his chair a smidge, and with it, his confidence. Making it worse, no reinforcements followed. Nobody else stepped up to the plate to hit one out of the park or to pick up the slack of their fallen teammate; their colleague who had just whiffed in front of a home crowd.

A flickering flame kindled in Josh's gut, sparked by one of his pet peeves—when everybody lacked the onions to speak up for a colleague for fear of failure. Falling way short, no one else so much as left the dugout, let alone strolled from the on-deck circle to the batter's box. With that, the umpire announced the call; Josh shuttered at the thought of being shamed by his own flesh and blood.

"That's correct! The trust of the jury." George eyed his great-nephew and dipped him the slightest of nods. Josh sighed, thinking *Thanks for making me sweat, Uncle George*. With his confidence renewed, Josh hoisted his posture.

"How can you expect a jury to trust you and allow you the opportunity to convince them the defendant deliberately and intentionally killed the victim if you can't even *produce* a victim? After all, providing a victim is the easy part. It's simple. All it takes is a dead body, killed by unnatural means. In short, evidence there has been an unlawful death. It's proving beyond a reasonable doubt that the killing was deliberate and intentional which is much more difficult. But how can you expect a jury to find that you've proven the most difficult elements when you can't even prove the simplest part—that somebody is in fact dead?" George paused intentionally, then steadied on. "With no body, isn't it reasonable that the 'victim' is still alive?" George threw up air quotes on cue. "In other words, there is no victim. And no victim means no murder, making it easy for the jury foreperson to utter those two dreadful words—*not guilty*."

The silence of the students still lingered. But no longer an air of uncertainty. Not at all. Now, stares of hunger locked in on George, famished for knowledge. Not even having teased them with appetizers, the master chef had his students drooling at the bit. Ever so subtle, his tone, voice inflection, mannerisms, and strategic pauses captivated his audience, yearning to be fed.

In a matter of two minutes, Josh was taken back to his youth. As if time had turned back, Josh was reminded of how engaging a speaker Uncle George was, and how the still-sharp-as-a-knife prosecutor emeritus had earned his reputation as a legendary litigator. Just like that, Josh was twelve years old again, sitting in a courtroom for the first time, inspired and motivated by a master of the English language and a guru of persuasion. An artist of words.

George continued after scanning his eager audience. "What if he's sipping tropical drinks on a secluded island? What if he purposely disappeared to make it look like the defendant murdered him? What if, what if, what if? Sounds like a lot of doubt, doesn't it? Is it all reasonable doubt? Perhaps! Does *any* of it amount to reasonable doubt? Absolutely! And that's what makes it a 'perfect' murder."

The retired seasoned prosecutor stretched on. George detailed the barricades grounded on the path from indictment to conviction of a defendant charged with the murder of an unaccounted-for victim. He cited statistics reporting that over fifteen hundred Americans are reported missing on an average daily basis.

"You heard me right," he reiterated, "over fifteen hundred a day. Surely, all those people weren't murdered." He reminded his students that some people voluntarily disappear, and for a multitude of reasons: fleeing abusive relationships, substance abuse problems, mental illness, credit problems. The list was long. Also, without a body to inspect as to the cause of death, how does one prove the death occurred by unlawful means? Not to mention, proving the "crime" took place within the prosecutor's jurisdiction. A legal technicality—but required, nonetheless.

With each obstacle presented by the near-century-old instructor, his reading glasses shifted locations on his hunched upper body. They hung from a chain. Swinging back and forth on his surprisingly firm chest; the product of thirty push-ups a day. When in use, the fully magnified readers perched on his nose as he pointed to a section of his outline, pre-written on the twentieth-century relic in the form of a whiteboard. And periodically, his pinching grip lifted them to his forehead. And with their snug arms clinging to the side of his head for short stints between use, Josh was reminded of his renowned Constitutional Law professor from his studies at Ole Miss.

Pressed for time, George cut short further elaboration. The group of younger attorneys got the point, as he had eloquently set forth. "No body means no bueno," he summarized. After a ten-minute break—stretching, drinking water, then draining water—Mr. Dellucci moved on to the next "perfect" murder.

"While the first 'perfect' murder we discussed was centered on the victim or lack thereof, the next 'perfect' murder earned its spot on the list because of the skill and insider's knowledge of the perpetrator. Specifically, it's a murder committed by a top-notch prosecutor or skilled detective." George randomly pointed around to the attorneys in the room, ninety percent of whom were prosecutors. "Who better to avoid leaving a trail of incriminating evidence than someone who makes a living investigating, collecting, and proving the link between the evidence, the crime, and the accused?"

The rookie deputy district attorneys vigorously jotted down notes on their legal pads, mostly in cryptic law school shorthand only decipherable by its scrivener. The eager newbie lawyers hurried, trying to catch up while their elder instructor reached for a drink of water.

Austin turned to Josh, and mouthed, "He's incredible." The former smiled, then whispered to the latter, "Exceptionally bright and well-spoken. You sure you two are related?" The proud great-nephew just grinned as he flickered a thumbs up.

"How many of you have ever prosecuted a case in which the jury returned a verdict of guilty, after which you thought, *if I was the defense attorney, this is what I would've done to poke holes in the case to establish reasonable doubt*? And not just your idea of reasonable doubt, but a jury's version of reasonable doubt—enough to acquit the defendant."

A third of the room raised their hands, including Josh and Austin. George nodded while his eyes browsed the room. Leisurely, he too raised his hand.

"A good prosecutor is always a couple of steps ahead of opposing counsel," opined the legendary litigator. "A good prosecutor questions effectively, boasts rebuttals to defenses and quickly counters his opponent's objections. A great prosecutor is several steps ahead, seemingly out of sight. A murky shadow fading into the darkness. A great prosecutor anticipates questions, defenses, and objections so far in advance, that the opponent can't even raise them without appearing a fool. Preemptively eliminating his or her adversary at every turn, a great prosecutor can convince a jury of anything; that the earth is flat, the ocean's dry, or that Colorado skiing is just okay."

The attentive group of students chuckled, the locals grasping the absurdity of George's final example. The old man had a sense of humor. Who would've thought it? After all, this guy was of the generation of black and white family photos in which nobody hinted so much as a smile, let alone beamed a grin. Long before selfies, this man was so old he might've posed for Louis Daguerre, the guy behind the camera of the earliest known photograph of a human. If *one* of the tech-gen attorneys was thinking those things, they *all* were.

As George continued, Josh listened intently. He hadn't been around his uncle in a long time. Too long. He'd almost forgotten how witty he was. Josh saw in himself a lot of his uncle. But Uncle George was next level.

To his credit, Josh was an extremely successful prosecutor, with a track record to prove it. But just when he thought he was at the top of his game, doubt emerged. There was an intangible element in Uncle George that Josh couldn't quite pinpoint, but it most certainly was there. A bright star from the dark sky to which you couldn't quite point your finger.

Josh thought to himself, *If I can figure that out, I can be a better version of myself.* Until the novice mate could solve that piece of his own puzzle, the success of his relationship with Kristen stood in doubt. At least in his mind, it did. And as Uncle George often told Josh, "If you think it, you're right."

Intermittently engaging the group in constructive discourse, Mr. Dellucci laid out the "perfect" murder by a prosecutor. "Just like prosecuting a criminal trial, you first start with the elements of the offense. Just as a deputy district attorney must prove all the elements of the offense beyond a reasonable doubt to get a conviction, conversely the 'perfect' murder should make that impossible. For instance, let's take the element of 'a deliberate or intentional killing.' A death resulting from an 'accident' might be a good place to start. Don't you think?"

The young prosecutors continued to take notes fervently. As the lecture went on, a couple of them gradually reduced their obsessive notetaking, as if afraid their meticulous notes could come back to haunt them should they become a person of interest in a future homicide. One, clearly the smartest, with the makings of a great prosecutor, stopped writing entirely. Prognosticating the next part of a "perfect" murder, leave no trace of any incriminating evidence.

"And the alibi. Don't forget about an alibi," he continued. "In the event that you didn't cross every 't' and dot every 'i,' you need an alibi. And not just a good alibi. A solid alibi, stronger than concrete. And unlike the ozone layer, one without holes. Such that it would appear impossible that *you* could've done it."

George elaborated on his opinions; planting ideas never hatched in the minds of law-abiding lawyers. The old man, with years to circumspect on the mistakes made by the countless criminals he escorted to prison, seemingly every feasible "perfect" murder filled a file in his Rolodex. Those ill-fated the moment their cases crossed George's desk. Presumably convicted after the words "Ladies and gentlemen of the jury" left the great orator's mouth.

Winding down, George voiced a few more witty comments, threw in a "prosecutor walks into a bar" joke, and summarized how it all tied together with the seminar's theme topic. In closing, he snatched the attention of everyone, especially those who didn't know him on a personal level, leaving half the room wondering if the crazy old timer was serious when he voiced his closing comment.

"You never heard this from me." George looked around cautiously, as if sharing the greatest secret ever kept. "But I could've murdered ten people and never so much as be a person of interest."

An uncomfortable pause floated over the room with the weight of a military hovercraft. Joshua and the District Attorney burst into laughter. Following the cue that the old man was joking—or so they hoped—the rest of the room roared with amusement. Though, if facial expressions were suggestive, some less convinced than others.

George Dellucci gazed at the room, his face as straight as a ruler. "But just to be safe, don't go digging around my yard."

Chapter Sixteen

FOR ALMOST TWO decades, the white-collar scam artist rotted away in relative isolation, opting for a slow death over a quick one. With moderate-to-high levels of violence, this was no federal "country club" prison. Who some might call a squirrely nerd, he might as well have been a peanut in a closet of starving elephants, destined to be devoured if not crushed first.

Early on in his prison sentence, the risk to William's life became evident after two attempts on it, both undertaking tortures to extract details from the swindler about the whereabouts of the treasure. Both times, the beatings were severe. Both times, he crossed the bridge and saw "the light." But somehow, both times, he survived without cracking as if someone's life depended on it.

The Machiavellian inmate did the calculation. Even with the federal prosecutor throwing the book at him, and after the federal judge poured salt on the wound by tacking on consecutive sentences, William's life expectancy had given him hope. Hope that he'd someday make it out of prison with time to spare. Time to recover the loot and live lavishly in whatever remaining time lady justice allotted him.

But life had a way of laughing at his plans, recently chewing them up and spitting them out. Now, even by employing the craftiest math, it didn't add up. Multiply this number, then square that, plus outlive the prognosis; too little too late. Whatever way he computed it; freedom preemptively rejected his post-dated ticket, branding it with a big red stamp—*Admission denied.*

Clybourne was no longer knocking on death's door, nor taking a battering ram to it. Rather, he had one foot in the room and a Sherman tank pushing him from the rear. He'd successfully scammed thousands for millions, but it only took a measly six-letter-word to end any hope of splurging it—ever.

William's prison cell took on a minimalist design. As if he had much choice. Unlike his comparable female felons who could seek firsthand the advice of a world-renowned decorator, Martha Stewart hadn't been housed in his all-male facility. That being the case, he made do with the resources available to him.

Three feet above the prisoner's hard, lumpy bed, a bookshelf displayed a handful of items. A cheap wooden frame, battered with more dings than a prison cafeteria tray, displayed a 3x5-inch photo of Geoff's mother. Next to it, four books stacked on one another lay flat on their back covers. Lastly, and to the right of his mini library, leaned an empty picture frame, encased inside black plastic trim as depressing as its imageless presentation.

Among his choice of publications, two should've come as no surprise: *Think and Grow Rich* and *Rich Dad, Poor Dad*. Regrettably, as empowering and innovative as those bestsellers were, clearly the conniving con artist missed their message. William opted for the "get rich quick" path to wealth, ostensibly favoring the shortcut. Unlike most that chose that route, it actually worked for him. Until it didn't.

The third book was a paperback book of famous quotes by famous people. From its appearance, it'd been well read. Worn ink. Wrinkled pages. Bent corners.

The fourth book on the prison cell shelf was of the nonfiction variety. The top right corner of the cover was missing, and the bottom right corner bent. The pages appeared swollen, puffed up from condensation, and crinkled from routine handling and periodic mistreatment. Folded inside page eighty-two was a sheet of standard-size college-ruled paper. On it, was a note. An aged note. A sentimental note. A revealing note. Read thousands of times, but only by its author.

Perhaps feeling nostalgic trailing the visit from his son, he grabbed the largest book from the shelf. He blew the dust from its cover, forming a cloud near his watering eyes. A cough followed.

As the days and the years drifted by, the books received less and less attention. The fact that he knew what pages it was between, as if strategically placed, made finding the note efficient. With the resulting separation in the book, Clybourne could find the note blindfolded.

The prisoner sat in the middle of his bed. His left hand clenched the book, while his right slid out the note. His compressed pillow hardly sank when the tossed book did a back flop onto the worn cotton-stuffed noise suppressant. Compacted by more than William's sleepy head, it also served as a therapist, a sounding board of sorts. If he had a nickel for every time he screamed into it, he'd have a million dollars, maybe two. Of course, he didn't need the cash. Allegedly, that was only a fraction of the monetary worth of his hidden, ill-gotten gains—or so legend had it. Wistfully for him, the treasure's value to this caged prisoner was equal to the value of his pillow-snuffed shrills—worthless.

Although he hadn't read the note in months, he knew it by heart and better than the *Pledge of Allegiance*. He unfolded the note with gentle precision as if handling the original Declaration of Independence. To the author, the note had no monetary value, for it was all in his head. To the casual reader, should it ever fall into the hands of one, realistically it bore no value, for it was too cryptic and personal with its amateur prose.

Sliding the note back in its place, William squeezed the book and pressed it against his forehead. His eyes were glued shut. Looking confused, he tapped the book at his hairline, as if seeking through osmosis the solution to an unanswered question. Or perhaps he could've been praying, preparing for what would follow his last breath.

Living on borrowed time, perhaps he was seeking forgiveness in the hopes of meeting his maker. Undoubtedly, he believed that given his past sins his next escalator ride would be headed down, not up. So, what did he have to lose by searching for reconciliation? Lord willing, it might change the direction of his moving staircase.

Whether he was immersed in anticipative absolution, or slowly beating himself with a hardback, he didn't hear the first couple of calls of his name.

"William," called the rookie tight-end-sized guard. Then louder, he hollered again, "Clybourne!"

Still, no response.

A massive fist pounded on the solid metal bars. "Hey, Bill! You alive?"

Disengaging from his subliminal state, the hazy prisoner shook his head in a brief, rapid motion, like a wet dog shaking dry. "I'm sorry. Yes."

William looked up. His eyes focused on the baseball-size tattoo displayed on the left side of the twenty-one-inch neck. If the newly God-fearing inmate was thinking anything now, it had to be in awe of this guy's neck being thicker than his usual guard's thighs. "Where's Cody?" asked the inmate.

"Day off," responded the guard arduously like English was his second language, which it wasn't. "Outdoor time. You want it?"

"You Tarzan. Me Jane," joked the prisoner, foolishly mocking the mammoth of a man.

More King Kong than Tarzan, the colossal guard replied, "That's a dangerous thing to say in a men's prison. Like you're auditioning to be someone's bitch."

"Good point," said the scrawny convict, who graced the idyllic build of a prisoner's girlfriend.

"So," the apathetic ape said, "you want your outdoor time? Let's move it. We're on a schedule."

William squeezed the sacred book for good measure, then placed it on his bed with reverence. He stood; shoulders slouched. Staring down at his book, he inhaled deeply, then exhaled. Bordering his previous hypnotic state, the sliding prison bars opened his cell while the sound closed his meditative mindset. He puttered through the opening, pinching past the guard who reached half his age and twice his size.

The prison yard looked empty of prisoners. A partially deflated basketball, with leather worn down to the rubber, set idly on the damp concrete underneath the rusted netless rim. Although the snow in the yard had melted, the ground was still moist. In the far corner of the yard, opposite the entry door to the prison hallway, laid two weight benches, upon each which rested a forty-five-pound Olympic bar. Two racks of weights of varying poundage filled the tarnished metal pyramid frame positioned between the two workout benches.

William was a creature of habit, first by nature and further exacerbated by his prison routine. One could set his watch to the inmate's outdoor habits. Shoot hoops first. Three lay-ups, Thirty-three free throws, and three three-point field goals. Next, three laps walking the perimeter of the yard. Finally, some light weightlifting. Not enough to bulk up, but enough to avoid atrophy. And mechanically, all in sets of three.

With William poised to begin the third phase of his ritual, a few other prisoners entered the yard. While not unheard of, it was rather unusual for others to fill the yard before his time was up. And from habit, his time routinely ended with Clybourne pumping some iron to close out his exercise schedule. Perhaps sluggish from his melancholy state, he must've slowed down during his routine, falling slightly behind schedule. But since Godzilla hadn't called him over yet, William proceeded with some bench press.

With a forty-five-pound plate on each side, William laid back and raised the bar to begin his three sets of ten reps of one-hundred-thirty-five pounds. While half the prisoners could one arm dumbbell press a buck-thirty-five, the pencil-necked prisoner could comfortably, but not effortlessly, bench it with the pair of toothpicks protruding from his shoulders.

The warming sun dropped a tad, sheltering behind the protection of the solid prison walls. With that, the warmish winter air cooled in a heartbeat. William finished his first two sets, then sat up. He took a deep breath, then exhaled. Two other inmates approached, then stopped, waiting their turn. If looks were any indication, these two thugs could've graced the cover of the prison's annual calendar if such were a thing. One kissed the anchor tattooed on his chiseled bicep and grinned at Clybourne. They stood over their fellow inmate patiently but said nothing.

"One more set guys," William said. "Then I'm done." Taking another deep breath, he planted his back firmly on the bench, reached up, and lifted the bar, exhaled, closed his eyes, and began to pump his final set.

With a slight onset of fatigue, his fading voice counted out his final reps, "Five, six, sevvvennnn—"

His counting cut short. The Olympic bar, resting in the down position, stopped moving. At each end of it, the *next-up* inmates took on the role of an anchor rather than a spotter. Pressed down, the assisted barbell slid from William's emaciated chest, crushing his throat and larynx. The cracking sound mixed with the hissing of a leaky inner tube dissipated with his last breath.

In seconds, his twigs-for-arms went limp. With the seven-foot steel barbell strategically steadied on the flattened neck, the "spotters" each grabbed a forty-five-pound cast iron plate and simultaneously slid one on each end, balancing the two-hundred-twenty-five-pound load on the lifeless lifter.

The inmates stepped back. Knowing their weight bench of choice would be occupied for a while longer—with free weights replaced by dead weight—they strolled over to the basketball court and began shooting the rock while casually shooting the breeze.

Chapter Seventeen

T HE HOUR WAS well past midnight. Light snow has been dusting the Rockies for about an hour, with heavier dumping expected in the early-morning hours. The forecast called for an additional five inches of snow on the nearby slopes, followed by an abrupt Colorado-like flip to sunshine expected no later than 10 a.m.

Colorado was unique in that way. One minute, unloading more white powder than an overturned *Hostess Brand* truck of donuts. The next minute, flaunting nothing but blue skies and sunshine within an arm's length atop a 14er. The proud state also distinguished itself as home to fifty-eight mountain peaks soaring over fourteen-thousand feet above sea level; more than the other forty-nine states combined.

The top dog never met face-to-face with his lackeys. Dealings were achieved through other means—phone calls via burners, sealed envelopes delivered to a mailbox secured under a fake name, encrypted messages through classified ads in the local newspaper.

Only one person under his thumb knew his identity. And as certain as one could be, his right-hand man would never reveal his boss. For one, he was paid handsomely. Five times more than the seventh-grade dropout could make doing anything else, assuming lawful employment. More convincingly, his loyalty had withstood the apex of torture, bordering martyrdom.

The loyal deputy did as had been requested of him, bringing the underling with him to the late-night impromptu meeting. The compliant agent wasn't told the nature of the covert conference, but he could make an experienced, educated guess—with one-hundred-percent accuracy.

Given the lateness of the hour, all the retail shops and restaurants at The Village at Copper Mountain had been closed for some time. Save for a few dimly lit nightlights, the canopy of condos above the retail district was dark and quiet. Their occupants, out cold from the debilitating exhaustion in the wake of a full day crushing the slopes. A bomb could've been dropped in the center of the village, and at most, a few side-sleepers might've switched shoulders.

Nonetheless, the boss hadn't selected the venue for its late-night tranquil setting. From firsthand experience, his deputy surely figured as much—painfully familiar with the hot spot. On the flip side, the low man on the totem pole was oblivious. Naïve and in over his head, he took no clue as to the reason and location of the clandestine meeting with the head honcho.

Almost smack dab in the center of the paver-pathed corridor of the condo-topped retail buildings of the village burned a massive fire pit. But it was no ordinary firepit. Unlike the typical ski resort firepit, hosting a traditional open-flamed round pit surrounded by Adirondack chairs, this blazing spectacle more re-sembled a work of art.

Situated nearby the entrance to one of the local gift shops, flashed a majestic metal fire globe more than six feet in diameter. With its rusted copper appearance, it looked more suited for a pretentious art gallery on Rodeo Drive than the practicality of providing warmth to the frost-bitten snow junkies. Artistically, it was stunning. Practically, its heat could melt gold.

The boss had arrived fifteen minutes prior to the scheduled meeting time, assuring their privacy and taking his place opposite the scorching globe from his soon-to-arrive guests. A goose-down hooded parka warmed his shoulders down to the top of his knees. Its waterproof, breathable nylon shell easily turned away the thick snowflakes that floated softly from the sky. The premium down insulation, tested successfully in subzero temperatures, heated its occupant without the need for assistance, especially from the propane-fueled, rounded, torrid metal ball. His heavyweight fleece face mask exposed nothing but a pair of deceptive dark brown eyes that provided the visionary path to a demented mind.

In the distance, about forty yards out and closing, his subordinates plodded their way toward the flaming fire globe. His right-hand man was bundled from head to toe, including snow gloves warming his hand-stuffed coat pockets. A furry layer rimmed the front of his hood and fell to the top of his eyelids, replicating the untrimmed hairy unibrow of the transformed high schooler in *Teen Wolf*. The younger man, coatless with only a short-sleeve t-shirt covering his hypothermic upper body shivered along with increasing speed.

As instructed, the elder assistant and his subordinate stopped five feet shy of the unique, massive sphere of fire. Just before coming within identifiable sight, the boss shielded himself behind the giant metal ball. The younger peon took an extra step closer, frantically seeking the heat seeping through the artful openings to thaw his frozen limbs.

"I still don't understand why you wouldn't let me wear a jacket," quivered the sparsely clothed minion.

"They found the body," snarled the heavily wrapped superior.

"What?" hollered his right-hand man. He lifted his right hand to his ear, visibly struggling to hear the nature and tone of his angry boss over the vociferous hissing of the pressurized burning propane that oozed from its fuel source.

"They found the body!" the boss yelled, voicing more fury than before.

The bundled right-hand man faced his junior. Displaying mannerisms consistent with having a better understanding of the purpose of the meeting, he gazed a fiery look to his understudy comparable to the blistering fire globe glaring at him.

"You said you took care of it."

"I did, but—" he hesitated before finishing his sentence. With his brain permanently stuck in second gear, it couldn't catch up to his five-gear mouth.

"Do you know why you were asked to take care of that problem?" asked the boss.

Shaking feverishly, the minion responded, "Because he made a big mistake."

"Correct," the boss escalated his volume. "But even worse, he went rogue. Lack of loyalty. And as you've seen firsthand, I have zero patience for that. Mistakes, eh? Some mistakes actually create teachable moments."

"Lessoned learned, sir. I promise. I learn from my mistakes." His shaking voice mimicked his hands. "And I've learned from this one."

"Did you?" questioned the alpha male. "First, no notebook. Now this!" shouted the boss. "I have little tolerance for mistakes. I have no tolerance when one doesn't learn from his mistakes. And clearly you haven't."

"I'm sorry," the fearful, crackling voice stuttered. "I won't let it happen again. I promise. I'm so sorry boss." As tears evaporated from the profuse heat, his panicked eyes stared at the deformity burned into his supervisor's face, giving him a glimpse of what fate awaited him.

"Young man don't think of this as punishment. Think of it as a rite of passage. A birthmark showing me that you're part of our family now."

"You don't need to do this!" he begged. "You have my loyalty. And I won't screw up again. I swear! Please! I'm sorry!"

"I know you are son. I hear your anguish," comforted the commander, just loud enough to be heard. "In the words of Karl Marx, 'The only antidote to mental suffering is physical pain.' And to quote World War II legend Chesty Puller, the most decorated Marine of all time, 'Pain is weakness leaving the body.'"

The boss wandered around the fire globe, now sweating from its blistering heat. With his head down, a human-shaped figure of winter clothing shouldered beside his right-hand man. "I taught you the importance of loyalty and diligence."

Staring straight ahead past the star and snowflake-littered openings of the artsy, blistering metal globe, the two subjects focused their eyes on the dancing flames.

The boss took two steps forward, placing him back-to-back with his puppets. He stopped abruptly. Then, twisting his neck to the right with his fleece-covered chin resting on his padded shoulder, he said, "His time has come."

Slithering away into the muted darkness of the pristine white snow, the leader's accelerated pace indicated he trusted his message was clear.

Fifteen seconds of silence followed, almost quiet enough to hear the fluffy snowflakes feathering to rest on the soft powdery base of its recently fallen kin.

"Ahhhhhhhhhhh!" In an instant, a piercing scream polluted the silent white air. The distressing wail escalated in volume for four seconds. Abruptly, it stopped—either swiftly muffled or from pain-induced unconsciousness.

Chapter Eighteen

A DAY ON the slopes did the couple some good. Fresh powder, fresh air, and a fresh start. Even if momentarily, it took their minds off dodging a pair of bullets two nights prior. While both proved flexible with their vacation itinerary, getting shot at was not an acceptable alternative to their penciled-in plans.

The packed powder of the recent fresh snowfall made for epic runs. And the late morning and early afternoon weekday crowd were just right; short-to-no lines on the mid-mountain lifts, and very little wait time at the bottom. The sparse crowds allowed for numerous runs in a short period of time. Almost too many if there was such a thing. And for the casual skiers, a limit was inevitable.

Before long, Kristen's legs were burning, forcing her to throw in the towel earlier than expected. Feeling the same, but too macho to admit it and faking disappointment, Josh agreed to hang up their skis a little early. His partner knew he was spent, but she gifted him his pride, apologizing for not sticking it out longer.

Ignoring the giant pink elephant in the room, neither made any mention of the specifics of finding the dead body nor peeped a word about the shooting. *This is our vacation, for crying out loud*, Josh thought, *and we're not going to let a dead body or attempted murder ruin it. It's not like we're not used to it. Practicing law and dodging bullets—that's our thing.*

Josh's stance to keep Kristen partially in the dark on the matter was understandable. His decision not to enlighten her of the high probability they were the targets—hopefully forgivable. Justifying his decision, he believed he was protecting her. Not understanding women, he was deciding for her and what he thought best. Though oblivious to this one, it was yet another reason why Josh sensed he was blowing his relationship with the love of his life.

As they had originally planned, before playing dodge ball with bullets, they'd ski, shower, and change, then go to the cabin to cook Uncle George dinner. But by ending their ski day a little sooner than anticipated, they had time to spare.

Making the most of their found time anew, Josh and Kristen took in the Frisco Historical Park and Museum prior to heading to Uncle George's cabin. Just a short walk from the B&B, the charming local museum incorporated the well-manicured park-like city block on Main Street located between 1st and 2nd Avenues.

Despite their burning legs screaming at them to sit and chill, Josh and Kristen were delighted they chose to ignore the pain. Aside from learning the history of the charismatic town and making a new friend, the results of the nerds' cost-benefit analysis paid dividends more than they could've anticipated.

Unlike any museum they'd ever visited, the compilation of original historic buildings scattered around slightly less than an acre of park-like land left an indelible memory on the intellectual couple. Its features included the Schoolhouse Museum that housed the town's first schoolhouse, the Log Chapel, Trapper's Cabin and original Jail, and a plethora of photographs, artifacts and exhibits chronicling the spirited history of Frisco.

As an unexpected bonus, the touristy duo gained an advanced insider's knowledge of the history of the "Main Street of the Rockies" listening to stories from the museum's longest-tenured employee—Mabel Lespron. With two-and-a-half decades at the museum under her belt and being a direct descendant of one of the first lot owners in the inaugural subdivision development at Bill's Ranch, Mabel was armed with tales she could've told for days and would happily do so if you let her. And like the spunky, kind-hearted, and engaging nature of Josh's two grandmothers, God rest their souls, the visitors didn't want her to stop. Even if they did, good luck with that.

But with plans to visit another Italian old-timer, the endearing couple had to go. They said thank you and goodbye and exited the museum's main building—formerly home to the old schoolhouse.

"Oh, I forgot," said Josh, reaching into his pocket.

Kristen stopped on the paved area outside the museum facing the corner of 2nd Avenue and Main Street. "What'd you forget?"

"I meant to leave a donation." He pulled out a five-dollar bill. With it, a quarter fell to the ground, and with the snow fully melted on the sun-drenched concrete, the coin rolled about eight feet away, resting where the pavement, building, and grassy edge of the manicured grounds met. Josh bent down, paused, then picked up the quarter and shoved it in his pocket as he stepped toward the entrance. He opened the door, turning his head toward Kristen. "I'll be right back."

Josh entered the museum and quickly dropped the five into the donation box placed directly left of the entrance, gave a quick wave, turned, and attempted to flee undeterred. But chatty Mabel had other plans. Seizing the opportunity to extend her hospitality, she waved the young man over and insisted on punching her cell phone number in Josh's phone should the "cute couple" have any more questions. Josh knew better than to refuse the gesture. And after spending an hour with the hospitable employee, he wasn't about to argue, else they'd be lucky to make dinner at Uncle George's cabin a week from Tuesday.

* * *

WHEN IT CAME to directions, Josh had an incredible memory. He could visit a place once, come back twenty years later, and navigate his way around as if he lived there a lifetime. With each turn, as they got closer to his uncle's cabin, it was as if the time gap between his visits had shrunk. Flashes of his childhood visits poured through his nostalgic brain, prompting a childlike smile he hadn't expressed in years.

Josh missed his uncle but didn't realize how much until the site of the old cabin breached the last turn. Drawing Josh in like a high-powered magnet to a chunk of metal; the force seemingly pulled him in at an increasing rate of speed. Perhaps that, but more likely from his excitement that manifested itself by weighing down his foot to the rental car's floorboard.

Josh cracked his window down, excited to have his sense of smell jolt childhood memories of Colorado. He inhaled deeply. His nostrils flared, relishing the crisp, cool smell of the Rocky Mountain evergreens that drowned the modest cabin in a teal-blue sea of Colorado Blue Spruce. Kristen's left hand cranked up the heat in her desperate attempt to offset nature's air conditioner blowing steadily through the creased window opening on the driver's side.

Up the private dirt road, mostly covered in snow, the visitors cruised toward the cabin under the guiding light of a full moon and setting sun. Two deer glided across the roadway, not a care in the world. In a flash, Josh slammed on the brakes. The rental car slid about ten feet forward and to the left before coming to rest inches shy of the decayed trunk of a dead Aspen tree.

The startled couple looked at each other and sighed. Josh took another deep breath, unglued his shoe from the brake pedal, and gingerly lowered the gas with his trembling foot. Two minutes later and several deeper breaths, they pulled up to the dark cabin, lit only by a dim porch light and the flickering light in the window reflecting the flames of the indoor fireplace.

Kristen settled in nicely, cozying up to the warm fireplace, engrossed in the stories told by the old man. Slaving away in the kitchen, Josh insisted on being the chef for the evening, giving his girlfriend an unencumbered heart-to-heart with Uncle George. Josh had heard all the stories, some more than once, and stored them in a special file in his brain.

Baked Ziti with Ricotta was the dinner of choice selected by the two chatterboxes, gossiping akin to a couple of schoolgirls huddled in the gymnasium corner at a junior high dance.

The novice chef was happy to oblige, savoring the smell while he diced and sautéed white onions, then added a tablespoon of minced garlic for taste and scent. It had been a while since he'd made the decadent Italian delicacy, loaded with spicy meat sauce, mixed with creamy curds of ricotta to douse over an abundance of ziti pasta shells, topped with mozzarella and baked to perfection. The cabin in the Rockies smelled more like a *ristorante* in Rome.

Side-hustling as a waiter, Josh brought his customers each a glass of wine—a red blend flaunting aromas and flavors of juicy rich black fruit, ripe plum, and boysenberry and hints of toasted vanilla oak leading into an edgy, lingering fruit finish. The silky-textured flavors from Paso Robles became a local favorite of the California Coast couple. After their first romantic getaway following their transition from best friends to paramours, they established a special affinity for the fruity red blend from the nearby winery.

"Here's some cheese and crackers to nibble on until our main course is ready," Josh said, setting a plate of quick-n-easy appetizers on the end table placed between the old man and the young beauty. "I don't want you both plastered before dinner. I'm more than happy to cook dinner, but I don't want this to turn into an episode of *Cheers* or *Will and Grace.*"

"Huh?" Kristen said, partially confused.

"Don't be putting away the alcohol like Norm Peterson and Karen Walker." Josh chuckled. "You know, the famous TV boozers."

"I like to think of myself more like a Sam Malone," George said, flashing a flirtatious wink and smile at Kristen. "Kept the ladies warm. During the Cold War era, of course."

Kristen smirked during a brief awkward pause, which didn't last two seconds before the three broke into hysterical laughter, causing George to start coughing. "You okay Uncle George?" Josh asked, hustling toward the sound of a barred owl gagging on a crayfish.

Kristen stood up, ready to pat the old man on the back. George lifted his hand, signaling he was fine and breathed "I'm good. I'm good." Clearing his throat, he whispered, "Thank you."

While her area of expertise focused on business law, Kristen would've thrived as a therapist. Her soft, gentle features and genuine smile put strangers at ease. Methodical questions, easing from small talk to personal matters never shared with a soul, flowed from the talented attorney smoother than soft serve ice cream at the Iowa State Fair. In seemingly a matter of seconds, Uncle George had her up to speed on his decades-long treasure hunt. Next, effortlessly she transitioned him to the couch-laying psychoanalysis.

"So, I hope you don't mind me asking," said Kristen, "but did you ever marry? Any kids?"

"No and no. Joshua is the closest I ever came to having a child. We've always had a special connection."

"And never married, huh?" Kristen dug further.

"No, ma'am. I was always married to my work." George paused, stared toward the fire, then gazed at Kristen. The blazing light from the fire highlighted the moisture forming in his eyes. He took a sip of wine.

"I don't mean to pry," Kristen said. "But I'm sensing there's more to it than a straight no."

"You're as perceptive as you are smart," replied George. Swirling the three ounces of wine left in his glass, he stared deep into the red blend. Tilting the glass, the bottom rim pressed below his nose. As George smelled the aroma, Kristen sniffed out a romantic tragedy.

Kristen patiently waited for more details. After a gentle whiff, he opened up; unable to resist the pretty young lady's charm.

"I almost got married. Much later in life—well after halftime."

Kristen leaned in, ostensibly sensing that the lonely man had been waiting years to pour out his soul to sympathetic female ears that would listen attentively and refrain from teasing jibes.

"I met a lady shortly after I retired from the District Attorney's Office." George's voice softened. Kristen grabbed a cracker and cube of cheddar, signaling to the old man there was no rush. His words were clearly shaken with emotion, hinting to her patience was in order.

Josh, plugging away in the kitchen, just heard the words without seeing the clues. And even if he had seen them, his keen perception of physical evidence wasn't proficient in recognizing human emotion. Partially innate to the Santa Barbara Deputy D.A., and partially embedded from years of prosecuting crime, Josh preferred a "just the facts, ma'am" approach. His nature simply lacked the patience to endure the subtleties of sentiment surrounding the facts.

"Uncle George, you never told me that." Josh cracked the oven door, checking on the status of the heavenly scent rushing through the six-inch opening. He noted the cheese, visibly inching toward its bubbling phase.

"Because it didn't end well," George replied. "Not something I often rehash."

"I'm sorry," Josh said, sliding on an oven mitt older than him. "I had no idea."

"It was a long time ago. Yet sometimes it feels like it was yesterday."

Kristen dabbed a sympathetic nod. "True love plays funny tricks with time."

"Speaking of time, Joshie my boy." George eased the tension. "I'm living on borrowed time, son. Are we going get a taste of some baked ziti, or did you switch the menu to burnt cheese?"

Kristen grimaced, chuckling "Joshie?" Her signature snort followed.

"Don't ask," stated Josh, embarrassed by the name of affection coined by his great-uncle when he was a boy.

Pulling the sizzling cheese-topped Italian entrée from the oven, Josh set the baking dish on the cast iron stovetop. He closed his eyes, inhaled deeply, and gently waved his open palm beneath his drooling chin. "It's ready," he said. "We just need to let it cool for a few minutes."

Josh strolled around the kitchen island, grabbed the vino from the countertop, and refilled the empty long-stemmed glasses. He felt certain the glasses must've had holes in the bottom, draining faster than a sick kid's nose.

"Why did the two of you end the relationship?" asked Kristen tossing an empathetic lean toward the heartbroken old-timer. "What happened? Why didn't it work out?"

Josh listened intently. He envied that about Kristen. She possessed a special ability to get one to open up easily. Organically. If he asked the same questions, it seemed contrived, almost nosey. But when she inquired, the recipient's flood gates burst open, followed by the most personal information never before revealed. Josh's ability to effectively question another was second to none in the courtroom but heavily flawed in real life.

"She disappeared," responded George. A tear dripped down his cheek, diluting his wine. With his voice cracking, he continued, "Vanished . . . on the day I was going to propose to her."

In their classic synchronized fashion, the two guests blurted out. This time, on different wavelengths. "Vanished?" hollered Josh. "Propose?" cried Kristen.

"Just disappeared. Gone. Faded into the night."

"Oh my gosh!" Kristen looked ready to cry. "Do you have any idea how or why?"

"Misplaced. Lost. Fled. Snatched," George shrugged his timeless broad shoulders. "I can't say for certain." He paused, swirling his glass, staring at the sugary layer forming in the wake of the swirl. "I have a theory. But that's all it is—a theory. It's not something I like to talk about, so we'll just leave it at that."

Kristen, ordinarily the one to keep conversations moving, was speechless. Josh was dumbfounded. George chugged his glass dry. A refill couldn't come soon enough.

The three broke bread, enjoyed more wine, and chatted intimately. Josh relished every minute, valuing the company of two of his most loved people. Not until they all yawned simultaneously was it time to call it a night. George hugged Kristen, then Josh.

Saturated in fermented grape juice, Kristen stumbled to the car after refusing Josh's help. He was halfway out the door when George stopped him, saying, "Joshie, my boy. I can't tell you how great it is to spend time with you and your wonderful young lady. She's a gem. Definitely a keeper." He shook his hand, discreetly slipping a tiny box into his great-nephew's hand in the process.

Chapter Nineteen

T HE DARKENED SKY completed its magical shift, getting lighter as the evening drew later. After a sabbatical from snowfall since mid-morning, a progressive drift softly glided its way to the white-blanketed mountain road. The highly reflective nature of the pure white snow, working in combination with the thick cloud covering overhead, made it noticeably brighter than a full moon at its most radiant phase. The mesmerizing snow glow enhanced visibility in the otherwise blackened mountain acreage.

Preselected as the designated driver, Josh limited his alcoholic intake to one glass of wine. Kristen and George happily finished off the bottle, then another, which paired nicely with the evening's entrée created by the ever-improving amateur Italian chef. Uncle George, born to Italian immigrants, expressed his enjoyment of Josh's culinary talents. "Your great-great-grandmother would've labeled that dinner an emphatic *delizioso*," he had complimented when the two youngsters stepped down from the front porch.

With the roads getting a little sketchy, Josh eased his way down the cabin's long, private roadway. Once he reached the end, it was just three more turns and a few additional miles, and they'd hop on I-70 heading east, then exit onto Main Street a few blocks from the heart of Frisco.

* * *

GEORGE'S WELL-MANNERED GUESTS had organized the sealed-up leftovers in his fridge, cleaned the dishes, and left no conspicuous trace of their presence in his cabin. After the rarest of entertainment gigs by the cabin master, George looked around, admiring their diligence, and smiled. Although he'd never admit it, the old man had to feel lonely in his secluded cabin. He had no blood relatives nearby and, other than shooting the bull with a couple of ol' cronies, minimal human contact. So, after sharing a home-cooked Italian meal with his favorite kin and his enchanting partner, George's stomach was filled, as was his emotional bucket.

The old-timer walked over to the inset nook nestled in the wall of the great room just to the left of his bedroom door. Rectangular shaped, measuring two feet wide and three feet tall, two wood shelves evenly separated the space. Alone on the bottom shelf, an AM/FM radio rested on the pine wood insert. Permanently set on his favorite station, George flipped it on to listen to the local sports station. According to the announcer, the Colorado Avalanche were up 4-1 with three minutes left in the second period, and well on their way to their eighth straight home win.

With his life past the third period, and well into overtime, the still-sharp senior erred on the side of caution. When home alone, he'd keep his private notebook handy, should an idea pop up in his tireless mind. Though becoming increasingly more difficult, he triggered the secret lever and the hidden room opened. George grabbed his notebook from its designated spot, set it on the right arm of his fireplace-warmed reading chair, and closed the hidden passageway.

A little lightheaded, George tossed a log on the fire, plopped himself down on his favorite chair, and cozied up near the fireplace for some light reading. He reached for a paperback fiction novel set on his side table as he gazed into the fire. When he blindly touched the tabletop item, his head jerked to his left, revealing Kristen's hand purse placed next to his book.

Without his own phone, and George being wise enough not to filter through a lady's purse to see if her cell was inside, he'd have to wait for them to turn back after she realized she forgot it. If not, it could wait until the following morning when the young couple had planned to meet him at his favorite coffee shop, conveniently located a stones-throw away from their temporary residence at the B&B.

George grabbed his book and reread the chapter preceding the bookmarker. He hadn't read in a few days. And at his age, he was lucky to remember to unzip his pants before taking a leak. So, recalling the specifics of a so-so novel he had read more than twenty minutes prior carried less favorable odds than winning the lottery.

The radio volume was set low, just loud enough for the old man to hear over the crackling fire. In the distance, it sounded as if a car door had closed. If not, it wouldn't be the first time his hearing deceived him. With his ears, nothing was certain.

With the book in his left hand, George lowered his reading glasses from his nose, pinching them as he rested his right hand on his thigh. He tilted his head fifteen degrees to the right, evidently a senior citizen's secret to enhancing one's hearing. A second door closing slammed, this time unmistakably heard by the old man.

"Hmm, I guess they realized Kristen forgot her purse," George mumbled to himself.

"Bam!" The front door burst open. The deadbolt crushed through the splintered wood door jamb, taking the secured metal plate with it. George froze, his heart stopped.

Three men in ski masks crashed in, the first two with guns drawn. Covered from head to toe and fingertip to fingertip, only six angry eyes were visible to the attentive victim.

For a brief second, as the intruders' eyes cleared the room for any unanticipated occupants or spring-loaded rifles, the nimble-minded, quick-handed veteran tossed his notebook faster than a pin-pulled hand grenade.

"Where's the notebook old man?" demanded the non-armed ringleader.

Unaccustomed to entertaining two visitors, let alone three masked intruders on the heels of his mini family reunion, a response eluded the panicked homeowner. His physical demeanor appeared calm, his bladder not so much.

"I said, where's the notebook?" repeated the lead member as his two cronies hastily searched the area.

George's heart kicked in, too stubborn to call it quits just yet. "I don't know what you're talking about," he replied.

The top dog made eye contact with one of his gunmen, tipping his head toward the old man who now appeared stuck to his chair. Stomping toward his prey, the thug pressed the muzzle to the back of George's gray-haired noggin, stamping a circular imprint into the old man's occipital lobe.

"I will only ask you one more time," growled the dark, beady-eyed criminal. "Where is your notebook?"

Drawing on his world champion poker face, George calmly responded, "I don't have it."

"How unfortunate for you," snarled the bully, giving a nod to his hitman.

The trigger slowly edged back. George didn't move. He breathed steadily, offering a stubborn grin to the aggressor. "Go ahead. Pull the trigger. . . and you'll never find it."

"Click." The empty sound of an unloaded gun suggested temporary victory for the old man. He grinned.

As if feeling defeated by the seemingly helpless old geezer, the leader nodded to gunman number two.

"Bang!" George's body jerked, nearly falling from his chair. A bullet punctured the aged hardwood floor, grabbing the hard, aged man's attention, though not his cooperation.

"You think this is a game, old man?"

George snidely replied, "Well, it sort of is a game."

"Wham!"

A crushing blow thrown to the back of George's head, intensified by the heavy metal handle of the 9mm gun, packed the lethalness of a fully loaded weapon as it pierced the skin of the defiant opponent's skull. His antique head, although hardened from decades as a criminal prosecutor, was no match for the metal instrument. He was out cold!

Chapter Twenty

T HE MORNING SUN shined bright, rising unobstructed into the clear sky that surrounded the grandiose mountain range. Josh tiptoed quietly around the B&B suite, careful not to wake his sleepy companion. Skiing, ice skating, scavenger hunting, dead body finding, bullet dodging, wine drinking, and more skiing; they'd had a busy week. Josh functioned well on minimal sleep, but Kristen, not so much.

The plan was to meet Uncle George at the coffee shop across Main Street. Enjoy some freshly brewed java around the fire pit, fuel up with a tasty breakfast burrito, and relax and listen to war stories from the old men.

The best-laid plans . . . Kristen was still out like a light. Physical exhaustion from a full day of snow skiing mixed with generous consumption of heavy Italian food and a bottle of vino proved too much for the lightweight. Her Mona Lisa Vito alcohol-consuming law school days, barely a speck in her rear-view mirror.

Kristen hadn't twitched or peeped in hours. Josh placed the back of his hand under her nose to ensure she was still breathing. A gentle flow of air warmed his cold hand. *Thank God.* A glimpse of worry ended with a deep exhale. She was alive and breathing. Perhaps comatose; but breathing, nonetheless.

Josh debated whether to wake her as he grabbed a pen and notepad from the side table nearest the couch. He paused. Lifting the pen to his mouth, ready to bite it, he realized it wasn't a pen from his office or house, triggering him to faux spit. He stared at Kristen in deep thought, computing the pros and cons several GHz faster than Intel's fastest desktop processor. The cons had it. Jotting a quick note on the pad, Josh grabbed his wallet and phone and strolled to the coffee shop.

One store away from the coffee shop, Josh glanced at his watch. It was 7:32 a.m. According to Uncle George, the old-timers would arrive around 7 a.m. Josh saw only one man sitting around the firepit, his head on a swivel as if looking for a lost puppy. He approached. It was Sam, alone with his coffee, his eyes shifting back and forth.

"Good morning, Sam," Josh greeted him.

"Good morning, Joshua," Sam replied.

Josh noticed that older people tended to call him "Joshua" more so than younger generations, typically going with the shorter "Josh." *Is that because older generations are more formal, or younger generations are lazier? Probably both*, thought Josh. Either way, he didn't mind. Aside from being called dipshit or asshole—common terms of affection uttered by countless defendants when addressing the prosecutor—Josh was fine with whatever.

"How are you?"

"I'm fine," said Sam, looking at his watch. But I'm a little concerned."

"Where's Uncle George?"

"That's my concern," Sam said, pointing to the east. "I live only a few blocks over. But even still, your uncle usually arrives here before me."

"Perhaps his ride is running late." Josh sat facing Sam, whose back was to the coffee shop's entrance. "Where's Hank? Maybe he knows."

"Hank's out of town for a week or so," said Sam. "And I texted George's ride about five minutes ago, but I haven't heard back."

Just then, a Subaru whizzed into an open parking space directly in front of the coffee shop. Its screeching stop suggested the person was in a hurry. The driver nearly tripped while jumping out, slammed the door, and ran toward the heated outdoor patio of the coffee shop.

With his back to Main Street, Josh turned his head and shoulders enough to get a glimpse out the corner of his eye. Unless his periphery deceived him, Josh recognized the driver. But before he could utter a word, the driver spoke.

"I got your text," the driver told Sam, visibly flustered from something. "George is gone!"

"What?!" blurted Josh.

The driver made eye contact with Josh. "Josh, what are you doing here?"

"Me?" Josh said, even more surprised. "What are *you* doing here, Hannah? And how do you know my uncle? And more importantly, what do you mean he's gone?"

"Your uncle?" Hannah said in a puzzled tone. "George is your uncle? I'm usually his driver."

"Well, great uncle to be precise. But yes." He pointed at Hannah. "*You're* his driver?"

"Yes," she replied. "I also happen to be Sam's granddaughter. He's the lawyer I told you about. The one who talked me out of going to law school in favor of my passion for skiing."

"Okay," Sam interrupted, unquestionably concerned by Hannah's assumption. "Now that we all know each other, what do you mean George is gone? You think he's *missing*?"

"So, I went to pick him up, like I always do. And when I knocked on the front door, it crept open. I peeked in and noticed the door jamb was busted. I called out for him but got no response. So, I went in. The place looked ransacked and there was no sign of George."

"Could he have been outside?" asked Sam. "Maybe he went out for an early morning walk or to chop some firewood."

"Possibly," Hannah responded. "But I looked around the cabin and hollered out for him. And other than his radio on, nothing."

"You said his place was ransacked," said Josh. "How badly? Maybe he'd been looking for something and turned his place upside down."

"It's possible, but not likely," said Hannah. "It looked far too messed up for that. George keeps a tidy ship."

"Was the fireplace blazing, or flickering?" asked Josh.

"Huh?" Hannah looked at him in confusion. "Flickering. But why do you ask?"

"Because that's the primary source of heat in the main living area," Josh responded as a panic-stricken shadow cast upon his face. "If the fire was only flickering, that means he hadn't placed any cut logs on it since last night when Kristen and I were there."

Josh paused. The film reel in his mind recapped the recent events, from the time Sam told George that the original scavenger hunt almost led to them finding his dead body to the sequence of "unfortunate" events that had followed since. Individually, the events were, at the very least, scary. Added together, tragic. And as Josh frequently said, too many "unfortunate" coincidences equaled evidence of a crime.

With Josh buried in thought, he stared blankly into the fire. Hannah stared at her grandfather. Sam gazed at Josh. With the three of them fretting over George's whereabouts, a stealthy Kristen drifted up unseen. Her mouth opened to greet them. But before her words escaped, her breath was cut short.

Sam's worried gaze penetrated Josh's mind. "You don't think—"

Josh swallowed hard. "Uncle George has been kidnapped!"

"Uncle George has been kidnapped?!" Kristen parroted Josh, triggering three heads to whip in her direction.

Chapter Twenty-One

T HE PHONE CALL came in a few minutes after Hannah left the three abashed attorneys to attend to her other gig. Despite Hannah volunteering to call in sick, Sam insisted that she keep her private ski lesson scheduled for 9 a.m. at Copper Mountain. Private instructions paid the most, making them her bread and butter. Adamant that there was nothing more she could do that they couldn't, Sam vowed to update her when they learned more about George's whereabouts, knowing she thought of George as if he were her own uncle.

Josh glanced at his cell phone. "Unknown Caller" flashed on the screen. Sam gazed at the buzzing phone. Kristen's eyebrows raised. Josh's shaking thumb hovered over the screen.

Life's unknowns— the greatest source of anxiety.

Uneasiness aside, Josh answered the call. "Hello." Empty air hushed from the other end. "Hello," he said again. He pulled the phone from his ear, then checked the screen display— "Call Ended." Likewise, so did his hope.

Before anyone could utter a sound, Josh's phone rang again. Uneasiness thrust to nervousness. Afraid to confront the unknown alone, he held his phone forward, tapped the answer button, then pressed the speaker icon.

Uncertain if he'd be able to hear over his heart palpitations, Josh spoke, "Hello." A brief pause followed, then a filtered voice spoke from the dark side.

Technologically modified, the voice asked, "Is this Joshua?" From the tonality and pitch, Josh's mind translated it to *Luke, I am your father*.

Hand trembling, Josh leaned his chin toward his phone and answered, "Yes, who is this?"

"You can address me as 'Sir' . . . I believe I've earned it. I have *someone* you want, and I believe you can get me *something* that I want."

"Joshie. Tell him no. No matter what," a familiar voice hollered, but distant and muffled as if behind closed doors.

"Uncle George are you okay?" hollered Josh, his bulging eyes shifting from Kristen to Sam.

"There's a certain notebook I need. And, *by George*, I think he's got it. My terms are simple. You get me the old man's notebook. I give you your uncle. Say no, he dies. Call the cops, he dies. Don't follow my instructions, he dies. Are we clear?"

With no other alternative response he could contrive at that moment, Josh answered, "Yes."

"Across the street, on the corner, is a small retail shop—*Blissful Boutique*. There's a bench in front of its bay window. See it?"

Josh turned toward Main Street. Familiar with the bench after seeing "Peeping Tom" sitting on it a few days earlier, he confirmed. "Yes, I see it."

"There's a burner phone taped underneath it. Get the phone. You will receive a call on it at 1:37 this afternoon. That call will give you instructions. Should you choose not to follow them, the old codger dies. Are we clear?"

"Yes, we're clear," whispered Josh.

"Are we clear?" the kidnapper asked again, raising his volume.

"Crystal," responded Josh.

The call ended.

"Look around casually," Josh mumbled without moving his mouth. "I think we're being watched."

Without a moment's hesitation, Josh bolted toward Main Street. Not bothering with the crosswalk, paying no mind to traffic, and in total disregard to his *Frogger* training, he raced across the street. Slipping and sliding on the wet patches of ice and snow along the way, Josh managed to cross the street without cracking his skull or taking a fender to his ribs.

He shuffled along the sidewalk toward the empty wooden bench. Fortunately for Josh, the bench was minus a peeping Tom. Otherwise, Josh would've appeared the pervert, reaching between an old-timer's legs, face first in his crotch.

Reaching underneath, he felt around aimlessly, similar to the first time he'd attempted to cop a feel back in high school. Reminiscent of his search of the pre-blossomed Susie, he felt nothing. On the other hand, with his second teenage fling, he'd struck gold—or rather melons. *Where are Paula's peaches when you need them?* With an open palm, he swiped back and forth, front to back, grabbing in a frenzy. *Oh, the memories.*

"Son of a—" he said, jerking his hand back to pull a splinter the size of a Louisville Slugger from his thumb.

Dread overcame him. *Was Darth Vader jerking with him? Where was the phone? Why not give him instructions now? And what's the deal with 1:37 p.m.?*

The normally unflappable litigator regained a semblance of composure. Taking a deep breath, Josh went from a squatting position to taking a knee. He leaned to his left and down, scanning the underside of the old wooden bench. The sight of countless wads of gum, unnoticed by his frozen hand, had him warding off the inclination to vomit.

The panicked prosecutor patted profusely like probing for Paula's produce. *Jackpot!*

There it was. Duct taped in the far-left corner. Focused, he averted hurling and tore the flip phone from the seat's underside and stood up. Always the prosecutor, Josh checked his coat pockets. Bingo. The interior pocket of this ski jacket contained a small plastic sandwich bag. Josh kept one handy whenever he skied, employing it as a poor man's dry bag. He used it to secure his wallet from moisture in the event of a major wipeout, which was known to happen—frequently.

He placed the phone and tape in the sealable baggie and tucked it into his pocket. Fingerprints. The villain might have been careless enough to leave his prints on the evidence. However unlikely, it was worth a shot. Meticulous in his ways, you could take the prosecutor out of the courtroom, but you couldn't take the courtroom out of the prosecutor.

The Deputy District Attorney marked the box on his mental checklist and hustled back to the coffee shop. His mother was wrong. It turned out the thousands of hours he seemingly wasted on *Frogger* in fact were useful in real life, as Josh instinctively weaved and dodge traffic without giving it a thought. And by early morning traffic on Main Street—meaning two cars.

"Did you find it?" Kristen asked anxiously.

"Got it." Josh patted his coat pocket.

Kristen looked back and forth between Sam and Josh, waiting for the lead. "So, what's the plan?"

"We need to get the phone and duct tape checked for prints right away."

"But no cops. Or George is—" Sam couldn't finish his sentence, choked short by the lump in his throat.

"I'll take it to Austin at the D.A.'s office," said Sam. "He's got to know someone who can get it done ASAP and under the radar. If not, I'm sure I can run down an old source still lingering around from back in the day."

"And what's with the notebook?" Kristen asked.

"Yeah, Sam," Josh said, hoping George's best friend knew more than his nephew. "Uncle George mentioned keeping notes of his progress of the treasure hunt, but he didn't go into details. What do you know about that? I'm assuming that's the notebook referenced by the kidnapper."

"George became very hush-hush about the notebook after Helen."

"Was that the name of his lady friend that disappeared?" asked Josh.

"Yes," Sam continued. "Her name was Helen Windimere. George and I were working together from day one to solve the riddles. He kept diligent notes of clues, our theories, findings—the whole nine yards. But shortly after Helen disappeared without a trace, possibly related to our quest for answers, I took a back seat. I decided it wasn't worth the risk anymore. With family in the area, I had too much to lose. Still do. Since then, it's been all George."

"Why is he so adamant about pursuing it?" Kristen said with rising concern reflected in her tone. "He doesn't need the money. And he knows the risk, first-hand. So why?"

"It's his life's obsession," replied Sam. "Josh, as you know, George was a legendary prosecutor. The best I've ever seen."

Josh nodded emphatically, but said nothing, figuring Sam had more to say.

"He established quite the reputation for himself. One former President had offered him the position of Attorney General of the United States," Sam bragged about his friend. "George turned it down. He simply wanted to fight crime in the place that he loved. His impact on this county has been immeasurable. His court record was perfect. But just before he retired, he encountered his white whale."

"What do you mean by that?" Josh asked while glancing at his watch. His gut told him all this newly learned information might piece some of the puzzle together. The three sat down next to the fire pit. Josh patiently listened to his uncle's best friend.

"So, you obviously know about the convicted *Gold Scammer* from a couple of decades ago. The one that inspired the annual scavenger hunt in Vail," said Sam. "Right?"

"Yes, of course," Josh replied.

"Well, the feds prosecuted him for a myriad of federal crimes, which carried way more time than any state offenses we could throw at him. But, in addition to the white-collar crimes, George firmly believed that not only did the convict have a partner, but that he'd killed his partner, or hired someone to do it, and disposed of the body."

"Murder!?" blurted Kristen as she leaned toward Sam.

"The guy was relatively young when he was convicted. So even with the harsh federal sentencing, absent an early death, the guy probably figured he'd be paroled in time to retrieve the ill-gotten fruits of his crime and move to a remote, non-extradition island. And with that, he'd not only get away with murder, but he'd also live lavishly during his remaining days."

"Meanwhile, the victims of his scam would be left staring at bank statements of empty bank accounts." Shaking her head in disgust, Kristen moaned, "Mm."

"The only thing necessary for the triumph of evil is for good men to do nothing," Josh quoted Edmund Burke.

"Precisely." Sam nodded. "And George is as good a man as there is. Far from doing nothing, he's devoted to doing everything."

"I can see why that would eat away at someone like George," noted Kristen.

"Speaking of Uncle George," Josh announced, "I've got a plan."

Chapter Twenty-Two

THE NEXT CALL guaranteed itself as the most important conversation of Josh's life. That spoke volumes for a man who negotiated for a living the lifelong confinement and loss of freedom of human beings. In a handful of hours, George's closest support system was on a time-sensitive mission to tip the scales in their favor, as slightly as it might be. And it would start with the next call.

Josh's first thoughts: *Besides Sam, who else knew about the notebook—other than the kidnapper, of course? And how did the kidnapper know about the notebook? Did the notebook contain enough information to allow the crook to locate the treasure? By itself, most likely not; otherwise, George would've found it by now. Perhaps it contained the missing piece to a bigger puzzle, solving a twenty-year-old riddle.*

Sam raced to the District Attorney's Office, his old stomping ground that had since been refreshed with a younger breed of altruistic lawyers, eager to save the world, ridding it of one criminal at a time. Despite years since his retirement, Sam never strayed far from his roots at the D.A.'s office.

Having mentored the current D.A., Nathan Jesper, back when the future politician had first joined the office, Sam never went more than a few months without dropping in to say hello. He'd enjoy a donut and coffee in the break room sharing war stories with the younger armed forces of the criminal courts and he'd provide a sounding board to the D.A.—assuming the latter couldn't get a hold of George for advice.

As a bonus during his routine visits to his old workplace, Sam couldn't get enough of District Attorney Jesper's incessant quotations from his favorite movie, *A Few Good Men*. His Oscar-winning imitation of Jack Nicholson's character, Colonel Nathan Jessup, was uncanny, nailing every nuance down to his intensely eyed scowl. Not surprisingly, it was in sharing a nearly identical name to the iconic character that initiated and fueled the highest-ranking prosecutor's cinematic infatuation.

Kristen was tasked with a desk job. A master of legal research, she holed herself in the comfort and safety of their deadbolted B&B room and clicked away on her laptop. Browsing old newspaper articles covering the investigation and prosecution of the *Gold Scammer*, digging up excerpts of the court transcript of his trial, reading the court opinions of his appeals grasping at straws for some judicial error in hopes of overturning his conviction. She scanned for red flags, looked deeper for the convict's connections, and scrutinized the web for the slightest of clues.

With the assistance of a mild hangover and all the stress and panic of the early morning revelation, Kristen hadn't realized that her phone was missing. And with her face buried in her laptop, she didn't figure to do so anytime soon.

Meanwhile, Josh searched for the holy grail. Having raced to George's cabin, he tiptoed a fine line by driving so fast that it almost slowed him down permanently, as he was inches from wrapping the rental around a bristlecone pine, nearly replacing its dangling tree-shaped air freshener with the real thing.

Josh pulled up to the cabin and noted the front door wide open, looking as if it had been rushed by a frightened deer or an angry bison. Approaching the entrance, he scanned the ground for clues. He recognized his and Kristen's shoe imprints in the snow based on where they had parked the night before, approaching the right side of the cabin facing the front.

Tire tracks much wider than his rental marked the snow on the opposite side of the cabin front. Several jumbled footsteps appeared coming and going to the old cabin's porch steps. Crossing the path of human footsteps were several animal tracks dragged over them, making a positive headcount extremely difficult to decipher. Best guess, it appeared that two men, maybe three, had nabbed his uncle.

Before entering, Josh looked carefully over the front porch's weathered wooden planks. Perhaps the kidnappers dropped something. Maybe Uncle George managed to leave a bread crumb of sorts, in the hopes of giving the slightest nibble to his familial protégé. Josh's head hung low. Nothing jumped out. Hoping better luck was through the busted door, he proceeded inside, past the cracked and splintered door frame.

By this time, the fire was completely extinguished, paralyzed by the cold breeze overnight that had transformed the warm, cozy cabin into a shivering meat locker. Not an orange ember remained. Flames were replaced by crispy cubes of frost.

Although he felt clueless and helpless, Josh realized he knew more than he first thought. He pressed rewind in his mind and replayed a moment earlier in the week. When they first met, Sam had mentioned to Josh of George's cabin getting ransacked. Now, once again, George's cabin had been invaded by strangers, and likely the same trespassers, who this time stole its most valuable asset—the owner.

Josh scanned the room quickly, hoping for some obvious clue to spring up from the floor and knock him over. Woefully, the only thing that floored him was the hideous-looking, loudly colorful coffee mug screaming beside the stove atop the kitchen island. Oddly, it looked familiar. Sadly, Josh knew why. The nostalgic nephew recalled he had made the unappealing kindergarten craft, further triggering an onset of memories of his past visits to the cabin.

Pressed for time, a thorough examination of the cabin would have to wait. With no indication of the identity of the invaders, the anxious nephew focused on priority number one—finding the notebook.

While the possibility of the notebook hidden in one of the hundreds of books lining the bookshelves, Josh knew his uncle better than that. Too risky. Perhaps Uncle George had a hidden compartment somewhere inside the cabin. But if so, Josh didn't have the time to go down a potential rabbit hole searching based on potential alone. Time was of the essence.

Every second could be the difference between life and death—literally.

As far as Josh knew, only a few people alive knew about the cabin's hidden room. And they were all blood-related. So, it had to be in the secret room. The concealed room. Essentially, an old-school version of a panic room. The perfect hiding place. There was only one problem. A simple, yet major problem. Although Josh was one of a few who knew of the secret space, he had no idea how to access it.

Perplexed, his angst grew as he stared at the bookcase and randomly felt around for some type of triggering mechanism. Once again, he flashed to floundering for Susie's stack, equally discouraged that he'd come up with only a handful of dust.

Suddenly, he stopped. Pressing his eyes shut with all the force his lids could muster, his forehead all but burst a blood vessel as he strained to picture the room. In his mind, he could see the inside. Once, many years ago, he'd been inside the mysterious room. *But how did I get in? Why can't I remember?*

For a man with an incredible memory, why, when his uncle's life literally depended on it, could he not remember? Was he experiencing some type of stress-induced amnesia?

"Think," Josh demanded out loud. "Come on, man, think!"

He examined every nook and cranny within ten feet of where the bookshelf likely could open. Certainly, the lever would have to be in proximity. Pulling books back, twisting lampshades, titling a bronze-coated scales of justice gifted to George upon his retirement; Josh tried it all, but nothing worked.

The sullen face gazed at his watch. *Impossible!* How could time escape so quickly? The thought of going out back, grabbing an ax, and destroying the bookshelf crafted by his great-great-grandfather had once seemed inconceivable. With each tick of his watch, such an unimaginable alternative now seemed more viable. Feasible approaching likely. Now obviously necessary.

His stress level continued to rise. A stress ball would've had the life squeezed out of it if Josh had one handy. Clenching his fists, and rotating one hand over the other, Josh's knuckles cracked repeatedly. Suddenly, in a moment of forced calmness, he interlapped his fingers in a prayer-like fashion. With the tip of his right middle finger's posterior, he felt an indentation on the back of his left hand.

The chip in the bone of his hand had been there as long as he could remember. How it got there, he couldn't remember. His mother had told Josh it was an accident when he was little. The details of which she refused to recount. It happened. He lived. That's all he needed to know. Realizing the sensitivity of the topic, he never inquired again.

After a quick prayer, Josh unfolded his hands, then began to run his right thumb gently over the notch in the metacarpal bone. A habit he didn't even realize he had; he'd fiddle with the deformed bone when he was nervous. Years earlier, after the rookie prosecutor's first jury trial, Josh's colleague asked him why he was rubbing the back of his left hand during his entire closing argument. Josh had no answer because he had no idea he was doing it. For Josh, the only hand that mattered was the jury handing the defendant a guilty verdict.

A small wooden table pressed against the wall was situated at a right angle to the trick bookcase. Centered on it, a forty-year-old table lamp laid on its side, hanging over the edge and collecting dust. Its bulb, scattered in a thousand pieces. Josh stared at the bottom lip of its rounded fabric shade; its circular shape was slightly flawed.

Then it happened. In a flash, Josh remembered knocking it over as a kid, the bulb shattering glass all around. Next, as if the lamp turned on the lightbulb over his head, more memories of his visits to the cabin resurfaced.

His eyes began to water, then a couple of tears crawled down his cheek. Lowering his head and raising his hand, Josh softly wiped the falling drops. He noticed the frayed condition of the cord, corroborating the age of the light source. His curious eyes followed the cord as it snaked its way to the plug in the bottom terminal of the wall outlet. Above it, a sensor-controlled nightlight was plugged into the top terminal.

"Hmm," Josh mumbled aloud, scrunching his eyebrows.

Two things jumped out at the observant novice investigator. First, it was an odd place for a nightlight—underneath a tabletop and canopied by the table. Even more suspect was its capability to illuminate. Under the shade of the table, the area around the outlet was dark enough that the nightlight should've been on. But it wasn't.

Josh's head tilted to the right; his eyes glazed with deliberation. He rubbed his depressed metacarpal again. Abruptly, he froze.

"Oh my God!" he cried, at this point presenting more astonishment than reverence.

All at once, major, life-altering questions were answered. With flashbacks of his childhood colliding with his adulthood experiences, a repressed Rocky Mountain memory inundated Josh's brain with the ferocity of a Colorado avalanche.

Chapter Twenty-Three

H IS FIRST INSTINCT was to question the flashbacks playing in his mind. Although Josh usually trusted his gut, his memories were typically triggered by smell or taste, not touch.

Since age seven, the distinct smell of damp, freshly mowed springtime grass always sparked thoughts of baseball as a child, including his game-winning double in the Little League championship game and winning the batting title his senior year in high school. And from age thirteen, the taste of diet cola generated a smile on his face, prompting a distant memory of his first kiss with his eighth-grade sweetheart, who drank three cans a day.

Rare was the case in which his sense of touch initiated such vivid recollections. In fact, nothing immediately jumped to mind where a certain caress provoked memories from his past—save for Paula of course. But today was different. Perhaps cognitively appreciating the urgency, the deformed feel in his hand bone unleashed his stifled memory.

He pressed the crack again. The chipped bone was unmistakable. With his thumb gently stroking the back of his hand, Josh closed his eyes, allowing the darkness to bring clarity to his memory. He saw himself standing in the exact same spot, but a quarter century earlier.

The Rizzetti family had set aside two weeks during summer break for a road trip to Colorado. One warm summer day in Copper Mountain, Josh's family drove to Frisco to pick up ice cream at the grocery store. Josh had stayed behind at the cabin with his Uncle George playing *Go Fish* and *Old Maid*. After having drunk three glasses of lemonade, Josh needed a restroom break, during which time his great-uncle had gone out back behind the cabin to bring in a load of cut fire logs in preparation for the evening cool down amidst the canopy of blue spruce and pines.

Waiting impatiently for Uncle George, Josh picked up a baseball that rested on a small wooden stand, adjacent to a lamp, displayed atop an end table pinned against the wall. He looked closely at the ball, reading the signature of Larry Walker of the Colorado Rockies. He tossed it up a few times, spinning it along his child-size fingers. On the third toss, he dropped it. The autographed memorabilia bounced off the hardwood floor, then rolled toward the back of the table. Anxious to replace the ball back to its proper place—before getting caught with his hand in the cookie jar—Josh dropped to a knee to pick it up.

The youngster leaned underneath the table. As he reached for the ball, his eyes and ears were overcome with wonder. In the wall outlet underneath the table, a nightlight had been knocked sideways to a ninety-degree angle with the vertical outlet, as if on a swivel. Simultaneously, a heavy furniture-dragging-like sound came from less than ten feet away.

Josh quickly grabbed the ball, placed it on its stand, and looked up. His eyes fixated on the custom bookcase, as it appeared to split in half, creating a door-size opening. A look of amazement coated his face. Like most young boys, his curiosity instantly shut down any bit of common-sense gathering cobwebs in his brain. Impulsively, he zipped to the opening. First, with just a peek, his head entered the dark hidden space just enough to satisfy the boy's sense of wonder. The light from the great room peeped into the otherwise black hole of space, but enough for Josh to notice a chair and a bucket. Other than that, nothing more could be seen without entering.

But, before the curious young boy could explore any further, the heavy wooden structure began to close steadily. Jumping back, Josh slipped and bumped his head on the bookcase and fell to the ground. And before he could escape, the several-hundred-pound structure had closed . . . but tragically, not entirely.

The small, innocent left hand of the little boy stopped it short, wedged in between the bookcase and the adjoining wall. His fragile developing bones—crushed.

A high-pitched scream resonated throughout the Rocky Mountain region. Animals fled for safety. Skiers plunged off chair lifts. Avalanches rushed down the mountainside, closing several sections of Interstate 70. That's certainly how his mother would've described it just before she entered the room.

Five seconds later, both the front and back doors to the cabin busted open. Josh's mom saw her precious son in the corner. Helpless and in excruciating pain. His body flopping in place like a goldfish, his hand limp. With his favorite youngster screaming and bawling his eyes out. Uncle George rushed in, dove to the floor, lunged to the "nightlight" and triggered the bookshelf to release its death grip on the suffering young boy.

Snapping to the present, Josh jerked back. His eyes burst open. After years of staring into a hazy fog of his mother's hardened heart toward her beloved uncle, in the blink of an eye, the muddled air of the unknown had cleared. The mystery of an inexplicable falling out between the two made sense—whether justified or not. Mystery solved.

A mother's obsession to protect her child from harm knew no bounds. And with the freaky bounce of a ball, her trust in Uncle George had been crushed like the bones in her son's delicate hand. Were it not for Josh's idolization of his great-uncle, she may have never let the youngster set foot again in the cabin. As it stood, it wasn't until four years post-incident that she let Josh reunite with his great-uncle again.

And while Josh's revelation answered an age-old question, it didn't put his mind totally at ease. At this juncture, it was the urgency of Uncle George's life that burdened his mind. But, with one step in the right direction, he'd uncovered the secret of how to access the hidden room. And if Josh knew his uncle as well as he thought he did, surely the infamous notebook would be perched on the arm of the chair that occupied a good portion of the tiny, secret room.

Josh dropped to the hardwood floor, shards of glass and all. Numbed by the moment, he didn't feel the pain that later would set in from his bruised and poked knees. The underside of the table was just as he remembered it; a lamp plugged into the bottom outlet, and an apparent nightlight plugged in above it. Setting his left hand to the hardwood for balance, he reached toward the "nightlight" with his right hand and tilted it ninety degrees. Then, "click."

Anxious to enter the room that undoubtedly housed the holy grail, Josh hopped to his feet. His jaw dropped. The door wasn't opening. How could that be? His recollection was so vivid, surely it was real.

Shuffling to the end of the bookcase, he noticed a slight separation between it and the wall. He squeezed his chunky fingers into the slot and pulled. To his surprise, the heavy rectangle of lumber opened.

With his hand firmly pressed on the side wood panel, he felt a metal clasp. Next, Josh looked to the wall side, noticing a latch mechanism that locked and unlocked the rolling bookcase. His first thought, he figured Uncle George had modified the automatic door post-accident, downgrading it to operate only manually. That may've explained why his mom finally caved when twelve-year-old Josh was permitted to visit his great-uncle again.

Josh checked the time on his phone, then tapped on its flashlight icon, and entered the dark, musty cave-like space. Time had stood still. An armchair sat in the middle of the closet-size room, with a bucket nearby. Shining his flashlight around, he noticed a few gallons of water, canned food, a blanket, and a gun. Nothing else. Closing in on the chair, there was no notebook. Reaching into the crevices of the seat cushion; no notebook. Shaking the folded blanket, still no notebook. And although not many of them were in the tiny space, the panicked explorer searched every inch. Wall to wall and top to bottom. No notebook.

Josh rushed into the great room and whipped his head around. Where would he have put it? Josh shut his eyes. He envisioned Uncle George sitting by the fire, when "bam," some lowlifes barge in, catching the old-timer by surprise. Imagining himself in his great-uncle's shoes, Josh contemplated what the genius would've done. Pretending he was sitting in the comfy old chair, with his prized notebook in hand. When suddenly, he's caught with his pants down—the object of their desire in his strong, wrinkled hands.

The thugs knew about the notebook, meaning they did their recon. Having scouted the old man, they may have anticipated a surprise booby trap ready to greet any unwelcomed visitors. So, they would've cleared the room when first entering. Albeit only a couple of seconds, the intruders' eyes would've wandered elsewhere, and off their target.

The lightbulb beamed brightly. Josh hopped to the fireplace. To the right, a set of cast iron fireplace tools hung from their rack. He grabbed the poker, envisioning Uncle George contemplating driving it into the gut of one of the thugs but thinking twice knowing he couldn't take out more than one without suffering the wrath of another.

Poking around the fireplace, Josh shuffled around the ashes that dusted the air. Then, pulling the right front leg of the log stand that bedded two burnt logs that had dwindled down to the size of a brick, he shifted it forward five inches while turning it forty-five degrees. Torn between relief and crestfallen, the poking prosecutor spotted the missing evidence. Two charcoaled inches of the spine of a notebook remained somewhat intact, somehow evading incineration. It was just enough to pinpoint the item's identity, but not remotely sufficient to provide any substance.

Josh's head dipped down, dropping alongside his hope. His heart punctured like the bullet hole in the hardwood floor. Whatever smidgen of the notebook survived, embodied a painful reminder of what little remained of Uncle George's life.

Chapter Twenty-Four

T HE HANDS ON the face of Josh's watch spun at record pace like straight out of a cartoon. He gave it a glance as he pulled into the back parking lot reserved for B&B guests. He'd texted Sam around 11:30 a.m., immediately prior to leaving the cabin. The time now showed 11:55 a.m., but his eyes saw the watch hands reeling faster than a pro bass fisherman. *Did they find prints on the phone? If so, whose? And why haven't I heard back from Sam?*

His hands were empty, having nothing to show for his thorough search of Uncle George's cabin other than freshly burned ashes dusting his jeans. After the secluded home had been ransacked a second time in a week, it appeared nothing was missing. One invaluable item had been destroyed, but nothing was missing.

Josh thought about it further. Actually, two things had been destroyed: the notebook that could save his uncle's life; and Josh's hope that he'd ever see Uncle George alive again.

With his empty hand, he wiped the cold sweat from his forehead. As the outside temperature slowly settled near freezing, his anxiety quickly soared past dejection. But being a man accustomed to pressure, he gathered his composure as he ran up the stairs to the B&B suite where, with any luck, Kristen had made more progress than him.

Frustrated and unnerved, Josh's trembling hand kept dropping the key card each time the door sensor blinked the dreaded red light. Inside, Kristen reacted to the fidgeting of the door handle, visibly terrified considering recent events. She grabbed a solid bronze candle holder set on the fireplace mantel and tiptoed toward the door prepared to crack someone's skull.

Ready to unleash her high school softball swing, Kristen raised above her right shoulder the only "weapon" in sight. "Josh. Is that you?"

"Yes, it's me," Josh said with his words projecting to the floor as he picked up his key card for the fourth time.

Clearly afraid to stand too close to the door should it get kicked in by the kidnappers, Kristen only heard a muffled response.

"How do I know it's you?" she hollered.

"You're standing there with some mock weapon in your hand," he predicted. "And like Pat Benatar, you're ready to 'Hit Me with Your Best Shot.'"

"Only Josh," Kristen said, shaking her head as she opened the door. "Mr. Eighties' Music Freak."

"I hope you've had better luck than me," Josh said in a somber tone.

"That depends," replied a curious Kristen. Her hand brushed aside a pinch of hair that covered her right eye. "What kind of luck did you have?"

"Absolutely none. The notebook was burned."

"Burned! What do you mean, burned?"

"I found remnants of a notebook in Uncle George's fireplace, and paper ashes all around it." Josh dusted his pants, then motioned his right hand as if tossing a frisbee. "He must've tossed it in the fireplace when the kidnappers barged in. And I'm guessing they didn't see him do it, otherwise they wouldn't be asking for us to get it to them."

Josh locked eyes with Kristen. Her eyes were watering, caving to her emotions. She turned to him, reaching for a sign of hope. "So, what are we going to do now?"

"I guess that depends," said Josh. "Did you discover anything new that might help us?"

"I hope so," Kristen said. Her facial expression looked desperate to find a reason to crack a smile. Even a glimmer of optimism would suffice. "But I guess it depends on what you already know from what your uncle may've told you previously."

"I think you're pretty much up to speed with what I know, but it's certainly not enough."

"Okay," she said with a smile. "That's good."

"Good? How do you figure?"

"That means I learned some new information that's hopefully new to *you* as well and might be helpful."

"I'm all ears," Josh said eagerly as the two sat at the four-foot round dining room table next to their kitchenette and where Kristen had been pecking away on her laptop keyboard.

"So, you know how your uncle has been gathering clues and such over the years, trying to figure out where or how the *Gold Scammer* hid assets that escaped the reach of the feds? And, of course, also trying to figure out if the convict killed his partner, and if not, what happened to the second con man?"

"Yes. I'm listening."

"Well, it seems that the treasure hunt has more than one map to find it."

Confusion masked Josh's face. "What do you mean more than one map?"

"After his trial and conviction, the Court offered the *Gold Scammer* an opportunity for some leniency in his sentencing if he gave up the location of the hidden assets."

Josh interrupted. "Obviously, he didn't. Right? Otherwise, this might've ended two decades ago."

"Well, yes and no," Kristen said, then paused for a breath before she continued. "He said that he already had."

"What? When?" Josh looked more confused than ever.

"That's all he kept saying, 'Your Honor, I have given up the location of the hidden assets.' It pissed off the judge so badly that he threw the book at the snide scammer when he dished out his sentencing."

Kristen stopped, giving Josh time to absorb what she'd revealed. She then clicked the spacebar on her laptop screen to wake it from sleep mode. Spinning it around for Josh to see, she said, "Check this out."

Josh peered at the screen, recognizing it was the front page of a local newspaper, the *Summit Star News*. The headliner article was entitled "Taunting or Flaunting?" He pulled the laptop closer, adjusted the angle of the screen, and read the following article, which comprised two-thirds of the front page:

> On the commencement of his long prison sentence, William Clybourne, locally identified as the *Gold Scammer*, has not disappeared quietly into the night. Months after his sentencing from a slew of federal fraud-based convictions, the *Gold Scammer* resurfaced with a series of riddles he sent to local Deputy District Attorney George Dellucci.

> Mr. Dellucci is the Deputy D.A. who'd been assigned to prosecute the state crimes alleged against the *Gold Scammer* in the event he was acquitted of the federal charges—crimes that carry much harsher sentences. However, after the latter received near the maximum sentences for his federal crimes, at least for now the state of Colorado has decided to employ its limited resources elsewhere.

> In addition, Deputy D.A. Dellucci indicated that if the state does prosecute Clybourne, they preferred to try him on all charges at once. That statement is be-

lieved to be referring to an investigation by local law enforcement into the disappearance of Mr. Clybourne's partner in crime, who disappeared shortly after apparently agreeing to meet with prosecutors to testify against his partner in lieu of a plea deal.

Did the *Gold Scammer* "get rid" of his partner before he had a chance to spill the beans? Deputy District Attorney Dellucci responded to that question by saying, "That's a strong working theory."

Months into his federal sentence, the infamous prisoner started periodically sending cryptic messages to Mr. Dellucci. At first, the veteran prosecutor believed Mr. Clybourne simply was taunting him, gloating he'd gotten away with murder. Then, one day, the mocking messages took on an altered state: shifting from teasing to enticing.

According to a reliable source, Deputy D .A. Dellucci has received a handful of letters from the convict, written in a style most accurately described as a riddle. Do these riddles reveal the entire story behind the infamous scam? Or is a man with nothing but time on his handles merely harassing the local prosecutor? Is he taunting or flaunting? And if flaunting, how many more riddles are needed to solve the puzzle? The answers to those questions remain to be seen.

Folding his arms, Josh took a deep sigh after reading the final word. He continued staring at the online newspaper page for a few more deep breaths, then gazed up at Kristen.

"So, assuming the *Gold Scammer* wasn't jerking with the judge at his sentencing hearing, and that he hasn't been jokingly tormenting my uncle for years, the notes in Uncle George's notebook are not the only path to the hidden treasure." Josh scratched his vacation stubble peeking from his chin. "Somehow, somewhere, he provided another clue or set of clues to its whereabouts. Is that what we're thinking?"

Kristen nodded her head in agreement. "That's what we're thinking."

"That means, if we can figure out *that* piece of the puzzle, we might be able to provide the kidnappers what they want, even without Uncle George's notebook."

"Exactly!"

"There's one problem, Kristen."

"What's that?"

Before Josh could respond, his cell phone vibrated. He had a text from Sam. It read "I'm at your front door and . . ." Josh glared at Kristen and said, "Correction. Two problems."

"Two?"

"I just got a text from Sam," Josh said, tossing his phone on the table, then getting up to open the suite's front door. Oozing with despair, Sam shook his head as he handed over the burner phone. "Sorry son."

"No latent prints. And—"

Josh gazed at his watch. As quickly as the revelation of Kristen's research had inflated their bubble with an air of positivity, a pin-size hissing leak from the other end burst open when Josh responded, "We're out of time!"

The often-merciless timing of the universe reared its ugly head—echoing with a sound more deafening than a firehouse alarm. The burner phone rang.

Chapter Twenty-Five

WITH NO TIME to panic, Josh quickly tossed the death alarm in the air as if it was a hot coal, then flung it on the table. His eyes lifted to Kristen, then back to the phone. Time had run out. He hadn't prepared what he wanted to say. It was supposed to be as simple as, "I have the notebook. Give me my uncle, I'll give you the notebook."

For a young man who made a living thinking and speaking on his feet—not to mention very successfully—and with peoples' lives and freedom at stake, at no time was it ever personal. Seemingly born with the ability to say the perfect thing at the spur of the moment, perhaps this time would be different for Josh. After all, there's pressure, and then there's *pressure*. A slip of the tongue, the wrong choice of words, and his great-uncle would be dead. *That's* pressure!

Don't think. Just trust your instincts. Ripping off the band-aid, Josh grabbed the phone and answered, "Hello, this is Joshua." While talking slowly, he pulled out his cell phone, pressed an app, and started recording the conversation.

"Did you get what I asked for?"

"No, not yet, but—"

"Not yet?" said the distorted voice. "That's very unfortunate. I'll let your uncle say goodbye to you. Because that's the kind of guy I am."

"Wait, I can—"

Before Josh could finish, he heard his uncle holler, sounding distant in the background, "In the words of my second favorite Josh, 'Life consists not in holding the good cards but in playing those you hold well.' That's how to beat a wheeler and dealer. And always treasure our wild trip to the Monterey Bay Aquarium when you were twelve and you found the answer you'd sought during that chapter of your life. I love you son."

"Uncle George—"

"Times up Joshua."

"No. Wait! I just need more time."

"Sorry, Joshua. Wrong answer. Your time's up. And so is your uncle's. I'll leave his body where you can find it." Click.

The call ended. Josh dropped the burner; his leaded jaw and the phone hitting the ground at the same time.

Josh had failed his family. In a matter of seconds, his poor choice of words cost a life. And Uncle George would pay the price.

Inspired by the great wordsmith, George Dellucci, the young man hadn't reached the level of his idol and perhaps never would. If he had, Josh would be discussing arrangements with the abductor to get Uncle George back . . . alive. Instead, he'd be discussing funeral arrangements with a mortician.

Chapter Twenty-Six

JOSH DIDN'T MOVE an inch. His eyes fixated on the burner phone, laying on the floor next to his stunned jib. He heard nothing. His glazed-donut eyes, as blue as his mood, saw nothing. Paralyzed in place, wearing an empty stare as void as his emotional state. Disbelief, anger, despair, rage, grief, and numbness rolled into one.

Kristen burst like a frozen water pipe, unable to fight the tears. Sam calmly picked up the burner phone, set it gently on the table, and paused, giving the two young attorneys a moment to feel whatever it was they needed to feel, the entire time staring at his gunmetal *Fossil* watch crinkling his right wrist. Exactly one minute passed when George's best friend put an end to the mourning.

"What's with the long faces? This isn't a horse stable." Sam declared, throwing Josh and Kristen into a different kind of shock. "Here's what we know. We just heard George's voice. Speaking. Alive! And from the sound of it, seemingly unaffected for an old man who's been kidnapped by Lord knows who."

Josh embraced Kristen as Sam handed her a tissue. "You know what? Sam, you're right. First, we must operate under the assumption that Uncle George is alive until proven otherwise. Second, we must do all we can to ensure that *otherwise* never happens. It ain't over until the fat lady sings. And I don't see any fat lady. Are we all in?"

Kristen removed herself from Josh's grip. With the first tissue heavily saturated, Sam handed her another. She dabbed her eyes, wiped her upper lip, and slowly nodded her head, acting somewhat convinced to forge onward. With a deep sigh, a semblance of peace graced her innocent face. Then, throwing Josh for a loop, in a moment of sports-inspired antics, she put her right hand forward and said, "All in for Uncle George."

Josh threw his right palm down, dwarfing the back of Kristen's dainty hand. "All in for Uncle George."

Sam joined in with his left hand, parroting "All in for Uncle George."

"Sam, you mentioned George's voice sounded unaffected," Kristen said. "I agree. He sounded very lucid."

"You're right. He did," said Josh. "We have to take that as a good sign."

"And from what you two have said about him," Kristen opined, "and from what I've seen for myself and recognizing that there's a lot of him in Josh, I'm guessing he was *telling* us more than he actually *said* to us."

"I think you're spot on young lady. And he quoted his second favorite Josh." Sam paused, then landed a firm pat on Josh's muscular right shoulder. "As we all know Joshua, you, young man, are his favorite."

"Ya know, you're right." Josh's tone perked up a bit. "With Uncle George, words are never wasted.

They are meticulously chosen. Like every grape of a fine wine. Like every brush stroke of a world-class painter. Michelangelo. DaVinci. Dellucci. The masters of their craft. Generational artists. The first two with the brush, the latter with his silver tongue."

Sam handed Josh another pat and gentle jiggle to the shoulder. "It sounds like the leaf from George's vineyard didn't fall far from the grapevine."

Kristen plopped down at her seat, spun her computer around, and started typing away.

Josh continued. "And he loves to quote Josh Billings." With raised eyebrows, Sam nodded.

"Here it is," Kristen said, reading verbatim from her screen. "I searched for famous Josh Billing quotes, and bam, 'Life consists not in holding the good cards but in playing those you hold well.' Now, what did he mean by that?"

Sam added to the puzzle. "Yes. What does he mean? And *Josh*, what can you tell us about your trip to the Monterey Aquarium as a kid?"

"Nothing."

"Nothing!?" Kristen said. "What do you mean nothing?"

"Listen, son." Sam placed a comforting hand on Josh's other shoulder. "I know this is stressful, and stress can make it difficult to remember things. And I know that was a long time ago. But surely you can remember something. Anything. Any bit of information might help us."

"Sorry, I can't," replied Josh. "Because we never went on to the Monterey Bay Aquarium. I've never been there before in my life."

Chapter Twenty-Seven

C ALLING THE POLICE crossed Josh's mind, given the fact that the kidnapper all but admitted he would kill Uncle George. But the statement seemed rather abrupt under the circumstances. The abductor wanted one thing, Uncle George's notebook. Josh didn't mention it was destroyed, only that he didn't have it *yet*. Why would this criminal mastermind give up his leverage so easily? Chances are, he wouldn't. God willing, he was bluffing. So, giving the conniving criminal another reason to kill Uncle George by calling the cops wasn't worth the risk.

And at the possibility of being overconfident, what brainpower could the local police department assemble that could even scratch the surface of Josh's team? He'd call them when he needed law *enforcement*. But for now, bringing them in the loop likely wouldn't amount to anything more than putting his uncle's life further in danger, assuming, of course, he was still alive. And for purposes of investigating and fact-finding, Josh felt confident pushing all his chips into the pot, and banking on his own legal dream team.

And while confident, Josh wasn't stupid. The fewer who knew of the abduction, the better. But having a local resource was imperative. And with Austin already in the know, after getting someone to run prints on the burner phone and duct tape, he kept the circle of trust to a minimum.

Austin joined his fellow attorneys at their B&B headquarters thirty minutes after he received the text from Josh. Hustling from the D.A.'s office in Breckenridge to Main Street in Frisco, the impact of his arrival was felt immediately. It turned out Austin was more than an additional bright resource to contribute to their think tank. Playing the part of a reporter, he rolled in with staggering news.

"Our thousand-piece puzzle just became a five-thousand-piece jigsaw mess," Austin declared with his trailing foot still in the suite's doorway.

Josh responded, "I'm afraid to ask."

"The *Gold Scammer* is dead; murdered in prison."

Josh threw his arms up in the air. "Are you serious?"

"That can't be a coincidence," Kristen said. Recognizing they had a long afternoon ahead of them, she prepped the coffee maker sitting below the corner cabinet of the snug kitchenette.

Sam nodded his head. "No, it can't be." Now seated at the table, the elder member of the impromptu-formed abduction rescue team for the FBI—the *Frisco Barristers of Investigation*—continued. "Other than George's efforts, the dust collecting atop the Gold Scam has gone mostly untouched, accumulating for well over a decade. And just like that, within a week's time, George's cabin is ransacked, then he's abducted, and the convict responsible for causing the chain of events is suddenly murdered—twenty-some years after tipping the first domino."

Josh and Austin joined their team seated at the table. Josh leaned over in his chair, stretching to pick up the burner. He glanced at his watch as if timing when it would ring again. Praying it would ring again.

"It'll ring again," predicted Kristen, apparently reading Josh's distraught mind. She locked eyes with Josh, giving him a subtle nod sweetened with her comforting smile.

Less convinced and struggling to crack a smile, Josh acknowledged her consoling gesture with a receptive nod.

Instinctively, Josh jumped to the front of the line, thrusting himself into the role of the leader. Since birth, he had the makings of it. In elementary school, group projects almost automatically started with the group choosing him as the leader. During recess in the schoolyard, somehow, he'd always be selected as a captain, picking his team for the seasonal sport. Never shying from it, he led with confidence and respect for others' input. But make no mistake about it, if opinions were on the fence, or a sway vote was required, Josh's way prevailed. Period.

"Okay, let's get started," said Josh. "We need to divide and conquer. Sam, Austin. First, we need to bring you up to speed with what Kristen uncovered with her thoroughly efficient research skills. Then, we'll divvy up assignments with the goal of finding more answers than questions."

Giving way to Kristen, Josh closed his eyes as she shared her findings with the others. Josh replayed Uncle George's last statements in his head. What was his intent? Should he focus on Josh Billings, or the quote itself? Why would he reference a trip they never took? What was its significance? And why age twelve? Did it have to do with something that happened when the twelve-year-old Josh visited Uncle George? Or was it something else?

Overwhelmed with the possibilities, Josh took a deep breath. When swamped with options, only one approach was the best—take it one step at a time. So that's what Josh did. Starting with the first statement, Josh whispered it out loud several times—*Life consists not in holding the good cards but in playing those you hold well.*

As if on cue, as Kristen concluded her update to Sam and Austin, it clicked. Seamlessly, as the last word exited her mouth, Josh blurted out, "That's it! The cards. It's in the cards."

Chapter
Twenty-Eight

NOT THINKING MUCH of it at the time, other than noting the eccentricity of his great-uncle, the special occasion cards Josh had received periodically contained a riddle-like segment. Birthday cards and Christmas cards alike. Not all, but some. But not one to be a hoarder, most cards were read, appreciated, and tossed in the trash after being displayed for a week or so by the thankful great-nephew.

Knowing Uncle George loved to cite famous quotes, more often than not Josh concluded it was just that, a random expression of an entertaining quote or an anecdotal riddle. Now, in hindsight, Josh criticized his ignorance in brushing it off to its simplest form. Turns out, they were much more than arbitrary. And fortuitously for Josh, if not just by dumb luck, he had saved the cards containing the famous quotes.

Why? He couldn't be sure. Sentiment, maybe. Possibly, to feel closer to his hero who resided on the plus side of a thousand miles away. Or perhaps it was the eighties-obsessed aficionado's longing to identify with someone who, as he, seemingly had an uncontrollable urge to quote others.

But with Uncle George, nothing was random. With Uncle George, everything had a deeper meaning, sometimes far greater than appearing on the surface. A man with an aversion to leaving things to chance. And a man far too intelligent to put all his eggs in one basket or, as it were, all his notes in one notebook.

Very few people possessed that top-tier level of intelligence. George had it in spades. Missing the added significance of the cards for so many years, Josh now questioned whether he had his uncle's gift. If he did, unquestionably the student's level of brain power fell far short of his teacher.

Fortunately, owing to the urging of a close friend, the California prosecutor's Santa Barbara bungalow was not sitting vacant. With Josh's house being centrally located within walking distance to the famed State Street and the beach, finding someone to house-sit was never an issue. Typically, it came down to a matter of choosing one of several eager volunteers. This time, his buddy Tyler won the house-sitting lottery. Directing his house sitter to their location, Josh summoned the content of the special occasion sentiments. Within an hour of his request, the cards riddled with riddles were being scanned and emailed to the *Frisco Barristers of Investigation* team.

"Okay team," Josh directed, "once again we have to divide and conquer." Sliding his chair back, he stood and paced the room, emulating the likes of Vince Lombardi and Knute Rockne. "Kristen, you and I will start with deciphering the cards Uncle George has sent me over the years. Tyler is going to scan and email them to you and me. The email might be in your inbox by now. Sam, use your contacts to find out everything you can about the *Gold Scammer's* murder. And Austin, get a hold of the full trial transcript and review it with a fine-toothed comb. From there, we'll all compare notes, and shift tasks to get fresh eyes on everything."

* * *

THE TEAM OF four separated themselves into working sections of the suite. The California couple set up shop at the dining table. Sam, with his mobile phone in hand, plopped his thinner skin in the comfy chair nearest the warm fireplace. Austin topped his head with a Denver Broncos knit beanie, wrapped his neck in a black and gray plaid fleece scarf, closed the door behind him, and dropped his cold butt on the one chair small enough to furnish the modest balcony overlooking Main Street.

With Kristen's laptop at her fingertips, Josh cozied up his dining chair next to hers as she read from it, while he jotted notes on a small notepad that'd been collecting dust next to the suite's landline. First, he wrote verbatim as she recited the following "clues" from the cards:

> *History is an endless repetition of the wrong way of living* by Lawrence Durrell.

History is indeed little more than the register of the crimes, follies, and misfortunes of mankind by Edward Gibbon.

Time is the school in which we learn, time is the fire in which we burn by Delmore Schwartz.

He who opens a school door, closes a prison by Victor Hugo.

Money is human happiness in the abstract; he, then, who is no longer capable of enjoying human happiness in the concrete devotes himself utterly to money by Arthur Schopenhauer.

All the gold which is under or upon the earth is not enough to give in exchange for virtue by Plato.

Prepping Josh for disappointment, Kristen briefed Josh on the entirety of the conversation she'd had with Uncle George during their dinner visit the previous night. In short, the final piece of the puzzle intentionally had not yet been released.

Perhaps in hope that some miracle would befall the crook who surely didn't deserve one, in his final letter to George the *Gold Scammer* alluded to a hitch in the generous disclosures he'd been feeding the old man over time. The catch—the con man wouldn't send the final clue until his deathbed. Until then, George would carry the weight of not knowing the entire tale behind the scam, and likely forever wallow in the mystery behind the disappearance of his true love. Ironically, the weight of an Olympic barbell saw to it that relief of that burden might evade the tirelessly patient altruist.

Josh scratched his head, staring down at the notes he had taken. "So, what you're saying is, even if we correctly decode these riddles, we'll still be one clue from solving the puzzle?"

"From what your uncle told me," Kristen said in a dejected tone, "apparently so."

Just then, Sam, who'd been making phone calls from the armchair warmed up to the fireplace, pushed himself up whimpering his old man groan. Josh cringed when he heard it. Not from sympathy, but with empathy; self-conscious that he was prematurely entering the old man stage—thirty years too early! Had the years of being a three-sport star, rapidly racking up high mileage on a newer vehicle, caught up with him already? He straightened his posture as Sam took the seat opposite Kristen.

Sam's face indicated he was ready to burst. Patiently, he took a deep breath. Kristen lowered her screen and locked in on George's former colleague and dearest friend. Josh tossed his pen on the six-by-nine-inch notepad and leaned back in his chair. A creak sounded. Josh couldn't be certain if it was the chair or his bones.

"Whatcha got for us Sam?" asked Josh. "Please don't tell me the *Gold Scammer*, on top of being murdered, left nothing behind."

Sam nodded to Kristen, then to Josh. "My dear youngsters, not only did he leave *something* behind, but he also left *someone* behind."

Josh's head pulled back, then jerked toward Kristen. Kristen gazed at Josh, then snapped her head toward Sam. "Say what?" she said. "What do you mean, he left *someone* behind?"

"After twenty years of no one other than his lawyer visiting him, it seems Mr. Clybourne recently had another visitor to his modest cage in Florence, Colorado."

"How recently?" asked Josh. "And more importantly, who?"

"This week," Sam said nonchalantly as if the timing was no big deal. In fairness, in comparison to what followed, it wasn't. "And the who—his son!"

"His son!?" said Kristen. "I could've sworn I read he had no living relatives. George told me that as well; that basically, the guy was a loner. His girlfriend ditched him after his arrest, and that's probably why he started playing this riddle game. He had no one in his life to reap the rewards of his crime, so he'd either get paroled someday and live the high life or die in prison while surrendering the treasure to the druthers of a worthy sleuth."

Sam was a Colorado-lifer. Born in Durango, raised in Denver, college in Grand Junction at Colorado

Mesa University, and law school at the University of Colorado in Boulder.

His family ties to the Centennial State were long and deep. His father had been Colorado's Attorney General serving under two different governors. His uncle died in the line of duty as Chief of Police in Pueblo and his grandfather spent years as a State Senator on Capitol Hill in Denver. And that was just on his paternal side. His mother's side also had a few members in the inner circle.

With his pedigree packing more ingredients than Dog Chow, Sam had connections well-situated throughout the state. And not being one to misuse his network pull, when he'd call upon a favor, invariably the response would be along the lines of "Certainly. What else do you need?" After making one phone call, he had three people taking action; two calls, and he could have the National Guard awaiting his direction.

"I don't suppose we'd be able to track him down to find out if his old man told him anything." Josh nibbled on his pen cap. "But even if we could, it's not likely he'd talk to us anytime soon."

Straight-faced, Sam responded, "You're right—"

Kristen interjected, "We'll have to make do with what we got."

"You didn't let me finish," Sam said as the corners of his mouth crept north. "You're right. He can't talk with us anytime soon. He can *meet* with us even *sooner*!"

"George told me you were quite the prankster, Sam," spilled Kristen, shaking her pointer at his face. "I hope you're not yanking our chain."

"Other than the metal-wrapped tires entering the avalanche-sandwiched Eisenhower-Johnson tunnels, there's no chain yanking going on around here."

"Go on!" Josh whirled his right hand as if rolling up the window of a 1974 *VW Bug*.

"It appears his son was staying at a hotel, nearby the prison. He'd scheduled a follow-up visit for next week. The warden thought it best to break the news to the young man in person. After dropping the bomb on him, they gave the kid the few possessions his old man called his own. Apparently, from there his kid was headed up to Denver, to take care of some business. From Denver, he'd be traveling west to Salt Lake City, which means he'll be coming right through Frisco tomorrow."

"So, you think you can get him to stop on his way through and meet with us?" Josh's appetite increased, from nibbling on the pen cap to biting the entire pen. Recognizing his nervous habit, earlier he'd poured boiling water over the writing stick.

"I don't think so," said Sam.

"Let me guess," Josh jumped in, "you *know* so."

"You're a quick study young man. Just like your uncle told me. The warden gave me the kid's number, I spoke with him, and he'll be here tomorrow. Sounded like he's eager to speak with us. I got the impression he felt he might be able to learn more about his father from us than we can from him. For George's sake, I hope the kid is wrong."

Knowing firsthand what it's like not to know one's father, Kristen empathized. "Hopefully, it turns out to be equally beneficial to everyone."

Her warm sentiment didn't linger long before a cool chill entered the room from the sliding balcony door, with Austin quickly following. He tossed his cap and scarf on the end of the bed that jotted out from the wall opposite the fireplace. He leaned toward the fireplace, extending his hands toward it, rubbing them furiously to thaw his fingers. Kristen rushed him a hot cup of coffee.

"You're a Godsend. Thank you."

"Tell that to your friend," Kristen said with a smile, tipping her head in Josh's direction. "And you're welcome."

Austin took a sip, then wrapped his frozen paws around the warm ceramic mug doubling as a hand-warmer. "So, I tracked down the court reporter who transcribed the *Gold Scammer* trial. The good news, she still has an electronic copy of the transcript stored on an external hard drive at her home. Bad news, she's away from home right now. She said she'd email me a copy of the transcript as quickly as possible, but it could be a day or two."

Shadows fell upon the Main Street to the Rockies as the sun relaxed west of ski country. On paper, it appeared the group was closer to solving the puzzle. But were they closer to finding George? It didn't appear so. And if and when they found him, would he still be alive?

Kristen scanned the room, reading the demeanor of her newest colleagues. Surely Sam missed an afternoon nap and dinner before sunset and appeared on the threshold of passing out any second. Austin, who wasn't on vacation nor retired, now found himself juggling his profession as a prosecutor, a newlywed at home, and now a side-hustle as an amateur gumshoe. Catching Josh's eye, Kristen's raised eyebrows jerked her head in the direction of their guests. Her subtle way of tipping off Josh the tank warning light was flashing, and the team was running on empty.

"Okay. So, we won't have the transcript for a day or two," Josh recapped. "And we're meeting with the Clybourne's son tomorrow. So, I think we should get our rest and reconvene tomorrow morning. Austin, I'll email you a copy of the scanned cards with the clues and we can touch base with you during your lunch tomorrow."

"Lunch?" Austin broke in. "I've got a ton of vacation days piling up. I already texted our HR lady and let her know I'd be taking one tomorrow."

Josh cracked a smile and gave his friend a nod. "Thanks, man. I owe you big time."

"Don't mention it. And don't worry, I'll collect."

Turning to Sam, Josh said, "Sam, I'll email the same to you as well. Do you have an email?"

"Have an email?" responded Sam, looking insulted at the subtle age jab. "I'm not that old." He paused, then smiled. "Okay, I *am* that old, but I'm hip to the times."

"*Hip*," cracked Josh. "The fact that you said hip screams otherwise."

In a needed moment of levity, the four chuckled.

"Next," Josh continued, "you'll be telling us everything will be just swell."

"Hey young man," Sam replied, "don't be knocking *The Brady Bunch*. Assuming you've heard of them."

Kristen almost choked on her laughter before throwing out her retort, "Oh, he knows *The Brady Bunch*. Are you kidding? He's a walking TV Wikipedia."

"Wikipedia?" corrected Sam. "You mean encyclopedia."

Lazily shaking his sunken head, "Oh, Sam," Josh said in his most sympathetic tone. "You're not helping your argument any. How 'bout I send you a telegram and we'll call it a day?"

"Ring." The terrorizing sound captured the room, taking prisoner its moment of solace.

In a flash, the levity was lost. A single ring from the burner phone robbed the room of its welcomed but fleeting reprieve. Like Austin's buttocks, the entire room froze.

Another ring. Quicker than a frog tongue-snatching a fly invading the airspace above its lily pad, Josh's reflexes took over. He grabbed the phone and answered it.

"Hello. Hello." Nothing. Dead air.

Josh pulled the phone from his ear and glared at the screen. As sudden as the vanishing laughter in the room, the call ended.

Nobody said a word. Staring at the burner phone, they just waited. In total silence. Hoping it would ring again. Praying it would ring again.

The clock above the mantel ticked. The fireplace below blazed. The room's occupants held their collective breath, leaving sufficient oxygen to fuel the phone. All for naught. The damn burner had flamed out—failing to ring again.

Josh looked more torn than a teenage girl's jeans. The wheels were in motion. Progress appeared on the horizon. If their leads panned out, the united brain power of the *Frisco Barristers of Investigation* was on the brink of solving a twenty-year-old mystery. And with it, on the precipice of finding a treasure worth millions.

But all the gold around Mr. T's neck wasn't worth anything if Uncle George's life was the cost. A return on investment in which Josh had no interest. And even if the kidnapper had been bluffing with his ill-fated comment, at some point he'd put his money where his mouth is if Josh didn't comply with his end of the deal.

If not already, eventually no notebook would mean no Uncle George.

Chapter Twenty-Nine

T HE TWO-BEDROOM CABIN couldn't have been too far from Frisco and Copper Mountain. After being nabbed, the thugs had zip-tied the old man's strong, wrinkly hands behind his back, tossed a thick, black pillowcase over his head, and weaved around for an hour and a half until they reached their destination.

George knew the area from Keystone to the east extending to Vail to the west as well as anyone. A ninety-minute drive west on I-70 could've got them as far as Glenwood Springs. But from the speed, frequent turns, and topography of travel, they couldn't have trekked that far. Some turns must've been intended as a distraction; being too frequent and seemingly taking them in several circles.

The captors locked the old man in a ten-by-twelve-foot bedroom, equipped with a full-size bed, a nightstand topped with a table lamp, and a thirty-two-ounce cup of water. The tan hardback fabric shade of the industrial-style lamp topped its elongated, Eiffel-Tower-shaped bronze neck welded to a five-by-five-inch square, two-inch-thick base, The head of the brass post bed was centered on the twelve-foot back wall, with a two-by-three-foot window on each side of it and boarded from the outside with more nails than a beauty salon.

The mattress felt new and surprisingly comfortable; a far cry from what one would expect from a kidnapper's hideaway. With hardwood floors that appeared newly refinished in a Hickory Oak shaded satin sheen, the mountain cabin had the makings more of a vacation home than a criminal's refuge. A masked thug entered every few hours to escort the decades-old enlarged prostrate to the can and throw him a bite to eat every other trip.

Periodically, with his ear to the door and his hearing aid cranked up, George's laboring ears could hear the voices whispering in the main room. Best he could tell, at times there may've been three, and sometimes as few as one. But with his impaired hearing, it just as likely could've been a radio or television in the other room, or three bears eating porridge.

Slight imperfections in the wood securing the boarded windows allowed slivers of natural light to poke in the cold sparsely furnished room. If George made it out alive, his online reviews would dole out an earful. *Poor natural light, stuffy rooms, and armed guards. But the mattress was like sleeping on a cloud. For that, I bumped it up to two stars. You'd have to bound and gag me to stay here again, much like my first stay. Go with the nearest Best Western.*

With nothing but time on his hands, whatever limited amount he had left, George paced, sat, laid down, and repeated. All the while, his brain worked overtime. Replaying the involuntary rideshare trip he'd endured the night beforehand. Listening to the outdoors. Thinking. Planning.

The tired captive sat slouched forward on the side of the bed, his elbows pressing on his knees, his hands clasped. Annoyingly, a tickle triggered his right hand to rush to his ear, swatting his hearing aid as if it were a pesky fly buzzing in his earhole. Whacking too closely, he flipped the middle finger to his hearing device, flinging it from his ear. After receiving "the bird," the ear-trumpet flew over the edge of the mattress, bounced from the floor, ricocheted off a spindled wooden leg of the nightstand, and rolled awkwardly under the bed.

George exhaled deeply, softly closed his eyes, and shook his head. "Are you kidding me?"

Frustrated and weary, he lowered his knees to the hardwood, leaning heavily to his right with his pointy elbow digging into the mattress. A booming groan bellowed, waking the dead and prompting his armed air bed and breakfast host to holler, "You alright old man?"

Choosing not to respond verbally, George's left hand released a second bird airborne in the direction of his "concerned caregiver."

Caged like an animal, fittingly the old-timer got on all fours, then lowered his left elbow to the impressively stained flooring. In a sweeping motion, his right arm surveyed beneath the bed, his palm collecting dust, dirt, and debris faster than a *Hoover*. Rubbing cracker crumbs from his fingertips, George mumbled, "With a mattress from the Ritz, you'd think the housekeeping would sweep the *Ritz*."

George's aidless ear couldn't be sure if he said that out loud or merely mouthed it, continuing to explore. His right hand stopped upon hitting the headboard leg closest to the nightstand. His long boney fingers reached around the tapered metal leg. And just as he felt a familiar object, he cried, "Ouch!" His hand pulled away for a second, then gently reached back to grab his hearing device and the pin-like assailant.

Struggling to get upright, George raised his dusty elbow from the floor, rested his butt against his heels, and opened his right hand. Two objects rested on his palm. A drop of blood dotted his middle finger. With his left hand, his fingers pinched the hearing device, lifted it to his mouth for a cleansing blow, then set it on the edge of the nightstand.

He peered at his open palm. Luckily George already had blown the dust from his hearing aid, because he found himself out of breath. His eyes locked in on the tiny object, raised twelve inches from his nose, open palm to Heaven as if offering it to God. His entire body shut down. Catatonic. Nothing moved, including his lungs. Years searching for answers. Right now, yearning for air. A single breath evaded him, but the answer had appeared. His saddened eyes glared at the object; dried, then glazed, then flowing.

* * *

HIS FALSE TEETH took a bite of the apple set on the plastic food tray that had been placed on the nightstand about an hour earlier. His meals and snacks were finger foods, requiring no utensils and thus depriving the old man of makeshift weapons. The tray was a thin, cheap plastic; incapable of wounding an ant. Despite their victim's age, which minimized the risk factor, plainly his abductors left nothing to chance.

Entering his second night in the foreign quarters, George had taken enough trips from his locked quarters to the restroom to take an inventory of the cabin. It lacked a phone landline, and the television was connected to a DVR, but nothing else. The stove was gas, probably fueled by an outdoor propane tank. Underneath the bathroom sink cabinet and beside a plunger, a nineteen-ounce box of powdered *Rid-X* was half-full, suggesting the cabin had a septic tank. A septic tank generally equated to having no city sewer system access, which in turn meant they were somewhere in the sticks.

In the small kitchen, no heavy pots or pans were visible. Nor were any knives. For a man in his eighties, getting ahold of a weapon in the kitchen before getting whacked by someone less than half his age seemed impossible—even on George's best day.

The rural resident, accustomed to making good use of limited resources, found himself at a loss each time he'd scanned the cabin on his way to and from the john. No visible ticket to freedom was available; the concert—sold out. There'd be no singing "The Pina Colada Song" for George—no "Escape." No Rupert Holmes. No going home.

Only two things were apparent from his thorough observations upon scanning the main living area. One, he never spotted a potential weapon. And two, the coffee table in front of the television had a mini-megaphone-looking device; likely the source of the voice distortion used to communicate during the ransom call to Josh and the limited communication with the cabin's annoyed guest.

George sat up on the bed. In tune with his prostate's schedule and given the last time he'd taken a leak; in four minutes a warm puddle would be forming below his feet. Donning a crinkled facial expression and dazed stare at a naked wall, he looked on the verge of a tactical breakthrough. If not that, perhaps desperate planning for a desperate man. His time had to be running out. It was now or never. And never wasn't an option for a man obsessed with lady justice.

Taking a deep breath, George walked to the bedroom door and pounded twice. "Hello. Excuse me. I need to use the restroom." He thumped one more time, rushed back to sit on the side of the bed nearest the nightstand, and waited. It was late. Odds were, only one goon covered the overnight shift. George banked on it. If he was wrong, like the victims of the *Gold Scammer*, his savings account would be worthless.

A metal-sliding noise ending with a click ensued. The outer-locked deadbolt sounded before the bedroom door squeaked open. One of the masked kidnappers entered, his notable scorched hand grasping the doorknob. Without saying a word, he motioned his head toward another head—one of the nautical origins. George stood up slowly, exaggerating his old-man groan.

He reached for the food tray, where only a used napkin and once-bitten apple lay. "I'm done with this," he said. Just as his right hand grabbed the tray, he cried, "Oh, my back!"

Dropping the tray, both his hands reached around to grab his lower, hunched-over back. George froze and groaned, exhibiting the primary signs of a thrown-out back.

The thug sighed in frustration and walked toward the nightstand. George didn't move an inch. He just stood there, bowed like Quasimodo, and reverberated his pain. "Ugh! My damn back went out." He inched his butt toward the edge of the bed. "Sorry about the tray. I'd help, but I can't move."

Embittered, the captor squatted down in front of George, took a knee, and reached for the tray. At that very moment, a timely blessing from above miraculously cured the old man, now seemingly more limber than an Olympic gymnast. The former All-Region slugger grabbed his "bat" and swung for the fences. The pre-loosened lamp shade popped off with ease, giving George more leverage for his bottom of the ninth, two outs, full count swing for the ultimate championship prize—his life.

The crack of the bat on the masked skull resonated beyond the bleachers. The once-heavily-recruited baseball star had crushed more than a few in his prime. But never had he made contact like that. Like one of the Blake Street Bombers launching a fastball over the Coors Field fountains back in the Rockies' slugging heydays, George squared it up good, splitting the skin-coated oversize baseball at the seams.

Flipping the goon from his knee to his back, the unconscious hired hand played the part of a bear rug. Flat, sprawled, and immobile. For how long? George couldn't be certain. He had to act quickly.

First, he rushed to the doorway. He looked around. It appeared they were alone. Scampering back to the losing end of a solid connection, he pulled the mask from the punk. His identity—no clue. George proceeded to pat him down. No wallet. No ID. No car keys. No weapon. No phone. Turned out that the guy was more worthless than George must've originally thought.

Adrenaline kicked in. The old-timer maneuvered around the cabin like he was seventeen again. Apparently, the swing of the lamp base had done more than emulating George's classic swing. It seemed to reverse time as he moved around akin to the way he use to circle the bases in his prime.

First, he peeked out the front window. Not a car in sight. He'd have to leg it out.

On a wooden coat rack to the right of the front door, hung an empty backpack and a heavy coat. A promising start to a winter's hike in the snow-covered Rockies. George threw on the coat, and with the open backpack in hand, scurried to the kitchen pantry.

He tossed in a few items, then suddenly stopped. Did he hear something? With his hearing, who could tell? He reached for a can of pineapples, tossed it in the backpack, pulled up his compression socks, then froze again to listen. A car engine sounded, increasing in volume, then disappeared in an instant. Out front, a door slammed shut, then another.

* * *

TWO MEN ENTERED the cabin, masks covering everything but their beady, ruffian eyes. The door to the snatched senior's bedroom was open. However, it wasn't *that* open door that got their attention. A bitter cold gust of wind blew through the back of the cabin, forcing the open back door to slam against the wood-paneled wall. One hooligan rushed to the bedroom doorway, the other to the cabin's back door.

The first goon slouched on the threshold of the bedroom door and yelled, "Oh shit!"

The lead goon, after scanning a look out the back door and seeing nothing but darkness, stepped inside and slammed the door shut with such force that his unconscious crony began to moan and squirm. "Son of a—that old bastard is gone!" Then, after a deep sigh, he remarked, "Well, some mountain lion or hungry black bear waking early from hibernation will be feasting on some aged white meat tonight."

Chapter Thirty

J OSH HADN'T SLEPT well, if at all. The combination of worry over Uncle George and a late-night spat with Kristen occupied his overworked brain, preventing any restful sleep.

After Sam and Austin had left for the evening, the "vacationing" couple studied the clues from the cards sent from Uncle George to his great-nephew. In the course of recapping the events of the past week, Josh slipped up, inadvertently mentioning the dead body they stumbled upon during the scavenger hunt was that of The *Midnight Vandal*.

After being informed by Austin of the dead body's identity, Josh intentionally withheld that information from Kristen. In hindsight, he'd made a mistake. In his defense, or so he justified, with knowledge of that fact Kristen would've concluded that she and Josh were the targets of the drive-by shooting outside the Italian restaurant. Her bright-but-stupid boyfriend didn't want to add further worry to the already highly stressful night. Instead, Josh simply delayed adding more stress.

It was 6:12 a.m. when Josh tiptoed out of their room and headed to the coffee shop. He returned with two large *Mountain Mogul Mocha Madness* drinks and four of Mocha Mountain Java's famous breakfast burritos as a peace offering. With a brown bag of burritos dangling from his clenched jaw, he balanced one cup on top of the other's lid and slowly opened their suite's door with his free hand. Not expecting Kristen to be awake, somehow, he managed to balance the coffees like a circus act when she ambushed him as he stepped inside their room.

"So first, you hold out on me by delaying telling me you wanted to visit your uncle during our vacation. Which was no big deal, so I'm not sure why you waited. Then, *you* decide I needn't worry myself over knowing the identity of the dead body. Mind you, the man set for a criminal trial stemming from his entanglement in the biggest mystery this county has ever seen. What else are you keeping from me? And who are *you* to determine what and when *I* should have the privilege of knowing?"

"I'm sorry," apologized Josh. "What can I say? I'm an idiot."

"No argument from me."

"Not that it's a good reason, perhaps more of an excuse, but I'm new to this relationship stuff. Other than you, the longest relationship I've ever had lasted only a few months." He paused, having hit a fork in the road. His next statement could've taken two different paths. He chose the shorter one. "And let's just say it didn't end well."

"You're right," she replied. "It's not a good reason. It's not a reason at all. It's an excuse."

"Please," he begged, "be patient with me. I'm learning as I go."

"Trust me. I'm very patient with you." She smiled, in a moment of peace. "Well," she said, holding a pause, "learn faster."

"I'll try." Josh returned the smile. "Is there a *Dummies* book on relationships?"

"Probably," she said. "But I'm not sure you'd be bright enough to understand it." A quick snort surfaced.

"Touché." While taking gunfire, Josh had managed to safely set the food and drinks on their modest dining table. As if to shield himself from the barrage of shots, he grabbed a mocha and burrito, raised the edible *Kevlar* in front of his chest, then handed them to Kristen, and said, "I come in peace, bearing gifts."

"It's going to take a lot more than this mister," she said, freeing Josh's hands, then taking a sip and raising the treats in a gesture of thanks. "But speaking of dummies. What kind of dummy would I be to turn down this delightful mocha and a tasty breakfast burrito?" She took a swig, followed it with a bite, then mumbled out a thank you.

By the time Kristen ate half her burrito, Josh had scarfed down two and was on the last gulp of his mocha. He rubbed his gut, thinking he'd tacked on a good five pounds since their plane touched down in Colorado.

Dropping to the floor, Josh punched out two sets of twenty-five pushups. Then, flexing his right bicep, he squeezed it like an orange and shook his head in disgust. He couldn't remember the last time he'd gone so many consecutive days without pumping iron. Missing more than a couple of days in a row, he felt weak. Skipping more than a week, his limbs flapped like noodles. Or so that's how he felt.

An hour later, the two had eaten, showered, and dressed; ready for day two of their work with the *Frisco Barristers of Investigation*. The other members of their team would be arriving shortly, refreshed and ready for answers.

Kristen fired up her laptop. Josh flipped to a fresh page of his notepad, then began brewing a fresh pot of coffee. Austin had called ahead, saying he'd pick up a dozen donuts on his way to *FBI* headquarters. *I might have no choice but to move here,* Josh thought, *because no plane with my fat ass aboard is getting airborne.*

As startling as an unexpected smoke alarm screaming at midnight, the burner phone rang. In dual mode, its vibration prompted it to dance on the table. Leaving nothing to chance, Josh grabbed and answered it after the first ring. Before a word was uttered, he pressed the speaker phone option.

"Hello," Josh said, silently praying for anything other than dead air.

The same distorted voice spoke. "You're lucky, young man."

"Excuse me?"

"I said, you're lucky. Your uncle convinced me that he's of more value alive than dead—at least for now."

"Yes," Josh's heart started beating again. "Alive. Of course he is."

"So, the notebook. Tell me you have it, and your uncle lives."

"I figured out where it is," Josh said, thinking quick-ly, just outpacing his mouth. Knowing he needed to distract the kidnapper from focusing on the fact that he didn't have it *yet*, the fast-brained barrister had to redirect the focus. Josh needed to create a diver-sion. Wave a shiny red ball. "I will have it by the end of today. Let's arrange the exchange for tomorrow morning."

"Hey, kid! I'm making the calls. Not you."

"First," the ballsy *kid* insisted, "I want to talk to my uncle. I need to know he's okay."

"Listen kid. Like I said. I'm making the calls. And you don't *tell* me what to do. You gotta ask me nicely. The old man is being held somewhere safe and he's fine. But I'm not at that location right now. So, you'll just have to trust me."

"Trust you?" Josh choked out a fake laugh. "Trust the man that kidnapped my uncle? You can't be serious?"

It only took a few push-ups, but Josh was pumped, and his ego inflated. He continued, "If you kill my uncle, it will guarantee only two things for you. You will get no notebook—ever! And a life sentence in prison." With his juices flowing, Josh found himself as an action hero in the script of a Hollywood movie. "You listen here, and you listen cautiously. I have a very particular set of skills. A set of skills I've acquired over a period of time and perfected over the years. And I promise you this. If my uncle isn't released unharmed . . . I will find you . . . I will have you arrested . . . and I will convict you."

The distorted voice cleared his throat. "Please tell me that you have something more, Deputy D.A

. Rizzetti. Your uncle is on trial for his life. Please tell me his lawyer protégé hasn't pinned his hope on his arrogance." He paused, then cleared his throat again. "I'm afraid you don't have much choice but to follow my demands. I'll call later with the arrangements. And remember, no cops, or else—"

The call ended. The adrenaline rapidly faded into a cloud of realism. Worry dripped from Josh's face. His frustration was exposed as he tossed the burner on the table.

Kristen looked befuddled. "How are you going to get the notebook? What're you going to do, sweep up the ashes and glue it back together?"

"I'd love to do that and shove it down that bastard's throat. Pardon my French." His face turned fiery red. "But I was thinking we'd recreate the notebook. We'll write in the clues from the cards my uncle sent me. Then we can throw in some other random notes. Notes logically related but intended to misdirect him."

"Do you think that'll work?" Kristen poured a cup of coffee, sweetened it up, and handed it to Josh. He grinned and nodded.

"I don't think it'll even come to that."

"What do you mean?"

Josh paused to swallow the lump in his throat. "I think he already may've killed Uncle George."

"No," Kristen insisted, despite seeing the pain in her partner's face. "Why do you say that?"

"He had to know I'd ask for proof of life. There's no way he would've called without Uncle George present, unless—"

Just then, a knock at the door accompanied Austin announcing the arrival of donuts. Kristen opened the door. Austin and a box of donuts entered behind the heavenly smell of sugary treats. And just as the door was closing shut, Sam hollered out from the end of the hallway. He hustled to the entryway, extending his arm to catch the door before it slammed shut.

"Good timing Sam," said Austin.

As soon as the donut box landed on the dining table, Josh put on another five pounds just looking at them, reminiscent of his days at "The Bakery" law firm. For good measure, he added another ten eating them.

Josh's carb-loaded sugar-filled mouth finished his gloomy thought, ". . . unless Uncle George is dead."

Chapter Thirty-One

F EW PEOPLE COULD'VE survived such harsh conditions overnight. Navy Seal. Special Forces. Wilderness Survival Instructor. Top-notch Eagle Scout—perhaps. Old, creaking litigation attorney—unprecedented. Freezing temperatures, wild animals, and minimal supplies. Any one of those factors, independent of the others, could've been fatal. Combined, they most certainly should've finished the job that the incompetent kidnappers failed to accomplish.

By 4 a.m., the low plummeted to three degrees Fahrenheit. Snow flurries took the evening off, but thanks to a prosperous winter that had been kind to ski enthusiasts, trekking along the thick white terrain without snowshoes was backbreaking. Shaded most of the day by the towering evergreen trees, George's path consisted of slushy ice, slick frozen patches, and protruding bowling-ball-size rocks. But the challenges his trail presented were minor compared to the unpredictable behavior of the indigenous inhabitants of the outdoor Rockies.

In hindsight, George probably regretted not bringing the lamp base with him as a weapon. It did the trick on the hardened skull of a two-legged creature and could've proven useful to ward off any four-legged ones. As it were, a three-inch-thick tree branch measuring almost four feet long had to make do, serving as both a weapon against pernicious greeters and as a walking stick for his frosted and aged bones.

Unaware of his exact whereabouts, George had to pick a strategy and stick with it. His strategy seemed simple, walk in the same direction until he came across something helpful. Preferably, an occupied residence, an open business, or even a well-traveled road. If not that lucky, at least something familiar to indicate his location.

He'd spent the first few hours of his escape trudging in one direction, distancing himself as far from the abductors' headquarters as possible. Every ten to fifteen minutes, he'd walk in a giant circle, creating multiple tracks in the snow, leaving little chance for searching kidnappers to track him down.

Once George's old limbs were burning hotter than thermite from over-activity, he set up camp to cool his legs and warm his body. Perfected by his days as a prosecutor, he was always prepared, even for unexpected challenges. In the courtroom, he owed his preparedness to his work ethic. In the wilderness, he owed it to his grandfather.

When George was ten, his rural-raised grandfather instilled in the youngster the importance of never leaving the cabin without two items: a book of matches and a pocketknife. When Josh reached the same age, Uncle George passed the invaluable lesson along, and replaced the pocketknife with a Swiss army knife, progressing with the times.

Indicative of the old man's advanced thought process, it wasn't a coincidence that the kidnappers didn't find those items in his pockets. After narrowly escaping the intruder from the prior break-in, George had wisely stowed the book of matches in his left sock, and the Swiss army knife in his right. Unaware at the time, his foresight saved his life. At least to this point.

George constructed his first campfire nestled up against a small manmade rock formation. The fireproof obstruction minimized the likelihood of signaling a flare to his captors. And as much as his thin-skinned body needed the heat, he had to be vigilant in not increasing the heat of the kidnappers' pursuit. He refueled his stomach, warmed his frigid appendages, and took a much-needed rest.

Without his watch, George didn't know exactly what time it was. If he could survive until sunrise, his chances of staying alive on a more permanent basis would improve significantly.

Clenching his survival stick close to his core, he sat and leaned against a towering lodgepole pine tree and closed his eyes. He desperately needed to sleep but knew better. He was in the wild, where untamed animals could surprise you at any time. As much as he required the sleep, the fear of waking up to a wild animal turning him on a spit over the firepit had to be at the forefront of his mind.

With the best of intentions to stay awake, life scoffed at George's plan. The nearby howling, branches cracking, and snow slushing didn't make a difference. After two deep breaths, exhaustion and the warmth of the fire overcame the trekker's inclination to stay awake and alert. He was out for the count. And depending on the intentions of his wild co-tenants, perhaps permanently.

* * *

A FEW HOURS later, a heavy thump on George's leg woke him in shock. And while nearly terrifying him to death, the frightened and disoriented squirrel proved itself a blessing in disguise.

It was nearly pitch-black outside. Only a single flame of George's fire, a few inches tall, flickered in the darkness. While it was closer to sunrise, when that was coming was unclear. What was clear was the roar in the distance, and likely what had startled the small furry animal. A tiny friend; seemingly sent to warn the snoring prey.

As familiar with the dangers of the Rocky Mountains as a park ranger, George shuttered at the signal announced by the hungry black bear. While typically avoiding close contact with humans, black bears would approach and could be dangerous if hungry enough. But despite George knowing that and not intending to fall asleep, the old man's limited food supply was enough to attract the keen-smelling bear, up early from hibernation.

Quickly, George tossed snow on the dwindling fire. Then, throwing the backpack over his shoulders and with the leverage of his weapon, he slowly stood up, making as little noise as possible. Gently, he tiptoed in the direction opposite the vicinity of the growling noise. He couldn't see it, but the disturbance trailing him indicated the animal was tracking the old man, mimicking his sluggish methodical pace.

Careful not to change his pattern, George proceeded in the same fashion for two-hundred yards, periodically looking back to make certain it wasn't gaining on him. And while the creature didn't appear to be closing the distance on George, nor did the old man seem to be outpacing the sly bear, which was tracking him easily with home field advantage.

Now faced with a lose-lose situation, George decided to remove his remaining food supply from his backpack. All that was left were a few canned foods. But with smell sensitivity vastly more potent than a human's, a bear could smell the food no matter how tightly it was packaged. Knowing that, George couldn't chance it. He dumped the last of his food supply and with it, nearly the last of his hope to survive.

Although less likely to attack humans than other types of bears, if the black bear did strike the old man, George would be dead in minutes. If the old-timer could manage to escape, even without food to eat, he'd be buying more time, improving the odds of his survival from impossible to highly improbable. And while not the best of odds, it was the only line Vegas was offering.

A few more minutes passed, but nothing changed. The canned goods didn't appear to slow the two-hundred-seventy-five-pound furry-coated male. The bear either ate on the go or anticipated more plentiful fuel up ahead.

Initially energized by adrenaline, George began to tire. His pace slowed. Sadly, for the sluggish hiker, the bear's didn't. The time was approaching to prepare for the worst. Still moving forward, but with a laboring trod, George repositioned his grip on his tree branch, from walking stick to a weapon, flaunting his best Zorro impression.

George plugged onward but slackened with every step. He couldn't have had more than fifty steps left in him when he stumbled upon a paved roadway through a clearing. More encouraging than the road itself was the label on a road sign announcing the best three words he had ever read: *Baby Doe Campground*.

Just like that, George had gone from a potentially dead John Doe in the wilderness, to a re-energized native, knowing precisely where he was and what he needed to do.

Baby Doe Campground was a small campsite located on the eastern shore of Turquoise Lake in the San Isabel National Forest, roughly thirty-six miles from Frisco. George had been fishing there countless times. He knew its layout well. He knew what to do and where to do it. The only problem was it was winter. And winter meant the campground was closed. More importantly, it meant his only shelter would be locked up for the winter. That aside, he had to give it a chance.

George's furry stalker was relentless, getting closer as the old man reached the two-door wooden shack that housed the campground's vault toilets. As was typical in the winter months, both doors were locked shut. No matter how hard George shook, the handles wouldn't budge. The heavy steps of the lumbering bear loomed closer. George's effort was pointless. And unlike his angelic squirrel friend from earlier, neither locked door was doing him any favors.

His left hand looked as if it was frozen to the Men's door. He continued to jiggle it, though nothing changed. Slowly, George turned his head. Behind him, breathing heavily, a black bear stopped thirty feet behind him. Likely familiar with humans frequenting the campgrounds, and associating food with those campers, the black bear didn't appear frightened by the frozen old man. He was simply hungry and had selected a frozen Italian T.V. dinner as his meal.

George leisurely leaned his nature-made weapon against the front wall, reached into his right coat pocket, and cautiously removed his Swiss army knife. In slow motion, he flipped the flathead screwdriver from its slot and inserted it into the key slot of the door handle and jiggled it. Turning his head slowly to check on his tracker, George continued to fidget with the lock at a more vigorous pace.

The bear took two steps toward George, then stopped, roaring something at the old man. Perhaps the indigenous bear needed to use the can first, possibly hoping to get *Charmin* clean. Normally, a courteous George would've deferred to the native inhabitant on his home turf. But tonight, survival outweighed social etiquette.

Led by another roar, the hairy beast traipsed forward. Stomp. Stomp. Stomp. George's heartbeat increased at the tempo of the bear's lumbering steps. The Swiss army knife jiggled faster than Santa's belly at a Chris Rock performance. Not from lack of effort, the lock wasn't budging.

Informed of being "black bear aware," George raised his arms, waved them slowly, and talked to the bear in a normal voice. Shocked? Yes. The bear stopped, tilted its head, and stared at the old man. Scared? Hardly. The bear roared back as if mocking the old man. After another roar for good measure, the bear thumped his way closer to George, seemingly tormenting the old geyser with his sluggish stride.

George slowly reached for his branch, then thought twice. At best, the stick would buy him seven extra breaths. With his back to the wall, literally and figuratively, he gradually redirected his attention back to the lock.

"Click." George heard a promising sound. Either that or his knife broke. Hopeful the result emulated the sound, he slowly turned the handle. It kept turning, followed by another click—the sound of a door latch sliding open.

Almost at a standstill, George softly, lightly, and calmly caressed the door open with his left hand; his eyes now locked in on the bear. His right hand subtly placed the knife in his pocket and reached for the branch, all in one slow, fluid motion.

With the door opening cracked about twenty inches, the old man gradually repositioned his aching frame, aimed to slide in, and slam the door shut. Judging by his disciplined approach, Smokey had other plans. Either his hiney longed for the diamond weave texture of the mega roll and he was seizing the opportunity, or the grass-berry-fruit-nut-and-plant-deprived animal was hangry, and the two-legged aged white meat was at the wrong place at the wrong time.

In slow motion, the bear continued his approach, now twelve feet away and closing. Eleven. Ten . . .

Silently mouthing a countdown from three, George prepared to make his move. "Three, two—"

Chapter Thirty-Two

L IVING TRUE TO his name, Geoff Summons arrived on time and ready to testify to the group of amateur sleuths as if he'd been subpoenaed to court. A far cry from formal testimony in a court of law, his information could prove more fruitful than any sworn court statements. Perhaps unlocking the mystery of the golden treasure. More critically, aiding the *FBI* in their search for George.

The *Gold Scammer's* son looked considerably younger than his early twenties. His boyish face, lanky build, and pale skin could've passed for pre-pubescent years. Were it not for his height, measuring six feet two inches, he might've snuck by purchasing a kid's lift ticket had he been in the ski mecca for recreational purposes. But tubing or snowboarding would have to wait.

As it were, the lean young man arrived with a box filled with his father's prison belongings. Prior to Geoff introducing himself and fortunate for his toothpick limbs, Josh's buff arms relieved the visitor of the box before it snapped the twigs hanging from his droopy shoulders.

After introductions, the hosts seated Geoff at one of the comfy armchairs nearest the soothing fireplace. Two of the dining chairs had been placed facing the armchair, for Josh and Kristen to sit, while Sam and Austin sat at the two chairs still grouped with the dining table. The plan was to make the pasty stranger feel welcome, increasing the likelihood he'd open up and speak freely.

Not certain if the young man was a coffee drinker, Kristen had a cup of hot chocolate ready for him once he was situated. Sporting the face of an eleven-year-old, the guest thanked her with child-like gratitude. With her comforting smile and delicate voice, Kristen took the lead.

"Geoff," she said. "First, we want to thank you for taking the time to talk with us. I know this can't be easy. I understand you just met your father for the first time in the past week. And before you got a chance to see him again, he died. Our sincerest condolences for your loss."

"Thank you," Geoff replied. He tilted his head down, stared at his feet, and shook his head. "I still can't believe it. I mean, what are the odds of that?"

"It certainly appears to be more than a coincidence," responded Kristen. "That's why we needed to talk with you."

With Kristen having broken the ice, Josh jumped in. "Geoff. I'm not sure what the warden told you—and I'm sorry if this makes matters worse—but," he paused, leaned forward slightly, and softly uttered, "we believe your father was murdered."

Kristen gazed over the youngster, quickly getting a read on him. "You don't look surprised."

"Quite honestly," Geoff said, "I'm not."

The response took Josh by surprise, causing him to blurt out, "You're not? I'm surprised you're not surprised. Shocked, more like it. If you don't mind me asking, why not?"

"A few things. First, when I left the prison with my father's possessions, I got a strange vibe from a couple of the guards. Like they were trying to rush me out. Not to mention, they insisted they could just toss his stuff so that I didn't have to lug around his worthless junk. Like they'd be doing me a huge favor. And of course, the timing of his death, relative to my visit and scheduled follow-up, seemed uncanny."

"You're certainly right about the timing." Josh investigated the fire, hoping the flames would spark his thought process. "Hmm. That's interesting. You said a *few* things. Was there something else?"

"Yes. I can't be certain, but I think somebody may have been following me on my drive up to Denver. About fifteen minutes into my trip, I noticed a car mimicking my actions—you know, like my speed and lane changing. By the time I was driving through Colorado Springs, I was almost certain."

"That's scary," Kristen said.

"Yeah. I was starting to feel a little shaken up. So, when it seemed like I was near downtown Colorado Springs— you know, taller buildings and all— I exited I-25, made a few quick turns on some crowded streets, zipped through a yellow light, and the suspicious car on my tail got nailed from the side trying to clear the intersection. I heard the crash, checked my rear-view mirror, then hustled back to I-25 toward Denver and didn't look back."

"Quick thinking," said Kristen. "Thank goodness you made it here safely. We're glad you're okay."

"So, why don't we start with what you can tell us about your father, the infamous William Clybourne," Josh said. "Then you can show us what's in the box. After that, we'll see if or how everything ties into what we know and then see if we can start to make more sense of this."

"I'll do my best. Unfortunately, I knew very little about my father. Until recently, he's been a mystery to me my entire life. When my mother finally told me who he was, she said very little about him." Geoff stopped. His eyes watered. He took a deep breath before he was able to finish. "And now she can't tell me anything more. She died this past year."

"I'm so sorry," comforted Kristen. "Do you need to take a break? Or can I get you some more hot chocolate? Or how about a donut?"

"No, thank you. I'm fine." Geoff took another deep breath, exhaled, and continued. "On the plus side, because my mother told me so very little, I probably remember everything she said about him."

"That's looking at the glass half-full," said Josh. "Why don't you just tell us what you remember, and we'll go from there?"

"My mother met him on a blind double date twenty-something years ago. Went to a concert. They hit it off, became serious, then my mom became pregnant with me. But, before I was born, she learned about the scam he'd gotten involved in, so she left him. She'd told him she was pregnant, but then she left shortly after. So, he didn't know a thing about me until I visited him a few days ago."

"Did your mother tell you anything else about him?" asked Josh.

"She said he grew up in Summit County. I believe in Frisco. Never got past high school, but he was very smart. A computer whiz. Talked about getting rich someday by starting his own tech company. Until then, to pay the bills, he worked mostly as a day laborer. Some building construction type of work. You know, blue-collar stuff. He loved riddles and was obsessed with numbers. Particularly, the number three. And he loved music. Even more so because he met my mother at a concert."

"Obsessed with the number three?" Kristen asked. "What do you mean by that?"

"Well, my mom told me that he always said things happen in threes, and the third time's a charm. And it just so happens they met on his third blind date which occurred on the third day of the third month. Crazy, huh?" Geoff closed his eyes, looking deep in thought. Suddenly, they popped open. "Oh yeah, another thing. When I visited him, I noticed he had the number three tattooed on the back of his hand."

"Hmm. That's interesting," remarked Josh. "Interesting and helpful."

Sam and Austin sat quietly at the table, sipping coffee, and nibbling on donuts, all the while discreetly listening in while Austin took notes.

"Other than the tattoo," Kristen said, pointing to the back of her hand, "did you learn anything else during your visit with him?"

"Not really. I'm not sure if you all were aware, but he was terminally ill. He mentioned that. I also told him my mom had recently died, which came as a shock to him. Other than that, there wasn't much said. It was very short and awkward. Quite simply, I just wanted to meet him and hear him apologize. To say he was sorry for lying to my mom and hurting her. Sorry, that I had to grow up without a father because he placed greed over family. Just sorry." Geoff stared into the fire.

"From your tone," Kristen said softly, giving a sympathetic head tilt, "I'm guessing you didn't get the apology you were hoping for?"

"Not really," Geoff replied, shaking his head. "It wasn't until I walked away that he kinda clued in."

"Why do you say that?" asked Josh.

"Well, as I walked away from him, he started babbling something, then finally yelled he was sorry."

Josh leaned in toward Geoff. "Babbling? What was he babbling?"

"Something like come back. I'll tell you everything. Where the gold is. The bank account information. Everything. Then the guard shut the door behind me, and I was gone." Geoff paused, sniffled, took another breath, then continued. "I'm not sure if he knew it, but I scheduled a follow-up visit with him. But, of course, before that could happen, he died. Or, as you suspect, was killed."

"Geoff, you said that you got a strange vibe from a couple of the guards when you returned to pick up your father's belongings." Josh crinkled his eyebrows, as he pondered a possible link between a couple of things Geoff mentioned. "Did you happen to notice if one of those guards was the same guard standing by when you visited your father?"   Geoff didn't answer right away, seemingly thinking about that for the first time. "Now that you mention it, I think he was." After a short pause, he looked at Josh and asked, "Do you think that's a coincidence?"

Kristen responded, "Josh isn't a very firm believer in coincidences."

"It's likely that William was silenced to prevent him from telling you what he knew," Josh said. "And what he knew likely was more than any living person on Earth. Speaking of which, did your mother ever mention any of his friends or associates?"

"Not a one. At least from what I can recall."

"Alright then," Josh sighed. "Now that we know what your father told you before he died, let's see what his belongings can tell us."

Chapter Thirty-Three

EVEN THE COLD mountain air couldn't mask the stench of a dead body. The pre-dawn bout between the tenacious, hefty creature and the drained, geriatric was such a gross mismatch that Vegas had stopped taking bets. The size and strength comparisons were a joke. Not to mention, the bear enjoyed the perks of home-field advantage. But somehow, defying overwhelming odds favoring nature, brains beat brawn.

Despite age, exhaustion, elevation, and numbing temperatures, George bought himself more time with his soon-to-be-patented *shift, shimmy, and slam* move. Fred Astaire never looked so graceful. Justin Timberlake, never so smooth.

But for the grace of God, George survived one force of nature—the hangry bear. His reward, he now had to survive another—the ensuing odor *when nature calls*. Specifically, the putrid air polluting campground vault toilets.

Undoubtedly, George would've preferred the stench of a corpse over the wretched smell of the six-by-eight-foot solitary confinement space of the vaulted toilet room. The former prosecutor had sat in on his fair share of autopsies. The gases and compounds produced in a decomposing body were utterly disgusting. But with a dab of *Vicks* under the nose, the noxious odors could be neutralized. Unfortunately for George, he hadn't passed a twenty-four-hour pharmacy before caging himself into the campground's cesspool.

On the plus side, the vault had been emptied for the winter season. That's not to say that it smelled like a flower shop. Undeniably, it smelled like crap. But at least it wasn't ninety degrees in mid-July, with a vault filled to the same capacity as the fifty-one campsites at the peak of camping season.

George's furry nighttime shadow had scratched at the door for a few minutes, then calmed and sat outside the door for quite some time. Evidently, soft toilet paper was at the top of the bear's bucket list. Unfortunately for the patient paws, the old man had other plans for the lone roll of toilet paper. Tearing out one-foot strips, George had placed several in the sink, lit it with a match, and warmed the septic ice box. Meanwhile, the vented opening near the top of the side wall exchanged the indoor smoky air with the outdoor frigid air.

After the smoke had cleared, the tired old-timer dropped to the concrete floor with his back resting upon the door. He sighed deeply. His eyes grew heavy. Unzipping the backpack fully, George placed it on his lap like a blanket, then snuggled his limbs into his chest, utilizing every inch of his warm coat.

From the heavy breathing on the opposite side, George must've figured one of two things was happening: either his furry friend was still hanging around; or he was being rescued via human intervention, albeit by a phone sex operator. With the likelihood of it being the former, George sat patiently. Within two minutes, the old man was doing his best imitation of his outdoor companion, seemingly hibernating for the rest of winter.

* * *

BY THE TIME he came up from his long winter's nap, the sunshine was beaming bright, with rays of light peering through the vent as if sent from heaven. How many hours had George been sleeping? Heck, how many days?

The temperature was considerably warmer. Only two things could account for that. One, Colorado weather was infamous for changing drastically on a dime, especially during winter. Going from ten degrees to sixty-five in less than twenty-four hours was not uncommon. The other possibility was the old man, from sheer exhaustion, had slept 'til springtime. For all he knew, there was a camper waiting outside the door, desperately seeking relief after a stainless-steel-percolated morning cup of joe.

George's enlarged prostate hadn't gone so long without waking the old man in thirty years. Conveniently, he simply had to stand, take two steps forward, and voila—a toilet. Sadly, standing was far from simple. Problematic, burdensome, and laborious more aptly described the effort needed to pull his aged and weary bones to the standing position. And after it'd taken him a minute to stand, he spent another ninety seconds peeing, rivaling Tom Hanks' pee scene in *A League of Their Own*.

Outside the putrid confines of George's overnight shack, it was tranquil. Other than a few birds chirping, it was quiet. From the sound of it, or lack thereof, the thick-coated creature couldn't wait any longer, perhaps settling for *Angel Soft* or *Quilted Northern* at another vault toilet facility. But still, he waited. And with his eyes shut, he listened. He knew the black bear was smart. George had to be smarter.

Like Moses holding his staff at the parting of the Red Sea, George clenched his branch and parted the door from the jamb. Edging it open, he pinned his ears back with his eyes peeled open. Then, with both hands gripped to the stick, he pointed it outward, ready, willing, and able to ignore one of nature's hard and fast rules—don't poke the bear.

Using his hip to prop the door, George raised the stick as it led the way out the door with his head closely following. He peeked to his right. Clear. Suddenly, a rustling noise to his left caused him to whip his head around, and with it, his "weapon." His eyes shifted back and forth. Nothing. Nothing—until something appeared. Something very familiar from his "dead man walking" stroll the preceding night.

Swiftly, a squirrel scampered across George's path, then stopped. Raising to its hind legs, it turned to the old man, paused, and squeaked out something. If George had to guess, the same bear-warning squirrel had returned to him looking for a little gratitude.

"What the heck," George said aloud to himself. Then, with a smile and a nod directed at the tiny furball, he muttered, "Thank you for saving my life." George chuckled as the swift little animal appeared to dip him a nod, then scurried off into the woods.

Just as night had turned to daytime, like the clear morning sky, George's future looked brighter. He knew his location. He knew the road into it. And more importantly, he knew his way out and where it would take him.

Just six miles away rested the second most populous city in the state of Colorado—if it was the late 1800s. Presently, Leadville, Colorado hardly could be described as populous. In fact, that'd be the last word used to describe the former silver mining town summiting more than ten thousand feet above sea level. The town, covering slightly more than one square mile, now had a population of only half that of its heyday, when it had reached more than five thousand residents during the peak of the gold rush. Now, it was famous for two things: having a view of multiple 14,000-foot mountain peaks, and the distinction as the city boasting the highest elevation in the United States.

George scanned the area, orienting himself as to which direction he'd come from when he outpaced his furry stalker just hours earlier. Why? He needed fuel. At an average of three miles per hour, at best given his age and fatigue, he'd be in town in two hours. But, looking weak and depleted, a six-mile walk might as well have been sixty for a man over eighty and dragging along on an empty stomach.

After careful examination of his surroundings, he spotted it. Ten yards from the toilet facility was a large garbage bin, with a padlock in place for the off-season. Two giant steps to the left of the bin marked two tracks of steps, George's, and those of the bear. It was a longshot, but the old man was riding a hot streak, having beaten the house all night long. And like most die-hard gamblers, he was willing to parlay on his luck until it ran out.

With lady luck still on his side, George backtracked the short distance, praying his dumped food supply remained undisturbed. He paced the distance until he figured he'd be in the ballpark, then meticulously searched the area. With a fresh trail from the human and the animal recently pressed into the snow, elation or disappointment was nearby. George's stomach growled, crying for food.

Then, as George gazed between a towering subalpine fir and a two-hundred-year-old lodgepole pine that had thwarted countless fatal attacks from the mountain pine beetle, he spotted it—food packaging intact. And with it came elation at elevation. But for the time being, his celebration would have to wait. Not wasting any time, eight minutes later he'd refueled, backtracked on his backtrack, and was on the road toward downtown Leadville.

Pushing himself east on County Road 9, George slowed for a break some fifty-three minutes into his journey. Perhaps it was good karma following a good man—the weather was cooperating. Well, maybe not good karma, as he'd just escaped his abduction and near-murder the previous day. But, all things considered, his prospects were looking up. The sunshine was beaming, the temperature was moderate, and civilization was only a short distance away.

Beside the road, the old-timer's taxed legs led him to a sizeable, flat rock, begging to be used as a bench. George's legs obliged, irrespective of his desire to tread forward. He wiped the ten-inch patch of shaded snow that had escaped the melting powers of the close winter sun and plopped his behind on the chilled stone slab. *Better my butt sitting on this frozen granite slab than my back lying on a cold metal slab* undoubtedly crossed his mind.

George took a deep breath, then grumbled as he struggled to stand up. Another deep breath, and once again, he puttered east on the quiet road. An unexpected sound prompted him to stop and scan the forest. Despite the rustling, he didn't see the source of distraction and pushed forward.

"Oh my gosh," he said aloud, squinting to focus on the image approaching east to west. "Thank God!" He hustled to the middle of the road, ready to flag down an oncoming vehicle that eased in his direction at a purposeful speed.

"Hey! Help!" George waved his arms over his head, practicing his audition as a jumping jack instructor at a Florida retirement community. "Please, stop!"

Forty yards away and closing, the vehicle slackened from slow to slower. With the sun in his eyes, George shielded them with the palm of his right hand. Aside from the prominent glare, there appeared to be two people in the vehicle, both dark-complected.

Now twenty yards away, it became evident George's cry for help had fallen on willing ears. The vehicle slowed. George stepped back two steps to allow the vehicle to pull up beside the tired and hungry escapee. And while George may have been craving pancakes, surely he didn't want to become one.

Crawling to a stop, the vehicle that had poured relief over the old man two seconds earlier, now had him praying for relief. The two occupants weren't dark complected. Or maybe they were. George had no way of knowing because their faces were hidden. Ski masks once again disguised his unrelenting abductors.

Before George could make a run for it, the passenger had jumped from the vehicle, grabbed the old man, covered his head, and zip-tied his wrinkled wrists. George wrestled for his life, but age and fatigue were not on his side. Nonetheless, George squirmed and wrestled, determined to make his abductor show his worth. The old man was educated as a lawyer but born a soldier.

Suddenly, George found himself floundering untouched. Next, he heard the back door of the vehicle open. Two seconds passed. George took one step to make a run for it. His second step never reached land.

"Whack!" George fell to the ground as his back felt a blow akin to the one the old man had delivered to a devilish skull the previous night. Rising to his knees, George refused to stand as the thug labored to pull up the stubborn old goat, aiming to toss him into the back seat like a sack of groceries.

"Oh shit!" yelled the driver. "We gotta get outta here."

Blinded by the dark pillowcase over his head, George had no clue what had hurried the driver's plan. Nor did he have time to think about it.

"Wham!" The hollowing knock of a nightstick walloping a human head echoed through the soaring evergreens, reverberating loud enough to trigger an avalanche or two. George was out before the speed of sound could relay to his ears the crack of his skull. He flopped to the unyielding roadway, one that unkindly delivered a second blow to the fossil's smashed cranium as it flopped to the asphalt.

Habitual failures, the vehicle's tires screeched as they peeled west toward Turquoise Lake. In a flash, the kidnappers were gone. Or at least far enough to escape identification as a second vehicle stopped beside the lifeless, I.D.-less body.

Chapter Thirty-Four

THE PRISONER'S BOX of belongings didn't contain much. His son retrieved it so quickly the corrupt guards hadn't gotten around to sifting through the *Gold Scammer's* limited possessions. Not to say they hadn't done so on numerous previous occasions.

Having read the note several times, Geoff had removed it from its home amid the pages of the thick, heavy book, and secured it in a blank white envelope. Josh cleared a small end table next to the bed and set it beside his chair. Geoff pulled out four books, two picture frames, and the crisp, new envelope and placed them on the table.

"That's it?" asked Josh, as he lifted the empty box from the floor, aimlessly reached inside, then looked up to Geoff with disappointment.

"That's it. My father allegedly went from millions to this."

"Talk about downsizing," Kristen snickered.

Josh flipped through the two "money" books, looking for notes, marks, bent corners, anything. A clue. A hint. A speck of evidence. What he found, was nothing. It'd looked as if they'd been read several times, but nothing else. He repeated the process with the book of quotes. And while it seemed like it'd been read thousands of times, no indications of any clues stood out.

Optimistic that the fourth book would be their savior, Josh reverently placed the *Holy Bible* on his lap. "Say a prayer that we find something useful in this book," he said, then looked up to Good Lord and added, "besides the obvious, of course."

Like the God-loving disciple that she was, Kristen gestured a sign of the cross. Josh, a former altar boy, parroted his girlfriend, then began flipping pages until he fanned all the way through it. He repeated the same process four times, each slower than the last; his eyes laser focused. But like the other books, the large book looked well read, but nothing more. His super-scanner baby blue eyes didn't catch anything. Absolutely nothing jumped from the pages.

With it closed and resting on his lap, Josh rested his overlapped hands atop the good book. He sighed deeply, then sneezed. As his hands rose to cover his mouth, he felt the book expand on his lap. Curious, he pressed it down on his thighs, then released it. Like an accordion, it spread out as quickly as the weight of his muscular arms had compressed it.

"Did you see that?" Josh asked Kristen.

"Yep. And look," she responded, "there's a distinctive gap right here." She pointed to the prominent page separation in the twelve-hundred-page book.

Josh opened the *Holy Bible* to the parting, wherein the following passage of Genesis: 6:1-3 was circled in pen:

And it came to pass, when men began to multiply on the face of the earth, and daughters were born unto them, that the sons of God saw the daughters of men that they were fair; and they took them wives of all which they chose. And the LORD said, My spirit shall not always strive with man, for that he also is flesh: yet his days shall be an hundred and twenty years.

"Hmm. We'll have to circle back to that. No pun intended." Josh looked Geoff in the eyes, pointing to the #10 envelope in his hands. "Was that envelope in here?"

"Not the envelope," Geoff answered, pulling out the tattered letter encased by the pristine envelope. "But this was." He handed it to Josh.

Carefully, Josh unfolded the fragile paper. It had been folded and unfolded so many times, the frequent handling of it aged it such that, if the first three words written on it were "We the People," Josh wouldn't have been surprised. Half expecting to be reading the preamble to the U.S. Constitution. Josh glanced over the letter, then read aloud:

To My Sole Survivor,

Never in a million years did I ever think it would end like this, not even in my wildest dreams. I'm sure it's too late, but I hope this can make up for my years of absence. Time and time again, I wanted to reach out to you, hoping to meet you, praying you were well. And days like these, I wish I had.

Your entire life, your mother possibly created a false image of me to protect you, or more likely, never mentioned me at all. If that was her choice, we did not see eye to eye. Whatever she told you, you'd be lying to yourself to pretend I never existed. It's time to open your eyes to the true man that I am, which is hardly a man at all.

Now, only time will tell how you remember me. However that is, please don't cry at the darkness shadowed by my past but ride easy toward the daylight that lies ahead.

First, however, to reap the rewards of my past sins, you must <u>remove</u> the unnecessary and go to the start. The links to the present wealth are at the beginning of my past. You don't need to travel the ups and downs to Palmer Lake, Colorado, or put your wet suit on, in order to unriddle how to find the fruits of my crime.

In the words of British physicist Oliver Lodge, "Life must be considered <u>sui</u> generis; it is not a form of energy, nor can it be expressed in terms of something else."

In the words of Ronald Reagan, "Within the covers of the Bible are the answers for all the problems men face."

In the words of Robert Frost, "In three words I can sum up everything I've learned about life: it goes on."

In the words of actress Julie Andrews, "If you're not educated to enjoy the arts, if you're not taken to a concert, or you don't hear something beautiful, you don't know what you're missing."

Love,

William (your father)

Josh gazed at Geoff and asked, "Does anything jump out at you?"

"Nope," a discouraged look masked Geoff's face as he shook his head at Josh. "I was gonna ask you the exact same thing. To me, it's very confusing."

"Very cryptic," said Kristen.

"Very puzzling," commented Austin.

"Very obscure," remarked Sam.

"Very familiar," declared Josh. "I can't put my finger on it just yet. But there's something poking at my brain. Do you mind if I take a picture of this?"

"Help yourself."

Josh snapped a photo of the letter, then reached forward to hand it back to Geoff. His thighs angled slightly downward, causing the Bible to slide down. Josh's quick reflexes lurched his hands forward to grab it mid-air, but the heavy book slipped from his fingertips. Awkwardly, the good book hit the ground with the cover flapped open like a soaring eagle's wings, and hundreds of pages smashed against the floor. Swiftly and respectfully, Josh picked it up. As he did, a note fell to the floor.

His eyes focused on the surprise laying at his feet. "Hey, what's that?" he said, placing the Bible on the table, then grabbing the note.

Josh read it aloud, "In everyone's life, at some time, our inner fire goes out. It then burst into flame by an encounter with another human being. We should all be thankful for those people who rekindle the inner spirit. — Albert Schweitzer."

"Oh my gosh! I forgot to tell you," Geoff blurted. "There was something written on the back of the photo of my mother. And that's what it was." He picked up the photo of his mother, popped out the cardboard backing of the picture frame, and handed the rest to Josh. "See."

Kristen turned to Josh. "Hmm. Do you think—"

Josh read her mind and completed her sentence, "That it's the final message that was never sent to Uncle George? It's certainly possible."

"Hey guys," Austin jumped in as he dragged his chair ninety degrees to his left. "Sorry to interrupt, but I just got an email from the court reporter about the transcript request."

"Please tell me she found it," Josh said, crossing his fingers.

"Better," Austin said. "She attached it to her email."

"Well Geoff," Kristen added, "your father harped on things happening in threes. Looks like he practiced what he preached. If the transcript has any riddled clues to the puzzle, confirming what he had claimed at his sentencing hearing. That's one. The messages he sent to Josh's uncle. That's two. And the cryptic letter to you. Three."

"Kristen. If you're right, we'll now have an advantage that no one has ever had in the past twenty years. Three different paths to solving the mystery." As quickly as Josh's optimism rose, reality swiftly shot it down. Josh's eyes dropped to the floor, shaking his hand in disgust.

"What's wrong Mr. Rizzetti?" Geoff asked, clearly confused by Josh's demeanor. "Isn't that a good thing?"

In tune with Josh's mind and his feelings, and essentially seeing the heavy lump form in his throat, Kristen spoke for him. "It may lead us to whatever your father hid, which could be worth millions. But will it help us find whoever abducted Josh's uncle?" She paused, then whispered, "Assuming he's still alive."

Josh stood from his chair, returned the photo to Geoff, then squatted next to the fireplace. "There *is* one other thing I can think of to help us find Uncle George's kidnappers. Though time is not on our side, so it's gotta be done tonight."

"What is it?" asked Austin.

"To give you all plausible deniability, I can't tell you." Josh hesitated to speak further, then confessed, "And there *is* some risk to it."

The oldest and wisest jumped into the mix. "*Some* risk," Sam repeated. "Exactly how much?"

"If I get caught, at best, I'll be disbarred."

"Disbarred! At *best*?" Kristen shrieked, seemingly terrified to inquire further. "Dare I ask the worst outcome?"

Josh held a long pause, inhaled deeply, then stammered, "I'll get killed."

Chapter Thirty-Five

T HE OLD MAN lay peacefully in a new bed of the recently opened $26-million hospital in Leadville, Colorado. He hadn't experienced such comfort in three nights. Were it not for the minor disturbance—a coma—he might've appreciated the accommodations.

The witness had described the thread-shredding thump of the maple stick striking the baseball-shaped head of the old man to the first responding officer, who in turn relayed the same to the hospital staff. The treating physician emphasized it was nothing short of a miracle that any victim could survive such a crushing blow, let alone an elderly man. "He must be some kind of superhero," the doctor had commented.

For all they knew, George could've been Superman, Spiderman, or even Ironman. Bottom line was that they had no clue who he was. He had no I.D. on him, and they hadn't received a single inquiry from any panicked relatives trying to track down the whereabouts of an Alzheimer-suffering patriarch. Nor had there been any recent missing person reports in a seventy-five-mile radius.

Both curious and alarmed as to why someone would deliver such a beating to a defenseless old man, the chief of staff requested a uniformed officer sit guard outside George's room. The Leadville Police Department obliged, sitting in a rookie uniform outside the ancient John Doe's room.

*　*　*

AUSTIN HAD FORWARDED a copy of the *Gold Scammer's* trial transcript to the rest of the team, as well as to Clybourne's son for good measure. Before doing so, he highlighted the portions in which the defendant had testified to save them time. Likely, had the criminal left clues to the whereabouts of his ill-gotten gains, it would've been in his testimony.

Of particular note, his testimony tight roped the edge of insanity. Mostly a combination of nonresponsive drivel and pleading the fifth, one would've wagered he had entered a plea of not guilty by reason of insanity. The kicker was that he entered no such plea. Rather, he entered a simple plea of not guilty. No claim of insanity. No pipe dream to spend his time institutionalized in a mental hospital rather than caged in the federal pokey.

It was as if the *Gold Scammer* acted insane, after failing to enter the requisite plea. Why? Possibly to claim ineffective assistance of counsel on appeal down the road. After all, what attorney worth his salt would've bypassed requesting a psych evaluation on someone who incessantly broke out in gibberish? And, as Josh read through the transcript, he concluded that, while it was *a strategy*, it was a bad one. Had Josh been defending the con artist, *that strategy* not only wouldn't be advised, it wouldn't have garnered a breath.

Setting aside his legal criticisms, Josh read through the defendant's testimony four times. Each time, the same things gripped his attention, almost blinding him from the rest of transcript. In part, it was the quirkiness of what was said that captivated Josh's attention. But perhaps more so, it was the way in which the defendant's testimony was delivered. According to the court reporter's rendition, the accused sang two of his responses.

Trying to make heads or tails of it, Josh jotted the following excerpts of the defendant's cross-examination on his notepad:

> *Q: If your business was on the up and up, why did you feel the need to open a bank account in Grand Junction under a false name?*

> *A: (Defendant sang) Grand Junction junction, what's your function?*

> *Q: You heard the testimony of our expert who traced the website, and its money funneling system, as coming from your IP address. Isn't it true that you were the tech wizard behind this?*

A: I plead the fifth, located between first and second.

Q: In fact, isn't it true that you were not only the techie but also the mastermind behind the entire operation? Essentially, the jack-of-all-trades?

A: Jack-of-all-trades, you say. Hardly. (Then defendant sang) I'm just a Bill. Yes, I'm only a Bill. And I'm sitting here on Capitol Hill.

Josh interrupted the group's study time and read his notes aloud. "Is it just me, or does Mr. Clybourne imitating a Broadway musical throw up a red flag? What's the deal with that?"

Sam laughed, then responded to Josh's semi-rhetorical questions. "Huh. That's right. None of you are Gen Xers, are you? So, you're all too young to have watched it as a kid."

"Watched what?" asked Austin.

"When my children were grammar school age," Sam said, "there was a kid's show called *Schoolhouse Rock*. It had a bunch of short segments that taught certain subjects—like grammar—by way of catchy, jingle-like songs. Two of the most memorable were 'I'm Just a Bill' and 'Conjunction Junction.'" He paused, then chuckled. "Great. Now those darn things are stuck in my head."

"Hmm. I just looked up *Schoolhouse Rock*," Kristen said. "It says here that the pilot episode was entitled 'Three Is a Magic Number.'"

"*Three*," said Geoff. "My father's favorite number."

"Alright then," replied Josh. "I'd say that Bill's attempt to win a *Tony* certainly warrants a red flag."

Bouncing back and forth between the three sets of clues, the *Frisco Bureau of Investigators* and their guest read, studied, noted, and brainstormed for hours, undoubtedly losing track of time. In the midst of it, Kristen had ordered some pizzas that were eaten in their entirety within twenty minutes of delivery. Once again, Josh was more than impressed with the pizza pies of the Rocky Mountains. And plainly unable to limit his consumption, soon his frame would mimic the enormity of the majestic peaks.

Kristen heard the groans as her rubbernecked gaze read the room. Josh's moans stemmed from overeating. Everyone else appeared to be hitting the wall. And although Kristen was the one most capable, and accustomed to reviewing documents for hours—nonstop—someone had to put an end to it before a head exploded or eyes started bleeding. At the very least, it'd be best if the collaborative effort halted for the evening. Determined to see things through to the end, Sam and Austin stressed their commitment to plugging away when they got home as Kristen shoved them out the door.

As to Geoffrey Summons, Josh offered to spring for a room at the B&B if the *Gold Scammer's* son wished to stick around a while longer. With a new job starting in a week, and no family waiting for him, the young man graciously accepted and strolled downstairs to the only available room at the inn.

As the door shut behind Geoff, Kristen spouted, "So, what's the plan that could get you killed? Whatever it is, count me in."

"Are you kidding me?" Josh snapped. "No way. I may've already lost Uncle George." His voice cracked. His eyes moistened. "I'm not putting your life at risk too. Period!"

"Josh, I appreciate your concern. I do. But again, it's not for you to decide. You are not my keeper."

"I know I'm not. It's just that—"

"It's just that—nothing," retorted Kristen. "If I say I'm in, I'm in. You can't stop me."

Josh inhaled deeply from his nose, then strongly exhaled out his mouth. "I'm not going to win this one, am I?"

"I think we both know the answer to that. Don't we?"

Josh raised his eyebrows at Kristen, shook his head, then exhaled in defeat.

"Okay, you win," caved Josh. "We need to buy a couple of decent flashlights and rubber gloves."

Chapter Thirty-Six

THE MIDNIGHT VANDAL'S place, only nine short blocks from Main Street, had been taped off by the Frisco Police Department immediately upon the discovery of his untimely death preceding his upcoming criminal trial. His murder added the final piece of evidence indicating his random act of vandalism was in fact not random at all. Rather, as speculated, it not only tied into the hunt for the golden treasure but also corroborated a theory that the lone actor might be part of a larger crew; his murder being necessary to ensure the anonymity of the mastermind and perhaps punishment for a greedy underling going rogue.

To safeguard potential evidence, the police draped yellow tape across the front door that blocked the entryway to an indoor staircase that led to the deceased's second-floor apartment. Around the back, police tape marked a giant "X" across the wrought-iron gated balcony that overlooked a fifteen-by-twenty-foot grassy patch, dormant for the winter, and outlined by acres of wild forest. A ten-year-old Aspen tree centered the grass area, with its leafless branches just beyond the reach of the cantilevered balcony.

* * *

TO MINIMIZE THE risk of getting caught, the fearless duo planned to break in around midnight. With no snow in the forecast, darkness would be their friend. Already equipped with ski caps to keep their hair under wraps, the rubber gloves eliminated the possibility of leaving behind print evidence. And though the apartment would've already been swept, printed, and analyzed for evidence, the legal geniuses left nothing to chance.

Cross every "t", dot every "i." Josh ran a replay in his mind of Uncle George's seminar before the couple discussed the details of their plan. Next, a quick drive to the store, where they purchased their supplies; paying cash—of course. A credit card purchase of rubber gloves and two flashlights for a couple on vacation—while innocuous if the breaking and entering escaped attention—could pave the way to a slam dunk conviction if discovered.

They hit a drive-thru on the way back to the inn, grabbing burgers and fries to fuel up for their midnight adventure to the *Midnight Vandal's* valueless probate estate housed in the confines of a one-bedroom apartment. Of course, the value to Josh and Kristen wasn't in the murdered victim's possessions. A torn piece of notepaper with an address could prove more valuable to them than if they were to stumble across the fifty-nine-point-six carat *Pink Star* diamond. The former could lead them to the location of the kidnappers' headquarters; the latter could lead them to serve two dimes in "the big house." After all, the mission was to save Uncle George's life, not ruin theirs.

Two double-cheeseburgers, a large order of fries, and a thirty-two-ounce cola had Josh five pounds heavier and ten times sleepier. And given that he was already half asleep, they decided he'd nap for a couple of hours, then Kristen would follow suit. While having no prior experience, they assumed being well rested for an illegal nighttime scavenger hunt in a dead man's apartment was crucial. While awake, each could do research and attempt to decipher the clues, while also standing guard should the burner phone ring.

Josh's snoring rivaled the peak decibel record set at Mile High Stadium during a Denver Broncos' sellout. Kristen repeatedly shook her head and sighed, obviously distracted by the sleeping locomotive fifteen feet away. She probably thought of smothering his face with a pillow, then hesitated at the thought of committing two felonies in one night. She hadn't so much as got a traffic ticket her entire life, so burglary *and* murder in one night may have seemed a bit too ambitious.

Music. She needed music to drown out the infuriating disturbance. She grabbed her earbuds from the nightstand, then patted her pockets for her phone. She paused, then surveyed the room. Its whereabouts, unknown.

In the pandemonium that had followed George's abduction, Kristen hadn't once needed her smartphone. An entire day, and she hadn't thought of it once. It was only now that she searched for it, desperate to muffle the foghorn sprawled across the king-size bed. It was nowhere to be found.

Unsuccessful in her hunt, she sat back down in front of her computer and closed her eyes in reflection. Her rolling eyeballs combed the corners of her mind on a quest to recall her phone's last known location.

"Oh," she exhaled, then whispered, "I must've left it at George's cabin." From a thirty-something-year-old's reference, she'd gone ostensibly forever without "needing" it. The world kept turning. Who would've thought? That being the case, recovering it could wait.

Making do, she grabbed Josh's phone, connected the Bluetooth to her earbuds, and focused on the music in one ear; albeit stifled by the deafening roar lounged over the bed. She snickered as she stared at Josh, noticing that he'd undone the top button of his pants. Either that, or it had shot across the room faster than a New Year's Eve cork when the expanding prosecutor's butt hit the sheets.

Without question, finding George was the most pressing matter. Focused on that goal, Kristen redirected her attention to the cryptic message, as recorded by Josh. She listened intently, then listened again. Then again. The music was distracting her, the snoring was disturbing her. Before she could get beyond what they had already figured out about the cards, Josh awoke and sat beside her.

"Here," Kristen said, handing Josh his phone. "You should focus on the recording while I focus on the back of my eyelids."

Exhausted, Kristen was asleep before Josh could finish round one of listening to Uncle George's enigmatic message:

In the words of my second favorite Josh, 'Life consists not in holding the good cards but in playing those you hold well.' That's how to beat a wheeler and dealer. And always treasure our wild trip to the Monterey Bay Aquarium when you were twelve and you found the answer you'd sought during that chapter of your life. I love you son.

Josh replayed what he already knew, careful to make sure he hadn't missed anything before moving on to the final half of the message. The second favorite Josh was a reference to Josh Billings. The quote about the cards was made famous by the nineteenth-century writer and humorist.

Impatient and ready to make new headway, Josh moved on to the next part, assuming for now they'd deciphered the meaning behind the quote. The "wheeler and dealer" blurb simply may have referred to the cards, like a dealer at a casino. So he put that on hold.

For the final two sentences, Josh focused on certain words, namely: *treasure, Monterey Bay Aquarium, twelve, found, answer, sought,* and *chapter.* He faced Kristen's laptop, his posture upright. First, he opted to search the most prominent clue, the *Monterey Bay Aquarium.* He typed it into the search engine, first to scan the results to see if anything popped, then to delve further.

The results of his search included the main website of the tourist attraction that summarized itself as being "located at the ocean's edge on historic Cannery Row, the Monterey Bay Aquarium is your window to marine life." Josh dug deeper, woefully finding no mention of the words *treasure, twelve,* or *chapter.* He crossed out the other words, concluding they were too generic, especially when researching an attraction centered on informing and educating its visitors.

Clicking and scanning the search results, Josh's eyes grew heavy. Reading had that effect on him, particularly gazing into the eye-straining blue light of the computer screen. It started when he was in college and had continued ever since. Twenty to thirty minutes of reading, and his tired eyes more resembled weighted barbells. Forty minutes into Kristen's nap time, Josh's forehead dipped slowly toward the keyboard until his muscular neck stopped it just shy of his chin plopping to his chest.

Far into dreamland, the sleepy lawyer fell from his chair at the sound of his phone alarm, which inadvertently had been set to the highest volume. His reflexes launched Josh upward before gravity plummeted him to the floor. And if the piercing alarm didn't wake Kristen, the heavy thump of her expanding pizza-dough-waisted companion—followed by him bellowing "What the?"—most certainly did.

The meticulous couple reviewed the plan one more time. Responding to Josh's text request, Austin had sent him the address of the *Midnight Vandal*—no questions asked—keeping plausible deniability somewhat intact.

Conceivably within walking distance, nonetheless, the criminally bound couple elected to drive the three-quarters of a mile and parked one block from the murder victim's apartment, then hoofed the rest. Decked in black from head to toe, it was as if two sets of the Invisible Man's footprints left tracks in the snow. Meticulously planned down to their underwear, they could hardly see one another walking merely three feet apart.

They reached the target's apartment, first walking by to catch a glimpse and get a lay of the land. The building was modest, maybe seven thousand square feet. It was encased in wood siding, freshly stained a dark redwood tone, and topped with a gray slate tile roof. It appeared to house eight symmetrical units; four on top and four below. Each set of top and bottom apartments had the entry doors side-by-side; the first being the door to the bottom unit, the next to the apartment above.

Fortunately for the rookie criminals, the *Midnight Vandal's* unit was in the final set of apartments, meaning his door was the last. That was significant because neither attorney was well-versed in picking locks. And the longer they stood there cramming and jiggling a Swiss army knife into the door lock, the greater the likelihood of getting caught. If someone opened and leaned out the neighboring door, they'd be close enough to kiss the fumbling intruder.

Centrally positioned to the length of the building, Kristen stood about ten feet from the walkway that led to all the entry doors, ready to signal Josh if a witness approached. Two lamp posts, positioned about twenty feet apart, illuminated the walkway. And with the B&E gods presumably on their side, only one lamp dimly lit the pathway running parallel to the front of the complex, while the other lamp—the one closest to Josh "The Lock Picker" Rizzetti—was burned out.

Their last-minute casing of the joint confirmed the present time was as good as any. If the indoor lights were any indication, it appeared that all the neighbors were either asleep or out of their residence, save the second downstairs unit. From the flickering light shining through the thinly draped picture window up front, mixed with some sporadic noise, it appeared that the resident was awake watching late-night television. Alert to that possibility, Kristen stood nearby with her head on a swivel, stopping every five seconds to give extra attention to *The Tonight Show* fan.

"Psst," Josh sounded to Kristen, then waved her over.

Josh couldn't help but chuckle with pride as Kristen scampered toward him; shocked that he'd successfully picked the lock, let alone in short order. Kristen ducked under the police tape and entered, followed by Josh, who caressed the door closed behind him. In unison, they clicked on their flashlights and scuttled up the narrow staircase to the living area of the dead man's apartment.

At the top of the stairs, faced a door behind which housed a four-by-four-foot coat closet. To the left of the stairs was the living room-dining room space, situated towards the front two-thirds of the unit. On the back one-third stood the kitchen, open-faced into the dining space. Walking across the living space were two doors, side by side. One led to the unit's only bedroom, the other to the bathroom. The kitchen cabinets and counter on the backside of the unit set out along three-quarters of the back wall, with the final quarter occupied by a sliding glass door leading to the unit's rear cantilevered balcony.

The painstakingly prepared partners had a plan of attack designed to minimize their time in the apartment. Josh was to search the main living area and kitchen; Kristen would check all other rooms and closets. Kristen hurried to the bedroom and began her search of the room from top to bottom. Josh decided to start with the kitchen when he noticed a space at the end of the counter, open underneath like a built-in desk, clearly designed as a small bill-paying station, or the like.

Atop the counter was a pen holder, filled with several pens, a highlighter, and a pair of scissors. Beside it rested a bamboo two-slot mail organizer, filled with miscellaneous papers—bills, paystub receipts, junk mail, realtor postcards, and a letter on law firm letterhead. First, Josh flipped through everything to see if something jumped out. Perhaps he'd get lucky and find a note that wrote "Criminal mastermind's headquarters" with name, address, and phone number. No such luck. *Sadly, there'll be no cashing in my lottery ticket tonight*, he thought.

Josh paid particular attention to several paystub receipts, evidently from the *Midnight Vandal's* employer. The astute attorney noted how fortuitous it was that the criminal, who'd been caught red-handed—or more specifically, jack-hammer-handed—tearing up the sidewalk, worked for what appeared to be some type of construction company named Vail Valley Contractors. Apparently, his tools of the trade came in handy for both his occupations, legal and criminal alike.

Suddenly, Josh stopped moving and held his breath. He heard something, possibly a door slamming. He froze in his place, listened closely, and stared at the large window at the front of the unit. A ray of light flashed across the window, then disappeared. Just then, his phone vibrated. Josh pulled it from his pocket and looked at the screen. It was Kristen calling.

Thinking she'd found something in the bedroom or was calling to alert him that she'd heard or seen something worth calling attention to, Josh answered, "Did you find something?"

A muzzled, male voice responded, "I think I may have found you." An evil snigger preceded a beep and the call ended.

Fifty-three seconds later, a bizarrely scarred masked man stood at the top of the *Midnight Vandal's* stairs. Ready to scratch his itchy trigger finger, he followed his loaded partner, a *Ruger Mark IV*, into the living room.

Chapter Thirty-Seven

HANGING AROUND ONE night during their stay in Frisco, relaxing by a fire and sipping a Chilean Cabernet or an Argentinian Malbec had been penned on the agenda for the workaholic attorneys. Hanging by their fingertips from a second-story balcony, desperate to avoid gunfire, was not. A dichotomy truly emblematic of their vacation—in a nutshell.

An intruder infringed upon the trespassers. The cats had become the mice. With only one door in and out of the unit, Josh and Kristen had two options. Dive headfirst down the stairs and hope they landed on their uninvited guest, but not on his gun, and knock him—but not them—unconscious. But with the experienced criminal armed with a loaded gun, and the rookie criminals only armed with sparkling new flashlights, that option greatly lacked in appeal.

Choosing the lesser of two evils, they elected to sneak out the slider, step over the railing, hang from the balcony, and drop to the ground. Fully extended from their freezing fingertips to their bitter toes; Josh's drop wouldn't be more than four or five feet, and Kristen's, about a foot farther.

As each stepped over the wrought iron railing, a flash of light beamed inside, going from their left to right as they faced the unit's interior. With fluidity the likes of which Spiderman would've been proud, they inched their way over and down. By the time their fingertips were the only things clinging between them and the snow-covered ground below, the slider skidded open.

Shoulder to shoulder, Josh and Kristen locked eyes. Josh felt helpless, spotting absolute terror in his partner's eyes. In an instant, he flashed back to months earlier when Kristen had dived for her life to dodge a bulleting SUV aimed straight at its female target, and secondary to its main prey—Joshua. Now, once again he had placed Kristen in harm's way, metaphorically knocking on death's door while literally hanging from its balcony.

With their minds in sync, they knew their landing would make some noise. At the same time, they knew the hunter would spot his prey in about four seconds, assuming they could hang on that long. And in less than ten seconds, they'd go from hanging bats to sitting ducks.

Banking on the moderate noise created by a stiffened slider to be enough to mask the subtle crunch of two bodies falling to the snow, Josh gave a nod to Kristen, then mouthed "Now."

The one second between their fingers sliding down the balcony edge to their toes hitting the icy snow, time slugged at a snail's pace. In a flash, the moment gravity triumphed over their dangling bodies, the noise of the slider stopped. Fortunately, before

Josh could blurt out an expletive, the gunman beat him to the punch.

The gunman vigorously shook the obstructed slider, nearly forcing it off its track. "Son of a bitch," snarled the frustrated stalker just as the fleeing prey tumbled to the ground.

A few more choice words and forceful shakes later, the jammed slider released, rocketed all the way open, and then slammed to a halt. The criminal removed his flashlight from his clenched bite with his unarmed hand, then stepped onto the dark balcony. He flashed the light around the modest yard area, then beyond to the forest of trees. Nothing.

Next, leaning over the balcony, he shined the light straight down, onto the first-floor neighbor's tiny patio space, situated directly below the balcony. Plastic chairs, four stacked one on top of the other, leaned up against a covered outdoor propane grill. He leaned farther over the edge and scanned his flashlight underneath, exploring the entire space below.

"Clank." The railing jerked forward two inches, then stopped.

The poorly maintained aspect of the building revealed itself. Clearly, the aesthetics of the recently stained siding took precedence over safety. A few loosened carriage bolts nearly popped out of place, causing the railing to budge a little more, jumping forward another inch.

"Oh," uttered Kristen, with a kneejerk reflex.

The hunter stepped back quickly; noticeably afraid the railing was about to give way. "Gotcha!" he hollered, then whipped around to race through the open slider.

In eight seconds flat, the gun-toting predator bolted through the unit, down the stairs, and around the building. Illustrative of the sound of fear, footfalls sprinted across the backyard and into the acres of trees, with two dark figures just ahead of their footprints.

In the direction of the fleeing felines, the gunman fired into the trees turning trail on the cat burglars' tales.

Chapter Thirty-Eight

DRESSED TO KILL, they were not. Dressed to freeze, they nailed it.

The plan was simple. Drive less than a mile. Break into the *Midnight Vandal's* place. Gather whatever evidence or clues they could find. Get out. Cruise back to the B&B. And finally, brainstorm and research for answers. None of which necessitated layering up for an arctic expedition.

The best-laid plans.

Cuddled up against the intersection of two fallen Aspen trees, one crossed over the other, Josh and Kristen froze—both intentionally and through the force of nature. Intentionally, to avoid being spotted and killed. By nature, because the temperature had fallen to eleven degrees and was plunging by the minute. The forecast called for clear skies and no snow but predicted a low flirting near zero. Chilling the air further, the hunter was hot on their ice-covered behinds.

"Come out, come out, wherever you are!" the hunter hollered, eerily sounding like the deranged voice of Robert De Niro in his Oscar-nominated performance of Max Cady in the spine-tingling remake of *Cape Fear*. He too terrorizing an attorney. Hearing it sent flashbacks through Josh's mind in accord with the chills it shot up his spine. He'd seen the movie countless times. With each word breathed by the real-life predator, Josh could almost smell the cigar smoke clouding De Niro. Now, if he ever watched it again, it'd be too soon.

"Counselor," he bellowed, chilling Josh quicker than a polar vortex. "I know it's you."

Falling brittle to the freezing air, Kristen shivered. Hearing the chilling voice, Josh shuddered. With slow, deep breaths, they tightly huddled, struggling not to move an inch. The approaching voice and footsteps appeared to be thirty or so feet away and closing in on their less-than-ideal hiding spot. Fittingly, the crossed Aspens would mark their grave site.

Josh expected one of two sounds to resonate in a matter of seconds. One he prayed for, the other he feared. The predator was five steps away from spotting his prey and blasting the sound Josh feared most—gunfire. Four steps away. Three steps away. Then, before the next step landed, Josh's prayer was answered.

Sirens blared through the lofty trees, stopping the hunter in his tracks. The gunshots he had fired moments earlier from the rear of the apartment complex were sure to prompt a call or two to 9-1-1, and luckily for the cuddled couple, it had. And with no time to spare.

As quickly as the sirens rang through the ears of the novice prowlers, their pursuer disappeared.

Balled up and frozen like snowballs, Josh and Kristen patiently waited for law enforcement to canvass the area and then retreat.

Hypothermia couldn't have been far off by the time the frostbitten attorneys returned to their rental car and shuttled around Frisco with the heat cranked up. Although the dash from the B&B parking lot to the back door of the inn was less than twenty yards, the frozen pair decided they'd fully thaw in their toasty vehicle before heading back to their room.

Twenty minutes at high heat did the trick, and blood once again flowed through their veins, and their toes remained intact. Josh turned onto Main Street, four blocks up from the B&B. With the car stereo tuned to a local news station, the clock on its digital display showed 2:17 a.m. Three blocks away from the inn, the radio host stated the following:

> *In nearby Leadville, St. Raphael's Hospital recently admitted an unidentified patient who, by witness accounts, was being severely beaten on a nearby county road on the outskirts of downtown Leadville. Seconds later, as the witnesses' vehicle pulled up to the elderly man, they found him unconscious in the middle of the road. Immediately, they called 9-1-1, after which paramedics transported him to the new multi-million-dollar hospital in historic Leadville.*

Thus far, the man remains a John Doe. The witnesses estimated the man to be in his late seventies or early eighties. Sadly, upon his arrival at the hospital, the unidentified man has remained in a coma, in critical condition.

Authorities have issued the following request: If anyone has any information about the attack or the possible identity of this victim, please contact the Leadville Police Department and St. Raphael's Hospital.

Josh slammed on the brakes at the intersection just one block shy of the B&B. He whipped his head toward Kristen. She flipped hers toward him. And showcasing more harmony than an REO Speedwagon eighties' love ballad, they both shouted, "Uncle George!"

Chapter Thirty-Nine

CONFLICTING EMOTIONS BATTLED inside Josh as he entered the hospital. Uncle George was alive. The grateful great-nephew wasn't sure or even hopeful that he'd ever see this day again; fearful that the kidnapper had made good on his threat. For his uncle's life, on shaky ground as it was, he thanked God.

Clashing with Josh's sense of gratitude, Uncle George's condition left him and Kristen praying for a miracle. The sight of the comatose man with his bandage-wrapped head and tube-injected body worried Josh that his thankfulness may be short-lived.

Upon their arrival, the anxious couple rushed to the front desk, explained what they'd heard on the radio, gave a description of Uncle George, and was granted access to see him. Given the prelude to his admission, Kristen pleaded with the hospital administration not to release the name of the patient to local law enforcement until she had a chance to speak with them first. With her charming personality, incomparable knowledge of the law, and a subtle hint of a potential wrongful death lawsuit should they ignore her request, Kristen delayed their costly mistake—but perhaps only temporarily.

With patient medical information normally protected, under an exception to HIPAA laws certain information could be disclosed to law enforcement officials without the patient's permission to prevent or lessen a serious and imminent threat to the health or safety of an individual or the public. The hospital administrator, though aware of the law on its face, had never been confronted with such ambiguity. That being the case and erring on the side of caution, the first-year administrator placed a call to the hospital's second-year counsel and briefed him on the details.

Ultimately concluding that the moderate risk to many people outweighed the substantial risk to one, the hospital decisionmaker disclosed the details to local law enforcement, but with all parties agreeing not to release the name of the victim. However, with the witnesses already having disclosed enough information to the press, simply withholding the name of the victim likely didn't mitigate the danger, let alone ensure George's safety.

All things considered, Kristen's success in persuading the hospital and law enforcement to keep most information under wraps didn't amount to much. The toothpaste was out of the tube. The news report had provided sufficient details to put the kidnappers on notice that the old man had survived the pounding. After all, the odds of another old man being beaten on the same remote county road on the same day made winning the lottery seem like a sure bet. The thugs knew all they needed to know. The man was alive and was being treated at St. Raphael's Hospital, the new hospital aptly named after the patron saint of healing.

Agreeing that George might still be at risk, the Leadville Police Department kept a uniformed officer outside the patient's room. Inside, Josh and Kristen sat on each side of Uncle George's bed anxiously waiting for him to wake from his vegetative state. Kristen's forehead rested against the patient's bicep, and with her eyes closed, she whispered prayer after prayer.

Meanwhile, Josh's eyes stayed glued to his tablet. Fortunately, he didn't have to travel far to take advantage of the larger screen as compared to his smartphone. Inadvertently, he had left it in the rental car a couple of days earlier. For ease and portability, he'd emailed to himself all the clues, key website links, and relevant research in case he needed to quickly access it from anywhere. Always steps ahead of his foes, and it paid off. Researching on the tablet was far easier on the eyes than on the small screen of his Android.

An hour into her prayers, Kristen's voice faded as her eyelids lowered. Following a slight snort, she dosed off. In response, Josh rose from his chair and walked around the bed to his exhausted partner. Gently, he eased her back in her chair, held her head upright, and cruised the roller-legged chair up against the wall opposite the hospital bed, beside a pleather love seat. Gradually, he leaned her head back with his left hand, and with his right hand reached for a decorative throw pillow that added an ornate touch to the bland love seat in the bland room. With Josh placing the pillow in between her and the wall, he softly propped Kristen's head against the cushion.

Every twenty minutes, a member of the hospital staff popped in to check on the patient. A nurse here, a doctor there. And though the personnel had changed, the patient's status remained static, and his prognosis grim. From jump street, the treating physician was frank with Josh about George's chances. Given his age and the apparent number and magnitude of recent blows to his head, his odds of survival decreased disproportionately to the time he remained comatose.

But Josh kept hope. He knew his uncle, but the medical staff did not. That man had proven himself more durable than the *Energizer* bunny. Whatever life had thrown at him, Uncle George kept going and going. So why should now be any different? Josh convinced himself as much, but then deflated a bit each time he eyed his motionless hero.

"Control what you can control," Josh told himself, diving back into code-deciphering mode.

Realizing that Uncle George's life was continually at risk until his abductors were captured, Josh opted to dig a little deeper into the clues dropped by his uncle the last time they'd spoken. His gut was telling him that somehow, someway, Uncle George either knew or firmly suspected who was behind his kidnapping. And with that knowledge, he may've dropped the subtlest of clues as to the chief captor's identity; too faint to be detectable by the mastermind, but hopefully sufficient for George's protégé to decipher.

Mixing and matching his search terms, next Josh typed "Josh Billings twelve Monterey Bay Aquarium" into the search engine. The first four results revealed different websites focused on the aquarium itself. The fifth result jumped out for two reasons: the emphasis was not on the aquarium, and it referenced an aside he'd previously come across in his research of the aquatic museum. The resulting headline read: "John Steinbeck's Cannery Row Literary Tour."

From his prior research, Josh recalled that the Monterey Bay Aquarium resided on a street named Cannery Row. But why would that come up in conjunction with Josh Billings and the number twelve? Eager to find out, Josh modified his search to "Cannery Row Josh Billings twelve."

At first glance, the predominant commonality amongst the results referenced chapter twelve of John Steinbeck's novel *Cannery Row*. Seemingly insignificant. But low and behold, upon further reading, Josh's research had come full circle. As Josh read on, *that* particular chapter of *that* particular book just so happened to chronicle the death of none other than the late famous writer, Josh Billings. *That can't be a coincidence*, the living Josh thought.

Once again, Josh listened to Uncle George's last words on the recording while reading them verbatim from the notes on his tablet:

> *In the words of my second favorite Josh, 'Life consists not in holding the good cards but in playing those you hold well.' That's how to beat a wheeler and dealer. And always treasure our wild trip to the Monterey Bay Aquarium when you were twelve and you found the answer you'd sought during that chapter of your life. I love you son.*

Sensing there was more to the two references back to Josh Billings—other than the "cards" quote—Josh dug deeper into George's favorite humor writer. Josh checked into the details on three credible websites, all of which led with the same information—*Josh Billings was the pen name of the nineteenth-century writer Henry Wheeler Shaw.*

"Hmm. Henry Wheeler Shaw. Henry *Wheeler* Shaw," Josh whispered to himself. "*Wheeler.* That's gotta be it. Hence the seemingly misplaced *wheeler* and dealer statement."

Josh closed his eyes and took a deep breath. "But why Henry Wheeler Shaw?" he asked himself. Obviously, the dead writer wasn't the kidnapper.

With his eyes still closed, Josh racked his brain. Like a high-speed projector, a hodgepodge of clues and images flashed across his brain faster than the speed of an Olympic downhill skier as Josh labored to make sense of it all.

Over and over, it replayed in his head, each time bringing him closer to solving simultaneously the two separate ten-thousand-piece puzzles. With each replay, he sorted information into distinct folders organized and filed in his brain. Blurry images gained clarity. Random words started logically linking together. He was close. He could sense it. He could feel it. The answers loitered at the tip of his tongue, ready to be spoken.

Then abruptly, as if someone had pulled the plug, the projector burned out, as did Josh. Hanging from the drab hospital wall, the chrome-rimmed circular clock ticked loudly to 4:25 in the morning, dulling Josh to sleep.

When it came to court battles, Josh had no peers. Every time he'd been forced to fight for his life, Josh prevailed. But head-to-head against overtiredness, slumber triumphed over the fatigued litigator without fail. If tired enough, Josh could sleep standing up. Clearly, he needed his rest.

Tragically, George couldn't wake from his.

Chapter Forty

KRISTEN WAS GONE when Josh woke up from his four-hour siesta. He rubbed out the kink in his neck as he exhaled his increasingly recurring "old man" groans. Next, rolling his head in a clockwise motion, the crackling of his neck replaced his moaning. He couldn't help but wonder when the noises generated from his body sounded less human and more like *The Munster's* floorboards.

Josh scanned the room. Time had stood still for Uncle George; his eyes still closed, his body still motionless, and machines still doing their thing. Josh's tablet was on the floor, battery low—and like Uncle George—close to dead. The sun was shining brightly through the window, but the mood could not have been dimmer. Meanwhile, Kristen's chair was empty, symbolic of her heart.

Josh panicked. Other than the fortune of successfully dodging bullets, fleeing a predator, and evading the cops, luck hadn't been on his side lately. His dream vacation had detoured into a nightmare. His reunion with his great-uncle had transformed into a final goodbye. And the love of his life seemed to be slipping away. Or was she? He couldn't be certain.

With nothing but past failed relationships from which to judge, Josh questioned whether he was unjustifiably paranoid, or accurately reading the writing on the wall.

The unsettling feeling he'd experienced in the past, just prior to getting dumped, was gnawing at his gut. That, or the heavy pizza pies, fast food, and lack of consistent exercise to which he was accustomed had finally taken its toll on his obsessively fit physique. On the off chance it was the latter, Josh dropped to the floor and pounded out thirty pushups. As he pressed out number thirty, the hospital room door opened.

"If you're doing one for every pound you've gained during our trip," Kristen giggled, "another ten might be in order." She entered the room with two large coffees and a medium-size smile.

Feeling self-conscious, Josh responded defensively, "I know all the pizza I've consumed coupled with a sabbatical from my workout routine has taken its toll. But is it *that* bad?" Josh popped up; afraid she might answer.

"You're fine Arnold." Kristen handed him a coffee. "And by Arnold, I mean *Different Strokes* Arnold, not *Predator* Arnold."

"Ouch! That jab's got more *sting* than The Police's *Synchronicity* album." He took a sip. "And thank you," he said, raising his coffee cup.

"I'm just teasing. And you're welcome."

They both sat in their chairs and beheld George. Kristen took a swig of coffee. Josh glanced at his flexed right bicep, checking to make sure it was still there. He caught a glimpse of his belly. It looked bigger, but his bicep, not so much. Josh's arm dropped to his thigh, pressing up against a lump in his pocket. The small surprise that Uncle George had slipped into his hand after their homemade family dinner had remained within Josh's reach ever since.

He gazed over Kristen as she stared at George with her watering eyes. Words aside, Josh sensed an immediate bond between the two of them. From the look on her face, it was as if she was losing her grandfather. Warming his left hand, Josh lifted his cup and guzzled three ounces of coffee. Occupying his right hand, he manipulated his pocket.

Kristen turned her eyes to Josh, wiping a tear from her cheek. "Josh, we need to talk."

Sentiment abruptly turned to dread. The four words that prefaced every breakup since the dawn of man froze Josh quicker than the snow-filled foxhole less than eight hours prior. The eloquent orator of the courtroom fell speechless. His paranoia had been justified. In one giant swoop, in one sixty-five-yard-field-goal-kicking boot to the crotch, in one room, he was on the verge of losing *two* of the people whom he loved most.

Just when *Predator*-Arnold, Josh, was about to get dumped by *Terminator*-Arnold, Kristen, the hospital room door opened. A young, cheerful nurse stepped in, and judging by the authenticity of her smile, undoubtedly had just started her shift.

"Good morning," she said, checking George and all his attachments. "One of the doctors will come by shortly to give you any updates and answer whatever questions you may have. In the meantime, can I get you anything?"

A time machine, thought Josh. *And send in Doc Brown from Back to the Future while you're at it.*

"I think we're fine," Kristen said. "Thank you for offering."

Josh's snappy wit wasn't limited to public disclosure. His voice resonated within the confines of his head, *Fine? Really, fine? Yeah, you're fine! Your fine ass is about to dump mine.*

The nurse exited the room. Kristen stood and snaked toward Josh. He knew what was coming and preferred it quick and painless. Knowing the hospital was well-stocked with the same, Josh opted to rip off the band-aid rather than get tortured by a long "it's not you it's me" speech.

"I know what you're going to say."

"You do?" Kristen said, looking confused. "How? Did you talk to Austin and Madison while I was asleep?"

"They know!?" Josh hollered loud enough to wake Uncle George. Sadly, it didn't.

"Well, my gut was convincingly telling me one thing," she explained, "but I wanted to get some feedback on making such a drastic decision and to be sure that's what I really wanted before I told you. So, I talked it over with Madison. And being they're married, I assumed she'd spill the beans to Austin at some point."

"Even though I'm not one to quote post-eighties' tunes, a certain early-nineties song still rings true."

"What's that?" asked Kristen.

"Del Amitri's 'Always the Last to Know.'"

"Well, even if you already know it, I still need to say it. So, as I was about to say," Kristen continued, then held a dramatic pause.

Josh sighed deeply. Humbled and embarrassed, his hand covered the lump in his pocket. Heartbroken, his dejected chin covered the lump in his throat.

"I think—" Kristen said, stopping herself mid-sentence, clearly slowed by her kind-hearted nature. Josh stood up tall posturing himself to take the blow; remembering a favorite Oscar Wilde quote Uncle George cited frequently, *True friends stab you in the front.*

"I think—I think—" she stuttered, clearing her throat. "I think we should move here."

Josh fell to the floor, but not for the reason he'd anticipated. "You what!?"

"I know it sounds crazy. And I know we've been here only a short time. And I know this trip is spiraling downhill faster than an avalanche. But I feel at home here. Austin and Madison are great. And I couldn't love Uncle George any more than if he was my grandfather. God speed!"

"Wow!" Flabbergasted, Josh couldn't mumble any other sound.

"I know. I know. It doesn't *sound* crazy. It *is* crazy. Forget I said it."

"No! No! That's not it," confessed Josh, shaking his head excitedly.

"It's not. Then what is it? You look way more shocked than I envisioned. Especially since you said you knew what I was going to say."

"I thought you were going to dump my sorry butt like a *Hefty* bag."

"Are you serious?" Kristen chuckled. "*Dump* you? Why would I dump you? I mean, of course, aside from the obvious of me being way out of your league." Kristen giggled. "I *love* you, you moron. I know your past relationships weren't ideal, but this is different. *We're* different. For a couple to go through one-tenth of what we've been through and not flee thousands of miles away from each other is love at its strongest."

"Whew! Thank God." Josh embraced Kristen with unprecedented relief.

"Easy, big guy," she said, releasing her hold and stepping back a bit. "Are you packing a surprise in your pocket, or are you just that excited that I didn't give you the *Heisman*?"

Josh's world-class microprocessor kicked into full gear, and within seconds, months-worth of contemplation, deliberation, and consideration reached a decision. *Carpe diem.*

"Rather than tell you," Josh replied, reaching into his pants. "Why don't I just show you?"

"Whoa! I'm flattered." Kristen blushed in an instant. "But keep it in your pants Rizzetti. Someone could walk in on us. And certainly not in front of your uncle."

"Trust me," Josh said, smiling ear to ear. "I think you're gonna be ecstatic when I pull this out of my pants."

"My my Casanova. Don't we think highly of ourselves?"

"Unlike Tears for Fears, I won't be 'Sowing the Seeds of Love' to make you 'Shout.' At least not right now."

Josh dropped to his right knee and flipping open the small box he'd pulled from his pocket, he held it up to Kristen. "My intentions right now are pure."

"Oh my gosh!" Kristen softly screamed, muffling her mouth with both hands.

"Kristen Grace Laney, will you marry me?"

She nodded feverishly and held out her left hand. "Yes, Joshua George Rizzetti. Yes!"

As Josh slid the ring on her left ring finger, Kristen, shedding a few *happy* tears, asked, "But how? When? Where?"

"It was my great-grandmother's ring. Uncle George slipped it to me as we left his cabin after dinner."

Kristen planted a huge kiss on Josh, then stepped over to George's bedside and squeezed his hand with her right as she held up her left and gawked at its sparkling new decor. "Uncle George, please wake up. We have some exciting news that I know you'll love. Plus, I'll need someone to walk me down the aisle."

Josh's eyes misted. Kristen's dropped a downpour.

"Are you okay?" Josh asked.

"Yes. It's just . . . this is a lot to take in at once. It's all so—"

"Crazy. Unexpected. Spontaneous. Overwhelming."

"Wild," said Kristen. "It's wild!"

"Wild? Huh," Josh chuckled. "That's funny. I was just thinking of a favorite quote from Oscar *Wilde* that Uncle George likes."

"What's—" Kristen stopped talking when Josh raised his hand to stop.

"Oh, sorry to interrupt!" Josh said eagerly. "You're not going to believe this, but I think I just figured out who's behind the kidnapping. And you're never going to guess who?"

Chapter Forty-One

KRISTEN WAITED ANXIOUSLY. It was a coin toss as to what would pop out next—her eyeballs or Josh's strong speculation about naming the identity of George's abductor.

For the umpteenth time, Josh played the recording of George's message:

> *In the words of my second favorite Josh, 'Life consists not in holding the good cards but in playing those you hold well.' That's how to beat a wheeler and dealer. And always treasure our wild trip to the Monterey Bay Aquarium when you were twelve and you found the answer you'd sought during that chapter of your life. I love you son.*

"Sorry to keep you hanging. But follow my thought process and tell me if I'm crazy before I potentially slander a prominent figure." Josh took in a lung full. "Of course, we know the quote is from Josh Billings, which led us to the clues written in the special occasion cards sent to me by Uncle George over the years.

But I think it also gives us a segue toward the person to whom he was pointing."

"I can't wait to hear this," she said. "Fire away!"

"The Monterey Bay Aquarium is on a street named Cannery Row. *Cannery Row* also happens to be the title of a book written by John Steinbeck. Chapter *twelve* of that book describes the death of the one and only Josh Billings. Well, Josh Billings was only a pen name. The writer's real name was Henry *Wheeler* Shaw. Hence the wheeler and dealer blurb. Henry Wheeler Shaw also happened to be born in Monterey. It all ties together. And not coincidentally."

"Okay, okay. That's all very logical and makes sense. But how does that tell us who kidnapped Uncle George? And more importantly, who is it?"

"Here's where it gets ultra-cryptic," Josh said. "As I said earlier, I never went on a trip to the aquarium with my uncle, let alone a *wild* one. And as you've seen for yourself, Uncle George is off-the-charts intelligent. That being said, we can be safe to assume every single word he said was intentionally and carefully chosen. Meticulously crafted to provide us with vital information. For instance, the clues in the cards and his use of the word 'treasure' were purposeful. Likewise, when he added the word 'wild' for a specific reason. I believe he was referring to *Wilde*, as in Oscar Wilde."

"And? The kidnapper is—?"

"Oscar Wilde had a famous quote that Uncle George loved to cite." Josh cleared the lump in his throat as he stared at his comatose uncle. "I should say *loves* to cite. 'True friends stab you in the front.' Okay, now let's circle back to Henry Wheeler Shaw. Well, a nickname for the name Henry is what?" He paused.

"No! That can't be."

"Yes. Hank! And Hank is someone whom—obviously until the abduction—my uncle considered a true friend. Uncle George must've seen or heard something that led him to identify Hank as being the man behind his capture, and then in oh-so-subtle fashion conveyed that to me."

"Hank! Really?" The outrage casing Kristen's face outweighed the shock in her voice. "I follow your deduction. I do. As odd as it seems, it flows logically. But you know that sounds insane, right?"

"Yes. It sounded crazy to me too. But now that I've said it out loud, I'm even more certain."

"Why's that?" Kristen said. "How can you be more certain with something so obscure?"

"Because as I said it out loud, it triggered something in my brain that put all the pieces of the puzzle together at once. And not only am I nearly certain that Hank is behind the kidnapping, but I'm even more confident about where the treasure is hidden. And it all fits together like a well-designed, albeit grossly convoluted, jigsaw puzzle."

"I hope you plan on simply telling me where you think the treasure is before you drag me through the muddle scrambled in that brain of yours."

"Where's the fun in that?" Josh said tossing a devious grin at his fiancé.

Chapter Forty-Two

J OSH DECIDED TO keep his speculation between him and Kristen for the time being. To implicate a respected, well-connected, former Deputy District Attorney of kidnapping was a serious allegation, and if wrong, would irreparably damage Josh's reputation and possibly his career. A slander suit would inevitably follow. And God willing, should George regain consciousness and fully recover, the native resident would be ostracized from Summit County if not all of Colorado. And for an old man, who knew nowhere else, that life-altering impact alone was enough to convince his great-nephew to pull back the reins.

Ideally, George would come out of his coma and confirm or deny Josh's deduction. At least that's what the confident young attorney had hoped. Practically speaking, Kristen and Josh could let his theory marinate for a while before taking more drastic action.

"Alright, Columbo," said Kristen with a drip of sarcasm. "Let's hear your hypothesis on the treasure's location."

"Before I disclose my theory as to the whereabouts of the golden treasure, I need to make two phone calls to clarify an image in my head."

"Are you kidding me?" Kristen said impatiently.

"I need to make sure my theory isn't unduly influencing something I *think* I saw but I'm not certain. I'm going to step out and make a couple of calls, grab us a bite to eat from the cafeteria, and then I'll be back. You keep an eye on Uncle George. I know there's a cop outside the door, but I still feel better if one of us is in here."

"Don't keep me waiting long." Kristen pulled up her chair to the side of George's bed. "After hearing how you concluded that one of your uncle's closest friends kidnapped him, I can't wait to hear your theory on the whereabouts of a twenty-year-old hidden treasure that even your brilliant uncle hasn't figured out yet."

"In Uncle George's defense," admitted Josh, "until now, no one had the benefit of all three sets of clues. Believe it or not, the *Midnight Vandal* wasn't too far off in where and why he tore up the sidewalk around the town's clock at the corner of Third and Main Street."

"Really?"

"*Really!*" Josh said as he was halfway out the door.

"Don't leave me hanging," hollered Kristen.

As soon as the door slowly latched closed behind the attorney, a doctor entered the room to check on the patient.

Josh shuffled down the long hallway in the direction of the closest waiting room. Typical of a large, new hospital in a small, remote mountain town, the waiting room was sparse and hushed. And while new cars boasted a new-car smell, the brand-new hospital couldn't brag the same. As bright, shiny, and new as it was, it still reeked of the same hospital stench. The smell of depression.

The only visitor occupying the waiting area was a young man huddled in the far corner closest to the windows. With earbuds in place, he waited with his head down. His tinted glasses, buried in his smart-phone, were hardly visible underneath his old-school Denver Broncos ball cap, highlighted by the bronco bucking out from the center of the giant "D."

Josh coughed lightly, seeing if the visitor reacted. Nothing. Feeling secure with his privacy, Josh sat with his back to the other guest in the chair farthest from the local football fan's location and placed his first call.

"Hello, Geoff," Josh said after being greeted from the other end. "This is Joshua Rizzetti."

"Oh. Good morning, Joshua. I was just about to call you and ask if you and Ms. Laney wanted to walk over to the coffee shop with me."

"Oh. That's kind of you. But we're away from the B&B right now. I'll explain later. But for now, I have an odd question to ask you about your mother and father."

"Okay. Hopefully, I can help."

"You mentioned they first met going to a concert on a blind date. Right?"

"Yes, that's right. Long before I was born."

"Do you happen to know if the band playing was the eighties' rock band named Asia?"

"As a matter of fact, it *was*," Geoff said with utter surprise. "I didn't mention that because it seemed totally insignificant. I had never even heard of that band until my mom mentioned it to me. Why do you ask? Is that significant? And how on God's green earth did you know that?"

"I can't get into it right now. And yes, I believe it's significant. But I'll tell you later. For now, I need to make another phone call. Are you going to be hanging around Frisco's Main Street for a while longer?"

"Yes sir," said Geoff. "I'll either be at that Mocha Mountain Java, here at the B&B or wandering Main Street."

"Great! Because I may need you to check on something a few blocks down Main Street if I can't get a hold of someone. If I do reach her, I'll touch base with you later and give you an update."

"Okay. Whatever you need from me, just let me know."

"Thank you, Geoff. I'll be in touch soon."

Before Geoff could press "end call" Josh had done so and moved on to his next call.

Never in a million years would Josh have thought having Mabel's cell phone number would be of any use to him. But clearly the sweet, elderly employee at the Frisco Museum and Historic Park knew better. Josh called the friendly lady who not only knew Frisco's history, but also was an integral part of it.

"Hello, this is Mabel."

"Hello, Ms. Mabel. This is Joshua. We met the other day when my girlfriend, Kristen, and I visited the Frisco Museum."

"Of course, Joshua. The cute attorney couple," Mabel said with delight. "What can I do for you, honey?"

"I know it's early and the museum isn't open yet, but by chance are you at work?"

"As a matter of fact," she replied, "I am. I came in early to work on an application for a government grant that we're trying to secure so that we can get caught up on some much-needed, overdue maintenance."

"Great! Well, I don't want to take up too much of your time. I just have a quick favor to ask. It's a very odd request, and I can explain later why I'm asking. But for now, I'd like to ask you to go outside, and in the paved area to your far left, as you exit the front door, you'll see some letters and numbers etched into the concrete, right up against the building. I need you to read those to me."

"Yes, I'm familiar with that. I was told that was some sort of reference to the street or block location or a utility line, or something like that."

"Perfect. Can you please go there and tell me what you see?"

"Okay. And you're right, that is an odd request," Mabel said, breathing heavily as she threw on her coat and hustled out the door. A few seconds later, she was ready. "Okay, here is it. 'A-five-one-A,' then there's a space, then it's 'three-forward slash-three,' then another space. And finally, the numbers 'one-four-three' and then some simple drawing of some sort."

"Perfect. One more favor. Can you please take a photo of that and text it to me?"

"My pleasure, young man," Mabel said. Not surprisingly, she had more to say. "It's funny you're asking about that. I remember when that pavement was laid. In fact, the money from the grant we're requesting will be used in part to repair some of the cracked and raised concrete throughout the park's walkways."

"Hmm. You don't say." Josh said, smiling even bigger than before upon hearing Mabel's bonus information. "Do you remember if that concrete in the patio area in front of the museum was laid about twenty years ago?"

"Yes, that sounds about right."

"Thanks, Mabel. You're the best. I'll be in touch." Before she could say anything, Josh hung up.

Josh stared at his phone, waiting for the sound of a text notification. Of course, when that would come was a crapshoot. Mabel was no spring chicken, and thus likely suffering from the common elderly ailment—technologically challenged. He waited eagerly. In hindsight, perhaps he should've requested her to carve it into stone and send it over on horse and buggy.

"Beep," sounded Josh's phone. *Shame on me for underestimating that lovely lady*, thought Josh.

He pulled up the text image and focused his attention on the imprinted concrete, which read: "A51A 3/3 143." He zeroed in further and further until all that was on the screen was "A51A." He zoomed in a bit more until only two characters remained visible on the screen. The "51" seemed off, but Josh felt inclined to second guess his own judgment. He feared his deductive reasoning might be influencing his perspective of the actual physical evidence itself.

Josh squinted tightly, intending to enhance his focus. His eyes started to play tricks on him, blurring rather than focusing. He shut them, counted to five, then took a fresh look. Sure enough, he confirmed what he had hoped. The "51" wasn't a number. They were letters—namely, "SI." He then zoomed out and refocused the photo on the drawing after the number three. It was simple, but concise, almost like an emoji.

In his head, Josh replayed all that Geoff had told them about his parents. How they met. Where they met. When they met. "That's it!" Josh hollered, prompting a gaze from the otherwise preoccupied waiting room visitor. Josh then whispered *"ASIA, March 3, I love you. And a sketch of a flame."*

Quickly, Josh closed out his text and once again called Mabel. "Hello Mabel, this is Joshua. Sorry to bother you again, but I wanted to ask you something. Is it possible that the "51" engraved in the concrete is actually "SI?"

Mabel held a pause before responding, "I suppose so, but I can't be certain." She sighed. "I *can* say for sure that the concrete was laid about twenty years ago. I remember it well because my expensive new shoes got ruined." She paused as if waiting for Josh to ask how.

Josh hesitated. The litigator in him questioned whether he should ask an open-ended follow-up question. Painfully aware, he knew that when questioning chatty witnesses, a broad inquiry invited wordy, irrelevant answers that could drag on ad nauseum. But then, recognizing that Mabel's superfluous information was proving surprisingly helpful, he rolled the dice and asked, "What do you mean by that?"

"I had just purchased brand new leather shoes I had been eyeing for months. The first day I wore them to work, I stepped into the freshly poured concrete out front."

"You don't say?" said Josh.

"It was rather odd. I remember the museum was closed to the public for a week or so for the concrete company to tear up the old and lay the new. Well, early one morning, I was in the museum unpacking and labeling some new artifacts we had just received. When I was ready for a break, I decided to grab a cup of coffee up the street. Well, when I stepped out the front door, I stepped into fresh concrete and ruined my pricey leather shoes."

"So, why do you say that was odd?" Josh asked. "Didn't you say you knew they were laying fresh concrete?"

"Yes, but not that *early*. I remember because my boss asked me to call it a day no later than noon because the concrete workers were scheduled to begin pouring between twelve and one. Well, when I stepped out for coffee, it was still kind of early. Easily before nine in the morning. Also, it seemed weird because only one guy was working. Apparently, he'd arrived early and had poured an entire section himself before the rest of the crew arrived. He even touched up where I had stepped. So I just used the back door after that. I remember thinking to myself what an ambitious worker he was to have done all that himself. It was impressive."

"Mabel," Josh said with glowing gratitude. "Do you have any idea how helpful you are?"

"I try."

"One more thing, maybe two," said Josh. "I know it was a long time ago. But do you remember back when the *Gold Scammer* was arrested?"

"Remember?" she cried. "How could I forget? It rocked this town. Our sleepy little town was making national news but in a bad way."

"You don't happen to remember—" Josh started but was interrupted by Mabel.

"In fact, the *Gold Scammer* was arrested not long after 'the shoe tragedy'—as I refer to it. I never bought such expensive shoes after that. Learned the hard way." She took a deep breath, then continued. "Anyways, I remember it so well because my cousin was a relatively new reporter for the local newspaper. And she had stopped by the museum to ask me questions about the new artifacts and such that recently had been added to the museum's collection for a historical piece she was writing for the paper. And I remember she was ecstatic because her editor had just assigned her to cover the *Gold Scammer* story. She couldn't stop talking about it because it was going to be her first big story."

"Mabel, you're a Godsend! Thank you. I'll let you get back to your grant application. I have a feeling the museum's going to need that money for a lot more than just overdue maintenance."

Chapter Forty-Three

THE NOVICE GUMSHOE immediately followed up his call to Mabel with a call to someone he could trust. Calling the police wasn't an option. If Hank, a former Deputy District Attorney, and respected local businessman, had in fact kidnapped Uncle George, Josh couldn't be sure who might be on the take. And rather than call the police and make the allegation of a lunatic, meanwhile potentially tipping off the scheming mastermind, notifying Austin presented his only viable option. To boot, if Josh were institutionalized, it could delay their wedding plans, making Kristen more of a threat to him than any killers.

Josh updated Austin on the events that had transpired since the local Deputy D.A. had left the inn suite that was doubling as the *FBI* headquarters. Conveniently, Josh failed to mention the details of the B&E committed after he and Kristen snuck out of the B&B in a frantic effort to locate Uncle George. That part he simply summarized as "we did some more digging."

Even though Josh kept the burglary under wraps, the information he dumped on Austin's lap was a bundle to consume for such a short period of time, making it sound even more insane. But Josh's deductions made sense, albeit a stretch—especially to anyone who wasn't an obsessed expert in eighties' music trivia. Trusting Josh's judgment and eighties' tainted mindset, Austin promised his friend he'd alert his closest law enforcement contact and keep the circle tight.

After speaking with Austin, Josh felt like a colossal weight had been lifted from his shoulders. He and Kristen had been enjoying a fun vacation when it had crashed abruptly, then spiraled downward. Now, on the tail end of the longest few days of their lives, their luck finally appeared to be changing directions—or at least leveling off.

Unquestionably a top priority, they had found George and he was alive. In a coma, yes. But he was alive. Tallying a couple more marks in Josh's "good luck" column, the sleuthing attorney was somewhat confident he had discovered the identity of his uncle's captor and solved in the process the mystery that had riddled the quaint mountain town for two decades. Columbus-like, no. But major discoveries, nonetheless.

With a flurry of thoughts and emotions storming through his brain, Josh took a pause after his call to Austin. He pulled a tissue from his pocket and wiped his runny nose, signaling the possible onset of a cold. Curling up in the freezing snow could have that effect. He closed his eyes, took several deep breaths, then shot out five sneezes in machine gun fashion. "Oh my. Excuse me," he said, turning to apologize for his unsanitary outburst.

"Huh. I guess I'm talking to myself," he muttered. The waiting room was as empty as Josh's stomach. The Broncos fan was gone.

Before heading back to his uncle's room, Josh swung by the cafeteria for a grub grab. Still prepping for the morning crowd, a staff member suggested he return in fifteen minutes. Josh thanked her, apologized for his grumbling stomach, and rumbled over to the vending machines.

The prices were high, the choices were vast. Sugar. Sugar with sugar. Sugar-filled sugar. Chocolate-coated sugar. Flavored liquid sugar. And "diet" liquid sugar. The new hospital certainly wasn't shy in its effort to increase revenue to cover the cost of its beautiful new medical center. Facilitating diabetes would bring them more lifetime paying patients.

Josh passed on the temptation to induce a diabetic coma. And he knew Kristen would endure the wait in order to avoid the consumption of more junk food. Josh, on the other hand, was a little more flexible with his dietary choices—borderline apathetic—but wisely deferred to his better half's preference.

The self-conscious counselor looked at his gut and questioned his knowledge of physics. *If things expand with heat and contract with cold, why is my belly getting bigger when the temperature is freezing?*

Despite the respite from his rigorous weightlifting routine, Josh still looked incredibly fit. He could have introduced himself as a middle linebacker for the Broncos, and nobody would've questioned him. But he felt like a slug, further pressuring him to sidestep the vending machines.

Two turns then straight ahead and he was strolling down the long hallway that ended at the intersection with another hallway. George's room was at the cross-section of the two hallways. To the right of the door sat the uniformed police officer, head down, fighting back the Zs. Josh noticed a new officer was on duty, as this one was wearing an officer's cap over his curly locks, while the other had been showcasing his shiny bald head.

Josh sauntered slowly, flipping his eyes from his phone to his path of travel. When he reached twenty feet from his uncle's door, his phone rang. The officer looked up, giving Josh a glimpse of his face before he glanced down at his screen. It was Austin calling. Josh answered, turned, and began retracing his steps back to the privacy of the tranquil waiting room.

* * *

WITH A HEAVY heart, Kristen sat beside George and chatted away as if they were old college friends catching up over a cup of coffee. The treating physician had left the room after checking on his patient, whose status remain unchanged. He assured Kristen they were doing all they could.

What had changed, Kristen and Joshua were now engaged. Not to be outdone by their other life-changing decision; to relocate to Colorado, not far from Uncle George. But with the patient loitering in the status quo, all that simmered on the back burner.

Kristen's stomach growled, impatient for her fiancé to return with some food. Her mind wandered, likely ready for her fiancé to come back with confirmation that he'd solved the clues of the decades-old puzzle.

"Uncle George," she said, then paused after catching herself. "I'm sorry. I hope you don't mind me calling you Uncle George. After all, we're going to be family. I know you're hearing is not the best, so maybe I should keep telling you until you wake up. Joshua and I are engaged. Can you hear me? Joshua and I are engaged."

With her right hand, she held George's left, then bowed in. "I pray you can hear me. Joshua and I are engaged." She lifted his hand, then slid her left underneath his, with his palm centered on the engagement ring that had been stripped of his proposal years earlier, after his love mysteriously disappeared. "Feel. It's your mother's ring. Joshua proposed. I said yes. We're going to get married. But not without you. I want you to walk me down the aisle."

Stacked like a Little League team cheering after a game, her right hand covered his left hand that in turn covered her left hand and the engagement ring. Kristen leaned her chest against the bed and rested her forehead over her right hand. Tears snuck past her closed eyelids, down her cheeks, and dripped onto the bed.

"Please, Lord, bless Uncle George. I know it sounds selfish, but we need him," she prayed, begging for his health. Her left hand twitched.

The spiritual young lady lifted her head, but her eyes stayed shut as she continued to pray. Her left hand twitched again. She pulled her head back. Once again, another twitch.

Slowly, she crept her eyes open. George looked like an old-school switchboard. Wires and tubes coming and going in all directions. Leisurely, Kristen raised her right hand and sliding it under some tubes gently placed it on George's stationary shoulder. Her left hand twitched again. With a crinkled brow, she gazed at it like it was possessed.

Kristen held her breath and stared at George's seasoned left paw that dwarfed her dainty hand. In a flash, she jolted her head back a couple more inches. Her hand wasn't twitching. It was George's hand. And it wasn't twitching. It was softly squeezing hers.

"Oh my Gosh!" she hollered, softly nudging his shoulder. "Uncle George. Can you hear me? Uncle George."

An old man's whimper sounded from the hospital bed. And unlike the prematurely depressing noise made when coming from her youthful fiancé, George's moan resonated like a choir of heavenly angels. Gradually, his eyes edged open. Kristen, in jubilant shock and left speechless, could only smile.

George softly slid his left hand around Kristen's, lifting it just so. Their hands pressed palm to palm His thumb caressed the familiar ring as if it recognized the heirloom to be in its proper place. Still speechless, Kristen's growing smile spoke volumes.

Returning the smile, George whispered, "Welcome to the family."

Chapter Forty-Four

T HE REPLACEMENT OFFICER on duty outside of George's room had surprised his colleague when he arrived an hour before the tired rookie's shift was scheduled to end. Exhausted from sitting motionless since midnight, and with a wife and newborn child awaiting his return, the bald probie graciously accepted the gesture from the "just transferred in" newcomer to the Leadville police force.

The old man's great-nephew hit the end of the long hallway and turned the corner, out of sight. On either side of George's room were a janitor closet and another patient's room. A candy striper exited the neighboring patient's room and meandered down the hall toward the nearest nurse's station thirty yards away.

The floor was quiet. The halls were empty. George's uniformed guardian stood from his chair, casually looked around, then softly slipped into the patient's room.

Kristen, with her back to the door, was chatting faster than a giddy schoolgirl, telling George about her perfect wedding that she'd dreamt of since she was ten. She had raised the hospital bed, making George more comfortable and rendering face-to-face conversation less neck-wrenching.

The visitor's entrance resembled a stealth aircraft, sneaking in undetected. Kristen continued gabbing at a record pace. She didn't seem to notice the officer until George's eyes shifted focus from her glowing face to the air space over her shoulder.

Kristen turned her head slightly, looking startled at first as she spotted a glimpse of a person standing behind her. But due to the angle, it allowed her to catch only a hint of a figure, but no more.

"Oh. Good morning officer," she said. "Your timing is perfect. As you can see, Mr. Dellucci just woke up from his coma. I'm so excited, I got sidetracked without buzzing the nurse. Would you be so kind as to notify the nurse's station?"

"That won't be necessary," the officer replied, pressing the silencer-muffled barrel of a pistol to the back of Kristen's head.

Terrified, she sat motionless, as fixed as George had been a few minutes earlier. George, once again immobilized, shifted his eyes around hurriedly. The corded nurse call button dangled beside the bed, just beyond the reach of his right-hand fingertips—at least not without extending his arm and triggering gunfire.

With his gun-free hand, the officer reached over Kristen's shoulder and revealed a filled syringe. "I want you to slowly take this from my hand," he said, waiving the needle in front of her mortified face and trembling lips. "And I mean slowly. You wouldn't want my trigger finger to slip." He paused for a moment as if expecting her to make some heroic attempt to disarm his scarred hand. "Then, you are going to pull the tube from that hanging bag to your right and inject the contents of this syringe into the tube. And remember. Very slowly. My job is to eliminate problems. So don't be a problem."

In a sloth-like motion, she reached up with her left hand to grab the liquified murder weapon. Her jittery hand gripped the syringe as her panicked eyes scanned her sightline, desperate for a way out. With the release of the syringe, the hitman increased the pressure of his preferred but messier murder weapon.

Kristen locked eyes with George, revealing her agonizing fear and repenting sorrow. George raised his eyebrows, then slightly tilted his head to his right, in the direction of his bedside table. Kristen squinted, looking confused. George repeated his eyebrow-raising head-tilting motion.

"Okay. It's time to say goodbye." The "officer" tapped the silencer against the back of Kristen's head.

"Please forgive me, Uncle George," mumbled Kristen, barely intelligible over her uncontrollable sobbing.

"Forgive you?" George said. "I want to thank you for these lovely flowers and this beautiful glass vase. Bring it to your wedding, and you'll know I'm right there with you. And remember the quote from the poet and playwright Derek Walcott, 'Break a vase, and the love that reassembles the fragments is stronger than that love which took its symmetry for granted when it was whole.' Can you *do that* for me?"

The fear on Kristen's face lessened, slowly replaced by a pondering gaze. Facing death, George spat out a famous quote. The last time he did that, it was a clue.

Geniuses thinking alike, Kristen responded to the old-timer's request. "Of course, Uncle George. And can we play a song in your honor?"

"Two, in fact," George said. "Since Joshua loves eighties' music so much, I think you should go with 'Push It' by Salt-N-Pepa and 'Hit Me with Your Best Shot' by Pat Benatar." His eyes shifted decisively from his left to his right.

"Consider it done," Kristen said, then mouthed, "on three."

"Alright. Enough with the long airport goodbye." The gun pressed harder against the young lady. "Penetrate the tube before a bullet penetrates your skull."

Still seated, Kristen sluggishly reached up and to her right with the syringe. She inhaled deeply. And keeping her eyes locked on George's, she mouthed "one." She pulled the tube from the hanging bag, then mouthed "two."

George readied himself, waiting for his cue. Kristen positioned herself just right, hanging on the edge of her chair, prepared to "p-push it real good."

"Three," Kristen mouthed in sync with a more profound exhale.

On count, all hell broke loose.

* * *

AS IF RE-ENACTING the movie *Groundhog Day*, Josh once again walked along the hallway, bouncing his eyes back and forth from straight ahead to his phone. His conversation with Austin was groundbreaking, in more ways than one, and Josh was eager to share it with Kristen. His walk progressed to a trot. But when he noticed the officer's seat empty, fear struck him like a flash of lightning. His heart dropped. Flashbacks of the attempted murder of a hospitalized Kristen walloped his heartstrings. Josh's trotting legs gave way to his racing concerns, and he hustled forward, anxious to alleviate his worst fear.

The now-absent officer was wearing a hat. The previous officer sitting guard was not.

In retrospect, Josh had seen several Leadville police officers wandering around the hospital. Not one had been wearing a hat. His mind pressed rewind, then stopped when it caught a glimpse of the officer as Josh had answered the last phone call from Austin. The haze obscuring his sense of vague familiarity cleared. The image, now precise. The pizza place in Idaho Springs. The curly mop. A companion of Scarface.

Josh sprinted to George's room door. At about fifteen yards and closing, he heard a commotion coming from inside the room. A second later, Kristen bellowed a piercing scream.

The panicked prosecutor thrust the door open, frantic as to what he might see. When he'd left the room, it had been occupied by a comatose old man and a fragile, sensitive, and petite young lady praying at his bedside. When he returned, his eyes immediately focused on his fiancé who was on the floor. But rather than on her knees praying, instead, she was screaming for help. His uncle, as seen in Josh's periphery, was still lying in a hospital bed. And the police officer, hunched over a flipped chair as if he'd taken a hefty thwack to his nuts, was pointing a gun at the love of his life.

"No," Josh yelled as he took a step toward the "peace officer" readying himself to lunge at the assailant. But a millisecond before Josh got airborne, Uncle George cracked a vase over the skull of the hitman, hitting him with his "best shot" before the thug could "fire away."

The assassin fell face first onto the floor. His gun separated from his grip, sliding away on the shiny hospital floor. Josh plunged on top for the tackle as the goon's insentient body flattened limp to the floor. The prosecutor-turned-linebacker narrowly avoided a yellow flag for the late hit. Josh reached for the firearm, grabbed it, and scrambled to his feet. He exhaled deeply, and with both hands clenched to its handle, pointed the gun at the unconscious attacker's bleeding head.

"Thank God you're both okay," Josh bellowed. "You *are* both okay, aren't you?"

George reached his left hand out. "Kristen, honey. Are *you* okay? I'm alive and conscious, so I'm assuming I'm doing better than I was fifteen minutes ago. But are you alright?"

"Couldn't be better," she chuckled as Josh released one hand from the gun to help his fiancé to her feet.

"Wow! I leave you two alone for what, ten minutes?" Josh shook his head in disbelief. "And I come back to Guns N' Roses' 'Welcome to the Jungle.'"

"Speaking of eighties' hits," said George. "I can tell you one thing Joshie. You rubbed off on this lovely young lady. Her knowledge of your favorite genre saved a life. Possibly *two*."

"Oddly enough, that's not the first time," Josh laughed, smiling at Kristen in recognition of her encore performance of their dance with death in Santa Barbara.

"For the record young lady." George smiled and snuck a wink at Kristen. "He developed his love of eighties' music from yours truly."

"Focus gentleman," Kristen said, pointing back and forth between the bloody floor and Uncle George. "We need to buzz the nurse's station. Let's not forget you just awoke from a coma. And needless to say, we need a cop, a cleaning crew, and a doctor in here."

"Speaking of eighties' hits," chimed Josh, tipping the gun at the split melon. "The only crew this thug needs is Mötley Crüe. Because when his cracked skull comes to, he's gonna want to see 'Dr. Feelgood.'"

Chapter Forty-Five

T HE ASSAILANT LAID unconscious, handcuffed to a hospital bed, with a real police officer watching over him. The crack on his skull appeared comparable to that of the vase that had created it. The thug's body had taken its toll, racking up scars faster than airline miles on a new credit card.

George had been moved to another room. This one, more peaceful and sanitary; free from broken glass and bloodshed. The treating physician had conducted a thorough examination of his evidently invincible elderly patient and gave his future a thumbs up.

"With all this chaos, we haven't had a chance to talk," Josh said. "I'll cut to the chase, and I won't sugarcoat it. Your 'friend' Hank is behind your kidnapping, isn't he?"

"I still can't believe it. Right under my nose." George sighed and shook his head. "Clearly, Hank wasn't a true friend. The greedy bastard knifed me in the back. Didn't have the loyalty to stab me in the front." He paused, then reached for Kristen's hand. "You know, you two will have brilliant children."

"If they're half as smart as you, they'll be off the charts," Kristen said with a smile and a wink.

"Young lady," George chuckled, "the second I met you I knew that Joshua had hit the jackpot. You sure know how to flatter an old man. Especially an ancient mountain goat like me."

Josh explained in detail to George his deductive reasoning, and how it led him to the conclusion that Hank was the likely suspect.

"How did *you* know it was Hank?" Josh asked. "I'm assuming the kidnappers wore masks unless they had planned on killing you from the get-go. Notebook or not."

"Three things clued me in. As I'm sure you've figured out by now, I was being held at a cabin outside Leadville. Near Turquoise Lake. They had me locked in a separate room and the goons wore masks whenever they were in my sight. But they all sported construction boots with concrete residue on them." George pointed to Josh's shoes. "By itself, the boots didn't mean much. But then I overheard one of them talking on the phone with their boss. I pressed my ear against the door to get a better listen. When the guy who appeared to be the right-hand man of the mastermind got off the phone with the boss, I could've sworn I heard him once inadvertently refer to him as Hank. They were whispering and surely thought I couldn't hear a thing. And for the most part, I couldn't. But I was almost certain I heard the name Hank." George paused, looking parched.

"Hmm. Nice detective work." Kristen handed him a cup of water. "What was the third thing?"

"Thank you." George took a sip, then continued. "Well, when I had to use the restroom, I did some snooping. It looked newly remodeled, with shiny, brand-new tile. Well, low and behold, when I looked inside the sink's vanity cabinet, behind all the cleaning supplies and toilet paper was a grout float. You know—the hand tool used to spread out grout and force it into the space between the tiles. One that also can be used to smooth concrete."

"Okay," Josh said, looking perplexed. "But a lot of people own one of those. Especially if they recently laid bathroom tile."

"How many do you think own one that has a label on it that reads 'Property of Ragsdill Masonry'?"

Josh pulled his phone from his pocket, texted "Green light on Hank Ragsdill" and tapped send.

"What are you doing?" asked Kristen.

"Confirming with Austin what had I alerted to him earlier. He's also got the wheels in motion looking into the location of the treasure."

"Excuse me, *what*!?" George grabbed the bed remote and elevated his torso another ten degrees. "You solved the puzzle and you're just mentioning that. Talk about burying the lead."

"Sorry Uncle George, but I beg to differ," replied Josh. "You abduction and well-being are the lead."

"Speak for yourself young man," George said. "That's remained a mystery for twenty-plus years. I'm not sure how long I was in a coma, but I'm sure it wasn't *that* long. If I was, you two must've drank from the *Fountain of Youth*, because you haven't aged a bit."

The three chuckled. The old man nearly lost his life, but his sense of humor remained intact.

"First, let me say that I'm embarrassed if you figured out the riddle in about a week after I couldn't do it in two decades. But more power to you. The student has become the teacher." George paused for a swig of water. "Alright, Joshie my boy. Don't leave me hanging. Remember, I'm on borrowed time. And my interest rate, like the great City of Denver, is a mile high."

"Don't beat yourself up, Uncle George. We received some new, valuable information over the past couple of days that has made all the difference."

"Go on," George said. "And please don't bury the lead. I don't want to die in the middle of you explaining your reasoning without knowing the riddle's answer. Remember, just because I'm retired doesn't mean I've forgotten how long-winded you young attorneys can be."

"A curse passed on from your generation." Kristen tapped George a jovial nudge.

"Touché."

"Fair enough," Josh said with a smile. "I believe the treasure is buried under the concrete in front of the Frisco Historic Park and Museum." He paused to give George an opportunity to absorb the treasure's location that had eluded him for what must've seemed like forever. Undoubtedly pouring salt on the wound, it was only a stone's throw away from where he sat for coffee almost every single morning for twenty years.

"Okay. Okay. I can see how the clues lead in that direction. History was a recurring theme. And there was a mention of school. And, as I'm sure you've learned, the museum is in Frisco's original schoolhouse."

"Exactly. So, I'll read the clues that you so astutely wrote in the cards you've sent me over the years. By the way, nice backup plan in case something happened to your notebook, like burning it in a fire." Josh shrugged his shoulders. "But what if I hadn't kept those cards?"

"Oh, I also placed a copy of the clues and some of my notes in the middle of a cookbook in my kitchen. With all the books on my bookcases, no one would ever think to look in a cookbook in the kitchen. And even if they did, they'd move on after scanning a few recipes."

"Huh. You're right," said Kristen, with raised eyebrows and a titled head.

Josh grabbed his tablet that he'd set on an unoccupied chair in the room and pulled up his notes. "Yeh, so here are the clues we found in the cards you'd sent me. *History is an endless repetition of the wrong way of living. History is indeed little more than the register of the crimes, follies, and misfortunes of mankind. Time is the school in which we learn, time is the fire in which we burn. He who opens a school door, closes a prison. Money is human happiness in the abstract; he, then, who is no longer capable of enjoying human happiness in the concrete devotes himself utterly to money. All the gold which is under or upon the earth is not enough to give in exchange for virtue.*"

"So, they mention *history* several times. Also, *crimes, school, money, concrete,* and *gold.* And *under or upon the earth.*" Kristen nodded her head. "I see what you guys mean. Those clues easily can lead in the direction of the museum. But to reach that conclusion definitively might be a reach."

"Alright Uncle George, so that brings us up to speed with what was provided to you by the *Gold Scammer*. In hindsight, now knowing the exact location of the treasure because of other clues we encountered, the Frisco Historic Park and Museum seems more obvious. But without the new information we received, those same clues could've just as easily led to countless places. Like the town's historic clock on Third Avenue and Main Street. With clues like *history*, *time*, and *concrete*, that location could make sense. And of course, that's where the *Midnight Vandal* believed the treasure was hidden."

"So, do you think the *Midnight Vandal* was working for Hank and got greedy, going rogue before Hank's team of goons could dig it up?" Kristen walked over to the window and adjusted the blinds to deflect a glare shining in George's eyes.

"I do," responded Josh.

"Okay," said George. "So, you mentioned other clues."

"Yes, of course. So first, Kirsten read an article which wrote the *Gold Scammer*, at his sentencing hearing, claimed he had disclosed the location of his ill-gotten gains during his trial. So, we got a copy of the trial transcript, and the only thing of note was a brief exchange during his testimony in which he sounded like a nut job. He sang excerpts from a couple of songs from the old kids' show *Schoolhouse Rock*. Again, the museum was the old schoolhouse. And *rock*, like concrete. Then, after pleading the fifth in response to a question, he followed it by adding 'located between first and second." Well, the Frisco Historic Park and

Museum is on Main Street, between *First* and *Second* Avenues."

"That's actually brilliant," commented Kristen. "Clybourne's *clues*, that is. Not *you*. I certainly don't need to inflate your ego any, seeing as how the *Goodyear* blimp pales in comparison." She hesitated, then continued. "In comparison to your ego, that is. Not your waistline."

"Ouch." Josh snickered as he touched his belly.

"Yes," agreed George. "William Clybourne is an extremely intelligent man."

"*Was*," said Josh.

"Was!?" George said, nearly choking on the word.

"He was murdered the other day," said Kristen.

"Murdered!?"

"Yep. Austin got word of it shortly after it happened. They said it was an accident, but given what we learned, it had to be the result of a hit put out on him."

Creasing his eyebrows, George asked, "What makes you say that?"

While alternating like championship tennis doubles partners, Josh and Kristen explained how they'd met William Clybourne's son, Geoff, and what had transpired since his visit to the prison. This included Geoff's first encounter with his father and the suspicious nature of events after he picked up Clybourne's possessions. Josh also detailed the content of the *Gold Scammer's* belongings, as well as his backstory, laying the foundation for what was to come next.

"So, Clybourne's 'accidental' death, occurring in the brief period between him telling his son he'd reveal everything if he'd come back and Geoff's scheduled follow-up visit, is far beyond being a coincidence." Kristen pointed back and forth between George and Josh. "And we know how you prosecutors feel about *strong* coincidences."

"Okay, with the entire background in place, that leads us to my deductions—the method to my madness if you will." Josh took a deep breath.

"This should be good," Kristen sat down and leaned forward.

"Alright. Now first, let's remember that Clybourne was obsessed with numbers, particularly the number three because of his history with Geoff's mother. With that in mind, I believe Clybourne gave out three sets of clues as to the whereabouts of the treasure. The clues in his trial testimony, the clues to you," Josh said, pointing to his Uncle George, "and the clues he left for his child in the letter to his 'Sole Survivor'—Geoff. Each separately, logically could lead to the museum, but certainly not definitively. But considered together, I believe they do."

"Okay," said Kristen, "you've established the trial testimony as pointing to the original schoolhouse with Clybourne singing *Schoolhouse Rock* songs and referencing the location between First and Second Avenues. And partially, how the clues given to George—" George cleared his throat, causing Kristen to pause. He tipped his head and tapped his right index finger onto his left ring finger. She smiled, then nodded to the elder attorney and continued, "I'm sorry, how the clues to *Uncle* George point in that direction. But those seem like more of a stretch. And as to the letter to Geoff, I don't see a connection at all."

"Fair enough," replied Josh. "First, let me address your first concern. Remember, Kristen, the clues to Uncle George weren't complete. There was one more. One that hadn't been delivered yet. The quote behind Clybourne's photo of Geoff's mom."

George jumped in. "And that was what?"

Josh quoted verbatim, "*In everyone's life, at some time, our inner fire goes out. It then burst into flame by an encounter with another human being. We should all be thankful for those people who rekindle the inner spirit.* By Albert Schweitzer."

Kristen shook her head. "Still not seeing it."

"That's understandable," said Josh. "I'll tie in that clue in a minute. Just keep it in the back of your mind for now, as I move on to the third set of clues. This is where even the smartest of people might get lost, even the two of you—the two smartest people I know."

"I'm not sure if we should be offended," Kristen said, gazing over George.

"Don't be," said Josh with a big smile. "Figuring them out had less to do with intelligence and more to do with luck. Believe it or not, my quirky obsession has paid off in spades."

George exhaled deeply. "Quirky obsession? I'm afraid to ask."

Chapter Forty-Six

K RISTEN HAD SEEN the same look on Joshua plenty of times. George, not so much. The elder pretended to plug his ears as if he was afraid he'd learn of some strange foot fetish, or perhaps worse. Kristen laughed, clearly having a good guess as to where Josh was headed with his off-the-wall statement.

"Uncle George," said Kristen, "after your surprising, and might I add live-saving display of familiarity with eighties' music, I have a strong suspicion you're going to want to hear this."

"She knows me well," Josh said with a chuckle. "So let me start by saying that the letter from Clybourne to his son was found in the *Holy Bible* on the page on which the passage of Genesis: 6:1-3 was circled. For purposes of its relation to the riddle contrived by a numbers-obsessed individual, all we need to know is that particular passage ends with the words 'hundred and twenty years.' So, let's focus on the number, *hundred and twenty*, and put it on the back burner for now."

"Okay," George said. "Hundred and twenty. It's simmering on the tiny burner."

"And finally, we are left with the focal point of the third set of clues—the letter to Geoff—which I will read verbatim. But, to make it less overwhelming, I'll break it down into two parts." Josh reached into his back pocket and pulled out two pieces of paper folded together, separated them, then handed Kristen and George each a sheet. "When I stepped out, among other things, I sweet-talked one of the nurses into letting me print out a couple of copies of this."

Josh lifted his tablet, and after two taps and a scroll, he began reading the first half of the letter as follows:

To My Sole Survivor,

Never in a million years did I ever think it would end like this, not even in my wildest dreams. I'm sure it's too late, but I hope this can make up for my years of absence. Time and time again, I wanted to reach out to you, hoping to meet you, praying you were well. And days like these, I wish I had.

Your entire life, your mother possibly created a false image of me to protect you, or more likely, never mentioned me at all. If that was her choice, we did not see eye to eye. Whatever she told you, you'd be lying to yourself to pretend I never existed. It's time to open your eyes to the true man that I am, which is hardly a man at all.

Now, only time will tell how you remember me. However that is, please don't cry at the darkness shadowed by my past but ride easy toward the daylight that lies ahead.

Josh held a long pause. George glared at Josh, then turned to Kristen and asked, "Are you sure you know where he's going with this?"

Kristen looked baffled, saying, "I thought I recognized that look. But now I'm second-guessing myself."

"Fear not," laughed Josh. "You were spot on. But it's a little more specific than just eighties' music. And seeing as how a certain group from that era is one of my all-time favorites, this letter hit me like a ton of bricks. Or should I say gold bricks?"

In unity, Kristen and George looked at each other in confusion, then shrugged.

Josh handed his smartphone to Kristen. "Kristen, I want you to humor me and enter the following search: *greatest hit songs*." He paused.

"That's going to pull up everything under the sun."

"Now, type in *Asia*, click search, then please start to read off some of them from the top."

Kristen did as Josh requested, then began to read, "Okay, so we have 'Heat of the Moment,' 'Only Time Will Tell,' 'Sole Survivor,' 'Time Again,' 'Wildest Dreams,' 'Don't Cry,' 'Daylight,' 'Eye to Eye,' 'Lying to Yourself.'" Kristen caught her breath, then said, "Should I keep going?"

"Keep going," Josh said with a nod.

"Okay," Kristen continued, "continuing on we have 'The Heat Goes On,' 'Never in a Million Years,' 'Open Your Eyes,' 'Too Late,' 'Days Like These,' 'Ride Easy'—"

"Okay," Josh interrupted. "You can stop there."

George raised his eyebrows in astonishment. "Wow! I know my hearing stinks, but it sounded like a lot of Asia's top hits were referenced in the first part of the letter, weren't they?"

"A dozen to be precise. Twelve out of the fourteen Kristen mentioned are in that letter." Josh bounced his glance back and forth, from Kristen to George. "And the only two missing from that letter are?"

Kristen jumped in like an anxious student wanting to impress her teacher. "'Heat of the Moment' and 'The Heat Goes On.'"

"Bingo!"

"How'd she—" cried George.

"My memory is—"

"Off the charts!" interrupted George.

"Believe it or not," Josh said, scrolling down to the second part of the letter, "those exclusions were intentional. And if the repeated references to Asia's greatest hits aren't enough, there's more. Way more. Recognizing the song references to hit songs by Asia, I called Geoff and confirmed my assumption—the main act performing at the concert where his parents met was none other than the eighties' rock band Asia. And, no pun intended, but the hits keep on coming."

"I'm sure the pun was intended," insisted Kristen, "but do tell."

"Okay, so now I'll read the second part of the letter." Josh read the following:

First, however, to reap the rewards of my past sins, you must <u>remove</u> the unnecessary and go to the start. The links to the present wealth are at the beginning of my past. You don't need to travel the ups and downs to Palmer Lake, Colorado, or put your wet suit on, in order to unriddle how to find the fruits of my crime.

In the words of British physicist Oliver Lodge, "Life must be considered <u>sui</u> generis; it is not a form of energy, nor can it be expressed in terms of something else."

In the words of Ronald Reagan, "Within the covers of the Bible are the answers for all the problems men face."

In the words of Robert Frost, "In three words I can sum up everything I've learned about life: it goes on."

In the words of actress Julie Andrews, "If you're not educated to enjoy the arts, if you're not

*taken to a concert, or you don't hear something
beautiful, you don't know what you're missing."*

Love,

William (your father)

"Don't tell us that the second part of the letter also recites more of Asia's greatest hits," George said with a smirk. "That would put them in a league with Elvis and The Beetles."

"Well, they *are* a highly underrated band. But I digress," the eighties-infatuated music junkie replied. "It's better than that. It puts all the pieces of the puzzle together. Confirming, if you will, the deductions drawn from the other sets of clues."

"I can't wait to hear this." Kristen leaned over and gave George a nudge on his arm.

"Okay, so point blank, Clybourne pulls no punches when he writes 'reap the rewards of my past sins' and 'go to the start' and 'beginning of my past.' The rewards of his past sins are the proceeds of his crime—the treasure as we know it. And the start or beginning of his past is in Frisco, where he was born and raised."

George and Kristen looked at one another, then nodded. "Alright," Kristen said. "We're following you. Carry on."

"Okay, now here's where it gets super-cryptic but very revealing." Josh tapped on his tablet. "Notice that in this entire letter only two words are underlined: *remove* and *sui*. Now, I want you to look carefully at the sentence that reads: 'You don't need to travel the ups and downs to Palmer Lake, Colorado or put your wet suit on, in order to unriddle how to find the fruits of my crime.' Now, Palmer Lake is a real place in Colorado, down near Colorado Springs. But Clybourne references it for another reason." Josh paused, took a deep breath, then continued. "Kristen, on that webpage you're on, does it reference the original band members of Asia?"

Kristen tapped, scrolled down, and read. Then, she gave a puzzled look to Josh and said, "Yes." She paused, then Josh dipped her a nod to go ahead. "Geoff Downes, Carl Palmer, John Wetton, and Steve Howe."

"And if you'll read a little further, I'm sure you'll see that when John Wetton—the original lead singer—left the band, he was replaced by Greg Lake."

Kristen read further, then responded, "Yes, that's correct. Man, the amount of useless information stored in that brain of yours is beyond description." Her eyes rolled as she shook her head.

Josh ignored the jab, choosing to prove otherwise with his riddle-solving skills. "Now, with that in mind, and looking at that sentence with leniency toward some poetic license, you'll note that it states: *downs*, as in Geoff Downes; *Palmer* as in Carl Palmer; *Lake*, as in Greg Lake; and *how*, as in Steve Howe."

Josh let his words sink in a bit before he continued. "But what about the original lead singer—John

Wetton— you ask? Clybourne really makes you work for that one. The grand finale if you will. Hidden in the phrase *wet suit on*. If you *remove* the letters *S-U-I* from the word *suit* in that phrase—as instructed by Clybourne when he underlined the two words *remove* and *sui*—and then combine the remaining letters of that three-word phrase, you're left with *wetton*, as in John Wetton. The original lead singer of Asia."

"Okay, so it's abundantly clear that Clybourne's referencing Asia throughout his letter." George swigged some water, then continued. "And how anyone could deduce that is nothing short of a miracle. Disturbing actually. You'd have to be an obsessed, restraining-ordered fanatic to put all that together."

Kristen tossed her hands in the air. "You have met your great-nephew, haven't you?"

"Good point." George shrugged. "But how does that lead us to the Frisco Historic Park and Museum?"

"I thought you'd never ask?"

"Huh," chuckled Kristen. "I thought you'd never tell us."

"Touché." Josh dabbed his head before continuing. "So next we have the Ronald Reagan quote telling us the *answers* are within the covers of the Bible. Now, recall I told you to remember *hundred and twenty* as the focal point of the Bible passage that was circled. Why is that number important, you ask? Because that's the address of the Frisco Historic Park and Museum—120 Main Street."

"Hurray, now we're getting somewhere," Kristen said with a sincere smile. "Keep going and I'll see if I can get *Asia's* restraining order against you lifted."

"Beautiful, smart *and* funny." George grinned, then gave the floor back to his kin.

"The final two quotes are somewhat interlinked. First, the quote from Robert Frost tells us a couple of things. It references *three*, as in the three sets of clues, Clybourne's favorite number, and the third day of the third month when he met Geoff's mother. Next, Frost states what he's learned about life: 'it goes on.' That, I believe, both references Asia's hit song 'The Heat *Goes On*' while also intentionally leaving out, or should I say *missing*, the word *heat*. That ties in with the final quote, wherein it mentions a concert—once again bringing us back to Asia—and states 'you don't know what you're *missing*.'"

Kristen poured Josh a cup of water and handed it to him. He took a sip, then continued his thesis. "Well, we do know what's *missing*. What's missing from Clybourne's letter are two of Asia's biggest hits: '*Heat* of the Moment' and 'The *Heat* Goes On.'

"May I?" Josh grabbed his smartphone from Kristen, pulled up the photograph of the concrete in front of the museum that Mabel had sent him, showed it to Uncle George, and then to Kristen as he handed her the phone.

"The final quote in the letter also references *educated* and *arts*, once again providing clues back to the schoolhouse museum. And finally, the icing on the cake is the inscription on the concrete in front of it. And thanks to our helpful friend at the museum—Ms. Mabel and her expensive shoes—they're markings I'm certain were engraved by Clybourne." Josh took a deep breath.

"Don't stop now," said his better half.

"He inscribed it for the world to see. 'ASIA 3/3 143' along with a simple sketch. He had met the love of his life at an Asia concert on March third. And the '143' is the numeric code for I love you. And last but not least, the sketch is of a flame, notorious for creatinnnggg—"

Kristen and George chimed in together, "Heat."

"Jackpot!" Josh hollered with his hands raised as if they'd just kicked a game-winning field goal.

Chapter Forty-Seven

GEORGE'S CONFIRMATORY NOD authorizing Josh's phone calls to Austin and Sam generated enough clout to drive the wheels of justice and jackhammers of concrete in motion. A warrant was issued for Hank's arrest and a private concrete company—one not named Ragsdill Masonry—broke ground in front of the Frisco Historic Park and Museum, digging for buried treasure. As a courtesy, Josh gave Mabel a special phone call layered with a thank you, a heads-up, and an apology for the incessant noise that was to follow.

Two new police officers—real cops this time— sat guard outside George's room. They were vouched for and verified by Sam, who had stopped by to visit his best friend. After exchanging their classic jabs at one another, Sam stepped out of the hospital after insisting that he pick up some quality food for everyone. Josh was more than agreeable, as he wasn't entirely comfortable with leaving his uncle's side just yet. Despite significant breakthroughs in the case, Hank and however many goons he controlled under his payroll were still at large.

Josh's pants nearly split down the middle when Sam suggested a great pizza place nearby. One of the officers rushed into the room a millisecond after the pizza-pie-stuffed prosecutor shouted, "No!" So, they settled on salads and light sandwiches from a nearby Leadville café to mitigate the likelihood of Josh being admitted to the hospital for an angioplasty. Any more cheese in his arteries, and he'd be trading in his professional expertise in criminal procedure for inpatient treatment for a coronary procedure.

Kristen sat in a chair at George's bedside, picking up where she'd left off detailing her wedding dreams. Captive audience or not, the old-timer appeared delighted to be the focus of the young lady's attention. The smell of fresh flowers she had purchased to replace the weaponized bouquet scented the room with a smell of life in a building acquainted with death.

Josh sat quietly in a chair beneath the large window with a view of the snow-white outdoors. Passively listening to his fiancé, his mind drifted into replaying the inconceivable events of their vacation. He chuckled and shook his head as he was reminded that their vacation getaway had been prompted by their need to get a break and distance from the life-threatening Santa Barbara murder mystery from which they'd recently escaped. *Out of the frying pan and into the fire*, he thought. Then he corrected himself. *Actually, we just jumped from one fire to another.*

Josh's smartphone rang, extinguishing his blazing thoughts, and with them any chance of burning calories. He eyed the six-inch screen. "Hey Austin. What's up?"

"I've got a few things for you," Austin took a deep breath. "There's no sign of Hank yet, but a team of officers has been formed specifically to find him. And my boss and the police chief took the necessary steps to break ground in front of the museum."

"That's great!" Josh said loudly, causing Kristen to pause from her monologue. "Hopefully the cops can find Hank before he flees to some non-extradition country. From what I understand, he's got the resources to get out of Dodge, never to be seen or heard from again. Even without whatever proceeds are buried in front of the museum." Josh paused and scratched his chin with his free hand. "That's one thing that has me confused."

"What's that?" said Austin.

"Hank's the owner of a very lucrative company. And for the icing on the cake, I think he worked at the D.A.'s office long enough to be receiving a decent retirement. It seems rather odd that he would risk everything by committing kidnapping and possibly be involved in a murder, all in the hopes of finding a treasure that may be a hoax or possibly worth nothing."

"That brings me to the final update I have for you. And it's a doozy. This might shed some light on your bewilderment. We had one of our investigators do some digging into Hank's past. It seems that the small law firm he had prior to joining the D.A.'s office raised a red flag."

Josh paced the room. "Do tell," he said impatiently.

"Well, when I say small firm," continued Austin, "I mean small. It was just Hank and his partner. And here's what we found out. First, interestingly enough, they didn't file a dissolution of their partnership with the Secretary of State until well after he had joined the District Attorney's office."

"That's not necessarily unusual," Josh interjected. "Maybe they wanted to secure other employment before officially throwing in the towel on their law partnership."

"True," Austin said. "But as you suspected, we figured there had to be some reason, some source of motivation, to cause Hank to risk everything; banking on a wing and a prayer simply in the *hope* of finding fortune. If he was broke, maybe. But Hank's wealth was more than most people dream of. So, we dug further."

"Don't tell me that you found evidence that he was somehow directly involved in the gold scam itself?" Josh said, uniquely blending rhetoric, sarcasm, and curiosity, stirring quite the mixed cocktail of speculation.

"Well, let me tell you this. Then *you* tell *me*," replied Austin. "We examined the firm's dissolution papers, which were filed six months after Hank came aboard as a prosecutor. We then compared his partner's signature on the Statement of Dissolution form to that on past court filings by his partner. The signatures didn't match."

"What is Hank's former partner's name?"

"His name is Sherwin Barlowe," said Austin. "And the *is* may be a *was*."

Josh stopped pacing to take a seat and stared out the window. "You have my undivided attention."

"Okay, so now it gets really interesting," Austin said with a sigh. "Not only is there no record of any activity from Hank's former partner during that six-month period, but there's also been no record of him ever since. Period. No credit card charges, no employment history, nothing. And state bar records indicate that's when he stopped paying dues, failed to complete his annual attorney registration, and never submitted the completion of his MCLE credits. Nothing. Literally, all traces of his existence disappeared, but with no death certificate nor any report of him missing."

"Very interesting. So, you think—"

"It's certainly a possibility."

"Hm. Okay. So, we have Hank's connection to his law partner. But Clybourne's connection to Hank is minimal—apparently briefly working for Hank's brother at Ragsdill Masonry. So that leaves us with one big gap. Have you checked to see if Hank's partner had any ties to William Clybourne?" Josh turned his gaze toward Uncle George and Kristen. "I'll bet if we dig deep enough, we'll find some connection."

"Great minds . . . my good friend. That's exactly what we're doing now."

"Perfect," said Josh. "Oh yeah, and one more thing." He turned and smiled at the chatterboxes.

"What is it?"

"Can you please ask your boss if I can interview for the Deputy District Attorney position with your office?"

"I wish," Austin said, then paused for the punch line. One never came. No hit, no strike, no knock. No punch, no *Kool-Aid*. "Oh—you're serious, aren't you?"

"As serious as a guilty plea. Kristen and I have decided to move here. Oh, yeah. And one more thing I forgot to mention." Josh said, throwing in a dramatic pause. "We're engaged."

"We *are*? I don't recall you putting a ring on my finger."

"Ha-ha. Very funny my friend."

"Can you say burying the lead?" Austin chuckled. "Congrats man. Madison is going to flip when she hears the news."

"Hey, if you don't mind," said Josh. "I think Kristen will want to tell her."

"My lips are sealed."

"Perfect. Just like the Go-Go's." Josh strolled to Uncle George's bedside table and took a whiff of the colorful winter bouquet and smiled. And while flowers smelled heavenly, Josh and Kristen had begun reeking of a more earthy scent. "Thanks Austin. Keep me posted. In the meantime, I'll do some research on my end. I have an idea that might shed more light on the mystery of the missing partner."

Chapter Forty-Eight

A FTER SAM RETURNED to the hospital with a tasty selection of salads and sandwiches, the four attorneys chowed and chatted until George's eyelids grew heavy. Sam had sworn not to leave the room until the newly engaged couple had a chance to shower and change. George had insisted they accept Sam's offer, teasing that their odor was likely to comatose him again.

Traveling precisely thirty miles north on CO-91, Josh and Kristen drove for thirty-seven minutes from the hospital in Leadville to their B&B in Frisco.

Outside, the weather was ideal. Cool, but sunny. The roads had been cleared and the nearly two-mile-high elevation made it easy for the blazing sun to quickly dry the blacktopped roadway. Josh quickly brought Kristen up to speed on his conversations with Austin, then changed the topic abruptly to reduce their stress level. Relishing the remainder of their beautiful drive, it was the most peace Josh and Kristen had enjoyed in days.

The spunky manager on duty greeted the disheveled couple as they hustled through the B&B lobby akin to the walk of shame; the pair being more worried about being sniffed than seen. According to Uncle George, they smelled more like a pair of sweaty gym socks than a pair of white-collar professionals.

By the time Josh and Kristen arrived in their suite, the hour approached noon. Josh showered quickly, ensuring there would be sufficient hot water for both of them. As Kristen showered and did whatever it is women do to take five times as long to prep, Josh hopped on the laptop and kicked his research skills into fifth gear.

Josh was keenly aware from first-hand knowledge that it was impossible for someone who had been licensed as an attorney to remain completely off the grid. So, he knew his research into Sherwin Barlowe would turn up something. Whether he'd find anything more than his public state bar records remained to be seen.

A search on the Colorado Supreme Court's website confirmed what Austin had told Josh about Barlowe's attorney status. Non-payment of his annual registration fees spiraled down his law license from delinquent to suspended to disbarment. Beyond the information already known, that route proved to be a dead end.

In the background, Josh heard the roar of a hair dryer pollute the air with its annoying sound, like a failing jet engine struggling for more power. That signaled Kristen was half ready. Time-wise, Josh estimated he had another four or five hours—maybe days—give or take, before his better half felt ready for public consumption. Funny thing was, with only five minutes of prep time, Josh thought she'd fly to the top of any beauty contest.

Josh continued his search, optimistic that if an uncommon name like Sherwin Barlowe turned up any information local to Summit County, it'd likely be the man he was researching. Query after query, page after page, he found nothing beyond Barlowe's status as a local attorney.

A couple of clients Barlowe had represented while partnered with Hank at the law firm of Ragsdill and Barlowe PLLC had made the local newspaper back in the day. One had been the Superintendent of Schools who'd sued the Summit County School District over a claim of wrongful termination. The other was a local high school teacher who had filed suit against the school claiming she'd been denied a promotion due to alleged gender discrimination. Nothing significant jumped out at Josh, other than him noting that both clients had been employed by the school district.

The hair dryer silenced. "How's it going?" Kristen hollered from the bathroom, while the jet engine cooled.

"Slow so far," shouted Josh. "I've found a little more information on Hank's former partner, but nothing yet that indicates a connection between him and the *Gold Scam*."

"Bummer," she said loudly, peaking her head out the door. "I'm almost done getting ready," she said, then prepared for takeoff as she rebooted the hair dryer.

Almost, Josh thought as he chuckled. *What a relative term.*

Josh picked up his smartphone and shot a quick text to Geoff, "Hey Geoff. Does the name Sherwin Barlowe ring a bell with you? Thanks, Josh."

Living up to the reputation of his generation—buried in his smartphone—Geoff texted back in seconds, "No, I don't think so. Sorry."

Josh cued up some vinyl jazz on his phone app, set it on the dining table and took a deep sigh. Running out of ideas, he shifted the scope of his search from broad to more specific, on the off chance of getting a hit on Sherwin Barlowe. Perhaps it was a coincidence that the two publicized legal matters in which Barlowe was counsel of record both had a connection to the school district.

Connected by chance? Maybe. But the seasoned prosecutor wasn't a big believer in coincidences. Josh typed into the search bar "Sherwin Barlowe Summit County School District."

Once again, his skeptical faith in coincidences proved accurate. Beyond the articles he'd already reviewed, he got another relevant hit. In fact, he got a few. None of them amounted to earth-shattering news. Barlowe wasn't a serial killer or the creator of some world-changing software company. But the articles did appear to be referencing the one and the same Sherwin Barlowe. *That's encouraging,* thought Josh. And better yet, they provided new information of which Josh was previously unaware. *That's progress.*

Eyes submerged in the screen; the eager researcher read three articles archived on the local newspaper's website. All three mentioned Sherwin Barlowe, two of which highlighted him for making generous donations to the local school system.

One article of note chronicled an interesting backstory that had given some context to the motivation behind Barlowe's donations. According to the article, Barlowe studied Computer Science in college. Later, after receiving his degree, he returned to his hometown and was instrumental in creating an afterschool computer learning program geared for local middle school and high school students. The article also referenced Barlowe contributing as an instructor until the time he left town to attend law school. Then, after receiving his J.D., he returned to Frisco once again to teach computer skills to local youth and continued to do so until he and Henry Ragsdill partnered up to form a new law firm.

Josh noted the time frame of Barlowe's ventures. It lined up with the theory forming in his head. *Coincidence? Possibly, but not likely.*

He snatched his smartphone from the table and called Geoff. "Hey Geoff. It's Josh. Sorry to keep bothering you, but I've got another quick question. Did your mother ever mention to you how or why your father got involved in computer programming?"

"Huh. Funny you ask. Your timing is impeccable," replied Geoff. "You know I was trying to think if there was anything else I could remember about what my mom told me about him. And one time I had asked her that very same question."

"Please. Do tell."

"She told me he loved playing video games as a kid, mostly because he had trouble making friends.

I guess he was kind of a loner. No sports. No clubs. None of that kind of stuff. So he became fascinated by what it took to create the games, and apparently, that's what started his interest in computer programming. Then one day he heard about an after-school program teaching the basics of computer science and programming. As I'm sure you can imagine, given the nature of his multi-million-dollar scam, he became very good at it. So good, that one of the instructors took him under his wing and gave him more advanced instruction. From there, the rest is history."

"Sadly, criminal history," Josh commented somberly, then paused before altering his tone. "Geoff, you're the man. Thank you."

"Is that somehow important?"

"More than you can imagine." Josh grinned with satisfaction. "I'll give you the full rundown shortly. Oh, and one more thing. Do you happen to know who his computer mentor was?"

"No. Sorry."

"No worries. You've told me more than I could have hoped for, so don't sweat it. I'll be in touch soon. Thanks again, Geoff."

As Josh ended the call, Kristen's hair dryer had dropped its landing gear, coasted along the tarmac, and came to a rest at the gate. A moment of peace and quiet followed, prompting Josh to close his eyes, take several deep breaths, and recharge.

With his personal battery near seventy-five percent, Josh opened his eyes upon hearing the concrete-shattering disturbance faintly sifting into their suite accompanied by the cool draft of the outdoors. With the power of the jackhammers tearing up the front patio of the museum, he too couldn't help but feel a bit of power. For it was Josh's deductions that had initiated the destructive action at one of Frisco's most revered historic landmarks. Good or bad, he was about to enter the history of Frisco for future generations.

For the third time, the hair dryer drowned out any nearby noises. Exhausted, Josh popped up his phone app, and with a slight variation and increased volume, closed his eyes to the sounds of smooth jazz. Seconds later, the muscular-necked prosecutor's chin stopped three inches shy of his chest, falling fast asleep in his chair. A minute later, the decibel level of his snoring took a close third place to Kristen's hair dryer and the Main Street jackhammers.

* * *

JOSH FELL FROM his chair when the blaring ringtone woke him from his brief slumber. Kristen's hair dryer was off, and she was singing softly in the restroom. Josh popped up, sat back in his chair, and momentarily adored the angelic voice before it was muffled by another loud ring.

Mesmerized by Kristen's soothing voice, he answered the call without bothering to look at the caller. "Hello, this is Joshua."

"Hey Josh, it's Austin."

"What's the good word, my friend?" With the back of his hand, Josh wiped a speck of drool that had leaked out the corner of his mouth. "Kristen and I are back at the B&B getting cleaned up. I can hear the commotion from our suite."

"Well, my friend. I have some news for you. Are you seated?"

"I am. And from the way you asked, you've got me worried." Josh leaned forward. He rested his elbows on the dining table, stabilizing himself for shaky news. "I'm almost afraid to ask. Is it good news or bad?"

Chapter Forty-Nine

J OSH BRACED HIMSELF for the news to follow. A once relaxing vacation had quickly shifted from ice skating and skiing to kidnapping and murder. And from sipping hot beverages cozied up to a midday fire to fleeing bullets amid late-night gunfire.

Oh, how quickly the tide had reversed. The vacationing couple's itinerary wasn't worth the paper it was written on; its plans had been crushed like the hammered concrete fronting the local museum.

"By the way," Josh blurted out before Austin could respond to his question, "There is a link between Clybourne and Barlowe. And I found out what it is."

"Funny you should say that," said Austin. "That'll put into context what we found buried in the annals of time. Or should I say buried under the cement of the museum?"

"Once again, my friend, you have my undivided attention." Josh walked toward the balcony, opened the door, and stepped outside, then faced the direction of the museum.

"We found a waterproof safety box buried underneath the concrete. Almost directly under the area with the inscription. It seems that Mr. Clybourne planned carefully in the hopes of one day being re-leased from prison. But if not, and in the event his riddle got solved, the box's contents filled in the twen-ty-year void in Frisco's history. And fittingly, it does so on the grounds that literally encapsulates Frisco's past."

"Man, do I sound like that too?" joked Josh.

"Like what?"

"When every time I'm explaining something, it's like I'm presenting a closing argument to the jury."

"Sorry, my friend. It's a habit of the profession."

"No need to explain. You're preaching to the choir. And no need to apologize. Glass houses, my friend."

"Be that as it may," continued Austin, "I'll cut to the chase. The box contained account information for a Swiss bank account. It also had a key to a safety deposit box at the Bank of Frisco, one giant gold bar, and a letter to end all letters."

Josh rushed back into the room, sprinting to the restroom as if symptomatic of food poisoning. The door was open. He tapped Kristen repeatedly on the shoulder, then put the phone on speaker.

Josh held out the phone and said, "Austin, I put you on speaker. I have a feeling Kristen is going to want to hear this." Josh then whispered to Kristen, "They found a safety box buried in front of the museum with information for a Swiss bank account, a key to a bank safety deposit box, a giant cold bar, and a letter."

"Sorry Austin," Josh said leaning forward as if the phone's microphone would struggle to hear his booming voice. "Please, continue."

"The letter is written by William Clybourne. I don't have it in front of me right now, but suffice it to say, the letter is a tell-all. It turns out he had *two* partners in the scam. None other than Henry Ragsdill and Sherwin Barlowe. It even goes so far as to tip off law enforcement. Obviously aware of the nature to which Hank would go to protect himself, the letter states that if either Clybourne or Barlowe ever turned up missing or dead, law enforcement need look no further than Henry Ragsdill."

"Based on that," said Josh, "I'm quite certain the value of the Swiss bank account and the contents of the safe deposit box will be quite lucrative."

"How can you be so sure?" asked Kristen.

"I think that when Clybourne realized he was going down for this, he thought about taking his partners down with him. Then, word leaked that an anonymous source was about to cut a deal with the prosecution. That must've been Barlowe. Hank got word of it and eliminated the risk. My guess is, after that, he threatened Clybourne if he sang. Perhaps even so far as to threaten to kill Clybourne's girlfriend—a.k.a. Geoff's mother—unless Clybourne kept his mouth shut."

"Barlowe?" Kristen said with confusion. "Hank's former law partner?"

"Yes," responded Josh. "While you were warming the inn with your hair dryer, I uncovered a link that connects Barlowe to Clybourne. So, we deduced that Barlowe must have been the suspected mysterious third partner in the scam."

"And as added security for Jessica Summons," Austin interjected, "Clybourne probably agreed to share with Hank the loot he had hidden. After he got paroled, of course. Basically, Hank used the threat of Clybourne's girlfriend as leverage to protect his butt and get a piece of the pie upon Clybourne's release. And Clybourne leveraged someday sharing the hidden proceeds he embezzled from their scam to protect Jessica and, assuming she had given birth and kept their child, Geoff as well."

"That actually makes perfectly good sense," commented Kristen.

"*Actually*?" said Josh. "Oh Yee of little faith."

"And there's more," Austin said.

Josh and Kristen walked toward the kitchenette and sat at the dining table.

Austin continued. "The letter also states point blank that if anyone ever gets too close to uncovering the truth behind Opulent Ores Inc. and then happens to be found dead or mysteriously disappear, the first person law enforcement ought to investigate is Henry Ragsdill."

"No honor among thieves," snarked Kristen.

"It sounds like Clybourne predicted his own murder long before it happened," Josh said as he stood and walked toward the door. "Are you still at the museum?"

"Yes," said Austin. "A marked vehicle just secured the box. They're taking it back to the police station now to enter it into evidence. Someone from my office is requesting a warrant right now so that we don't have any issues retrieving the contents from the accounts.

Then the detectives will go open the safe deposit box and secure access to the Swiss bank account. In the meantime, I'm going to stick around a while longer to see if anything else turns up. And as we speak, a cement truck is on its way to make the museum patio as good as new once the destruction is finished."

"Objection Your Honor. The State moves to exclude any concrete coming from a cement truck owned by Ragsdill Masonry?" Josh chuckled slightly louder than Kristen's adorable snort.

"Motion granted," Austin said with authority.

Josh signaled Kristen, prompting her to put on her shoes. "Thank you, Your Honor. co-counsel and I are going to walk over to your outdoor chambers right now. We'll see you in a few minutes."

"Counsel may approach," Austin said, just before the head-thumping noise picked up again.

Kristen grabbed both their coats hanging on a brass coat rack beside the door. They threw on their jackets while strolling down the hall. The outside clatter was muted, but still annoying nonetheless. As Josh's foot hit the first step of the stairs, the noise stopped again.

Josh dipped a head nod to an elderly man with bottle-thick glasses coming up the stairs as he and Kristen headed down to the lobby. The couple cautiously yielded extra clearance to *Mr. Magoo*, giving him two fewer things in which to faceplant.

Refreshed and no longer ashamed of their look and smell, the attractive twosome greeted the cheerful lady who had a special knack for making the inn feel like a home.

"Hi, Connie. How are you doing?" Kristen walked up to the front desk glowing with a rejuvenated smile and flashing her engagement ring. From the responsive look on the manager's face, perhaps Kristen should've toned down her joyous expression. Judging from her smirk-wink delivery, Connie may've thought the jack-hammering vibrations had been coming from the couple's upstairs suite rather than from down the street, outside the museum.

"Hi, Kristen. Congratulations! Are you all enjoying this beautiful Colorado day?"

"Yes, thank you."

"I bet you are," Connie snickered with a devious wink. "Have a great rest of your day."

"Thank you. You too," said Kristen, scooting toward Josh as he held the front door open.

Josh gave a toothless smile and a friendly wave as they stepped outside. "You're on a first name basis?" Josh asked with genuine surprise.

"Of course we are. It's not like we're only here for a night."

"You are a better person than I."

"You say that as if it was ever in question," Kristen giggled, ending with her signature snort.

"Touché," Josh said, then pointed to a police SUV slowly driving up Main Street as it approached the intersection with Fourth Avenue. "That's probably the unit transporting the golden treasure. Can you believe this? What a vacation!"

"If I wasn't living it, no, I'd never believe it."

The couple held hands while strolling along the sidewalk near the intersection of Main and Third. A middle-aged lady with a smile painted on her face approached them coming from the opposite direction. Glancing at her phone in her right hand, her left hand held one end of a leash with a pristine Alaskan Husky on the other end. Her chest was snow white, and her back was a light gray, sporting a medium-length coat over a heavy undercoat. The dog, not the lady.

Like all humans, the gorgeous canine took an immediate liking to Kristen, prompting her owner to let her fluffy-tailed dog soak in some affection. Kristen squatted and rubbed the underbelly of the appreciative animal whose tail wagged with pleasure.

"Wham!" A deafening crash caused the canine to snap back and Kristen to jump upright.

Josh jerked his upper torso one-hundred-ten degrees to his right. "What the—"

Storming from left to right of the marked police SUV, a black *Hummer* crushed the driver's side of the evidence-bearing vehicle, flipping the heap of smashed metal on its passenger's side, thrusting it scraping another fifteen feet across the intersection before coming to rest. Sparks of metal settled while the chilling shrill pierced the mountain air.

With airbags deployed, the two officers were trapped as they hung parallel to the ground from the straps of their seatbelts, blood dripping from their noses. Two masked men jumped out from the passenger's side of the massive military-grade SUV, one armed with a semi-automatic machine gun, and the other with a crowbar.

Instinctively, Josh had nearly tackled Kristen to the ground and covered her like a bear rug with his bear hug. The startled Husky barked incessantly, likely from a mix of fear upon hearing the booming crash and the protective instinct of her new friend who'd been taken down like a hung-out-to-dry wide receiver crossing paths with a head-hunting oversized strong safety.

Emulating the speed and precision of a NASCAR pit crew, the two robbers orchestrated a flawless heist as their driver reversed their vehicle and positioned it for a swift getaway. The armed felon waived his assault weapon around while pedestrians screamed and scampered for cover. In a matter of seconds, the tailgate of the police SUV was pried open and robbed of its valuable, ostensibly unattainable cargo. Then speedily, in their final orchestrated act, the pit crew jumped back aboard the *Hummer* and the street-legal tank tore east toward Lake Dillon.

The monstrous SUV screeched as it burned rubber, blistering its massive tires into a cloud of smoke, permeating the Main Street to the Rockies. The heist clearly was well planned, capturing the treasure in transition with minimal police security. But it was not without its weakness, as a barrage of officers stood guard only a stone's throw away after having secured the museum's perimeter only minutes prior. Eight seconds later, two police units coming from the historical site, now more prominent than ever, raced down Main Street in silver and bronze medal positions with sirens blaring, fresh on the tail of the golden getaway.

With Josh laying on top of Kristen, perhaps positioned like the B&B manager had envisioned moments earlier, they gazed in awe. The incident unfolding before their eyes generated greater shock than the freezing concrete beneath their merged bodies. Then, joining the sound of Kristen's furry friend, the couple barked, "Oh my God!" staring in astonishment at the high-speed gold heist chase.

A far-fetched vacation. Now, more so than ever. The hits kept coming—literally.

Chapter Fifty

J OSH AND KRISTEN hadn't walked another half block when their short journey was disrupted once again, first by multiple sets of screeching tires several blocks behind them, but out of their sight. Then . . .

"Crash!" A massive collision reverberated along Main Street with its sound waves vibrating faster than the concrete-hungry jackhammers.

Fresh off the stunning army-emulated attack only steps outside their temporary home, Josh and Kristen nearly fell to the ground. Automatically, they twisted and plunged their torsos downward like a corkscrew.

"What the—" Kristen hollered as she squeezed Josh's hand numb.

Josh regained his balance. He steadied his partner, and boosted their pace to a jog, pulling Kristen behind him. Their rush to the museum, now more urgent. They took short, quick strides, cautious to avoid any possible ice patches.

Ninety seconds later they reached Austin, who was standing on the street corner of the museum. Two police cars had already bolted from their location, racing toward the Lake Dillon shoreline, adjacent to the intersection of Summit Boulevard and Main Street—the scene of the second earth-shaking crash.

Standing beside Austin was an older policeman, a sergeant according to the stripes on his uniform. White-haired and sporting a crew cut, he was alternating between speaking into his walkie-talkie and holding it up for him and Austin to listen in on the police chatter. He was short and chunky, with the top of his cut not a hair above Austin's shoulders. His Santa-like belly suggested he could find the nearest donut shop while blindfolded. Undeniably, jelly had filled the inside of both for years. Seriousness dripped from his face, with a hint of raspberry, as he and Austin listened attentively to the thirty-eight-channel, weatherproof handheld device.

The power couple slowed to a brisk walk as they crossed Second Avenue and hurried toward Austin. Indistinguishable chatter popped around in the crisp thin air. Main Street, normally a peaceful pedestrian-friendly retail respite, looked flustered with tourists and police scampering in a frenzy.

Josh and Kristen stepped up the curb and wandered toward Austin and the sergeant-in-charge, slowing so as not to interrupt the official business painted on their faces. Abruptly, the senior officer on the scene held up a finger to Austin and stepped away, pacing about five steps in the direction of the museum's front door. He pressed the walkie-talkie to his ear and stared blankly at his black shoes, now dusted gray by the airborne concrete residue.

Austin turned, facing Main and Second, and made eye contact with his friends, then shook his head in disbelief.

"Given your timing and path of travel, I'm guessing you just had front row seats to the breaking news?" Austin pointed up Main Street, tightening his lips while continuing to shake his head.

"Front row seats?" exhaled Kristen. "I think we were in the game."

"And what about the encore performance?" Josh said, throwing his hands in the air. "What the heck was that crash?"

"So far, from what I know is that the getaway SUV got T-boned racing through a red light at the inter-section of Main Street and Summit. You know, right where it runs into the lake." Austin tilted his head toward the sergeant. "Sergeant Gartrell is trying to get an update now."

Josh and Kristen locked eyes and raised their eyebrows in sync. Austin exhaled heavily, ready to say more, but waiting for more information. As if recognizing Austin's yearning for more details, Sergeant Gartrell waved over the local Deputy District Attorney. Austin excused himself and zipped to the ranking officer on the scene.

Josh lasered his focus on Austin's face trying to read his friend's reaction. Austin nodded, then nodded again. Sergeant Gartrell spat out a few more sentences. Austin's chin plummeted to the ground. With eyebrows launched, his eyes appeared to pop out from their sockets. He nodded again, patted the sergeant on his shoulder, and strode over to his anxious friends.

Beyond impatient, Josh couldn't wait. "It's big news, isn't it?"

"I wouldn't say big," responded Austin, simulating his best poker face. "More like earth-shattering."

Chapter Fifty-One

NINETY MINUTES LATER, George's heavy eyelids crept open as he woke from a nurse-mandated nap. His best friend sat across the room, engrossed in a novel he had picked up in the unexpectedly impressive hospital gift shop. Sam's eyes remained glued to the pages, not noticing his friend had woken. George sat quietly, looking appreciative of his loyal friend.

The hospital room door edged open, evident of a cautious intruder. Not even a whisper of air accompanied its gentle sway. Sam flipped a page, leaning intently into the bestselling legal thriller. A head peaked into the room through the partial opening, its eyes scanning the room for clues.

Abruptly, the heavy door thrust open. Alarmed, George's head jerked to his left, catching the movement of the two entrants that had popped into his periphery. But before George could move an inch, or Sam could raise his head, the elderly patient shouted out, "What the—"

"Sorry," Josh said. "We didn't mean to startle you. The news we have will do that just fine."

Kristen recapped the details of what they had experienced since their most recent exit from the hospital room. George and Sam listened intently, looking dumbfounded as their heavy lower jaws weighed their mouths wide open. Exchanging turns, each kept repeating "Oh my God!"

Hanging on Kristen's every word, George and Sam were speechless as she stopped just short of the story's headline, respecting the priorities of the nurse that entered the room. The red-headed medical professional swiftly checked fluids and monitors and then promptly left the room, as if sensing the anxiousness of her departure.

Kristen nodded to Josh, signaling him to drop the bomb. Sam closed his book. George grabbed a glass of water from the mobile cart beside his bed.

"So, after Austin got a final update from the sergeant, he returned to give us the news." Josh took a deep breath, locked eyes with his great-uncle, and said, "Hank is dead!"

Sam dropped his book. George dropped the glass on his lap, soaking his frontside as if he'd just relieved himself.

Josh continued when he realized his news had rendered them speechless, but undoubtedly eager for more specifics.

"Turns out, Hank was driving the getaway Hummer. He flew through a red light at a dangerous rate of speed while attempting to turn left from Main Street onto Summit Boulevard. Likely, he was heading toward I-70, looking to hop on the highway and bolt some sixty miles west to the Eagle County Regional

Airport, where he'd chartered a private plane." Josh inhaled deeply, then continued. "Well, the Hummer got plowed when it was broadsided by a massive truck coming from its left on Summit Boulevard."

Kristen interjected, placing the ball on the tee for her partner to take the final swing. "And the massive truck that crushed the Hummer was none other than . . . "

Josh let the room hang quietly for a moment, then blurted, "A cement truck. Buckle-less Hank and his two treasure-heisting cronies were pronounced dead on the scene."

"Wow," shrieked Sam. "Talk about ironic."

"More like poetic justice" added George, looking relieved and saddened all at once. "It's hard to believe Hank gave up everything, including his life, for an unknown treasure."

Kristen jumped in, once again teeing one up for her partner who loved to put the cherry on top of every closing argument. "I wouldn't say unknown. At least not any longer."

"As we pulled up to the hospital, Austin called with a final update. First off, they confirmed the *Midnight Vandal* worked for Hank. His employer was a company called Vail Valley Contractors. Turns out, that was just a shell company. The detectives were able to link that company back to Ragsdill Masonry."

Kristen chimed in, "And there's more."

"And this time, it's not about the criminals. Rather, it brightly illuminates the light at the end of the tunnel. The loot. The elusive prize. The golden treasure. Turns out, for roughly the past twenty years, during which time gold has gone up in value from about two-hundred-seventy dollars per ounce to nearly two-thousand dollars per ounce, the Bank of Frisco has been sitting on gold bars that collectively, are now worth nearly twenty million dollars."

"I'm sorry," George said. "I'm old and my hearing isn't the best. Did you say *twenty million*?"

"Your ears haven't failed you yet," said Kristen. "You heard just fine."

"And the Swiss bank account," added Josh. "Eight million dollars in cash!"

Sam shook his head as he mumbled "Mm" repeatedly. "This is all so surreal. We worked with Hank all those years and shared our lives over coffee every week. You think you know someone, and then you find out something like this."

"Sadly, there's more," Kristen said somberly.

"More, what more can there be?" George said with his mind numbed from the news and his crotch still numb from the ice water.

"The detectives did some digging, and quickly were able to find a link between Hank and some property records of some real estate out near Turquoise Lake. They found the cabin where you were held hostage. The deed was in the name of a trust created several decades ago by the Ragsdill family." Josh paused to let the news sink in before he dropped the final bomb.

Kristen pulled up a chair beside George and held his hand.

"Clybourne's prognostication in his buried letter appears to be spot on. In a locked shed behind the cabin, police found two large steel drums that smelled as if they'd once been filled with acid. At the bottom of each drum, the forensic team recovered what appears to be the microscopic residue of bones, as well as some tiny undissolved fragments."

"Two drums?" said Sam. "You think—" Sam cut his comment short.

Kristen squeezed both her hands around George's cold and wet left hand.

"They have enough remains to run DNA," Josh uttered. "And I'm guessing the results will positively identify the bodies of Sherwin Barlowe and—" He paused, hesitant to upset the patient who'd already experienced more trauma in the past few days than a person should have to endure in a lifetime.

"And Helen Windimere." George's watered eyes looked sadly into Kristen's.

"Do you really think so?" Kristen's squeeze fell limp.

"At the cabin," George said, his gaze collecting moisture, "where I was being held, I found a tiny brooch pin. A rose, about the size of a dime. I had given it to Helen. She wore it every day after that."

Unable to contain her emotions, Kristen's tears flowed down her flush cheeks, dripping onto her lap, wetting it nearly to the tune of George's water-soaked mid-section. With his free hand, George reached to the tissue box atop his bedside's mobile cart and handed his consoler a tissue.

Sam shook his head emphatically and snarled, "Wow! The secrets people keep."

Josh's mind raced as he pondered the powerful words just spoken. He stared at Kristen, impressed with her organic ability to comfort those in need, feeling blessed to add her to his family—which without a doubt she already belonged. Now engaged, she would soon take the final step and officially become his wife. Someone with whom to experience the unknown. Someone with whom to share the unspeakable. Someone with whom to disclose the unforgettable.

His brain processed. His heart saddened. His throat swelled. It was time.

"Speaking of secrets," Josh muttered. "Kristen, since we're going to be married, there is something I need to tell you. Something I haven't shared with anyone in years. Something that happened to me when I was in law school. Something that made the most memorable time of my life, some of which I pray I wish I could forget. But unfortunately, it's unforgettable."

Kristen's face turned whiter than George's bed sheets. Her tears seemingly froze midway down her cheeks, in sync with the rest of her body.

Uncle George appeared to be relieved, likely thankful for the distraction as to how the love of his life had mysteriously disappeared. Giving his great-nephew the nudge he needed, George said "The Grove?"

"The Grove," confirmed Josh as a mixture of emotions gazed into Kristen's eyes.

A wardrobe of anxiety abruptly shrouded the tears masking Kristen's face. "The *Grove*? What about the Grove?"

About Author

Dean earned his bachelor's degree from California State Polytechnic University, Pomona ("Cal Poly Pomona") and his juris doctor degree from the University of Mississippi School of Law ("Ole Miss"). He has been a practicing attorney since 1996 and currently practices law in Colorado.

Dean is a former Assistant District Attorney who has tried seven first-degree murder trials, all resulting in guilty verdicts. Several of his ideas come from some of his nearly unbelievable real-life experiences as a prosecutor. After all, fact is stranger than fiction.

Today, in addition to practicing law, Dean dedicates much of his time to writing fiction novels. He lives with his amazing wife and their two incredible children in Colorado. He enjoys skiing, kayaking and coaching youth sports.

Dean is working on his third novel in the Joshua Rizzetti thriller series, ***The Grove Conspiracy***. Subscribe to Dean's mailing list at www.deancferraro.com to stay updated on its release and other exciting news.

Novels by Dean C. Ferraro:

- ***Murder in Santa Barbara*** (Book 1 of the Joshua Rizzetti series)

- ***Murder in Vail*** (Book 2 of the Joshua Rizzetti series)

- ***The Grove Conspiracy*** (Book 3 of the Joshua Rizzetti series) – Coming soon!

Websites:

- deancferraro.com

- twitter.com/DeanCFerraro1

- facebook.com/DeanCFerraro

- instagram.com/deancferraro